D1459287

‘i

—

2

To re
or vi.

The

05441738

Curtain Call
at the
Seaview
Hotel

GLENDA YOUNG

Curtain Call at the Seaview Hotel

HEADLINE

First published in 2022 by
HEADLINE PUBLISHING GROUP

1

The Seaview Hotel, the Vista del Mar and the North Mount Hotel in this story are
fictional hotels and are not based on any hotels in Scarborough.

Cataloguing in Publication Data is available from the British Library

ISBN 978 1 4722 8568 3

Typeset in Adobe Garamond by Palimpsest Book Production Limited, Falkirk, Stirlingshire

Printed and bound in Great Britain by Clays Ltd, Elcograf S.p.A.

HEADLINE PUBLISHING GROUP
An Hachette UK Company
Carmelite House
50 Victoria Embankment
London EC4Y 0DZ

www.headline.co.uk
www.hachette.co.uk

For Scarborough, my happy place

Acknowledgements

The Seaview Hotel, the Vista del Mar and the North Mount Hotel in this story are fictional and not based on any hotels in Scarborough. Likewise, Windsor Terrace and King's Parade are fictional streets.

My thanks go to the following:

Angie Pearsall and her rescue greyhounds Monty and Carla for help in bringing Suki to life; Lynn Jackson, vice president of the Scarborough Hoteliers Association; Norman Kirtlan; Andy Davis for surfing advice; Joe Parkinson; Gillian Galway. For lifting the curtain so I could take a peek behind the scenes into the world of theatre, my thanks go to Corinne Kilvington (Theatre Space North East) and to my brother Chris Young, Martin Wallwork and Gail Shepherd – thanks for the squirrel. To my husband Barry for his love, support and all the frothy coffees and cheese scones that kept me fuelled while writing. Thanks also to my wonderful agent Caroline Sheldon and to Kate Byrne, my editor at Headline, from whom I continue to learn a great deal.

I'd also like to thank everyone involved with the competition for a reader to have their name included as a character in this book, in aid of the amazing charity Dog A.I.D. (Assistance in Disability). To find out more about their wonderful work, visit dogaid.org.uk. My thanks also to my lifelong friend Lynn Stacey and her assistance dogs Bella and Nancy.

And last but by no means least – to Scarborough, my happy place, always.

Thank you, everyone. I couldn't have done it without you.

Act I

Chapter 1

Helen Dexter, landlady of the Seaview Hotel in Scarborough, gazed from her lounge window. She took in the pretty view of the North Bay beach, where the sea sparkled under a blue sky. It was early September, and the day was warm with late-summer heat. She pushed her bobbed brown hair behind her ears.

'Come on, you can't sit gawping out of the window all day. You've got guests arriving this morning,' she said out loud.

'What's that, love?' a voice replied from the hallway. It was Jean, the Seaview's award-winning cook. When Helen and her late husband Tom had bought the hotel, they'd inherited Jean as part of the fixtures and fittings. She was a no-nonsense Yorkshire woman in her early sixties, a dynamo of a woman with short blonde hair and oversized glasses. She was short and dumpy, but woe betide anyone who called her that as Jean described herself as cuddly.

'I'm just talking to myself again,' Helen called back. 'Don't they say that's the first sign of madness?'

Jean bustled into the lounge, where Helen was sitting on the window seat. 'It's when you start answering yourself that you need to worry,' she replied.

Helen swung around to face her. 'I've been talking to myself a lot since Tom died, you know. I talk to Suki all the time, but she's not much of a conversationalist.'

'Well, that's greyhounds for you,' Jean smirked. 'Anyway, you've always got me. Any time you want to chat, or need a shoulder to cry on, I'm here. And you can talk to Jimmy, too.'

Helen turned her head from Jean's enquiring gaze and looked out of the window again. 'Jimmy's still away, working on the cruise ship with his troupe of Elvis impersonators.'

'Yes, but he's coming back next week, isn't he? You must be looking forward to seeing him again and picking up where you left off. He's a good man, Jimmy Brown; you seem well suited.'

Helen picked up a cushion, plumped it and placed it back down. She wasn't ready to talk about Jimmy. He was the first man she'd had feelings for since her beloved Tom had passed away after thirty years of marriage. It felt like she was betraying Tom's memory, and she was struggling with the emotions that raised. However, Jean wasn't ready to let the subject drop.

'I don't understand why you didn't join Jimmy on the cruise when he asked you. It would have done you the world of good to get away.'

'How could I have left? I had the Seaview to run,' Helen said, more sharply than intended. She smiled an apology at Jean. 'You know how hard I've worked getting the place decorated and updated over the summer; there was no way I could have gone away. Anyway, I didn't want to. I wanted to stay and cherish my memories of Tom.'

Jean held her hands up in surrender. 'I'm just saying you could have done with some time out, that's all. It's been almost a year since Tom passed; it's high time you were moving on. You could do a lot worse than getting to know Jimmy better.'

'Sorry, Jean. I guess I'm feeling on edge this morning because of the new guests coming in,' Helen replied, happy to change the subject. She'd deal with her feelings for Jimmy when she saw him again. Right now, she had too many other things on her mind. 'They sound an odd bunch, this lot arriving today,' she went on. 'They've booked the whole place for a solid two weeks.'

'An odd bunch? In what way?'

Helen laid her arm along the top of the window seat. Jean sat opposite, straightening beer mats on a tabletop and turning them right way up. Helen appreciated her attention to detail.

'They're a theatrical group. They've booked eight rooms, though only seven people are coming to stay. They said they need one room to keep props and costumes in.'

Jean's eyebrows shot up in surprise. 'You didn't tell me they were actors.'

Helen shrugged. 'I didn't think you'd be interested. They're rehearsing a play that's going on at the Modernist Theatre on the seafront in two weeks' time.'

'Really? I'm sure I read in the *Scarborough Times* that the Modernist was in danger of closing down.'

'Well, the play our guests are putting on is the last chance to save it, so there's a lot riding on it. If the play's a success, sells enough seats and the audience returns, my friend Taylor says it'll be saved.'

'How is Taylor? I haven't seen him in ages,' Jean said.

An image of Taylor Caffrey, theatre manager, came to Helen's mind. He was in his late forties, a jovial, rotund man with slicked-back black hair that Helen suspected was dyed. He liked to wear a grey pinstripe suit with two-tone brogues and styled his look on gangster films from the black-and-white era. He was a well-known, well-liked, flamboyant character about town

5

who contributed to the arts page for the local newspaper, the *Scarborough Times*.

'Is he still living on the Esplanade with his mangy old cat?' Jean asked.

'Mr Phipps? That poor cat must be on its last legs by now, but as far as I know, it's still alive. Anyway, if the play's a success, it means Taylor will have enough money to carry out repairs and keep the Modernist open for another season. That will give him time to apply for grants to pay for repairs to keep it going long-term.'

'And if the play fails?'

'Then the theatre closes down. Poor Taylor will be out of work and the Modernist faces the bulldozers. He told me he's already been approached by a chain hotel who're after the land, as it's such a prime spot on the seafront. Actually, he was the one who recommended the Seaview to the cast; that's why they're staying here. They were supposed to go into theatre digs, but there's a problem with mice in the kitchen and they've had to close until it's sorted. All being well, the actors will move there two weeks today, on the morning the play opens.'

'Mice in the kitchen?' Jean wrinkled her nose in disgust.

'Anyway,' Helen carried on, 'they can't rehearse at the Modernist until the leaking roof's fixed, and that's why they're rehearsing here.'

'Here in the lounge?' Jean frowned, looking around.

'And the dining room and hall; I expect they'll use as much free space as they can. When the booking came in, it was a posh woman who made it, said she was personal assistant to Mr Richard Dawley, Esquire. I mean, who calls themselves Esquire these days? She referred to the actors as "creative artistes" and warned they could be temperamental. Creative types might have fragile egos, I guess.'

'And only seven are coming, you say?'

'Yes, only seven breakfasts for you to cook for the next two weeks, so your workload should be nice and light.' Helen bit her lip, remembering something else she had to tell Jean. 'Oh, but there's something you should know . . .' She paused before delivering the news she knew Jean wouldn't like. 'One of them is vegan.'

'Vegan?' Jean sucked air through her teeth. In all the years she'd worked at the Seaview, her full English breakfasts were consistently highly praised in reviews. They were renowned for their quality and quantity, and had even won the hotel an award for best breakfast on the Yorkshire coast. Jean took her work seriously. The range of items she cooked was limited, admittedly, but they were always cooked very well. Helen had recently, and very gently, encouraged her to add porridge and grilled kippers to her repertoire. After an initial resistance, Jean was now adept at cooking both, although she still swore under her breath when kippers were requested. However, there was something far worse for her to contend with than kippers. What she couldn't understand were guests who didn't eat meat. She'd been raised on meat and two veg, and if it was good enough for her, why wasn't it good enough for the Seaview's guests?

She took a deep breath, laid her hands on the table and gave Helen's breakfast bombshell some thought.

'Vegan, eh? Well, I'm sure I could give them an extra slice of toast with beans and eggs.'

'No eggs,' Helen said quickly.

Jean looked like she'd been slapped. 'No eggs?'

Helen shook her head. 'Vegans don't eat meat, eggs or any dairy products.'

'Then what on earth will I give them?' Jean cried.

'There's a box of vegan sausages in the freezer; you can grill a couple of those with beans and toast.'

Jean blanched. 'Vegan sausages? They're an abomination, that's what they are.'

'And that's not all,' Helen continued. 'Another of the guests is on a special low-fat diet. I've bought plenty of soy milk and skimmed milk, plus yoghurts, low fat.'

Jean threw her hands in the air in desperation. 'Low fat? Why does anyone want low-fat food when they're on holiday? They're here to enjoy themselves.'

'This lot will be working, Jean, they're not coming on holiday. Besides, we've always made a point of catering to guests' special requests. It's part of our requirements as a three-star hotel. And when we get our four stars, it'll be even more important.'

'Don't count your chickens before they hatch, love,' Jean said sagely. 'I wouldn't want you to be disappointed.'

Helen furrowed her brow. 'What makes you think we won't get upgraded? I've followed the rules for accreditation to the letter. In fact, I almost went cross-eyed double-checking them. All we need now is for the hotel inspector to pay us a visit and give us their official report. I might even be able to start charging more for the rooms when . . .'

'If,' Jean chipped in.

'. . . *when* we get the extra star.'

Jean slapped her hand against her forehead. 'Oh, now you've mentioned the inspector, I've got something to tell you.'

'What is it?'

'You know my friend Gloria, who cleans at the Royal Hotel? Well, she heard on the grapevine that the inspectors have started doing their rounds on the coast. Apparently, the one who inspected the Royal was a woman called Jane Jones, who booked in for one night to give the place a once-over before she completed her report.'

Helen was shocked to hear this. 'Gloria told you the inspector's name? But they're supposed to be anonymous.'

'There's not much gets past hoteliers around here, you should know that by now,' Jean said. 'When there's news as big as an inspector at large, you can bet that word passes on.'

Helen thought about this for a moment. 'Miriam next door at the Vista del Mar usually lets me know about such things. You know what she's like, always up on the latest hoteliers' gossip, but she's never said a word about this. Are you sure Gloria got it right?'

Before Jean could reply, Helen's phone rang.

'Oh, the number's withheld,' she said, before swiping the screen and announcing herself. However, there was no reply. 'Hello?' she repeated. 'Seaview Hotel? Can I help you?'

There was a beat of dead air before a woman's voice broke the silence. 'Stay away from him.' The line went dead.

Helen glared at the phone, an uneasy feeling settling in the pit of her stomach.

'Who was it?' Jean asked.

She was about to reply when her attention was caught by a white minibus pulling up outside. Along the middle of the bus the two masks of tragedy and comedy were painted, with the words *Dawley's Theatre Group*.

'Jean, they're here,' she said.

Jean bustled out of the room. 'Then I'll go downstairs to put the kettle on for our coffee while you check them in.'

Helen stood, watching the minibus doors open and those inside tumble out. She counted only six people, not seven as Taylor had promised: four women and two men. Two of the women looked around Jean's age, ladies of a certain vintage who carried themselves with grace and style. They were both smartly dressed, one clad head to toe in black – a long leather coat, well-cut trousers and boots – the other wearing a three-quarter white coat with a pale blue pashmina thrown over her shoulder. The pair walked across the road to take in the stunning view of the beach, but Helen noticed they kept well apart.

The rest of the group appeared to be much younger. The man who'd been driving stood on the pavement stretching his arms and back. He was tall and lean, with dark hair. Good-looking too, Helen noticed, with a dark beard and moustache. The second man, younger than the driver, was tall and skinny, dressed in an unflattering beige anorak, and seemed unsure what to do. He hovered by the minibus as the two younger women – one wearing a red cap over short brown hair, the other with long blonde hair – both pulled their phones from their handbags. Helen glanced at her own phone, wondering who had called, before quickly dismissing it as a wrong number.

The Seaview's doorbell rang and she stood, pushed her shoulders back and made her way to the hallway. She quickly checked her reflection in the mirror on the wall.

'Not looking bad, Mrs Dexter,' she said out loud, slipping her phone into her jeans pocket. She put a welcoming smile on her face and pulled the door open to greet her theatrical guests.

Chapter 2

'Welcome to the Seaview, come in,' Helen said, holding the green door open. In front of her was the minibus driver. He was tall, distinguished-looking, with piercing blue eyes and dark eyebrows to match his thick, lustrous hair. A pair of faded blue jeans covered his long, muscled legs. He wore black leather loafers, a white shirt under a black jacket and a beaming smile.

'I'm Chester Ford, playwright, director, lead actor. How do you do?' he said. His deep, husky voice fitted the look of him perfectly. He extended a hand to Helen. In his other he held an old-fashioned black cigarette holder that was more than a foot long. Helen was relieved to see it was empty, as the last thing she wanted was to have cross words with her new guest when he'd only just arrived.

She smiled warmly and shook his hand. Chester swung around and extended his cigarette holder towards the five people behind him.

'And this is my little troupe of merry men and women who've joined Dawley's Theatre Group for my special Scarborough play.'

Helen stepped back from the door to allow him to enter. As the rest of the group arrived at the door with their luggage, Chester introduced each one. It was clear to Helen from the way he confidently took the lead that he liked to be in charge. The young, skinny man wearing the beige anorak and a worried expression stepped into the hallway first. Chester pointed at him with his cigarette holder.

'This is Paul McNally, who looks after our behind-the-scenes work. Props, lighting, you name it, Paul does it. We'd be lost without him. He's the glue that keeps us together.'

'You don't act?' Helen asked.

Paul lifted his gaze from the carpet and looked at her briefly, then shook his head and shuffled awkwardly past Chester.

Next was one of the two elegantly dressed older ladies Helen had spied from the window. She had stylishly cropped grey hair, and although her face was lined with age, she looked relaxed and carefree. She reminded Helen of the women in holiday adverts for cruises for the over-sixties.

'You might recognise Audrey Monroe, she's a theatrical star,' Chester said proudly, waving his cigarette holder. Helen scanned the woman's soft features but was unable to connect her to anything she'd seen.

'Oh Chester, stop teasing,' Audrey said. Her voice was soft and serene. She leaned towards Helen. 'Yes, I was big once, but that was decades ago, another lifetime really, probably before you were born. I've devoted my whole life to treading the boards.'

She glided along the hallway to stand beside Paul as Chester waved in the next person. A young, attractive woman dressed in a bright red jumpsuit and yellow ankle boots bounded into the hallway. Her blonde hair fell to her shoulders. She grasped Helen's hand and shook it heartily.

'Kate Barnes,' she said, before Chester could announce her.

'I'm an actress, singer and model, and training to become a children's TV presenter.'

Helen admired her energy. 'Nice to meet you.'

Chester tutted loudly. 'Kate, dear, you should know better than to call yourself an actress. You're an actor, darling. An actor. You're not in some provincial am-dram group now. Dawley's Theatre Group is a professional outfit.'

Kate shimmied along the hall to join Audrey and Paul.

'Next we have the lovely Liza,' Chester said, waving his cigarette holder in circles. The young woman in the red cap stepped through the door. There was something about her that looked familiar to Helen, but she couldn't quite place it at first. It was when Liza spoke that she made the obvious connection. Her voice was soft and calm, her features relaxed and serene. Her red cap sat atop short brown hair that feathered around her delicate features.

'I'm Audrey's daughter,' she explained.

'Of course! The resemblance is startling,' Helen said, turning from Liza to Audrey.

Liza whipped off her cap and bowed. 'Liza Carter, actor and costume lady. That's Liza with a zee.' She strode along the hallway to stand next to her mum, and Audrey laid her arm around Liza's shoulders.

Chester cleared his throat, then, with a regal wave, he gestured with his cigarette holder once more. This time it flew dangerously close to Helen's right eye, and she determined to have a quiet word with him later.

'And last but by no means least, it's our leading lady and star of the show, the one and only Miss Carmen Delray.'

Helen peered out of the door to see the woman dressed all in black. She clocked her expensive-looking boots and long trench coat. The coat had shoulder pads that made her look more physically robust than she was. She wore a black beret atop a mass of black curls that fell to her shoulders. In fact, she had so much hair that Helen thought it must be a wig, for surely no one her age would boast such a luxuriant mane? She had never seen such an extraordinary-looking woman before. Carmen was wearing heavy make-up, and was undeniably attractive. She was of average height, but whippet thin, and she reminded Helen of an ageing American TV star from a soap opera she was struggling to name. She was incredibly glamorous, and if it hadn't been for the lines on her face, which no amount of make-up could ever hide, along with the shadows under her eyes showing a life well lived, Helen would have pegged her for a lot younger than she really was. A pair of smoky eyes flashed at her and a perfect scarlet smile beamed from Carmen's lips.

As Chester offered his hand to help her into the hallway, she pulled her arm sharply away. 'I don't want your help,' she hissed.

Helen felt a twinge of embarrassment at being caught in their crossfire. Chester stepped back and stroked his moustache with his free hand while Carmen stayed where she was, looking around.

'Is this really the best place you could book us into, Chester?'

Helen's jaw dropped in shock. She'd never felt so affronted. 'Now look here—' she began, but her words were cut off by Chester, who laid his hand on her arm while pointing his cigarette holder at Carmen.

'I'm sure Carmen didn't mean what she said. She's just overtired from the journey,' he said apologetically.

'And she's in one of her moods,' Kate added quickly.

Helen took a moment to pull herself together. She shrugged Chester's hand from her arm, then smiled sweetly at Carmen. 'I'll have you know, the Seaview is a quality hotel, Mrs Delray,' she said firmly. 'Taylor Caffrey wouldn't have recommended it to you if he didn't approve.'

Carmen grimaced. 'I'll be the judge of what I think is quality,' she replied archly. 'Oh, and it's not Mrs. I'm not married.'

'I'm surprised she can keep up with whether she's single or married, with all the men in her life,' Kate sniggered behind Helen's back.

Helen counted to five in her head, calming herself down, then looked around at the guests. 'Well, as we're going to be sharing the Seaview for the next two weeks, the least I can do is make sure I know everyone's name from the off.' She nodded to the lady with the blue pashmina, kind eyes and serene face. 'You're Audrey Monroe, right?' She turned to the younger woman, the double of Audrey. 'Liza Carter, Audrey's daughter.' The red jumpsuit and yellow boots couldn't be missed. 'Kate Barnes,' she went on. 'Chester Ford,' nodding to the man with the moustache and beard.

'At your service, at all times,' Chester replied, twirling his cigarette holder, an affectation which Helen was already finding annoying.

'Peter?' Helen said, looking at the boy in the beige anorak.

He shuffled from foot to foot but didn't look up. 'Paul,' he said softly. 'Paul McNally.'

'Ah, sorry, Paul, yes.' Finally she turned to the woman in the leather coat. 'And Carmen Delray, of course.'

She didn't think she'd forget Carmen's name. The woman was

one of the most unusual who'd ever stayed at the Seaview. She was old, yes, but there was an energy about her, and she certainly knew how to make an impression. She'd walked into the hotel with her head held high, even while criticising the place. Despite Carmen's sharp words about the Seaview, Helen was intrigued by her. It looked as if she was going to be a force to be reckoned with, and Helen knew she'd need to be on her mettle whenever she was around. Helen shook her head, pulled herself together, then led everyone to the lounge, where she handed out room keys.

'Now then, which one of you requested the vegan breakfast?' she asked.

Kate's hand shot up.

'I've had a word with the cook,' Helen said, although she kept quiet about the words Jean had replied with. 'Is there another person to come? Taylor Caffrey told me there would be seven of you checking in, but only six have arrived.'

'Ah yes, about that,' Chester said. He tapped his cigarette holder noisily on the bar. Helen gently placed her hand on his to deaden the noise. Despite his debonair appearance, she was beginning to find Chester Ford and his cigarette holder irritating, what with him constantly tapping and twirling the thing.

'This is a non-smoking hotel, Mr Ford,' she said calmly, removing her hand.

'What? This little thing?' Chester laughed, raising the holder. 'Oh, I don't smoke it, I poke it.'

'You do what?' Helen said sharply. As well as being irritating, she wondered if he was now having a joke at her expense.

'I poke things with it. See, I used to smoke,' Chester explained, 'and when I gave up, I found that I was so used to having this

17

darling little thing between my fingers that I carry it now just to have something to do with my hands.'

A burst of sarcastic laughter rang out. Helen turned, surprised to discover the outburst coming from Carmen. She waited a moment, expecting an explanation, but none came her way. There were a few seconds of embarrassed silence before, professional to the end, she plastered her smile on and turned back to Chester.

'So, is there someone else coming?'

'Yes, another of our troupe will be arriving later. Lee Cooper.'

'Worse luck,' Kate muttered, just loud enough for Helen to hear.

As the actors made their way to their rooms, Helen noticed Chester and Carmen hanging back in the lounge, whispering. A black suitcase stood on the hallway floor.

'Is this yours, Carmen? Let me carry it up to your room,' she called.

'Let me, I'll take it up for her,' Chester replied.

Carmen glared at him. 'There's nothing you can do for me any more,' she hissed. 'You and I are over. You knew we were finished when I signed up with Dawley's for this tour of your stinking play.'

Chester noisily tapped his cigarette holder on the bar. It sounded to Helen as if a machine gun was going off in the lounge. 'This stinking play, as you call it, is my murder mystery masterpiece, *Midnight with Maude*.'

Carmen crossed her arms. '*Your* masterpiece? How dare you!'

'Carmen, we've been through this already. We've talked about it and agreed not to mention it again.'

'You mean you paid me to shut up about it.'

'Can't we try to be civil at least?' Chester pleaded.

Helen lugged the suitcase from the hallway, leaving the two of them arguing. By the time she returned, Chester was outside, pulling a suitcase from the minibus. Carmen was holding a small round mirror in one hand, a scarlet lipstick in the other. Helen watched as she puckered up.

'Are you all right? Need anything?' she asked.

Carmen snapped the mirror shut, flung it in her bag with the lipstick, then smacked her scarlet lips together. 'Oh, I'm more than all right,' she said, sounding bitter. 'But I doubt very much there's anything either you or your dump of a hotel can offer me, whether I need it or not.'

'Now just a minute!' Helen said angrily, but Carmen stood, flicked her leather coat behind her and stormed out of the lounge. Helen let her go, relieved to get the woman out of her sight. She turned to the framed photograph of Tom behind the bar.

'Well, what do you make of this lot?' she said.

Her eye was caught by something next to the photo that made her smile. It was a plastic figurine of Elvis Presley, a tiny, fun ornament, no bigger than three inches high. Jimmy and his troupe of Elvis impersonators had presented it to her when they'd stayed at the Seaview earlier that year. They'd called it her good luck charm.

'Well, Elvis, here's to the next two weeks with this acting group. They're quite a bunch of characters. I think I'm going to need some of your luck.' She pressed his plastic head, and his hips shimmied from side to side.

Just then, her phone rang. She picked it up, glanced at the screen and saw that it was another withheld number. She swiped the phone into life, wondering who it was this time.

'Good morning, Seaview Hotel,' she said cheerfully. However, the reply she heard knocked the smile off her face, and she stood to attention. 'One night?' she gulped. 'You'd like to book a room in the name of Jane Jones? Yes, I'm sure that'd be fine, let me just check the diary.'

She took the tablet from behind the bar and opened the app she used to book guests in. Jane Jones wanted a room for a week on Monday, while the actors would still be there. Helen briefly considered asking her to choose another date, but if she lost her slot with the inspector, she might have to wait months for another. No, she wasn't prepared to wait; she needed to act quickly. The acting troupe were only using seven guest rooms, plus one extra to store props and costumes. That left two rooms spare. She hadn't signed anything with Taylor Caffrey to prohibit her from taking other guests while the actors were there, although she knew they wouldn't be overjoyed once they found out. Well, she'd cross that bridge when she came to it. This was an exceptional booking, one she wasn't prepared to refuse.

Decision made, she went ahead and booked in Jane Jones. When she hung up, she breathed a sigh of relief and looked again at the photo of Tom. He was dressed as Elvis Presley, his musical hero, wearing a white suit, black wig and quivering top lip. The photo had been taken at one of the Seaview's famous Elvis-themed party nights, which they used to enjoy before Tom fell ill.

'This could be it, Tom,' she said. 'Finally, the Seaview gets its chance to shine.'

Chapter 3

Once the actors were in their rooms, Helen walked down to her basement apartment. A cafetière of coffee sat on the kitchen table along with a packet of chocolate digestives. Jean helped herself to a biscuit and dunked it in her mug. At Helen's feet, her greyhound Suki lay sphinx-like, her long caramel limbs neatly tucked under her body.

'Did the actors check in all right?' Jean asked.

'Almost all of them,' Helen replied. 'There's another arriving later.' She took a sip from her mug. 'Strange bunch, though.'

Jean raised her eyebrows. 'How do you mean?'

Helen shrugged. 'One of them is possibly the most glamorous woman we've ever had staying here. But she was also very rude. I picked up on some tension between her and a fella called Chester; they were arguing and whispering once the others were out of earshot. Chester's a good-looking man, maybe in his thirties. There's a mother and daughter too; the mother is a big theatre star, apparently. She's called Audrey Monroe – have you heard of her?'

Jean shook her head. 'Can't say I have. Will you need me to stay after breakfast each day? Perhaps they'd like morning coffee and pastries, or lunch? I could turn my hand to baking quiches and pies if that's what they want.'

'Well, they've only booked in for bed and breakfast, but I'll ask them. It could be a money-spinner if it works out. Thanks, Jean, you always have the best ideas.'

Jean took another biscuit and dunked it in her coffee. 'What's she like, then, this rude woman who was arguing?'

The black-clad Carmen Delray flashed through Helen's mind. 'She's stylish, I'll give her that. Very well dressed, classy, lots of make-up, gorgeous hair. She had a beret on, you know, looked a bit French. But my word, she had an attitude. I think staying here's a comedown for her; it sounds as if she's used to the finer things in life, and that doesn't include three-star B&Bs. Chester, the director, called her his leading lady.'

'What's her name?' Jean asked.

'Carmen Delray.'

Jean almost choked on her biscuit. She put her coffee cup on the table and covered her mouth with her hand, coughing and gasping for breath. Helen leapt out of her seat and thumped her on the back until her breathing returned to normal, then handed her a glass of water.

'Thanks, love,' Jean gasped between sips. 'My word, that name's a blast from the past.' She put her hand on her chest and leaned back in her chair.

'Do you know her?' Helen asked.

'I used to,' Jean said. 'Give me a minute, love, while I pull myself together.'

She took another biscuit and bit into it, washing it down with a sip of coffee. Then she leaned forward. 'We went to the same school, though she's a few years older than me. I remember her from when I was growing up in Hull. But she wasn't called Carmen back then. I knew her as Janet Carstairs.'

'When did she change her name?'

'When she left school and started studying drama in London. She never returned to Hull; I heard through friends that she thought the place wasn't good enough for her. Plus, she's been married at least three times I'm aware of. She might be Miss Delray to her adoring fans, but to those who knew her back then, she'll always be Janet Carstairs.'

'How old is she, Jean?' Helen asked, intrigued.

'She'll be late sixties.'

'I hope I look as good as her at that age.'

'Well, I haven't seen her in years, not since Hull. I don't suppose she'll recognise me. What I do remember, though . . .' a faraway look came into Jean's eyes, 'was that she used to flirt with one of our teachers, Mr Gibson, the history master. He had a huge moustache, if I remember rightly.'

'Chester Ford, the director, he's got a big moustache too,' Helen noted.

'Do you think Chester and Carmen are carrying on?' Jean asked.

'It's none of my business, Jean. You know I don't like gossiping about the guests, but this lot are very unusual.'

'Is it all right if I come upstairs to say hello to her at some point?'

'Course it is, any time.'

It was on the tip of Helen's tongue to tell Jean about the hotel inspector's visit when the doorbell rang. She glanced at the screen on the kitchen wall, which showed an image from the camera by the front door. A tall, thin, bald man was standing rigid with a large sports bag at his feet. He had a long, pale face and thin lips, and was dressed in a formal black suit.

'That might be the final guest,' she said. 'I'll go and check him in.'

Jean drained her coffee, then bent low to stroke Suki. The dog whined with pleasure in return. 'I'll let myself out and head up to the care home to see Mum. She's still having trouble with her legs. I'll be back in the morning to cook breakfast.'

'See you, Jean, thanks for everything,' Helen said as she headed upstairs.

Helen pulled the door open and greeted the man standing outside.

'Lee Cooper,' he said, offering his hand. Then he pointed to the minibus. 'I'm with Dawley's Theatre Group. I see the others have arrived.'

Helen stepped to one side to allow him to enter. 'Yes, they're here, please come in. Welcome to the Seaview Hotel. Did you have a good journey?'

'Well, the train wasn't full and I managed to get a seat in the quiet coach so I could start learning my lines. I sometimes have a bit of trouble with them, so the more practice I can get, the better. But it would've been easier if I'd travelled in the bus with the gang.'

'Why didn't you?' Helen asked, curious.

Lee's face seemed to collapse in on itself and his bottom lip trembled. 'My fiancée . . . well, she's my ex now, she's part of the troupe. We broke up recently and things are still raw between us.'

'Oh dear, I'm sorry to hear it,' Helen said. She wondered which of the female actors was Lee's ex-fiancée. Was it Liza, or Kate? It wouldn't be Audrey, surely, would it? She was old enough to be the boy's grandmother. Oh, and please don't let it be Carmen, she thought. There was enough drama going on with that woman already.

'How Kate and I will manage to get through the next couple of weeks working closely together and living in the same place, I don't know, but we have no choice,' Lee continued.

'Kate? Ah, I see,' Helen said, relieved that he'd answered her question without her having to ask it. She didn't like to probe into guests' affairs.

'Because both of us are actors, we're often broke between jobs. So when we were offered the chance to perform in *Midnight with Maude*, we jumped at it,' Lee carried on. 'We were still together when we signed up with Dawley's for this play and we were happy, thought we had the world at our feet. And now, things have gone wrong and here we are, forced together. It's not going to be easy for either of us, Mrs . . .'

'Dexter, but please, call me Helen.'

She handed Lee the key to his room and offered to take his bag. She was relieved when he declined; his bag was big, looked heavy, and his room was on the top floor.

With her afternoon free, and the weather still mild, Helen decided to take Suki to the beach. She flung on her old fleece jacket, fastened Suki's lead to her collar and led the dog out of the back door and into the yard. Turning the corner around the Seaview, she walked down Windsor Terrace to King's Parade and from there followed the path down the cliff to the beach. When she let Suki off the lead, the dog bounded to the waves, stopping short of going in and getting wet.

'Not going for a swim today, Suki?' Helen called.

The sun sparkled on the water, light bouncing like diamonds. Oh, how she loved Scarborough. She took off her jacket and tied the sleeves around her waist, exposing her arms. Then she closed her eyes, tilted her face to the sun and let its warmth sink into her skin, breathing in the sea air as she listened to gulls and the breaking waves. She was still learning to claim Scarborough as her own. Since Tom's illness had taken him, her life had taken on a different tone; it felt empty now and subdued. After he'd died, she'd put all her energy, heart and soul, not to mention her bank balance, into the Seaview, upgrading and decorating as she learned how to cope on her own.

When she opened her eyes again, ahead of her was a stout woman with an ice cream in her hand. She was barefoot, paddling in the sea, the waves splashing her ankles. Her skirt reminded Helen of deckchair stripes as it billowed out. Her perfume reached her, the scent of freshly spun candyfloss on the breeze. She looked happy, Helen thought, a woman in the prime of life, sun-kissed and smiling. All that was missing was a Kiss Me Quick hat on her head. She wondered if the souvenir shops on the South Bay still sold hats like that. She hadn't seen one in years.

When she'd walked for an hour, she returned to the Seaview. Taking her phone from her pocket, she saw a missed call from her friend Taylor. She called him straight back.

'How are the actors settling in, dear?' he asked.

'Well, they're here,' Helen said. 'There's not much more I can tell you. They seem like a nice bunch.'

'You'll get to know them pretty well over the next two weeks. The landlady at the theatre digs still can't take them till then. The mice have gone, but the inspector from the council has found something else.'

'What?' Helen asked.

'Believe me, you don't want to know. Anyhoo, I hope it's all right that I landed the troupe on you. Because you're the one who has to look after them, feed them and keep them energised ready to perform. I should warn you, there are some big egos amongst them; things might get intense.'

'Oh, it's already intense.' Helen laughed, thinking of Carmen.

'Not Kate and Lee?' Taylor said. 'I heard they'd split up. Can't be easy on either of them being forced to live together. I just hope it doesn't cause you too much grief having a fighting couple staying at the Seaview.' He cleared his throat. 'And how's madam doing?'

'Do you mean Jean?'

'No, darling. I mean the dark diva, Carmen Delray.'

'Oh, well, she's . . .' Helen tried to choose her words carefully. 'She's unique, I'll give her that. I don't think I've met anyone like her before.'

'Just keep her away from the bar.'

'Why? Does she have a drink problem?'

'You mean you don't know?'

'I'd never heard of her before she turned up today.'

'Haven't you ever seen *The Singing Nurse* on TV?' Taylor cried. 'Carmen was its star, darling. She lit up the screen each time she came on. She played Wendy "Songbird" Wren and was in almost every episode for fifteen years. It made her a big name in television – before she got sacked. You must have seen it, surely?'

'I've never heard of it, Taylor. You know I don't watch much TV. Running the Seaview takes up all my time. I'll Google it later. Why did they sack her?'

'Well, therein lies a tale. She kept turning up drunk for work. And rumour has it that she only got the lead role in the first place after seducing the show's director. He was married, of course, and there's been bad blood between Carmen and Audrey since.'

'What does Audrey have to do with it?'

'I can't believe you don't know, dear. Everyone in our business knows what happened.'

Helen laughed. 'I'm a hotel landlady, Taylor, not involved in your creative world.'

'Well, you know me, I'm not one to gossip, but as it's common knowledge already, there's no harm in letting you know. Carmen seduced Audrey's husband. Not only that, but she also took Audrey's role in *The Singing Nurse*.'

'You mean the role was meant for Audrey?'

'That's exactly right, dear. After it happened, Audrey disappeared from acting for a very long time. The official line was that she'd taken herself away to a meditation retreat in the Pyrenees, but others – shall we say less kind people – maintain she had a breakdown and couldn't face the world. I guess we'll never learn the truth about what really went on. I still can't believe they both agreed to join Dawley's Theatre Group for this performance, knowing that they'd be working with each other. But actors always go where the work is, even when it means reuniting with an old enemy. Anyway, I thought it best to warn you that things might get ugly. Carmen isn't known for her discretion and tact.'

'She's going to keep me on my toes, that one,' Helen agreed.

'And how does Audrey seem?' Taylor asked.

'Oh, she's lovely, very Zen and chilled.'

'Don't let appearances fool you. Remember, these are acting professionals, dear. I know what they're like; I've spent my whole life amongst thespians.'

There was a beat of silence before Taylor spoke again. 'Helen, dear,' he said, lowering his voice, 'you will look after the actors, won't you? *Midnight with Maude* is make or break for the Modernist. You know how much Scarborough folk love to see a good show. If the play doesn't pull a decent-sized audience, the theatre closes down. It's as simple as that. Running the Modernist is my life, it's all I've ever known. The place is crumbling around my ears, but I'm determined to save it.'

'I'll look after your troupe, Taylor, don't worry. How are the roof repairs going?'

'Good. I've got your friend Gav working on it,' Taylor said brightly. 'He can talk the back legs off a pantomime horse, but he's doing a great job.'

'If Gav's on the case, it'll be done well. He's a hard worker, and the Modernist is safe in his hands – or at least the roof is.'

'Anyhoo, I'd better go. Mr Phipps needs his dinner and I've bought him a tin of luxury tuna chunks.'

'How is the old fella?'

'Getting old and fat, just like me.'

Helen said goodbye, but before she put her phone away, she decided to search online to find out more about *The Singing Nurse* and the enigmatic Carmen Delray.

Chapter 4

It was all systems go the next morning while breakfast was being prepared. In the kitchen, Jean sang along to a sixties hit on the radio as she placed hash browns on a tray. Helen didn't want to get in her way while she worked; she knew Jean's routine off by heart and knew the woman didn't like anyone to fuss around. Instead, she took Suki for a walk along the North Bay beach.

As she returned to the Seaview, she spotted Sally on Windsor Terrace. Sally was the hotel's cleaner – at least that was what it said on her job description. In reality, she was so much more, helping out in every way she could. The only thing she didn't do, that Jean wouldn't allow anyone to do, was help with the cooking. She was a determined young woman in her early thirties, slim with shoulder-length fair hair, and when she wasn't working at the Seaview, she was studying business and law at Scarborough college. She was also a single mother to four-year-old Gracie and a good friend to Helen and Jean. The three women formed a tight-knit, efficient bond.

'Morning, Sally,' Helen called cheerfully. 'How are you?'

'A bit tired, if I'm honest. I was out with Gav last night; we went to a Northern Soul gig at the Spa and didn't get home till late. But it was a great night, brilliant music, Helen. You should come with us one night.' Sally put her hand to her mouth to stifle a yawn.

Helen glanced at her pale face. 'You do look done in. I'll ask Jean to make us coffee before we start serving breakfast.'

'The acting troupe have arrived, I see,' Sally said, pointing at the minibus.

'Oh, they're here. You'll meet them at breakfast.'

'Nice bunch?'

'Nice enough,' Helen replied, putting an end to further questions.

Sally got down on her haunches and stroked Suki's head, making a fuss of the dog.

'How's Gracie?' Helen asked.

'She's fallen in love with Gav,' Sally laughed, standing up. 'He's all she talks about – it's Gav this and Gav that. On the nights when he doesn't stay over at the flat, she's asking where he is. It's tricky, Helen. I think the world of him, but I'm scared of bringing him into Gracie's life full-time. He might just disappear like her dad did, once the novelty wears off and the reality of having a child sinks in.'

'Gav wouldn't do that,' Helen said quickly.

'Wouldn't he? How do you know what goes on in his mind?'

'He's a mate of Marie's and she's been my best friend since we were little. She thinks the sun shines out of him, and he can do no wrong in her eyes. And I trust her judgement. If Marie thinks Gav's a good 'un, he is. She's rarely wrong about men.'

'Apart from her husband, you mean. What a mistake he turned out to be.'

Helen rolled her eyes. 'The least said about Daran Clark the better. And just for the record, she's gone back to using her maiden name now she's divorced. She's not Marie Clark any more, she's Marie Davenport.'

'Makes her sound like a character in a period drama.'

Helen laughed. 'Oh, Marie would love that, wouldn't she? I can just see her now as Lady Davenport of the manor.'

The two women walked to the back of the Seaview and let themselves in through the yard.

'Come through to my living room,' Helen told Sally. 'I'll bring coffee in to perk you up. We've got half an hour before breakfast begins.'

They made their way through the kitchen, greeting Jean en route but knowing not to stop and distract her. In the living room, Sally settled on the sofa with Suki's head on her knee while Helen returned to the kitchen to fetch two steaming cups of coffee.

'Before we start work, I've got a couple of things to tell you,' she said as she passed Sally a chunky blue mug. 'The first thing is that we've got a special visitor coming a week on Monday and staying just for one night.'

'Who?'

'Brace yourself, Sally. It's the hotel inspector.'

Sally punched the air with her free hand. 'At last we'll get our four stars!' Then she leaned towards Helen. 'Aren't they supposed to be anonymous? How do you know?'

'Jean's got a friend who works at the Royal Hotel and she heard on the grapevine that a female inspector called Jane Jones is doing the rounds on the Yorkshire coast. Next thing you know, I receive a phone call from a woman for a single night's booking.'

'Let me guess, in the name of Jane Jones?'

'Got it in one.'

'Oh Helen, this is great news. You deserve that extra star.'

'We all deserve it: you, me and Jean.'

'Does Jean know yet?' Sally asked.

'No. I was about to tell her when a guest arrived. I'll tell her after breakfast, when we have our daily catch-up. But seriously, Sally, I couldn't have got the hotel up to scratch without your help, and without Jean agreeing to expand the breakfast menu. Well, and without Marie's investment, of course. She's the one who encouraged me to update the place after Tom died. She thought it'd be a distraction for me, but now that it's done, I can see she was right: it did look dated and dull before.'

'It really does look much nicer now, Helen. It feels light and airy, and the muted colours in the dining room are a touch of genius. Did she plough all of her divorce settlement into the Seaview?'

Helen shook her head. 'Not all of it. Marie's savvy enough not to put all her eggs in one basket. She invested enough to get this place looking smart, and she's been true to her word so far and hasn't interfered in the business. She said she only ever wanted to be a sleeping partner, and that's what she's done. She'll get a good return on her money, I'll see to that. And your Gav did a wonderful job decorating it with the team of lads he brought in. They were really fast workers.'

'So what's the second thing I need to know?' Sally asked.

'Just that we have seven guests here for the next two weeks, apart from the night when the inspector comes. Oh, and one of them is vegan.'

Sally laughed out loud. 'I bet Jean's not happy about that.'

'Happy about what?' Jean said, walking into the living room carrying two plates. 'Here we go, hot bacon butties to get your engines revving before you start serving breakfast.'

Helen and Sally each took a plate.

'I was just telling Sally about the vegan,' Helen said, winking at Sally.

Jean padded out of the living room, muttering darkly under her breath.

Half an hour later, Helen and Sally were waiting by the dining room door. Both wore a smart navy tabard with the Seaview's name embroidered in white. It was Chester Ford who came down first, and Helen was relieved to see he didn't have his cigarette holder.

'Morning, Chester. This is Sally, my right-hand woman. If you or the troupe need anything, all you have to do is ask. We'll do all we can to help.'

Chester ran his fingers through his thick dark hair. 'Thank you,' he said.

'Oh, hasn't he got a lovely deep voice?' Sally whispered to Helen.

Audrey and Liza came down together, chatting amiably. Helen stole a quick look at Audrey, remembering what Taylor Caffrey had told her about her fall-out with Carmen all those years ago. She wondered if behind her calm facade Audrey still bore a grudge. Then came Paul, avoiding her gaze, mumbling good morning in reply to her cheery hello.

'He's a bit shy,' she whispered to Sally once Paul was seated.

Next to enter the dining room was Kate, dressed in another colourful jumpsuit, this time turquoise matched with snow-white trainers. She was the most energetic and alert of the group, greeting Helen loudly, telling her what a wonderful room she had and how well she'd slept. She was followed by Carmen, who looked every inch as glamorous as she'd done the previous day. Helen wondered what time she set her morning alarm for to give her time to do her face and fix her hair – or was it a wig? She still wasn't sure. Carmen wafted into the dining room without acknowledging Helen or Sally, and Helen caught the scent of dark, heady perfume as she walked by. She watched the woman hesitate at the door.

'Feel free to sit anywhere you'd like to,' she said.

Carmen chose a table at the opposite end of the room to the others. Not only that, but she positioned herself so that her back was towards them, which Helen thought rather rude.

Last downstairs was Lee, who paused at the dining room door, peeked inside, then smiled wanly at Helen. 'Would you mind seating me away from Kate? I don't want to upset her by sitting close by.'

'You can sit anywhere you want, there are plenty of free tables,' Helen replied.

Lee walked slowly into the room, where muted good mornings were exchanged, but Carmen still refused to turn around.

Helen and Sally got to work bringing in Jean's breakfasts, cooked to perfection. All except Kate's vegan sausages, which were cooked as well as Jean could manage. Small talk was exchanged between tables as the guests ate, although Carmen didn't join in, concentrating instead on a sheaf of papers in front of her. Each time

35

Helen brought more tea or toast, she tried to peek at Carmen's reading material. Well, it wasn't as if she was being nosy, or so she told herself, for the bold typeface wasn't hard to miss. It was the script for *Midnight with Maude*. She also couldn't help notice Carmen's nails, which were long, sharp and painted a deep shade of red.

'Are you starting rehearsals today?' Helen asked Chester when she served him more tea.

'No, today is a day for settling in,' he replied. 'We'll begin rehearsals tomorrow, in your bar lounge, if we may? Taylor Caffrey said you'd offered us as much of your public area as we might need.'

'No trouble at all, make yourselves at home,' Helen replied.

The group ate at leisure, and when they finally left the dining room, Helen noticed that Lee kept his distance from Kate, who refused to look in his direction. Only Carmen was left in the room, reading her script, and without glasses too. Helen wondered what woman of that age didn't need reading specs. Carmen might be rude and unpredictable, but physically she was a marvel for her age.

'More tea?' Helen asked.

Carmen leaned back in her seat. 'I'm all done, dear. Thank you, breakfast was delicious. Please give my regards to your cook.'

An idea struck Helen. 'You could give her your compliments yourself if you like. She's someone you might recognise.'

Carmen's face dropped before she forced a smile. 'Really? Oh, who on earth could it be?' she cooed.

'Sally?' Helen called. 'Be a love, pop downstairs and ask Jean to come up.'

36

Within minutes, Jean was walking towards the dining room door.

'What is it? Any problems with breakfast?' she asked.

'On the contrary,' Helen said, smiling. 'There's someone here who'd like to say thank you.'

Puzzled, Jean put her head around the door. Her eyes opened wide. 'My word! It really is you!'

Carmen didn't move, and her face gave nothing away. Jean hesitated.

'It's me, Jean Atkinson, from Hull,' she said. 'Don't you remember me? Chubby little Jean? Oh, I was such a fan of *The Singing Nurse*. I loved you in that show as Wendy "Songbird" Wren. Mind you, I'm old enough to remember you as Janet Carstairs.'

Carmen's top lip curled, and quick as a flash she whipped a pair of large sunglasses from her bag and snapped them on to her face. Helen watched, intrigued.

'Janet Carstairs is a part of my life I never discuss,' Carmen hissed. 'I have no wish to dig her up from the dead.' She scraped her chair back, gathered her script and bag and stormed from the room, almost knocking Jean over as she went.

When she was out of earshot, Jean sidled up to Helen. 'My word, that was rude. Did I say something wrong?'

Helen shook her head, remembering what she'd read about Carmen online. 'You did nothing wrong, Jean. Once I've finished clearing breakfast away, I'll join you and Sally for coffee, and I'll tell you all I know.'

Chapter 5

Helen, Jean and Sally huddled around Helen's kitchen table while Suki lay on the floor. Sally had taken her shoes off and was sitting with one leg tucked under her. Helen spotted her discarded shoes on the carpet, perilously close to Suki's mouth.

'You might want to move them away from the dog,' she said.

'Has she still got a thing about chewing shoes?' Sally tutted. She uncurled her leg, sat up straight and pushed her feet into her trainers.

Helen poured coffee into three chunky mugs. 'I bought these with Tom from the Coast art gallery in Cloughton,' she said, remembering the autumn day they had driven to the nearby pretty village on a rare day off work.

Sally took a sip of coffee and glanced at her quickly. 'You seem able to talk about him more easily these days, although I know you must still miss him like mad.'

Helen cradled her mug with both hands. 'Oh, I miss him all right. Every single day. Every minute of every day. I think about him all the time. I even talk to him. Is that mad?'

Jean shook her head. 'No, lass, it's not. I did that a lot after Archie passed on. Sometimes I still do.'

'Well, at least I can talk about him now without dissolving into tears and feeling like I'm falling apart,' Helen said.

'It gets easier. I told you it would,' Jean said sagely.

Helen bent low to stroke the dog behind her ears. 'I'd be lost without Suki.'

'What about Jimmy?' Sally said. 'I thought he was coming back soon?'

Helen reached for a packet of custard creams, knowing that Sally and Jean were waiting for her reaction. 'I'll deal with him when I see him. I'm still not sure what to think.'

'Well, you know what me and Jean think,' Sally said.

'You could do a lot worse,' Jean added. 'He's quite a catch. Good-looking, talented, sexy . . . if you like that kind of thing.'

Helen burst out laughing. 'Sexy? Jimmy?'

Sally nodded. 'He is, you know, for an older man.'

'Hey, you, I'm not that old and neither is Jimmy. I'm not even fifty yet.'

'But you will be next year. Are we having your party upstairs?'

'I'll think about that nearer the time,' Helen laughed. 'Let's get through the next two weeks with this acting group first.' She turned to Jean. 'There's something else happening, a week on Monday.'

'What's that, love?'

'The hotel inspector's coming in.'

There, she'd said it. She sat back in her chair and looked at Jean, waiting to hear what she had to say. For Jean always had an opinion. Helen watched her take a sip of coffee, a bite from her biscuit, but was surprised when she remained unusually silent.

'Well? Aren't you going to say anything?' she said at last.

Jean shrugged. 'I've already told you not to get your hopes up. I know how hard you've worked, love. I've seen this place transformed over the last few months. It's more bright and cheerful than it ever was; it feels like we've gone up a notch. And if an inspector can't see that when they come, we'll always know we did our best.'

Sally bit her lip. 'Dan, a friend of mine from college, works in the bar at the North Mount Hotel on the South Bay, and he said the inspector stayed there last month.'

'Was it Jane Jones?' Helen asked.

Sally shrugged. 'Don't know, he didn't tell me the name. All I know is that it was a woman. She had bobbed blonde hair and a gap in the middle of her teeth. Anyway, he said that she booked in for one night and asked all sorts of questions about tourist attractions in Scarborough when she arrived. They gave her all the information she requested, and when she was told that reception opened at seven a.m. and closed at eleven p.m., do you know what she did?'

Helen and Jean leaned forward.

'She rang at five past seven in the morning to order room service and again at ten fifty-five at night to ask for a bottle of water.'

'She was checking to see if the receptionist was doing their job,' Jean said sagely.

'What else did she do?' Helen asked. 'The more you can tell us, the more prepared we'll be.'

'Dan said she kept herself to herself and didn't talk to other guests.'

Jean leaned back in her chair. 'We'll have no problems with her breakfast report, I can assure you.'

'Let's just hope she doesn't ask for kippers,' Helen said.

'Blasted things,' moaned Jean.

A companionable silence fell over the three women as they

enjoyed their coffee. Jean helped herself to three custard creams. She was about to pop the first into her mouth when she stopped and looked at Helen.

'Go on then, spill the beans about her ladyship,' she said. 'You said you'd tell me what you knew.'

'Who's her ladyship?' Sally asked.

Helen placed her mug on a slate coaster and looked at the two women. 'Now listen, both of you,' she said sharply. 'You know we must never call our guests things like that. That nickname stays strictly between the three of us down here.'

Jean tutted loudly. 'Come on, Helen, you know me better than that.'

'Sorry, Jean, but there's something about this group of actors that unsettles me.'

'Who is she?' Sally cried. 'Will someone tell me what's going on?'

'Well, I shouldn't really tell you this, but as I said, what we say down here stays down here. Got it?'

'Got it!' Jean and Sally chorused.

'You remember the older woman dressed in black this morning at breakfast, Carmen Delray?'

'The one with the amazing hair? All those curls!' Sally said.

'That's her. Well, Taylor Caffrey rang, asking after the guests. You know how much he's reliant on their play turning the fortunes of his theatre around. He asked me how they were settling in and told me to make sure I looked after them as best as I could. I told him I would, of course. But then he mentioned something about Carmen Delray. He said to keep her away from the bar.'

Jean shrugged. 'So, she drinks too much. That's hardly a crime, is it?'

41

'Well, it's none of our business whether guests drink, but Taylor's advice to me was to keep an eye on her. He also said she used to star in a TV drama.'

'*The Singing Nurse*,' Jean told Sally. 'She was ever so good in it.'

'Oh, my mum watches that. It's being repeated on the classics channel,' Sally said.

'Anyway, I'd never heard of *The Singing Nurse* or Carmen Delray, so I decided to find out about her,' Helen said.

'You Googled her, didn't you?' Sally guessed.

'I was curious, yes,' Helen admitted.

'You mean you were being nosy,' Jean laughed. 'Come on, what did you find out?'

'Well, it confirmed what Taylor said, that Carmen was a big star back in the day. *The Singing Nurse* made her a fortune, most of which she drank away or lost investing in a bar in Spain, or so the internet claims. But it seems to be true – there was more than one news page that said the same thing. Then she was sacked from the show because of her drinking.'

Jean's mouth opened wide. 'No!'

'Oh my giddy aunt!' cried Sally.

'And that's not all,' Helen continued. 'I did a bit more digging, and in every picture I found of her where she had a man by her side, the man had a big bushy moustache.'

'Different men?' Sally asked.

Helen nodded. 'She's clearly got a type that she likes. And there were plenty of pictures of her with Chester Ford, too – with their arms around each other, kissing for the camera, posing at awards dos and press junkets.'

'Chester was the chap sitting at the window table this morning, the one with the moustache and beard, right?' Sally said.

Helen nodded, and Sally carried on. 'Oh, he's a nice-looking fella, distinguished, not bad for an older man.'

'Older man? For heaven's sake, he's younger than me!' Helen cried in mock horror. 'I think I can do without any more ageism from my staff, thank you very much.'

'Ah, you're only jealous because you're not young like me.'

Helen laughed and placed her hand on top of Sally's. 'You're right. Make the most of every minute, love.'

'Well, what did you find out about him?' Sally wanted to know.

'It confirmed that he and Carmen had been dating,' Helen replied.

'But she's old enough to be his mother!' Jean cried.

'Some women like a younger man. And by the look of her, Carmen's a force to be reckoned with, and a lot of men like that. Anyway, from what I can gather since they arrived, the two of them have fallen out. In fact, I'd go so far as to say they're in the throes of a nasty separation. I heard them arguing in the lounge, and they're staying in separate rooms, plus Carmen sat alone at breakfast, ignoring the rest of them.'

'She always was a lone wolf at school,' Jean said.

'What do you mean, at school?'

Jean told Sally about Janet Carstairs and her modest upbringing in Hull. 'Did you uncover anything else about Carmen?' she added, looking at Helen. 'Was there anything online about her Hull days?'

'Not much about her past life; it was mainly all fan sites and articles about her acting days. When Taylor rang, he also told me that she had history with another of the actors, a lady called Audrey Monroe. Apparently Carmen had an affair with Audrey's husband, who was the director of *The Singing Nurse* who'd originally written the lead role for Audrey.'

Jean and Sally's eyes opened wide.

'Never in the world!' Jean exclaimed.

'Go on, Helen,' Sally urged.

'Well, obviously I Googled that as well to see what had gone on, and I found that what Taylor said was true – not that I doubted him. I've always known him to be honest. Anyway, after Carmen stole Audrey's husband and her role in the show, Audrey disappeared from public life. The tabloids said she'd had a breakdown. But I found some quotes from people reported as being her friends saying that wasn't true and that she'd gone to a retreat in the Spanish mountains to get away from the media frenzy.' Helen looked from Jean to Sally. 'And this is the first time that Carmen and Audrey have worked together since. Their past animosity explains why I haven't seen them speaking to each other since they arrived. In fact, I'd go so far as to say they're deliberately keeping out of each other's way.'

'Blimey,' said Sally.

'Buckle your seat belt, Helen, you could be in for a bumpy ride,' Jean said.

'And as if that's not enough,' Helen continued, 'I found out something else about Chester Ford and the play they're rehearsing.'

Jean and Sally looked at her expectantly.

'There was an interview in the *Scarborough Times* that said the play, *Midnight with Maude*, is a murder mystery he wrote to showcase Carmen's skills.'

'Well, it's been a long time since her heyday,' Jean said. 'I expect she'll be wanting to get back in the public eye after being sacked from *The Singing Nurse*.'

'In the interview, Chester revealed that agents are coming to Scarborough especially to see her, agents with the power to put her back on TV. He said that if she can shine on stage here, she might be given a chance to star in a show he'll be commissioned to write. So you see, there's a lot more riding on *Midnight with Maude* than we first thought. Its success is crucial not just for Taylor and the Modernist Theatre, but for Chester's future and Carmen's career.'

'But now Carmen and Chester have fallen out . . .' Jean said.

'Indeed,' Helen said wryly. 'It makes you wonder what might happen next.'

Chapter 6

Once Jean and Sally finished work and left, Helen walked Suki along the North Bay beach, one of her favourite walks. Black-clad surfers were making the most of the rough sea, and she watched them with the dog by her side. Her mind was busy with thoughts of her unusual group of guests, and especially Carmen and the offhand way she'd treated Jean. Not to mention that Carmen had also bad-mouthed the Seaview, right in front of Helen too. What a strange woman she was.

She breathed in great lungfuls of sea air as she walked, which always helped clear her mind. On top of the tension brought on by the actors' arrival, there was the added anxiety of the hotel inspector's visit. And then there was Jimmy returning to her life . . . but that was too difficult to think about yet. She still hadn't made peace with herself about starting a new relationship, the first since her beloved husband had died. She walked on, pressing her boots into the damp sand, her worries tumbling around her mind.

When she'd walked far enough, she called Suki, clipped the dog's lead to her collar and returned home, deep in thought.

Back in her apartment, Helen changed out of jeans and T-shirt into smart black trousers, black heels and her favourite blouse, covered with forget-me-not flowers. She ran a brush through her shiny bobbed hair and went through her make-up routine. A slick of lipstick, a blush of rouge, a shadow of brown to darken her eyes, followed by a curl of mascara. She looked at her reflection in the mirror.

'Not bad for a woman your age,' she said.

She sprayed perfume on to her neck. It was a new bottle, a rose scent she adored. It used to make Tom sneeze, though, and so she hadn't bought it in years. As the perfume settled on her skin, she felt a twinge of guilt at enjoying the aroma.

'It's not selfish to want things for myself, so don't look at me like that,' she told her reflection.

She slid her arms into a black jacket, picked up her handbag and left the Seaview for the short walk to the Scarborough Arms.

As she approached the pub, she saw a scarlet sports convertible shining like a jewel amongst the other vehicles in the car park. It belonged to her best friend Marie, and was one of the many luxury possessions she'd fought hard to keep in her acrimonious divorce from Daran. Helen walked into the cosy pub and immediately saw Marie at their favourite corner table. It was perfectly positioned so that they could gossip and chat without being overheard. Marie was swiping her phone, and didn't notice her at first.

'You're looking gorgeous, as always,' Helen said when she greeted her friend. Marie had long and expensively coiffured auburn hair, which fell in silky waves to her shoulders. Her make-up was immaculate, her body firm and toned from time spent at the gym. She was the same age as Helen, but looked and dressed younger.

Marie stood and they hugged. Helen gazed admiringly at Marie's tight-fitting ruby-red trouser suit and red strappy sandals. 'Is that another new outfit?'

Marie nodded. 'Thought I'd treat myself. I deserve it, why not?' Marie pushed her phone away as they sat down.

Helen removed her jacket, hung it on the back of her chair and put her handbag by her feet. 'Business going well, then?' she asked.

Marie beamed. 'Both businesses are. The nail bar in town is booming, and I've taken on Sharelle.'

'What's that, a new brand of nail varnish?'

Marie burst out laughing. 'Sharelle's my new nail technician. I had to hire extra staff, as it's so busy. Anyway, she's great. I can even trust her to manage the place. Which works out fine, cos it means I can spend more time running Tom's Teas. I'm loving my new venture there.'

'I never had you down as the type of woman to own a café,' Helen said. 'Thought you wouldn't want to get your hands dirty or your nails chipped.'

'Well, think again. I feel like a new woman running that place, and I meet all sorts of interesting people. Walkers, tourists, locals, it's great. I didn't realise I needed a break from the nail bar until I started work in the tearoom. In fact, it's giving me food for thought.'

'I like the pun,' Helen smirked.

'Seriously, Helen. It's making me reassess what I want. I haven't mentioned it to you before, because I was mulling things over, but before I took Sharelle on, I was actually thinking of selling the nail salon and investing my time and more money in Tom's Teas.'

'But you've owned the nail bar since we left school. It's a little gold mine.'

'Well, getting divorced from Daran has made me look at things differently. Anyway, it's just something I'm thinking about. As for Tom's Teas, thanks again for letting me name the place after him. We've got his picture on the wall, framed behind the till.'

'I still don't know what he'd think of his name inspiring a tearoom,' Helen laughed. 'Now if you'd spent your money on a pub that sold real ale and pork scratchings, and named *that* after him, he'd have been over the moon.'

'The name gets the customers talking; they want to know who Tom was. It's the least I could do for my friend. We all miss him a lot.'

Helen gently squeezed Marie's hand. 'And I'll always be grateful to you for keeping his memory alive in the town he loved.' She turned to the bar. 'Now then, what are we having to drink?'

'White wine spritzer for me,' Marie said. 'I'll just have one, as I'm driving. And bring the lunch menu when you come back.'

Helen headed to the bar, ordered drinks and collected menus and was about to head back to Marie when the pub door flew open and a noisy bunch walked in. She recognised them immediately as her guests. She watched as Audrey Monroe and daughter Liza led the group to the bar. Audrey was dressed in a pastel-pink coat and matching scarf, while Liza wore a purple hat stitched from patchwork scraps. Behind them was Kate Barnes dressed in a turquoise coat, followed by the beige anorak of Paul McNally. Helen got the biggest surprise, though, when Chester Ford walked in. It was definitely him; she recognised his hair and the way he walked, the smart way he dressed, the way he held himself. And there was no mistaking the cigarette holder he carried, tapping it against his thigh. But there was something different about his face, and it took her a split second to realise what it was. He'd shaved his beard and moustache off. His top lip looked pink and raw, the bottom of his face looked naked and almost obscene.

Helen forced a smile as she headed back to Marie, having no choice but to walk past her guests. 'Good afternoon, everyone,' she beamed.

Audrey, Liza and Kate greeted her warmly. Paul stood to one side, gazing around, avoiding eye contact. Helen sensed his unease and gently brought him into the conversation.

'They do great pub grub in here, if you like that sort of thing, Paul.'

He flinched at the mention of his name, seeming surprised to be directly addressed. He stuffed his hands into his anorak pockets and glanced at Helen.

'Thank you,' he said, blushing pink.

Chester was first at the bar. 'Who wants what?' he called.

As the group gave their orders, Helen moved to stand beside Liza. 'Where are the others? Aren't Lee and Carmen joining you?'

Liza sighed pointedly. 'Lee told me he wanted to stay away from Kate so she doesn't think he's hounding her. If you ask me, he's broken-hearted over their split.'

'And Carmen?' Helen asked.

'She's gone out with some fella who came to the Seaview to pick her up in a white Porsche. I've no idea who he is.'

Carmen certainly didn't let the grass grow, Helen thought.

'And have you seen the state of Chester?' Liza laughed. 'He's shaved his beard and moustache off.'

'Has he done it for his part in the play?' Helen asked, curious.

Liza shrugged. 'Who knows? I liked him better with it; his face looks weird now.'

'Is he a good director?'

'Yes, he's good, and fair. Oh, but there's one thing he really doesn't like. You must never mention the Scottish play.'

Helen's eyes widened. 'You mean . . .' she glanced at Chester before mouthing the word, '*Macbeth?*'

Liza burst into giggles. 'No, not that Scottish play; the one he wrote for the Edinburgh Fringe. Carmen was supposed to be its star, but she was so drunk on stage that she ruined its first night. The play was taken off and Chester lost every penny he had.'

Chapter 7

At breakfast the next day, Carmen sat alone as before, reading her script with her back to the others. Lee sat as far away from Kate as he could, while the rest of the actors chatted amiably, commenting on how tasty breakfast was. As Helen served tea and toast, she remembered Jean's words about offering lunch and snacks.

'What a splendid idea,' Chester boomed when she put the offer to him. 'What do you say, gang?' He looked at Audrey and Liza, then from Kate to Lee and Paul. They all nodded in agreement. He cleared his throat before looking directly at the back of Carmen's head. 'Carmen, darling, what say you?' he called across the room.

Carmen laid her script on the table and straightened her back but didn't turn around. 'You should know by now . . .' she said, pausing to let the sarcastic emphasis of the next word land squarely on Chester's head, '*darling* . . . that Carmen Delray does not snack. However, I will take up the offer of lunch.'

'Does anyone have any special requests?' Helen asked.

'Assorted sandwiches will do us just fine,' Audrey said.

'Could I have vegan sandwiches, please?' Kate added quickly.

Helen took her notepad and pencil from her tabard pocket.

'And how about snacks? Shall I provide morning and afternoon coffee, tea and cakes? How does that suit?'

'It sounds perfect,' Chester replied. 'Just add it to the bill at the end of our stay.' He clapped his hands sharply. 'Come on, everyone, it's time to start work. Let's meet in the lounge in fifteen minutes. No rest for the wicked, not even you, Carmen.'

Helen turned to see if the barbed comment would elicit a reaction, but Carmen's head remained still.

'Please, make yourselves at home in the lounge and bar,' Helen offered. 'Move the furniture as you need, but please be careful not to scrape the walls. They've just been decorated.'

'What lovely muted colours you have in here,' Audrey said to Helen as she left the dining room.

Once again, as had happened the previous day, the group departed without Carmen, who remained at her table. Helen walked across the room to the lone diner.

'Is there anything else I can bring you?'

Carmen dabbed lightly at the side of her mouth with a navy linen napkin. It was the first time Helen had used linen napkins at the Seaview; previously she used paper ones. But now that her hotel was going up in the world, reaching for its fourth star, she hoped little touches like that might help influence the inspector's report.

'Yes, there is one thing you could do,' Carmen said.

'More tea?' Helen offered.

Carmen stood and rudely marched past her out of the dining room, across the hall and into the lounge. 'Come on, dear, keep up,' she barked.

Helen bit her tongue and followed. Carmen was edging sideways along the wall of the lounge, peering out of the bay window.

'Are they still there?' she hissed.

Helen looked out on to Windsor Terrace and the sweeping bay beyond. 'Who?'

'My fans. There were two of them here this morning. I saw them from my room; they were taking pictures of each other in front of the hotel. Two women in their late fifties – about your age. They were both dressed in red anoraks, as homage to the outfit I wore in *The Singing Nurse.*'

'Late fifties? My age? I'm only forty-eight,' Helen said, shocked. Her anger gave way to a sinking feeling. Marie was always encouraging her to dress more fashionably, but Helen was happiest wearing jeans and boots. But to be called out as being ten years older than she was? Perhaps it was time to take her friend up on her offer of a clothes-shopping trip to York.

Carmen looked her up and down. 'You're really not even fifty?'

Helen could feel anger rising. However, she'd never lost her temper with a guest before, and she wasn't about to start now. The reputation of the Seaview meant too much to her; she'd never bring it into disrepute. She bit her tongue to stop herself saying something she would regret, then kneeled on the window seat and glanced from left to right. 'There's no one out there,' she said.

Carmen sank into a seat and put a hand on her chest. 'No women in red anoraks?'

'No,' Helen confirmed.

Carmen sighed. 'They follow me everywhere. I thought I'd escaped them coming to Scarborough. They're somewhat obsessive, you see.'

'You know them?' Helen asked.

'They've been on my tail for years. They started off as autograph hunters, waiting for me outside whatever digs I was staying in. I remember they turned up twice in York, once in London and twice, no, three times in Torquay. They're very keen fans; a bit *over*-keen.'

Helen noticed Carmen's gaze quickly flick to the spirit bottles behind the bar and saw her lick her lips.

'Anyway,' Carmen went on, swallowing hard, 'They've been following me.'

'Have you told the police?' Helen asked.

'And say what? That two fans are interested in spotting a faded TV star? They'd tell me I should be flattered by the attention. Besides, those women don't *do* anything, they don't bother me when they see me. I just say hello and ask if they want an autograph or a selfie, that kind of thing. But I got a bit of a start when I opened my curtains this morning and saw them sitting on the bench across the road.'

'Did they see you?' Helen asked. 'Because there's a spare room I could move you to, at the back, if you wish.'

It was the room she had intended to put the hotel inspector in, but Carmen's peace of mind was her priority at that moment. When she spoke about her obsessive fans, a worried look clouded her face, and Helen noticed how tired she looked. She saw, quite suddenly, how vulnerable Carmen was under her mass of make-up and curls.

'No, they didn't see me, thank goodness.'

'I wonder how they found out you were staying here.'

'Oh, that's easy enough for dedicated fans of *The Singing*

Nurse. There's an army of them out there.' Carmen smiled wryly. 'In the old days, there was just a fan club. My secretary used to sign letters or autograph photographs, pretending to be me. Nowadays the fans keep in touch via an online forum, where news is passed on quickly.'

'Are all your fans as obsessive as the two ladies who turned up today?'

'Thank goodness, no. I haven't been on TV for so long that most people have forgotten who I am. There's been a resurgence of interest since *The Singing Nurse* started reruns on classic TV, but nothing that's led to offers to return to the box. Mind you, that could all change with Chester's play at the Modernist. I've been given a chance to shine in it, and shine I intend to, my dear.'

Helen glanced out of the window. This time there were plenty of people walking past the Seaview, families out for a stroll. Ahead of her the sun glistened on the North Bay beach, but Carmen's fans were nowhere to be seen.

'If I see them when I'm out and about, shall I ask them to leave you alone?'

'No.' Carmen was firm. 'No, don't speak to them. Don't give them confirmation I'm here. Chester used to protect me from fans, but I'll need to get used to handling them on my own now.'

Helen pushed her hands into her tabard pockets and looked at Carmen. 'Is everything all right between you and Mr Ford? I couldn't help but notice—'

Carmen turned her head sharply and her eyes flashed a warning. Chastised, Helen took her hands from her pockets.

'Sorry, forgive me. I should never have asked such a personal question.'

Carmen stood and marched from the lounge, but not without firing a parting shot.

'Chester and I have history; anyone will tell you that. But you should not be prying into my business. Who on earth do you think you are?'

Helen was about to apologise when the doorbell rang. She took a moment to compose herself, embarrassed after Carmen's rebuke, then went to answer it. It was Miriam Jones, who ran the Vista del Mar next door. Miriam was in her early sixties, ageing gracefully, with long grey hair that she wore in a plait down her back. She was a short woman who wore large tinted glasses that darkened when she went outdoors. Helen noticed that she looked unusually flustered.

'Morning, Miriam, what can I do for you? Come in.'

'I'm having trouble with my blasted oven,' Miriam said. 'I managed to get through breakfast, but now it's given up. You wouldn't have the number of the electrician you use, would you? The chap I normally call is on holiday and I can't get anyone else to come at short notice.'

'Sure, come on in while I find it.'

Miriam followed Helen along the hall and Helen indicated to her to wait in the lounge. Then she headed down to her living room and the desk where she kept her laptop and files. She flipped open her leather-bound address book and ran her finger down the index to the letter G for Gav. She smiled as she did so, remembering how it drove Tom round the bend that she filed contacts by first name rather than last. The page opened to reveal a long list of Gav's business enterprises. There was Gav's Cabs, his taxi firm; Gav's Baths, his plumbing business; Gav's Cams, his security business, through which she'd met him when he'd installed CCTV at the Seaview. She remembered how he'd charmed Sally while he'd worked, and they'd been inseparable since. There was also Gav's Grub, his sandwich shop in Filey; Gav's Garage, where his team of mechanics serviced cars; and Gav's Garden Services, for weeding, planting and laying patios and drives. Right at the end of the list was Gav & Maz Enterprises, the company Gav and Marie had set up to purchase the old Glendale Hotel, which they'd turned into Tom's Teas, their retro tearoom. Helen wondered which of Gav's companies he was using to charge the Modernist for its roof repairs. Knowing him, he'd probably set up a new building firm to cover those costs. He was nothing if not entrepreneurial; a man who got things done.

It was Gav's personal number that Helen scribbled on a bright yellow Post-it for Miriam. She took the number upstairs to the lounge. 'Here you go.'

Miriam took the yellow note. 'Thanks, Helen,' she said, then pointed out of the window at the minibus.

'Who are Dawley's Theatre Group?' she asked. 'Are they staying with you?'

'They're a bunch of actors, here for two weeks before they move into digs near the Modernist. They're rehearsing a new play that's going on at the theatre. It's called *Midnight with Maude*, and the theatre needs all the support it can get. If you can spread the word next door to your guests, I'm sure Taylor Caffrey will be grateful.'

'Taylor Caffrey? My word, is he still running the Modernist?

I thought he'd have retired to his bungalow in Filey with his mangy cat by now.'

'No, he's still in Scarborough, him and his cat,' Helen replied.

Miriam returned her attention to the minibus. 'But why are a group of actors staying here?' she said dismissively. 'Why on earth didn't Taylor approach me? Actors are quality guests; they like a touch of luxury, and I don't suppose they'll find it here, no matter how well the place has been decorated.'

'Now that's enough, Miriam,' Helen said firmly. 'You might think you're a cut above, with your extra star, offering croissants for breakfast. But the Seaview is clean and tidy and—'

'Only three-star,' Miriam chipped in.

Helen put her hands on her hips and glared at her. 'Not for much longer.'

Miriam's face looked like thunder, but that didn't stop Helen going in for the kill.

'The Seaview will get its fourth star, you'll see. Now, I'm sure you're a busy lady and there must be things you can be getting on with next door, like polishing your extra star.'

'Oh, don't worry, I'm going,' Miriam huffed. She marched out of the lounge and along the hallway towards the front door. But before she stepped outside, she nodded ahead.

'Are those two of your actors out there?'

Helen peered around her to see two middle-aged women in red coats peering through the minibus windows.

Chapter 8

Later that morning, Helen and Sally cleaned the guests' rooms. Jean cleared up in the kitchen, then prepared trays of sandwiches on trays covered with cling film for the actors' lunch. With all the chores completed, the three women sat around the kitchen table with coffee and a plate of Jean's freshly baked chocolate cookies. Sharing coffee and biscuits each morning after work had become a ritual for them, a chance to catch up on each other's lives. The conversation that morning started with the state of Jean's mum's legs. They were still not good, although Jean said the care home was doing a great job. Then talk turned to Sally's daughter Gracie, who was looking forward to having Gav stay at the weekend.

'He's going to be there all weekend?' Helen asked.

Sally's face broke into a smile. 'It's the first time he's stayed so long. He normally stays overnight a couple of times a week, but this feels more special.'

'Do you think he'd move in if you asked him?' Jean asked, direct and to the point.

'I'm not ready for that, Jean,' Sally said. 'I don't want Gracie to start thinking of him as a permanent fixture. It might not work out between us; I've only known him a few months.'

The mention of Gav's name prompted Helen to tell Sally about Miriam's visit.

'You can let Gav know that Miriam will be ringing him to fix her oven, if she hasn't already.'

Sally rolled her eyes. 'As if he hasn't got a million other jobs on the go. He's busy fixing the roof at the Modernist right now, and he's working non-stop, always doing something for someone.'

'That lad's got a heart of gold,' Jean said, helping herself to another cookie.

'That's not what you said the first time you met him,' Sally reminded her.

Jean dunked her biscuit in her mug. 'Well, he took a bit of getting used to, that's all. He can't half talk.'

'He can be a bit full-on if you don't know him,' Sally agreed. 'Still, my mum thinks the world of him. Gracie does too. But I'm taking things slowly for now.'

She pushed her coffee mug away, stood and gathered her handbag and coat.

'Anyway, I should be going. I've got to get to college for a tutorial, and then it's an afternoon learning about finance and tax.'

'Rather you than me, love,' Helen said. 'I leave all that to my accountant in town.'

Jean stood too, and biscuit crumbs fell to the floor. Suki was on them immediately.

'I've left the actors' sandwiches on the side,' Jean said. 'The kettles are filled and ready to boil.'

'I'd be lost without you, Jean,' Helen replied.

She received a kiss on one cheek from Jean, on the other from Sally, then she waved them both off. She remained at the table, stroking Suki behind her ear, wondering about going up to the lounge to see how the actors were doing. She needed to ask them what time they'd like lunch and their snacks. Once she knew what their routine was, she could fit her day around them: head into town, drive to the cash and carry, and take Suki for walks. She gathered mugs from the table and was carrying them to the sink when her phone rang. The display showed yet another withheld number.

'Good morning, Seaview Hotel,' she said cheerfully.

There was silence at the other end. She waited a few seconds and tried again.

'Seaview Hotel, can I help you?'

More silence, then a noise, a breath. A chill went down her spine. Was this the same person who'd called before? What did they want?

'Who is this?' she asked sharply.

A woman's voice answered with two cryptic words. 'Nice car.' Then the line went dead.

Helen stared at her phone. There was no way of knowing who'd called, and she would drive herself crazy if she tried to guess. She'd received crank calls in the past, people ringing up to book rooms in fake names; Mr Hugh Janus and Al Caholic were always popular with pranksters. Maybe it was another one of those, or a wrong number. But after the earlier call warning her away from someone, this latest one unsettled her. She shook her head to dismiss thoughts that wouldn't make sense. Then she wondered if there was a way to trace a call when the number had been withheld. She Googled it quickly but found nothing of use, then chided herself for being stupid to think such a thing was possible. If it happened again, she'd ask Marie for advice. Decision made, she pocketed her phone and headed upstairs.

* * *

At the lounge door, Helen peered inside, intrigued. She'd never watched actors rehearsing before. All seven of the troupe were there, six of them seated, Carmen and Audrey sitting well away from each other. Chester was on his feet, giving directions. He waved his cigarette holder from one actor to another, as if conducting an orchestra.

'Page seven, Carmen, that's your big scene. You must give it all you've got.'

'Are you saying there are times when I don't?' Carmen replied archly.

Chester stroked his bare upper lip and ignored her. 'Paul, this is where the lights need to be up bright, a spotlight on Carmen's entrance. Now, I know it's difficult working out lighting and stage arrangements without being in the theatre, but we'll have to muddle through. We should be able to get into the Modernist on the morning of our opening night to do the technical run-through and full final dress rehearsal. Until then, to all intents and purposes and for reasons beyond our control, the Seaview Hotel is our theatre set.'

Helen watched Paul making notes, typing into his laptop next to his open script. Audrey and Liza were sitting together on the window seat, two peas in a pod. Audrey was dressed in a soft blue sweatshirt with black leggings, while Liza was wearing another of her hats, this time a green beret with a bunch of red cherries stitched to one side. Helen wasn't sure if the hat was a costume, part of the play, or whether Liza simply wore it for fun. Kate was lounging on the floor, dressed head to toe in black – black leggings and a long black T-shirt – very different to the brightly coloured outfits she'd worn so far. She was barefoot, her toenails painted blood red. Her hair was scraped back from her face with a scarlet headband, her face serious, free of make-up, and she looked every inch the actor-in-training. Lee was sitting apart from the rest, on a stool at the bar. He beamed at Helen as soon as he noticed her.

'Chester, could we take a break?' he asked. 'Mrs Dexter is here.'

All eyes turned towards Helen, who felt herself blushing.

'Oh, I'm sorry, I didn't mean to interrupt.'

Chester glanced at his watch. 'Take fifteen, everyone,' he said.

Kate yawned dramatically, stretching her arms in the air, then bent forward, spreading her hands on the carpet in front of her. Audrey and Liza walked out of the lounge arm in arm.

'We're going to get a breath of fresh air,' Audrey told Chester.

Paul stayed where he was, typing furiously on his laptop, his body hunched over his work. Chester walked towards Carmen, but when she turned her back to him, he slunk across the room to Helen with a resigned look on his face.

'Would you like refreshments now?' Helen asked.

'That'd be splendid,' Chester said.

'Do you need any help, Mrs . . . ?' Lee offered.

'No need to be formal. I've already told you, call me Helen. And yes, a helping hand would be great. I'll send everything up in the dumbwaiter, and if you could help serve it once it arrives, that'd be great.'

Lee took up position by the dumbwaiter in the hall. 'I might as well help you,' he said, glancing at Kate. Helen noticed a touch of sadness in his voice. 'Kate still won't talk to me.'

Helen heard the front door open and close, and was surprised to see Audrey and Liza already making their way back indoors.

'There's been a bit of bother outside,' Audrey said.

'What's happened?'

Audrey pointed at a car in front of the minibus. 'See the blue car, the four by four? It's had its window smashed.'

Helen's stomach plummeted. She ran outside and down the steps, and stared in horror at her car. The passenger window was shattered. Her heart hammered, and she felt sick. Had someone tried to steal it? She could have kicked herself for not having an alarm fitted. She didn't know what to do. Should she call the police, tell them someone had broken in? But the stereo was intact, a bag on the back seat undisturbed. She walked around to check for more signs of damage, and was relieved to see the other windows intact. However, she spotted something else – a long line scratched in the paintwork along the driver's side.

Chapter 9

Helen ran back into the hotel. 'Did either of you see who smashed my car window?' she asked Audrey and Liza, but they both shook their head.

'It was already broken when we went outside,' Audrey said. 'And I'm very sorry to hear it's yours, Helen. Is there anything we can do to help?'

Helen pulled her phone from her pocket. 'No, but thank you for offering. I'll have to go and make a couple of calls before I send up the tea and coffee.'

She ran down to her apartment. When she walked into her living room, she found Suki by the glass doors that looked out to the small patio. There was something about the way the dog was lying, with her head on her front paws, pulling at something with her mouth, that Helen didn't like. 'Suki! Leave!' she yelled.

Suki dropped Helen's slipper and Helen whipped it away.

'Of all the dogs in all the world, why did I have to pick the one who likes to chew slippers and shoes?' she chided.

Suki's head sank to the floor. Helen dialled the number for the local police station to report the damage to her car, and the menacing phone calls too. The woman who took her call was helpful and efficient and gave her the details she'd need to report the crime to her insurance company. After another call, to her

66

insurer, she was advised to take her car in for repair. Wasting no time, she scrolled through her phone and selected a number.

'Gav's Garage. How can I help?'

'It's Helen Dexter from the Seaview Hotel, I need some work done on my car.'

'Helen! It's Gav speaking, missus. You caught me working here today. I've just popped in to collect a spanner I need to take to the Modernist for Big Mick, one of the lads I've got working on the roof. Anyway, what can I do for you?'

'Someone's smashed the car window, and keyed the paintwork. It's in a right state. The insurance company told me you were on their list of approved garages. I'll need full paperwork, of course.'

'Of course,' Gav replied. 'Not to worry, Helen, I'll send one of the lads over now to pick it up and we'll get it sorted.'

Helen breathed a sigh of relief. 'Thanks, Gav, you're a star.'

'And you're the best landlady in Scarborough.'

Gav's cheery voice was just what she needed to hear, and a smile spread wide on her face. 'Ah, you're only saying that so that next time you're here, I'll butter Jean up to give you one of her famous full English breakfasts for free.'

'As if I'd do that, missus!' Gav laughed.

Helen hung up and sat back in her seat, feeling troubled by what had happened. Was someone targeting her? Or was she being paranoid and reading too much into what might have been a wrong number and a thief looking for something to steal from her car, the two things unconnected? After all, the phone number of the Seaview was public knowledge, available to anyone. Each time the hotel landline rang, the calls were diverted to her mobile phone.

She glanced at her watch. 'Oh, heavens!' she cried out loud, causing Suki to scramble to her feet. 'Down, girl,' Helen ordered. 'I've forgotten to put the kettle on for the actors' tea and coffee.'

She leapt up and flicked the kettle on, then ran back upstairs and outside to her car, where she removed the bag from the back seat and the stereo from its holder. There wasn't anything else she could do until Gav's mechanic arrived. Back inside, she distracted herself preparing refreshments to send up in the dumbwaiter. She worked quickly, automatically, all the while trying to stop herself worrying about her car and the phone calls, but her uneasy feeling refused to leave. She sent cups and saucers up, and carried two large flasks of hot water herself. When she entered the lounge, everyone expressed their concern about her car.

'The mechanic's on his way. Fortunately, I've a friend who runs a garage. I'm sure it was just a kid looking to see if there was anything worth stealing, but there was just a bag of tinned food for the dog.'

'You have a dog?'

Helen was surprised to see Paul at her side. He'd not said two words to her since he'd arrived, and had avoided eye contact. It was obvious to her that he was painfully shy, but when she turned to answer, she was surprised to see him unusually animated.

'Yes, a greyhound called Suki. I got her from a rehoming centre.'

'I love dogs,' Paul said, and for the first time since he'd arrived, his face broke into a smile. 'Where is she?'

'Oh, I keep her downstairs in my apartment.'

'Could I walk her sometime? I mean, could I come with you on a walk when you take her out?'

Helen was surprised by the request, but pleased too. She always walked Suki alone, and it would make a nice change to have company. 'That'd be great, yes, I'll let you know next time I go out.'

Carmen stepped forward and took a cup of coffee. 'Dogs are unlucky. I won't have talk of them while I'm rehearsing,' she snapped.

'Unlucky?' Helen said.

'We're a superstitious lot, us actors,' Kate chipped in. 'For instance, I wear this black T-shirt each time I rehearse, and if the rehearsal's going badly, I change it. But if it's going well, I keep wearing the same one.'

'There's a definite whiff of body odour coming from it, dear.' Carmen sniffed.

Kate chose to ignore the comment and carried on. 'Some of us like to have the same routine each day while we're working, and if the routine is broken then we get scared it might bring bad luck and we'll have a terrible show.'

Audrey glided towards Helen to pick up a coffee for herself. 'My superstition in all my years in theatre is that I always take Cyril on stage to help ward off bad luck.'

'Who's Cyril?' Helen asked, surprised.

'Cyril the squirrel. It's a tiny little brooch in the shape of a squirrel my mother gave me before she passed on. I pin him to my bra strap before I get into costume, no matter what part I'm playing. The audience don't see him; he's far too small for anyone to notice. But he's always with me, for luck.'

Helen thought of her own good-luck charm, the tiny plastic Elvis on a shelf behind the bar.

'And we never wish each other good luck before we go on stage

– that's the worst thing to say. We say "break a leg" instead,' Kate added.

'We never whistle on stage either; now that's a portent of doom if ever there was one,' Chester added.

'My word, there's such a lot to remember,' Helen said.

'Oh, that's just a fraction of the things we do, or don't do, before we go on stage, while we're on stage, or off stage,' Audrey said. 'We're creatives, hypersensitive, superstitious, what more can I say?'

Everyone began to file from the dining room into the lounge and Helen followed. Liza made a beeline for the window seat and gazed out to the sea. 'Come look at these waves, Mum, they're huge,' she called. The tide was rolling in and the sea turning angry. Audrey sat down next to her.

'My daughter the city dweller,' she said, gently stroking Liza's arm with her free hand. 'Ever since you were a little girl, you've lived and worked in one big city after another. I know how much you love the sea.'

Liza turned to Helen. 'Those waves, they're incredible, such power. I've seen nothing like it before.'

'If you think the waves are big here, you should see them on the South Bay, especially during a storm,' Helen said. 'It's very dramatic. They lash up against the prom and break over the sea wall. You sometimes see teenagers who think it's all a joke pushing each other forward when the waves splash up.' She had seen dangerous waves at the South Bay many times and knew the damage they could cause. 'The council put signs up to warn people of heavy seas when the tide's high, but kids will be kids. They don't realise how dangerous it is.'

'The sea is a powerful beast,' Liza said, enthralled by the waves.

A movement outside caught Helen's attention, and she saw a red van with *Gav's Garage* emblazoned in white pulling up. There were two men in the front. The one in the passenger side leapt out, and she was pleased to see Gav. The van roared off as he made his way to the Seaview. Helen excused herself from the actors and walked to the front door to meet him as he bounded up the path. He was tall and lean, with shoulder-length dark wavy hair, a good-looking man in his thirties who was also kind and thoughtful. A perfect catch, she thought, if only Sally would see it that way.

'Morning, missus,' he beamed. 'Gav at your service. Let me take your car keys and I'll get one of my lads straight on it at the garage. Should have it back to you all fixed in a few days. The paintwork will take a while to sort out, but I'll get a replacement window put in today.'

'Thanks, Gav. I really appreciate this,' Helen said.

Gav winked and smiled at her. 'It's the least I can do for my favourite landlady.'

She was about to reply, but the words seemed stuck in her throat. She was feeling anxious about the phone calls, confused too. Why would anyone want to harass her? She felt baffled and unnerved. If someone was targeting her, who on earth was it? And what had she done to upset someone so much that they'd go so far as to damage her car? She glanced up and down the street. Was the culprit still around? All she could see were a mother and toddler walking hand in hand. What about Carmen's obsessive fans in their red coats? Were they involved somehow? Oh, it was too upsetting for words.

'I've got to dash, missus,' Gav said, breaking into her thoughts. 'Once I drop your car off at the garage, I've got garden decking to lay in Bridlington and a kids' birthday party to arrange in Filey. I need to hire a clown. I don't suppose you know any, do you?'

Helen gave a weak smile and tried to pull herself together. 'You could ask Taylor Caffrey; he might know where to find one. And speaking of Taylor, aren't you supposed to be fixing the roof at the Modernist?'

'My construction lads are on the job as we speak,' Gav replied. 'Give Sally my love if you see her before I do. Did she tell you I'm staying all weekend with her and Gracie?' Before Helen could reply, he gave a cheeky salute and jumped into her car.

As it roared away down Windsor Terrace, Helen returned to the lounge, where Chester was drumming his cigarette holder on the bar. The sound of it set her already frayed nerves on edge. Very gently, but firmly, she put her hand on top of his and brought the noise to a stop.

'Not on the furniture,' she said sweetly.

Chester gave a little cough. 'Mrs Dexter . . . Helen . . . I wonder if we . . . I . . . might ask you a favour?'

'Yes, of course, what is it?' Helen said.

Chester looked around nervously. Liza nodded at him. 'Go on, ask her,' she said.

'It's not a good idea; she's not a professional,' Carmen muttered darkly.

'Ask me what?' Helen said.

Chester stroked his bare upper lip. 'We find ourselves in dire need of someone to work as our prompt until our professional prompter arrives. And we, um, well, we were wondering how you might feel about stepping into the role?'

Helen laughed. 'Me? But I can't act, I don't know the first thing about it.'

'You don't need to act, dear,' Audrey said kindly. 'All you need to do is follow the script as we're rehearsing scenes, and when one of us falters . . .' Here, she shot a look towards Lee that didn't go unnoticed by Helen, 'you simply remind us where we are and give us a prompt to chivvy us along.'

'But why me?'

'Because you're neutral,' Chester said. 'You can remain objective and not get drawn into our petty battles.'

Battles? Helen wasn't sure she liked the sound of her guests going to war.

'Think of yourself as the Switzerland of Scarborough,' Chester said.

'No, I really don't think I'm the right person to ask,' she said, flustered. 'I mean, I couldn't possibly leave my dog on her own all day if I'm working upstairs with you.'

Chester's face dropped. 'Now that's a shame,' he said. 'Perhaps you could bring the dog up here?'

Helen gave this some thought. It wasn't the worst offer she'd ever received, but it was certainly one of the most unusual. She glanced at the eager faces of her guests.

'Please say you'll do it,' Audrey said.

'You'll be great,' Kate beamed.

Helen looked at Paul. 'Couldn't you do it?'

Paul opened his mouth to say something, but before he could get a word out, Chester replied, his cigarette holder twirling furiously.

'Paul's fully immersed in technical details, lighting and sound. He uses specialist software on his laptop to record the notes he needs to make the show a success. His preparation work is more important than ever, as we're not rehearsing at the theatre. He can't keep his eye on both the script and technical notes at the same time. We've tried it in the past and it never works out well. We need someone who can concentrate fully on the script and give it one hundred and ten per cent.'

'Sorry, Helen,' Paul muttered.

Helen looked at them all; everyone was waiting for her reply. Well, all except Carmen whose face was like thunder. She clearly wasn't happy about having an outsider, a non-acting person, join the group.

Ah, what the heck, Helen thought. Surely this had to be better than sitting downstairs on her own, worrying about threatening phone calls?

'Well, I suppose I could bring Suki upstairs. She *is* well behaved,' she said, crossing her fingers against the tiny white lie.

'No! I refuse to have a dog in the rehearsal room! It's bad luck!' Carmen yelled.

'I'll keep her out of the lounge; she'll stay put in the hallway,' Helen said, but this didn't make much difference to Carmen, who continued to scowl.

Chester clapped his hands. 'Then that's fixed. I'd like to appoint Helen Dexter as our prompter.'

The cast gave Helen a round of applause, leaving her wondering what she'd let herself in for.

Chapter 10

The following day, Helen nervously prepared to take up her role as the actors' prompt. She'd never done anything like it before. The nearest she'd got to any theatre work had been a few months ago, when Jimmy and Twelvis, his troupe of twelve Elvis impersonators, stayed at the Seaview. When one of the group had gone missing on the night of their show at Scarborough Spa, Jimmy had begged her to make up the numbers. If she didn't, he'd told her, they would have to perform as Elevensis and would be a laughing stock. Not wanting to let Jimmy and her guests down, she'd agreed. It had been a nerve-racking experience, and she'd vowed never to perform live again.

When she told this to Chester, he reassured her that she wouldn't be performing in front of an audience, which helped quell her nerves. All she had to do, he told her, was sit quietly in a corner of the lounge as the cast rehearsed *Midnight with Maude* and follow the script word for word. If one of the actors forgot their lines, all she had to do was remind them. It was as easy as that, Chester said; what could possibly go wrong?

As she was about to head up from her apartment to the lounge to join the actors again, the Seaview's landline rang. Normally calls would divert straight to her own phone, but the landline was right there in front of her, and she picked up the receiver.

'Good morning, Seaview Hotel.'

There was a beat of silence, and then a breath. Helen's heart sank. Oh no, not again.

'Hello? Who is this?' she demanded.

There was no reply, but then she wasn't expecting one.

'I've reported you to the police,' she said, bluffing, turning angry. 'They'll find you. They know who you are. In fact, they're probably on their way to arrest you now.'

She knew she sounded ridiculous, but she was so scared, she couldn't stop waffling.

'He's mine,' a woman's voice said calmly.

Helen pressed the receiver closer to her ear, desperately trying to recognise the voice or catch an accent.

'Who is this?' she demanded again. 'Who the hell are you talking about?'

The line went dead. She stared at the receiver, as if it would give up the caller. Then, in frustration and anger, she banged it back into the cradle so hard that it bounced straight out again.

'Bloody thing!' she screamed.

Suki looked at her, cocking her head.

'I don't mean you, sweetheart,' she said, more calmly.

Quickly she dialled 1471 in the hope of finding the number that had called, but as she suspected, the woman had withheld it. She got down on her haunches and pressed her face against the side of Suki's head. She stroked Suki's skinny body, letting the dog's steady heartbeat calm her. 'I won't let this get me down, Suki,' she said, determined. 'I won't.'

She stood and patted her leg, the signal for Suki to follow.

'Come on, let's go and see if we can take our minds off things upstairs.'

Upstairs in the lounge, Helen didn't say a word as she slid on to an empty chair by the door.

Suki stood at her side. Paul rushed to the dog, stroking her head, and Suki groaned with pleasure at the attention. Kate and Liza also walked over and made a fuss of her. The attention cheered Helen after the distress of the phone call. However, not all of the cast were happy to have Suki there. Carmen pulled Chester roughly by his arm to get his attention.

'You should know by now that I never work with animals. They bring bad luck to a rehearsal room,' she hissed.

'Don't worry,' Helen assured her before Chester could reply. 'I promise you she won't enter the room. You have my word. I'll sit in the doorway, out of everyone's way, and Suki will lie in the hallway behind me.'

As if to prove a point, Suki collapsed without being asked, her caramel limbs spilling to the carpet. She raised her soulful eyes to Carmen, but the woman remained unmoved.

'As long as she stays out of the room,' Carmen huffed.

'Oh, she will. She's an obedient bitch,' Helen replied.

'Which is more than can be said for others,' Carmen hissed, shooting a vicious look towards Kate.

There was an audible gasp, and Helen saw Liza put her hand over her mouth. The small bunch of cherries on the side of Liza's hat wobbled as she struggled to compose herself. Audrey turned her face away, as if she wanted no part of whatever was going on between Carmen and Kate. Helen was stunned by Carmen's outburst and wondered what tensions bubbled there. The more time she spent with the actors, the more she realised what a complicated web of tension was woven around them. It was a web Helen found herself being drawn into, and she didn't like it one bit. She wondered if she'd done the right thing agreeing to work as their prompt.

A loud tapping noise cut into her thoughts. She looked up to find Chester drumming his cigarette holder. She caught his eye and shook her head. He picked up her subtle hint and pointed the cigarette holder at Audrey instead.

'We're going from the top, everyone. Let's have a read-through to the end of Act One.'

He spun around and pointed the cigarette holder at Helen. 'We'll stop for coffee then, if that's all right with you?'

Helen gritted her teeth. 'That's fine, although I really don't need to be pointed at.'

Chester had the decency to look slightly embarrassed. 'Sorry, old habits die hard,' he said.

'Jean's baked one of her special chocolate cakes for you to enjoy on your break,' Helen said, more brightly.

Audrey patted her stomach. 'Oh, no cake for me. Too many calories for my delicate frame, and besides, I'm still full after your cook's wonderful breakfast.'

Chester pointed the cigarette holder at Audrey again. 'Audrey, dear, would you be a love and open your script? You're the only one who isn't on the page.'

Audrey rifled through pages, then straightened in her seat. 'I'm ready now,' she said evenly.

Helen admired her unflappable demeanour, the gracious manner she had about her; she always seemed mindful, together and calm.

Chester was about to raise his cigarette holder again, but he caught Helen's eye and thought better of it, grasping it with both hands instead.

'Just follow the words on our first read-through,' he told her. 'It'll help you become familiar with the work. You'll hear when we need to pause, or where there's a beat of silence.'

'Got it,' she said. She opened her handbag, searching for a pen in case she needed to take notes. She brought her phone out too and laid it on the table. Across the room, Carmen sprang to her feet and raised her hand like a petulant schoolgirl.

'What is it now?' Chester sighed.

'First it was the blasted dog, and now you're allowing phones inside our rehearsal room!' Carmen erupted.

Chester glanced at Helen's phone. 'Oh, Helen, I should've said, we never allow phones on the set.'

'But it's on silent,' Helen said. 'I need to keep my eye on it. I don't want to miss bookings coming in while I'm working up here. I'm sorry, Chester. But if you want me to be your prompt, you'll have to take me as you find me or not at all.'

Chester nodded, then looked at Carmen. 'You know we're working under difficult circumstances, Carmen. Mrs Dexter has kindly agreed to turn her hotel over to us as our temporary set. We have to work around the limitations of her business.' He sounded exasperated.

Carmen sat down heavily. 'This would never have happened if I'd gone on tour with the Alan Ayckbourn play in Cleethorpes,' she sighed.

Chester tapped his cigarette holder on the bar, this time ignoring Helen's shaking head, then pointed it at Kate. '*Midnight with Maude*. Page one. Act One. Scene One. Mrs Trullo rushes on stage screaming . . . and . . . action!'

'Heaven help us, he thinks he's Quentin Tarantino,' Carmen said under her breath. Helen noticed a wry smile make its way to Liza's lips; she'd heard the comment too.

Kate began to read. Her character was Brenda Trullo, newly wed wife of Jim, who to Helen's astonishment was being played by Kate's ex-fiancé, Lee. She imagined things might become awkward for them as the play progressed. What if there was a kissing scene for the warring lovers to act? Under the table, out of sight, she crossed her fingers and hoped Kate and Lee would be spared such embarrassment.

She followed the script word for word, using her pen as a guide, and making notes whenever a break in dialogue wasn't obvious from the typed page. She also made notes each time Chester gave direction to his cast: 'This is where Maude arrives and trips over the drinks trolley. Paul, we'll need all the props in the right place.'

'And don't you dare forget my spotlight,' Carmen added harshly.

'As if I would,' Paul replied, tapping at his laptop.

Helen was ready to continue following the script, but when Carmen began reading the part of Maude, the star of the show, a tingle of excitement ran down her spine. She laid her pen down, let the script fall to her knee and watched, awestruck. It was the first time she had ever seen Carmen act. There was something magical about the way she captivated her audience and made them fully believe in her portrayal. Helen understood in an instant how the woman had been a big star. The talent Carmen had possessed decades ago to help her carry the role in *The Singing Nurse* hadn't been lost. Oh, her voice might be husky now, and she had more lines on her face, more years under her belt than she'd ever admit. She also had an attitude that Helen found difficult to understand. She'd been very rude to Jean, downright nasty to Chester, vicious towards Kate, offhand to the rest of the cast and disrespectful about the Seaview. But when she read, Helen knew she was in the presence of a star. How else could she explain it?

She looked around at the others. Paul was hunched intently over his keyboard, typing. Liza and Audrey were following the script, but Helen noticed Kate watching Carmen closely. As for Chester, he couldn't take his eyes off her. His script, his dialogue, the words he'd written for his leading lady were coming from her mouth, and he looked moonstruck. His cigarette holder dangled from his fingers, forgotten.

The morning session went quickly, and before Helen knew it, it was break time. She busied herself downstairs, sending up cups and saucers and Jean's wonderfully gooey cake in the dumbwaiter, then carrying the hot water up the stairs. While the cast took their break, she headed outdoors with Suki, taking a breather in the late-summer air. As she went back indoors, her phone beeped with a message and her heart leapt when she saw Jimmy's name.

'Helen, darling, we're ready for you again,' Chester called from the lounge.

She quickly opened the message.

Can't wait to see you again x

'Helen?' Chester called, louder, more insistent. 'Mrs Dexter, we're waiting.'

Her mind spun with thoughts of Jimmy: tall, handsome, caring, polite in an old-fashioned way that never failed to impress her. The first man she'd had feelings for since Tom had passed away, the only man she'd ever kissed apart from Tom. And that was all it had been, just a couple of kisses while Jimmy stayed at the Seaview. He'd taken her into his confidence, told her about his daughter, Jodie, who lived in a hostel for the homeless in town. She'd even helped him track down the killer of one of his friends. It had been an upsetting business, one she would rather forget, but it had brought her and Jimmy close. And now he was returning to her life. She felt nervous about seeing him again, excited too, but unsure about how to move their relationship on when all she'd ever known was Tom.

She put a smile on her face and walked into the lounge. 'All right, everyone, I'm ready.'

Chapter 11

After her initial nerves, Helen settled quickly into her role as prompt. She sat on the edge of the group, by the lounge door, where Suki crept forward under her chair, resting her head on her paws. Helen enjoyed the play a lot. *Midnight with Maude* was sharp and funny. Carmen played ageing pub landlady Maude, who was looking for love and finding it with the wrong men, played by Chester and Lee. The play ramped up tension and suspense as the whodunnit continued, and when everyone turned the final page of their script and Carmen read the last line, the actors relaxed in their seats, exhausted. Helen burst into applause and leapt from her seat; she couldn't help it. She felt sure it would be a success. But would it be enough to save the Modernist? She crossed her fingers on both hands, for double luck.

'Bravo! Bravo!' she cried. 'That was absolutely fantastic!'

Chester gripped his cigarette holder with both hands. 'You really think so?' he said, nervously.

'Well, I'm no theatre critic, but I know what I like and I think it's superb.' She looked around the cast, from Chester and Carmen to Audrey and Liza, from Kate to Lee and then Paul. 'All of you did a wonderful job. I feel honoured to be part of it until your professional prompter arrives. And I swear I'll do my best to help you as much as I can while you're rehearsing at the Seaview.'

Audrey stood from the window seat, stretched her arms to the ceiling and headed out of the room. As she wafted past Helen, she gently laid her hand on her arm.

'Thank you, darling,' she whispered.

Chester clapped his hands. 'Everyone, take an hour for lunch. Helen, do you need help bringing the food from downstairs?'

'I'll send it up on trays in the dumbwaiter. It's sandwiches and fruit, I hope that's all right.'

'Sounds perfect,' Liza said.

'Oh, Liza?' Chester called. 'Let's try some costume items for this afternoon's read-through, just a few things before we do our first full dress rehearsal next week. It'd be good for us to have some of the clothes and props. Could you bring them from the room we're storing them in upstairs? We'll need, let's see, the blue scarf for Carmen to wear when Maude goes on her date with Trullo, a pair of specs for Lee, gloves for Audrey and the black hat for my character. Think you can find them all?'

Liza was about to reply when Kate rudely pushed forward, jostling Liza so that her hat wobbled precariously on her head.

'Steady on, what's your rush?' Liza said, putting a hand to her head to stop the hat sliding off.

'I'll do it. I'll get the props,' Kate said urgently. She seemed flustered and looked wildly from Liza to Helen. 'I mean . . . I'd be happy to bring them down. I want to.'

'But I'm in charge of costume,' Liza said petulantly.

Helen watched the exchange with interest, then excused herself and headed towards the door that led down to her apartment, Suki following. Before she reached it, however, she heard angry voices behind her, and turned just in time to see Kate snatch something from Liza's hand.

'I said I'd get the props!' Kate snarled.

'Go on then, take the bloody key to the costume room, if it's so important to you,' Liza yelled.

Kate ran up the stairs while Liza stormed into the dining room. Helen headed downstairs, wondering again about the acting troupe. The friendly facade they'd arrived with was slowly beginning to crack.

Once the sandwiches were in the dining room, Helen peeled cling film from the trays, then set out apples, bananas and grapes. The flasks of hot water were standing to attention with coffee and tea bags waiting. When all was ready, she called everyone to the dining room and told them to help themselves.

'Will you stay and join us?' Paul asked.

She shook her head. 'I'll leave you to it,' she said. 'I've got some phone calls to catch up on while you have lunch, and besides, I need to take Suki for a walk.'

Paul's eyes lit up. 'Could I join you?' he said.

'Don't you want to stay here with your friends?'

He cast his gaze to the carpet, avoiding eye contact again. Helen's heart went out to him.

'Of course you can come. I'd like that,' she said.

His face lit up with a smile.

'Give me half an hour to sort things downstairs, and I'll meet you at the front of the Seaview,' she added.

Downstairs in her apartment, she helped herself to one of Jean's sandwiches, brewed a cup of strong tea and flipped her laptop open. There were bookings to attend to and emails that needed her reply. She worked quickly, efficiently, happy with the new booking website, which was working as well as she'd hoped. Marie had encouraged her to upgrade from the paper diary she and Tom had used to an online system instead. There was an email from the insurance company about the work that Gav's Garage were doing on her car. At least that was one less thing to worry about. But still she felt unnerved, even scared, each time she thought of the anonymous calls she'd received. She decided to email her contact at the police station to let them know about the new call. It had been a woman's voice again on the phone, but she couldn't say for sure whether it was the same one as before.

All done, she read Jimmy's text again, then plunged straight in, not giving herself time to think in case she talked herself out of replying. She told him she was looking forward to seeing him too, and she even put a kiss at the end. His reply came through in an instant, with a smiling face, a kiss and a heart. The smile and the kiss she was more than ready for; it was the heart she wasn't sure about sending in return, whether virtual or real.

She put her phone in her pocket, then attached Suki's lead to her collar. 'Come on, girl, let's walk on the beach. We've got company this time too.'

When she reached Windsor Terrace, Paul was waiting at the Seaview's front gate. He wore his beige anorak, which wasn't the most becoming colour or style. But she knew she shouldn't judge what other people wore when Marie was always on at her to make more of herself. However, running the Seaview was hard work, physical too, and she wouldn't get much done if she dressed the way Marie did, in her strappy sandals and tight trouser suits.

Paul smiled when he saw her. Helen pointed to the crescent-shaped bay at the bottom of the cliff.

'Let's go down to the beach. We should have enough time for a quick walk before Chester needs you back at work.'

As they walked, Paul asked questions about Suki, about her past life as a racing dog and about the rehoming centre where Helen and Tom had found her. He revealed that his parents had dogs at home; he'd grown up with two red setters, and he said that he missed them a lot. Helen enjoyed listening to him talk, but each time the subject strayed from dogs and she asked him about his work with Dawley's Theatre Group, he clammed up. She tried to keep the conversation neutral, dog-focused; she didn't want to upset him or cause him anxiety. But behind his bashful eyes, she detected a sharp, intelligent mind.

Climbing back up the winding path from the beach, he finally opened up.

'Did you really enjoy the read-through this morning?' he asked.

'Yes, I did. I think the Modernist is on to a winner with Chester's play.'

He stopped dead in his tracks. 'You really think it's his?'

Helen stopped too. Suki pulled on her lead, expecting to keep walking. 'Suki, wait,' Helen said, then turned to Paul. 'What do you mean?'

Paul looked ahead to the minibus outside the Seaview. 'Dawley's Theatre Group was a cooperative once upon a time. Ideas were shared.' He shook his head. 'Sorry, I shouldn't be saying this.'

'No, go on,' Helen said gently.

He dropped his gaze for a second before meeting her eye. 'Chester didn't write *Midnight with Maude* without help; it was

87

a collaboration between him and . . .' He covered his mouth with his hand. Helen looked at him and noticed he was blushing.

'Do you mean he's taking credit for something that isn't his?' she asked. She'd been intrigued about this since overhearing Carmen and Chester's argument in the lounge the day they arrived.

Paul turned his head away, and when he finally looked back at her, he was biting his lip. 'It's not a secret, I think it's all right to tell you. But please don't tell Chester you heard it from me. See, he's the one who's finally brought the play to life, and he deserves credit for that. It might have gone unnoticed if he hadn't got involved. It could have ended up another script that no one sees.'

'Who else was involved?' Helen dared herself to ask.

'Carmen wrote a lot of Act Three.'

'Carmen?' Helen asked, willing Paul to go on, but he'd clammed up again.

'You won't mention this to Chester, or to any of them, will you?'

'No, of course not. You can trust me, I promise.'

'Lee also wanted a hand in writing it; he even drafted a scene, but Chester wouldn't accept it.'

'Lee's a writer too?'

Paul nodded. 'He dabbles.'

Suki whined and strained at the leash again.

'Come on, we'd better get back. I don't want to make you late,' Helen said.

She shot a glance at him as they walked. They were about to cross the road when she decided to ask another question. She knew she'd need to be subtle and keep her tone light.

'Chester looks different without his beard and moustache, eh?' she said, looking at him, trying to gauge his reaction.

Paul's mouth twitched at the side, but he kept his focus on the Seaview. 'I guess he shaved it all off in a fit of pique to spite Carmen,' he said.

Helen raised her eyebrows. My word, she really was finding out what a strange bunch they were.

'Chester and Carmen used to be lovers, until things soured between them not too long ago. They argued all the way here in the minibus; it was awful for the rest of us,' Paul said. 'Carmen is attracted to men with big moustaches, you see. I suppose that shaving his off was Chester's way of accepting that things are finally over between them.'

'Did they split up because Chester's taking credit for her work on the play?' Helen asked.

'I guess that might have something to do with it. Although I heard on the grapevine that she dumped him for a younger man with an even bigger moustache.'

Helen raised her gaze to the Seaview, where the tall figure of Chester Ford could clearly be seen through the lounge window. Standing next to him was Carmen. However, from where Helen stood, daylight reflected from the glass and she could see no further into the room. She could make out Chester's clenched jaw, furrowed brow and reddened cheeks. He looked furious. Carmen was pointing at him, jabbing him in the chest with her finger, before flouncing off, leaving him staring into the distance. He didn't seem to notice Helen and Paul outside the window, though they could see him clearly. He gripped his cigarette holder tightly, angrily, and then he snapped it in half.

Chapter 12

The afternoon rehearsals left Helen feeling drained, as the mood in the room became tense. She followed the script, as she'd done that morning, but this time she couldn't help wondering how much of it was Chester's and how much had been written by Carmen. She picked up on other tensions too. Kate and Liza kept shooting daggers at each other, and Helen heard them arguing again about the key to the room where the props and costumes were stored. Kate and Carmen exchanged menacing looks. As for Chester and Carmen, they barely said a word to each other, and Chester only spoke to the rest of the troupe when he was in work mode, directing the play. Plus, Kate avoided Lee and turned away from him each time he approached her. Thank heavens for calm and serene Audrey, Helen thought, and no-nonsense, shy Paul. The two of them were like a breath of fresh air in the poisonous atmosphere.

By now Helen was starting to be called into action whenever an actor faltered and forgot their lines. Each of them turned to her for help, some more politely than others. Carmen snapped her fingers and called out impatiently, 'Line!' each time she stumbled with her script. Audrey closed her eyes and rubbed her temples before turning to Helen with a pleading 'Would you mind, darling?' Kate bit her lip, while Lee turned angry, banging his fist on the nearest tabletop in frustration, calling out a loud 'Damn it!' As Lee faltered most of all, there was a lot of banging and damning. Only Liza managed to be word-perfect, almost from the start, and needed no help at all. Chester rarely faltered either, but then he had written the play, after all.

When afternoon break arrived, Helen was relieved to leave the room and rushed out before anyone could collar her. She headed downstairs to gather cups and Jean's home-made ginger snaps and sent everything up in the dumbwaiter. When she returned upstairs, she was pleased to see Lee working with Paul to unload cups and saucers.

'Thanks, chaps,' she said.

Paul nodded at the open door of the lounge. 'We were wondering if your jukebox worked. There seem to be a lot of Elvis songs on there.'

The jukebox at the Seaview was full of Tom's favourite tracks. He'd loved Elvis so much that they'd even had an Elvis ballad played at their wedding. The same song had been played at his funeral, and again at his memorial service.

'Are you a big Elvis fan?' Paul asked.

'My late husband was,' Helen replied. Oh, it still hurt to say those words, to give Tom that title. And now when Elvis was mentioned, not only did it bring Tom straight to mind, but Jimmy too, the man who made his living impersonating the king of rock and roll. 'Yes, it works fine. I can switch it on if you like?'

'It'd be nice for anyone who wants to stay in the bar for a drink one evening,' Lee said.

'Then I'll make sure I do,' Helen said. 'Will you be in the bar tonight?'

Lee rubbed a hand along the back of his neck. 'No, I've got plans,' he said, before quickly walking away.

Helen busied herself serving afternoon refreshments, then took up her seat by the lounge door and returned to the script. When the afternoon read ended, some of the cast returned to their rooms, while others headed out for a walk. Helen watched Audrey and Liza walk off arm in arm, down the cliff to the beach. Left alone in the lounge, she straightened chairs and tables while Suki stood by the door, looking in.

'It's all right, Suki, you can come in. Carmen's gone.'

The dog padded across the carpet and stood beside Helen, both of them gazing at the beach as it stretched away to Scalby Ness on the left. To the right, the view took in the impressive sight of the ruins of Scarborough Castle. Helen heard a clatter of doors open and close upstairs, footsteps in the hallway, then the front door slamming shut. She looked out to see Kate in a scarlet jumpsuit hurrying down the path, with Lee in hot pursuit.

'Leave me alone!' Kate yelled.

Lee ran to catch up. 'Kate, please. How many times do I have to tell you? You're my world. Please tell me what I've done wrong. We can't throw our relationship away.'

Their voices were soon lost on the breeze.

Helen was stroking Suki's ears when her phone buzzed in her pocket. Her heart dropped at the sound. *Please let it not be another strange call.* With trepidation, she pulled the phone out, relieved to see Marie's name displayed.

'How do you fancy having dinner at Tom's Teas tonight? My treat,' Marie said.

Helen didn't need to give it a second thought. 'After the day I've had, dinner and a chat are exactly what I need.'

'See you there about six?'

'Perfect . . . and Marie?'

'What, love?'

'I need to talk to you, about . . . stuff.'

'What stuff? Hot stuff?' Marie teased.

'Scary stuff,' Helen said grimly. 'I've been getting anonymous phone calls, and my car was broken into. There are other things on my mind too, things like Jimmy. He's coming back next week, and I'm—'

'Yeah, I can imagine exactly how you're feeling about Jimmy. No need to say more about anything; we'll talk later.'

After Marie hung up, Helen glanced at the clock on the wall. She had just enough time to take Suki for a walk, feed her, then deal with any new bookings and emails before getting changed.

That evening Helen sat at her favourite table in Tom's Teas, the one with a view of Scarborough Castle floodlit against the night sky. A bottle of red wine and two glasses stood on the table in front of her. 'Looks spooky, doesn't it?' said a voice. She looked up to see Marie striding towards her in a pair of black leather trousers and a low-cut red blouse. She was pointing at the castle.

'No, I think it looks enchanting,' Helen replied. She stood and hugged her friend tight. 'What a beautiful blouse,' she said.

Marie shimmied her shoulders appreciatively. 'What? This old thing?'

They sat down, and Helen poured generous measures of red

93

wine into glasses. She noticed Marie appraising the blue jumper and striped scarf she wore with her jeans.

'Marie, stop it. You're doing it again.'

'Doing what?' Marie said innocently.

'Giving me that look.'

'What look?'

'The one that says I should be making more of myself, wearing different clothes.'

'Did I say that?' Marie asked gently.

'Your eyes did,' Helen replied.

They both broke into smiles.

'You look a bit down, Helen, that's what I was thinking when I was looking at you.'

'Every now and then, when I think about Tom, I go spinning like a loose wheel. Just today, I had to refer to him as my late husband. It still doesn't feel right to call him that, but there's no other word for it.'

'Who were you talking to?' Marie said.

'One of my guests at the Seaview. He was asking about the jukebox.'

'That thing? Is it still full of Elvis songs?'

'I can't bring myself to replace them. They remind me of Tom.'

'But the jukebox is a valuable resource for the Seaview,' Marie said. 'It's a nice little earner. You know what you should do?'

Helen leaned forward, keen to hear Marie's suggestion.

'You should take the Elvis songs out and put songs in that *you* like.'

'Oh, I couldn't,' Helen said, flustered. 'No, I couldn't get rid of Tom's tunes. The Seaview's jukebox is what made our Elvis parties so popular.'

'And when was the last time you threw one of those?' Marie said, not letting Helen off the hook. 'Look, I'm not pushing you into anything, but since Tom died, the Seaview has changed. You've upgraded and updated the place, decorated it from top to bottom, and you're going after your four stars at last. Isn't it time you let Elvis go too?'

'Let Tom go, you mean?' Helen said, swallowing an unexpected lump in her throat.

'I know it's not easy, love. But here's the thing . . . you can either leave the jukebox as it is, unloved and gathering dust, or you can change the music to something your guests like. Ask them what they want to hear.'

'No, Marie, I couldn't.'

'You could, and you should,' Marie said, reaching for her hand. 'If you want to listen to Elvis to remind you of Tom, you can do that any time in your apartment. My advice is to separate your home life from the Seaview a bit more. You need to remember that not all of your guests are Elvis fans. If you change the music on the jukebox, include a mix of old and new songs, it could be a money-spinner.'

Helen thought for a moment. 'Oh, you might be right,' she said at last. 'I've been reluctant to change the songs, but I suppose I could . . . I mean, it's not as if I'd need to take *all* the Elvis songs out. I could leave a couple in there, Tom's favourites at least.'

'Attagirl.' Marie smiled.

'Perhaps it *is* time the Seaview had new sounds,' Helen said, more decisively now.

'And the best sound of all will be the clinking of pound coins when you empty the money tray each week,' Marie added.

They raised their wine glasses in a toast just as the waitress came to take their orders. The evening menu was more sophisticated than the daytime tearoom menu. With Marie's guiding hand on the tiller, it was becoming a Bistro at night. Helen ordered Caesar salad, followed by grilled chicken and chips. Marie asked for the same.

'So, tell me what's going on,' she said once the waitress was out of earshot.

Helen told her all about the phone calls and her car. Marie listened patiently.

'I have no idea who it might be,' Helen finished.

'You said the calls were from a woman, and the first time she rang she warned you to stay away from someone, a man. Then she said "He's mine." Do you think she could mean one of the actors staying with you?'

Helen shook her head. 'Surely not. I've never had any problems with guests like that in all the years I've run the Seaview.'

Marie lifted her wine glass, deliberately, slowly swirling the liquid before placing it back on the table without taking a sip. She looked hard at Helen. 'Of course, there's someone else the caller could have meant.'

Helen was puzzled. 'Who?'

Marie lifted her glass again, and this time she raised it to her lips.

'Think about it, Helen. Which man is coming back into your life?'

'Jimmy?' Helen said, startled. 'No . . . it couldn't be Jimmy. Could it?'

'That's a question you need to ask yourself. How well do you know him? He appeared from nowhere, with his considerable manly charms, and it's easy to see why you fell for him. You were vulnerable after Tom died, and Jimmy's a handsome man. Then he left to work on the cruise ship, and now he's coming back. He could have any number of women hiding in the woodwork of his past. And if one of them has found out he fancies you, she might be putting the frighteners on to scare you off.'

Helen picked up her glass and took a long drink. 'But it doesn't make sense for this to be connected to Jimmy, because no one knows he's coming here, apart from Sally, Jean and you. If what you say is true and he's got a woman elsewhere, why would he tell her about me and where I live? No, Marie, it doesn't add up. I'm sure Jimmy isn't involved.'

'Well, if you get any more calls, give DS Hutchinson a call at the station this time. He seemed a decent bloke when he was investigating the Elvis impersonator's murder,' Marie advised.

Helen shuddered. 'I don't want to think about Jimmy being tied up in this,' she admitted. 'I've fallen for him, Marie. I think he's a decent man.'

She took another drink, then began to reveal how nervous she felt about starting a new relationship when all she'd ever known was Tom. She also told Marie how excited she was to see Jimmy again.

'I haven't had butterflies in my stomach like these since forever. It feels like I'm a schoolgirl with a crush.'

Marie reached across the table and took her hand. 'I hope you're right about Jimmy being a good man. You deserve nothing less.'

'That's what Jean says.'

'Then listen to her, she's a wise old bird.'

Their conversation was interrupted when the waitress returned with their plates of Caesar salad. The two friends talked, laughed and ate, emptying the bottle of wine, and at the end of the night, more hugs were exchanged.

'You're not driving tonight after half a bottle of wine,' Helen said firmly.

Marie grinned. 'I'd never be so stupid, you know that. I've ordered a taxi; getting a lift home from Gav's Cabs.'

'Do you want me to wait with you?'

She shook her head. 'No need. I own this place, remember? I'm sure there's something I can do to help out in the kitchen before the taxi arrives. Text me tomorrow, Helen, let me know what's going on with your actors. I want all the juicy gossip.'

Helen rolled her eyes. 'Oh, that lot, don't remind me.'

'What's up? Something wrong?'

'Have you ever heard of Carmen Delray or Audrey Monroe? They were big stars in their day. Carmen was a huge TV star; she was on telly in a show called—'

'*The Singing Nurse*!' Marie cried. 'I used to watch it with my mum when I was a kid. It's being repeated on the classics channel. What about her?'

'She's one of the actors staying with me.'

Marie's eyes opened wide. 'No! What's she like?'

'A bit scary, if I'm honest. Intimidating. She dresses all in black, loads of make-up. She's a faded version of who she once was, by all accounts, but she's still amazing to look at, a real force of nature. And then there's Audrey Monroe, who it turns out lost her husband to Carmen, who had an affair with him. Audrey's very serene, seems to take life in her stride, but she and Carmen haven't said two words to each other since they arrived.'

'Won't they have to act with each other in the play?' Marie asked.

'Yes, they do. I've been watching them rehearse, even helping out when they forget their lines. But as soon as they're off stage, it's as if the other doesn't exist. Too much water's gone under the bridge for them to be friends again, I feel.'

'I hope *we* never fall out,' Marie said.

'There's fat chance of getting rid of me, mate,' Helen replied with a smile.

It was still early, not yet nine o'clock, when Helen stepped out of Tom's Teas and into the night, where sea mist was rolling inland. It was only a short walk to the Seaview; she could see the hotel as soon as she left the tearoom. A couple were walking up the steps, a man with his arm across a woman's shoulders. Who on earth was it? It wasn't Chester, for this man was taller than him. It wasn't Paul; the man on the steps had more self-assured body language and wasn't wearing a beige anorak. She was shocked to the core when he turned his head and she saw it was Lee. But who was the woman? She walked quickly, hoping it was Kate and the couple had made up. But when she neared the hotel and saw the woman more clearly, she had no clue who she might be.

She assumed Lee had met someone and brought her back with him. Well, there was no law against it, of course. Although for fire insurance purposes, if nothing else, Helen didn't like anyone except registered guests staying overnight. Still, she was surprised at Lee. He'd led her to believe he was heartbroken over losing Kate; hadn't she heard him earlier begging her to take him back? And now, after telling her how much he loved her, how much his heart was breaking, here he was taking another woman up to his room.

She walked past the steps on her way to the yard at the back and the entrance to her apartment. As she passed the hotel, head down, she overheard the woman give a saucy giggle as she cuddled close to Lee.

'Oh, you are a naughty man . . .'

Chapter 13

Jean was placing sausages under the grill, remembering to keep the vegan sausages away from the pork in a separate pan, when Helen walked into the kitchen with Suki.

'Morning, Jean! How are your mum's legs?'

'Morning, love. Oh, she's not so bad, thanks for asking,' Jean replied, without looking up. She was counting under her breath as she took hash browns from a packet and placed them on a tray. Helen pulled her fleece jacket around her.

'Just talking the dog out for a quick walk.'

'Take your time, I'm all right here. Oh, you might want to get wrapped up if you're going outside.'

'But it looks like another glorious day,' Helen said, puzzled.

'The weatherman on the radio says there's a storm on its way,' Jean replied as she opened a catering-size tin of baked beans.

Helen took no notice. When she'd looked out of the window earlier, the sky had been cloudless and blue. She fastened Suki's lead to her collar and headed outdoors to Windsor Terrace, ready to walk to the beach. However, as soon as she turned the corner of King's Parade, she saw the tide was in.

'We'll have to walk elsewhere, Suki,' she said. She crossed the road to take in the sea view, but instead of descending the cliff, she carried on until she reached Peasholm Park. The park was one

101

of her favourite places in Scarborough, whether walking Suki or not. It was peaceful there, with a tranquil lake and lots of ducks and geese. She breathed in the fresh morning scent of grass wet with dew. Leaves had begun falling, a sure sign the season was ready to change. Suki sniffed at the grass, curious about the leaves, and when a duck swam by, her ears pricked up.

They walked around the lake, exchanging good mornings and hellos with other early walkers, and Helen let her mind roam free. The worries and anxieties about the mysterious phone calls and the damage to her car seemed far away right then. It felt good to be out of the Seaview, to be on her own, away from the actors and the tension in the group. Walking Suki relaxed her, filling her with a sense of connection to Scarborough, the town she loved and where she'd lived all her life. It also filled her with optimism, and on this note of happiness her thoughts meandered to Jimmy.

'Come on, Helen, you're an adult, you can do this,' she muttered out loud. 'He's only a man. Starting a new relationship is as easy as taking Suki for a walk. You venture out, unsure about the weather or the tide. But once you get going, all you have to do is put one foot in front of the other until you hit your stride. You'll soon find your footing and be walking in step with him by your side.'

'Are you all right, love?'

She turned to the voice that had come from behind, and saw an older woman with white hair, tightly permed. She wore a blue raincoat and had two trim Yorkshire terriers straining on their leads. It took Helen a moment to realise that the woman was talking to her.

'Me?'

'I heard you talking to yourself.'

'I was? Sorry, I was miles away.'

'As long as you're all right, that's all I wanted to know.'

And with that, the woman was pulled away by her two little dogs.

'Come on, Suki, it's time we headed home,' Helen said.

Back at the Seaview, Helen was surprised to see Sally.

'You're early this morning,' she said.

'Gav gave me a lift. He's working on the oven next door at the Vista del Mar.'

'I hope Miriam manages to cook breakfast all right. She's got a full house; the No Vacancies sign's in the window.'

'I've got every confidence Gav will fix it. But if it's beyond repair and she needs a new one, he'll get her a good deal from someone he knows.'

The two of them made their way into the kitchen, where Jean brewed a pot of tea. Helen knew better than to get in Jean's way, so she and Sally took their tea to the living room until it was time to serve breakfast.

'I saw one of our guests in the pub last night,' Sally said.

'Which one?'

'The Angel Inn. Me and Gav like it in there. It's quiet and we can have a proper talk. We seem to be having a lot of serious talks lately.'

'No, I meant which guest did you see?'

Sally sipped her tea. 'Oh, one of the younger men, not Chester.'

'Paul?' Helen said. 'Was he wearing a beige anorak and looking a bit sad?'

'Is he the bald one with the long face and thin lips?'

'No, that's Lee.'

'Then it was him, Lee.'

'Was he on his own?' Helen asked. She remembered how Lee had returned to the Seaview the night before with his arm around a young woman.

'No, he was with a girl. They looked very cosy.'

'It wasn't Kate, by any chance, was it?' Helen said hopefully.

'No, it wasn't any of the guests. They seemed to be getting on well.'

'Well, whoever she was, I think he brought her back here last night. I saw them when I came home from Tom's Teas,' Helen said.

'Bringing a girl in, eh? That's a bit off, especially when he's supposed to be working.' Sally raised her eyes to the ceiling. 'Do you think she's still upstairs in his room?'

'She might be. I didn't see anyone sneaking out the front door this morning when I took Suki for her walk. Or she might have left in the dead of night.'

'Will you have a word with him about bringing unregistered guests in?'

Helen cupped her tea with both hands. 'It's tricky, isn't it? I don't want to come across as a prude, but I'm going to have to say something. I need to know who's in the hotel for fire regulations and insurance.'

'Do you remember those folk musicians we had staying last summer?' Sally laughed.

Helen rolled her eyes. 'How could I forget? They were a nuisance, that lot, all of them sneaking women into their rooms every night. They thought I never noticed. Ah, the perils of being a seaside landlady. Still, there are worse things, I suppose. But yes, I'll speak to Lee and tactfully ask him not to do it again.'

'Breakfast's ready!' Jean called.

Helen glanced at her watch. 'Oh blimey, we're on in five minutes. Time's run away with us sitting here chatting.'

She drained her mug and left it on the kitchen counter, then threaded her head and arms into her navy tabard before heading upstairs.

In the dining room, serving breakfast to the actors, Helen kept glancing at Lee, wondering when to have a private word and what she would say. She'd had to give the same speech to guests in the past, but this time was different. She knew Lee had been trying to win Kate back and was disappointed he'd given up so quickly. She'd warmed to both Kate and Lee and would have liked to see them happily reunited.

Her phone rang and her heart dropped. She pulled it from her pocket and saw *Number withheld* on the screen. Before she answered, she gave herself a stern talking-to. She wouldn't live in fear of anonymous phone calls. She had to deal with this once and for all. But she was shaking inside, scared that someone might be watching her from the street.

Fortunately, this time there was no heavy breathing, no woman with a warning message. It was a booking coming in, and Helen headed to the bar, where she kept her tablet, to book in a guest who wanted a top-floor room for a weekend to celebrate their tenth wedding anniversary. Relieved, she put the phone away and went back to work.

She'd been asked to work as prompt again, a task she was half looking forward to and half dreading now that tensions in the group had emerged. Well, the actors would have to wait until she'd helped Sally clean the rooms. The Seaview was her priority and would always come first. Besides, they couldn't rely on her for the full two weeks, could they? And what would happen when the play was being staged at the Modernist? She couldn't work at the theatre when she had the Seaview to run. Chester had already mentioned a professional prompter coming in and she hoped they would arrive soon.

She waited by the door as the actors left the dining room. When Lee walked towards her, she subtly moved to halt his progress.

'Would you mind coming into the lounge for a moment?' she said with a practised smile.

He followed her in and closed the door.

'Look, Lee, there's no easy way to say this. I don't run the Seaview with a list of iron-clad rules, but there are some things I need to point out . . . things that can affect the insurance on the hotel and the fire regulations, that kind of thing.'

Lee looked nonplussed. She gave him a hard stare to ensure her words hit the spot.

'What I mean is, only registered guests are allowed to stay overnight.'

'But I registered when I arrived, didn't I? Is there something else I need to do, fill in a form or something?'

'I don't mean you,' Helen said, holding his gaze.

'I'm sorry, Helen, I'm not with you.'

She sighed. This was going to be trickier than she'd hoped. She had no option but to come straight out with it. 'Lee, I know you had a woman in here last night.'

He rocked back on his heels. 'Oh, that,' he said quietly.

'Yes, that,' Helen said.

'She . . . um, she didn't stay overnight.'

'I'm glad to hear it. And I'd rather she didn't come back, if it's all the same to you.'

'She won't be back, I promise.' He spoke quickly.

She opened her mouth to say more when the doorbell rang. 'Well, I've said my piece,' she said as she turned to leave the room.

She opened the front door to find an attractive young woman with long brown hair. But she didn't even get the chance to say good morning to her before Lee was at her side, rudely forcing himself between her and the visitor.

'I'll take care of this. She's, erm, a friend of mine,' he said.

Helen looked from Lee to the woman. She felt sure it wasn't the one from last night. It had been dark then, of course, and she hadn't seen the woman's face, but the newcomer was shorter and stockier than the previous one, who'd been tall and slim.

'Bear in mind what we've just spoken about,' Helen said archly.

Intrigued and more than a little annoyed, she left Lee and the woman and returned to the dining room to clear away breakfast plates. She kept alert to sounds from the hallway, but try as she might, she was unable to hear anything of their whispered conversation. However, her many years of experience running the Seaview meant that her watchful landlady eye never missed a thing. As she paused with a pile of plates in her hand and peered around the dining room door, she saw Lee and the woman tiptoe along the hall, obviously thinking they were unseen.

'Oh, you are a wicked boy,' the woman giggled. Then Lee took her hand and they ran upstairs.

Helen stood there gobsmacked. Many saucy guests had stayed at the Seaview over the years. The sea air seemed to invigorate them. But Lee was one of the most brazen she'd ever met.

Chapter 14

Later that morning, as the cast assembled in the lounge to begin another day of rehearsals, Helen and Sally were cleaning guests' rooms. Helen always started on the top floor and worked her way down, changing towels, topping up shampoo and shower gel, replenishing milk pots and biscuits. The vacuum cleaner worked non-stop, humming and pulsing as each room was cleaned. Showers were scrubbed, bedding straightened, curtains tied back. It was hard, physical work that she had become used to.

When she took the master key from her pocket to let herself into Lee's room, she paused. To be on the safe side, in case he and the woman were still inside, she knocked loudly, twice. When there was no reply, she laid her ear against the door. All was silent, so she turned the key in the lock and stepped gingerly inside. Thankfully the room was empty, and she quickly got to work. She cleaned the bathroom first, as was her habit, then made a start dusting and vacuuming, following her usual routine. When she pushed the vacuum under the bed, sheets of paper scattered, and she gasped in horror when one of them was sucked into the nozzle. She turned the machine off and got down on her hands and knees, pulling the paper as gently as possible. However, the vacuum wouldn't give it up and the sheet began to tear.

'Oh please, no,' she whispered.

At last she teased the paper free, and it came out, crumpled and torn. As she reached under the bed to retrieve the rest of the pages, her hand fell on a red notebook. Now, Helen wasn't the nosy type of landlady, not like Miriam next door at the Vista del Mar. She didn't pry into guests' business and she certainly didn't snoop. But when she pulled the notepad towards her, it fell open and what she saw made her gasp.

She was still on her hands and knees, the vacuum silent at her side. On the open page was a list of six women's names, with two of them scored out of ten. Was Lee rating the women he slept with? She was horrified he'd do such a thing. She scanned the list. Kate's name wasn't there, but Carmen's was, and now a different kind of chill went through her. Was he intent on sleeping with the leading lady?

'Come on, Helen, you shouldn't be doing this. These are Lee's private papers,' she said.

She put the loose sheets together, placed them on top of the notepad and pushed it all back under the bed. It was a strange place for a guest to keep their belongings, not something she saw every day. However, if she'd learned one thing in her time as a hotel landlady, it was that there was nothing so peculiar as those who lived temporarily under her roof. What Lee got up to was not her concern, she told herself firmly. The Seaview was a business, he was a paying guest. She had no right to be interested in what he chose to hide under his bed.

Once she'd given herself a stern talking-to, she switched the vacuum back on and finished cleaning the room. She was about to pull the window closed when something outside caught her eye. Across the road, leaning against the railings at the top of the cliff, were two women in red coats. Each of them held a takeaway coffee, and Helen recognised the logo of Tom's Teas on the side. One of them was drinking coffee with her left hand and talking with her right, but even with the window open, Helen couldn't hear what she said.

She watched them for a few moments. They were about Jean's age, she guessed, homely-looking, a little overweight. One of them had short straight grey hair while the other had brown shoulder-length hair and wore glasses. She wondered if Carmen knew that her fans had returned.

She closed the window, gathered her cleaning materials and left the room, locking the door. It was quiet on the landing, and all the doors were closed. She was pleased to see it. Sally was a hard worker, quick too, and it looked like all the rooms were now done. She picked up the vacuum and was about to set off downstairs, looking forward to coffee and a catch-up. But when she put her foot on the first stair, she heard a raised, angry voice from Chester's room, and Carmen's voice yelling back. Helen knew she shouldn't listen. What her guests got up to in their rooms was their business, and Chester and Carmen were going through an acrimonious split. She decided to leave them to it. She walked down two more stairs when she was stopped in her tracks by the sound of an almighty crash. She paused and listened. Something had broken in the room. A window? A glass? Her heart pounded under her tabard. She should knock on the door, make sure everything was all right, but it would seem like she was prying. Instead, she stood still and waited, listening for more. It wasn't long before the fighting resumed.

'You could have killed me, you bloody fool!' Chester screamed.

'That just missed my head by an inch. An inch! Let's be reasonable, please!'

'Reasonable?' Carmen exploded. 'I've been nothing but reasonable.'

'Carmen, please calm down.'

'Get away from me, Chester. I'm going to the papers with this.'

'No, Carmen!'

'I'll tell Taylor Caffrey, I'll tell everyone at the Modernist what you've done.'

'You wouldn't dare.'

'Try me. I'll tell the whole world you're taking credit for my work on *Midnight with Maude*.'

'You know fine well your work was edited out,' Chester said, more gently.

Helen put her hand on the banister, ready to scuttle away the moment the door opened.

'Not all of it was taken out,' Carmen said evenly. 'My name deserves to be on the credits just as much as yours. This play might actually be a success. You heard what the landlady of this dump said after she heard us read through.'

Helen took a sharp intake of breath. *A dump?* How dare she!

'She loved it, she couldn't sit still at the end – she jumped up and down and gave us a standing ovation. If it can do that to her, just think what it'll do for our audience. Just think what it could do for *us*.'

'There's still an us?' Chester said. Helen couldn't miss the note of hopeful desperation.

'Of course not,' Carmen spat. 'You know I mean the play. Its success could make your name as a playwright and set me on the path to becoming a writer too. But I need my name on the credits.'

'Never! Forget about writing, Carmen,' Chester said softly. 'I think you know it isn't your strength. Isn't being the star of the play enough? That's what this play will give you, a chance to get back on TV. You'll be signing autographs for your adoring fans again before you know it. I know you, Carmen. I know how much you crave being a big star after years in the wilderness. And remember, I'm the only one who knows that you're still knocking back the booze.'

'You wouldn't dare tell anyone the truth,' Carmen hissed.

'Never forget that I could,' Chester said. 'And if the truth about your drinking gets out, you'll be ruined. No one in TV will hire you if they find out about that.'

Helen heard footsteps from the room and quickly carried on down the stairs, expecting the door to burst open. When it stayed shut, she backed up to her original spot and carried on listening.

'Then let's keep it our little secret,' Chester was saying. 'If you stop demanding a writing credit for the play, I'll keep things quiet for you. I'll even talk about how you've beaten your addiction when I give interviews about the play. And there *will* be interviews, Carmen, lots and lots of lovely interviews, and not just to the *Scarborough Times*. I'm talking about TV, international magazines, prestigious news websites, even talk shows if we play our cards right.'

'This is blackmail,' Carmen yelled.

'No, it's common sense. Now if you don't mind, we've got work to do or else there'll be no play to perform. They're waiting for us downstairs. You go first, I'll follow in a few moments. If anyone asks where we've been, tell them we've been running through our two-hander scene in the third act.'

Helen picked up the vacuum and headed down to her

apartment. When she arrived in the basement, Jean and Sally were sitting at the kitchen table, where a cafetière of coffee and Jean's lemon drizzle cake, still warm from the oven, were waiting.

'You took your time,' Jean said when Helen walked into the room. Helen kept quiet, too embarrassed to admit she'd been listening to her guests. As she slipped off her tabard and sat down, Suki padded towards her and collapsed at her feet. Sally poured coffee into her mug, while Jean cut a slice of cake and slid the plate across the table.

'There's been a bit of a ding-dong upstairs,' Sally said.

Jean nodded sagely at Helen. 'Wait till you hear this. Sally's just told me all about it.'

'What happened?' Helen said, biting into the cake.

'I was cleaning Room 6, where that girl's staying, the one who wears the black T-shirt and leggings,' Sally began.

'Kate? What about her?'

'Well,' Sally leaned forward, 'she was still in there when I knocked, so I said I'd come back later. But she wouldn't hear of it and insisted I went in. She said she was on her way down to the lounge and she pushed past me to get out.'

'And?' Helen said, wondering where this was going. 'Nice cake, by the way, Jean.'

'Thanks, love,' Jean said.

'And . . .' Sally continued, casting a quick glance at Jean, 'she had a handbag over her shoulder, a big sloppy canvas bag that had loads of papers in it – her script, I guess. When she passed me, she was in such a hurry to get out that the bag caught on the door handle and all her papers spilled out.'

'I hope you helped pick them up?' Helen said.

Sally tutted. 'Of course I did. Or at least I tried to, but she went berserk, she wouldn't let me near them. I mean, she went absolutely bat crazy, flapping her hands at me, telling me not to touch anything. And I didn't know why at first, but then I saw pictures, photographs, you know, the old-fashioned kind . . .' she picked a slate coaster off the table, 'about this big. And they were all of the same woman. I'm no expert, and I wasn't trying to look, I was trying to help her pick them up, but I recognised who it was. It was her from upstairs, the woman Jean went to school with.'

'Kate had pictures of Carmen Delray?' Helen asked, confused.

'They were really old pictures, with faded colours and a thick white border. In the photos she had the same black curly hair, the same dark eyes. I mean, she looked a lot younger, of course, but I'd swear it was her.'

'Well, there's nothing wrong with having pictures,' Helen said, looking from Sally to Jean.

Sally dropped her eyes to the table.

'Go on, tell Helen the rest of it,' Jean encouraged.

Sally looked up. 'The pictures were a bit . . . you know,' she said.

'No, I don't know. A bit what?'

Sally bit her lip. 'Saucy.'

Jean leaned back in her chair. 'What the lass is trying to tell you, Helen, is that it looks like Carmen Delray did glamour modelling back in the day. But what we can't understand is why the pictures were inside Kate's bag.'

Helen looked at Sally. 'Glamour modelling?'

Sally nodded. 'Completely nude.'

115

Chapter 15

Helen paused with her coffee mug in one hand, cake in the other.

'Nude?' she said at last when she found her voice.

Jean waved her hand dismissively. 'Oh, it's no surprise. Lots of young women had glamour shots taken when they were trying to break into acting back then. It was a different time, an era when the casting couch was part of female actors' lives. Or maybe she's done nude modelling in the past, who knows? I mean, really, who cares in this day and age?'

Helen laid her slice of cake down. 'But why does Kate have the photos?'

'That's what *I'd* like to know,' Sally said. 'You should have seen her, Helen. She went mad when she realised I'd seen them. I didn't say anything to her; I was polite and helpful and handed her the ones I'd picked up. Then she ran out of the room and I haven't seen her since. I think they're all in the lounge, rehearsing.'

'Not all of them,' Helen said quickly, then she picked up her cake and bit into it before Jean or Sally could ask her what she meant. She didn't dare admit that she'd been listening to Chester and Carmen argue; it wasn't seemly and might appear she'd been spying. She always impressed upon Sally and Jean never to pry into guests' lives. It would be hypocritical if she admitted that that was what she'd just done.

'What will you do about Kate and the photos?' Sally asked.

Helen gave this some thought as she chewed. 'Nothing. It's none of our business,' she said at last.

'I agree,' Jean said quickly.

'But don't you think it's strange?' Sally asked.

'Yes, I do, but I'm not getting involved. Look, Carmen Delray was a big star once and was very attractive – she still is, in a . . . menacing way. Maybe Kate has a crush on her? I say we leave things alone. Whatever's going on with Kate is her business. You know she recently split up with Lee; who's to say they didn't part ways because Lee found out about her attraction to Carmen?'

'You might have a point,' Jean said. 'It takes all sorts these days.'

'I suppose you might be right,' Sally agreed.

'That's settled then, and we won't mention it again, right?'

'Right,' Jean and Sally echoed.

They tucked into their cake and coffee, and there was silence for a few moments before Jean spoke again. 'Are you working with the actors today?'

'I've agreed to, and I won't go back on my word,' Helen said.

'Well, I've left trays of sandwiches for lunch, with crisps and fruit, and I've baked another lemon cake to serve with afternoon tea.'

'You're a good 'un, Jean,' Helen replied. 'And that reminds me, we need to think about adding something special to our breakfast menu before the hotel inspector arrives.'

Jean sat back in her chair and crossed her arms, eyeing her keenly. 'But we've already added porridge, kippers and vegan sausages this year; what more do you want me to do? I hope you're not expecting me to serve fancy foreign pastries, like Miriam next door does. I won't bake croissants, I'm telling you that now.'

'Don't worry, I'm not thinking about branching out into pastries and I'm not interested in copying Miriam.'

Jean breathed a sigh of relief as Helen carried on.

'Anyway, Miriam doesn't bake the croissants herself; she buys them in, warms them up in the oven and passes them off as her own.'

'She never does!' Jean said, eyes wide. 'She's all show, that one.'

'So, if it's not croissants for breakfast, then what *are* you thinking about?' Sally asked.

'We need a house special on the menu, something the Seaview can claim as its own, something unique,' Helen said.

'Smoked black pudding?' Sally offered.

'No, but that's not a bad idea. I was actually thinking about pancakes.'

Jean's face dropped. 'Pancakes? I have to admit I've not had much success cooking them.'

'Aren't pancakes a bit dull?' Sally said.

'They won't be with the Seaview's special range of toppings,' Helen said, eyes shining with excitement. She looked at Jean. 'What do you mean, you haven't had much success with them? I thought you could turn your hand to anything.'

Jean sighed. 'It's all a matter of timing. I never seem to be able to get the stupid things out of the pan without burning them. And as for flipping them in the air, don't even get me started. I've had pancakes land on the floor, the kitchen bench, anywhere but back in the pan.'

'Could you give it some practice, please, before the inspector arrives?' Helen begged.

Jean pushed her coffee mug away, leaned back in her seat and crossed her arms. 'Flaming pancakes,' she muttered.

Helen thought for a moment, then turned to Sally. 'When are you seeing Gav next?' she asked.

'Tonight, why?'

'Because I'd like to buy some planters to put outside the front door, with pretty flowers in them, and maybe two hanging baskets. What's in flower at this time of year, Jean?'

'Winter pansies are a good bet, and they'll keep going for months,' Jean replied.

Helen turned back to Sally. 'Great, then would you mind asking Gav if he can supply them from his garden centre?'

'I'm sure he'd be happy to help,' Sally replied. She paused, then looked at Helen with concern. 'Gav told me he's got your car in his garage. He said someone smashed the window and keyed the paintwork. Why didn't you tell me?'

'What's all this?' Jean bristled. 'You never said a word to me either.'

'What's to tell? It was probably some kid, that's all,' Helen said. She stood, putting an end to the conversation. She needed to rise above the strange phone calls and how scared they made her feel. She'd reported them to the police; what more could she do? And yet there was still that knot of anxiety in her stomach each time she thought of the woman's voice. Was it someone she knew? Who was this man she was being warned away from? Was it really Jimmy, as Marie had suggested? She didn't see how it could be; no one but her closest friends knew Jimmy was returning to

Scarborough. She would drive herself mad if she thought about it too much. She'd tried not to dwell on the calls, but it had proved impossible. Her heart still lurched each time the phone rang and it was a withheld number. She'd thought about not answering such calls, but it would mean missing bookings, and her livelihood depended on those. She pushed her shoulders back and lifted her chin. 'It's about time I got myself upstairs to help the actors,' she said.

'Are you sure about not asking Kate about the photos?' Sally asked.

Helen shook her head. 'I'm certain. There are some nasty undercurrents rippling between the actors. I'm going to stay out of whatever's going on as much as I can.'

'Good luck with that,' Sally said.

'What's that supposed to mean?'

'I mean that your whole life revolves around the Seaview, Helen. You say you won't get involved with your guests' lives, but somehow you always do. Do you know what I think? I think you need a distraction, and fortunately, you've got a big sexy one turning up soon.'

'You mean Jimmy?'

Sally gave her a cheeky wink. 'When he's coming?'

Helen shrugged. 'He just said it'd be this week, I have no idea when.'

'Well, enjoy every minute with him. If I wasn't taken already, I might be interested in him myself.'

Jean had been busy putting her coat and hat on, and now she reappeared with her shopping bag over her arm. 'I'm off to visit Mum in the care home; see you both tomorrow. And don't forget to take a brolly when you go out. There's a storm coming in from the sea.'

Sally left soon after Jean, and Helen walked up to the lounge with Suki. All seven actors were rehearsing. She didn't interrupt them, and neither did they stop to acknowledge her as she quietly slid on to a chair and picked up her script. Sitting so far back from the window, she couldn't see passers-by on the street and never noticed the two women in red coats taking photographs of the Seaview.

Later that morning, during break time, Jean's freshly baked oatmeal biscuits went down a treat.

'We don't get great food like this normally when we stay in theatre digs,' Paul told Helen. 'Jean's cakes and biscuits and the lunches you provide remind me of home. Plus, being able to walk with you and Suki, it stops me from getting too homesick.'

'Do you miss home a lot when you're touring?' Helen asked.

He choked back a tear and nodded before taking his tea and biscuit into the lounge. Helen watched him go. His shoulders were round and slouched, his eyes downcast and sad, his trousers a few inches too short, flapping around his ankles. She suddenly felt very protective towards him, wanted to wrap her arms around him and tell him everything would be all right.

Paul was the last of the group to take his refreshments, and once he'd left, Helen set about tidying things up to send down in the dumbwaiter. She'd just brushed biscuit crumbs on to a plate when she heard urgent whispering behind her.

'Those pictures are private! How dare you!'

She recognised Carmen's voice and spun around, surprised to

see Carmen with Kate. But the looks on their faces told her they were more shocked to see her.

'I thought this room was empty,' Carmen hissed, before she marched out.

'Kate?' Helen asked. 'Is everything all right?'

Kate's face fell, and then, as if a switch had been flicked on inside her, she beamed a megawatt smile. 'Oh, we were just running through lines,' she said over-brightly, before she too turned and walked away.

Helen closed her eyes for a second, letting Sally's words from earlier sink in. She wouldn't – shouldn't – become embroiled in what was going on with her guests. It was their business, not hers. A saying of Tom's jumped into her mind, something he'd learned from a Polish family who'd stayed at the Seaview. He'd liked to repeat it whenever the stress of running the hotel got to him: *Not my circus, not my monkeys.*

'Thanks, Tom,' she said out loud, returning to her task collecting teacups, while circus monkeys ran wild in her mind.

The rest of Helen's day went well as she settled back into working as prompt. The actors were using their scripts less, and she was beginning to recognise the signs when they needed help. Carmen continued to snap her fingers and rudely call 'Line!' when she stumbled over her words. Kate still bit her lip, and Lee, the worst of them all for forgetting his lines, banged the nearest table in anger. Liza remained as word-perfect as ever, a skill Helen admired a lot. Chester was confident, but even though he'd written the play, he sometimes jumbled lines up. Helen had to assert herself to remind him of where he'd gone wrong, as he didn't like to be challenged. Audrey, as ever, was polite and kind, even apologetic for needing a prompt.

The role was one Helen began to enjoy, and she could see its importance. During lunch, Chester complimented her on her ability to stay focused and calm, and said again how grateful he was for her help. She noticed that he hadn't replaced the cigarette holder he'd snapped. Instead, he'd taken to tapping the furniture with a ballpoint pen.

When afternoon break arrived, she served up Jean's lemon drizzle cake. Some of the group went outdoors for a breath of fresh air. It was very breezy out there, a portent of the storm on its way. Helen stood by the window, looking out, as Audrey and Liza walked arm in arm to the viewpoint across the road. Paul walked alone, while Lee trailed behind Kate. Helen wondered again what was going on with Lee. Did he want Kate back or not? Because if he did, he was going a strange way about it, inviting women up to his room. Chester and Carmen remained in the lounge, enjoying Jean's cake and drinking tea. Carmen was sitting on a stool at the bar, reading lines, mouthing the words as she ran a scarlet fingernail down the page. Chester walked across the room to stand beside Helen.

'Is there a chance we could have the bar open this evening?' he asked.

'Yes, of course,' Helen replied.

'We're all going out for dinner with Taylor Caffrey in town. He's booked a table for us at the Eat Me Café; we've heard good things about it. We won't be late back, and then we'll come into the bar.'

'I'll have it open. Will you all be coming in?'

'Count me out. I have plans after dinner,' Carmen barked.

Helen turned, but Carmen kept her back turned, hunched over her script. 'Then it's just the six of you?' she asked Chester.

'Yes, well, Carmen has clearly had a better offer,' Chester said, shooting a dark look at the back of the woman's head.

Outside, the first spots of rain began to fall. Audrey and Liza huddled together and hurried back to the Seaview. They were quickly followed by the others, all running for cover now that the rain was beginning to splash. Heavy clouds above the North Bay scudded across the sea, and the blue skies turned menacing and dark.

'Jean was right after all,' Helen said as the storm made its presence felt. She looked at the ancient ruins of Scarborough Castle under the darkening sky and a tingle of excitement ran through her. She loved watching storms over the sea from the safety of the Seaview's lounge.

Chester clapped his hands. 'Come, everyone. Let's finish reading Act Three, then we'll call it a day. Helen has agreed to open the bar tonight; we'll meet here for a social after dinner in town.'

Helen heard someone groan, but whoever it was kept a straight face and she had no idea who it might've been. Undeterred, Chester carried on, directing, advising, giving notes to everyone on their performance.

That evening, the rain continued to fall as the cast returned to the Seaview in dribs and drabs after dinner in town. Helen was ready and waiting at the bar, singing along to Elvis on the jukebox. She was wearing her good trousers with her favourite blue blouse, and had applied make-up and styled her hair. She poured herself a glass of chilled Chardonnay, then raised it to the photo of Tom behind the bar. The actors were in a jovial mood, laughing and joking, and even Paul had a smile on his face. Suki lay in the hall, and he sat next to her, stroking her. Kate and Lee sat apart, Audrey and Liza together.

The evening passed amiably, and with the exception of Kate and Lee, the actors seemed more friendly and the mood was light. There was less tension between them, it seemed. Helen wondered how much of this unusually carefree attitude was due to the absence of the dark force of Carmen's overbearing personality. Outside, rain belted at the windows while thunder rumbled in from the sea. Flashes of lightning lit up the night sky, causing everyone to turn and stare. More drinks were served, and the jukebox was turned up high for an impromptu Elvis singalong. Helen thought again about what Marie had advised her to do with the jukebox. Maybe she would change the songs in the future, but tonight was for rock and roll.

Finally, she called last orders, then bid everyone goodnight as they went upstairs to their rooms. She switched off the jukebox and the lights, then headed to her apartment with Suki to settle in for the night.

Helen was woken by the doorbell's insistent ring. She focused her eyes on the clock. It was early morning, almost time for Jean to arrive. She lay still for a moment, trying to pull herself together, as the noise of the doorbell competed with torrential rain against her bedroom window. Her first thought was that Jean had forgotten her key and needed to be let in. She thrust her arms into her dressing gown and stumbled into the kitchen, expecting to see her on the screen, wet through, mascara streaming, hair plastered to her head, glasses steamed up. But it wasn't Jean. It was two men she recognised, and her stomach turned over with fear.

The taller of the men held his ID card to the camera. 'Mrs Dexter, it's DS Hutchinson.'

Helen's heart sank, for whatever news he was bringing wouldn't be good. Was this in connection to the anonymous calls? What else would bring the police to her door? She ran upstairs, her dressing gown flying behind her and Suki at her heels. As she pulled the door open, the rain bounced off the pavement outside.

'Sorry to bother you so early,' DS Hutchinson said.

Helen stood to one side and fastened her dressing gown. 'Come in,' she said.

DS Hutchinson was tall, distinguished and silver-haired. 'This is Detective Constable Hall,' he said, indicating a short, round man at his side.

'I remember you from the awful business with the missing Elvis impersonator,' Helen said, taking in the man's familiar plump face and dark hair.

'Can we sit down?' DS Hutchinson said, shaking the rain from his hair.

'Of course, come into the lounge,' Helen said, leading the way. 'What's happened? Is it about my car? Have you found the anonymous caller?'

'No, Mrs Dexter. We're here about one of your guests, a Miss Janet Carstairs. I believe she goes by the stage name of—'

'Carmen Delray, yes,' Helen chipped in. 'What about her?'

'I'm afraid her body has been found on the beach.'

Act II

Chapter 16

Helen felt dizzy and sick. She sank into a chair before her legs could give way. 'She's dead?' she managed to say.

'I'm afraid so,' DS Hutchinson said.

Questions whirled in her mind, each one clashing into the other as her thoughts ran wild.

'Dead?' she said again, trying to take it in.

DC Hall nodded sternly. 'We'll need to ask you some questions. And we'll need forensics to go over her room. I'm sorry, Mrs Dexter. We know this can't be easy and I apologise for putting you through it. We'll need to speak to any of your guests who knew her, to see if they can shed light on what's happened. Perhaps they know if she had enemies, that kind of thing.'

'Enemies?'

'We, er . . . we suspect she may have been murdered.'

'Murdered?' Helen screamed. She felt the room spin and had to steady herself with her hand on the nearest table. 'How did she . . . I mean . . . what happened?' she said. She steeled herself for the details.

'We were called out by a surfer on the South Bay. There are thrill-seeking surfers who go out in storms like the one we had last night. As long as the moonlight's bright enough for these adrenaline junkies to see breaking waves, not much will stop them.

However, before one of them could get into the water, he saw what he thought was an injured seal on the sand.'

Helen grimaced. 'But it was Carmen?' she said.

'It was Miss Carstairs, correct. We identified her from her driving licence and credit cards in her handbag. The bag was still over her shoulder; she hadn't been robbed. We were able to contact her family, a sister, who told us where she was staying. The surfer who found her body recognised Miss Carstairs as Carmen Delray from reruns of *The Singing Nurse* on classic TV. He was a big fan of hers and he told his brother what had happened. His brother runs the North Mount Hotel with his wife and they're both big fans of the show. The landlady at the North Mount told us that Carmen Delray was drinking in the back room of the pub last night. She'd even asked her for her autograph and was put out when she rudely refused. She was with a man about half her age, the landlord said, and they sat in the snug at the back. He said they looked cosy, romantic, kissing and flirting. They attracted a few strange looks, what with her being much older than him.'

'Any idea who he was?'

DC Hall shook his head. 'Landlord said he'd never seen him before; he wasn't a local. All he remembers is that he drank pints of mild, and had dark hair and a thick moustache. There were just a few regulars in the snug, it was a quiet night because of the storm.'

Helen closed her eyes, afraid that she might faint.

'Mrs Dexter? Are you all right?' DS Hutchinson asked.

She buried her face in her hands 'No, of course I'm not all right. It's such a horrible shock.'

'We understand Miss Carstairs was part of Dawley's Theatre

Group, who are putting on a play at the Modernist, is that right?'
DC Hall said.

Helen nodded. 'Yes, that's their minibus outside. Carmen arrived in it with the others a few days ago.'

'We'll get forensics to check it,' DS Hutchinson told her.

'Do you think . . . Could it have been . . . I mean, she didn't seem like the sort of woman who'd . . . but you never know, do you?' Helen ventured.

'Do we think Miss Carstairs committed suicide, is that what you're asking?' DS Hutchinson said. 'No, it wasn't suicide.'

'How can you be sure?'

'Because she'd been stabbed.'

Helen's hand flew to her heart. 'Oh my word, no!'

'We found the weapon beside her body, on the sand.'

Tears sprang to her eyes and she pulled a tissue from her dressing gown pocket. This couldn't be happening, could it? Nothing seemed real any more. One minute she'd been fast asleep in bed, the next she'd been plunged into a nightmare, with two detectives telling her one of her guests had been stabbed. For a brief moment she thought she must be dreaming. She pinched her leg to wake herself up, but quickly realised the horror was only too real.

'What happens now?' she asked. 'Oh, my heart goes out to the actors. They have no idea of the news about to come their way. The woman was their colleague. And for one of them she was . . .' She faltered.

'She was what, Mrs Dexter?'

Helen blew her nose. 'For one of them, she was more than a friend. She'd been his lover until recently.'

'Which one of your guests is that?'

'Chester Ford, the director.'

DS Hutchinson locked eyes with her. 'You must learn a lot about your guests while they're staying with you.'

'A little,' she said carefully. 'Look, I don't want to become embroiled in another murder investigation. I didn't know the dead woman and I don't know the people she worked with, only what I've learned in the last few days.'

'But you must see the way they act with each other,' DS Hutchinson continued. 'You can pick up a lot, I imagine, while people are living under your roof.'

Helen nodded. 'Sometimes,' she said. She thought of Kate with the nude photos of Carmen, but decided to keep quiet. If Kate had a crush on Carmen, what use was dragging it into the open? The only thing Helen thought might be useful to share was that she'd overheard Chester and Carmen arguing, but as it was public knowledge that the couple had recently split, she didn't know if her input would be much help.

'And this Chester Ford, is he on the premises now?'

'As far as I know,' Helen said. 'They were all in the bar with me last night, apart from Carmen. She'd gone off on her own.'

'And she didn't return to the Seaview?'

'I never saw her,' Helen said. 'Chester told everyone she'd gone to meet her new boyfriend, the man she'd dumped him for.'

'And so Chester might have been feeling jealous about this, one would assume?' DS Hutchinson asked.

Helen didn't like the way he was leading her into answering questions she felt uncomfortable with. 'Look, I'm just a seaside landlady,' she said firmly. 'You've woken me up at the crack of dawn, I'm in shock and I'm horrified to hear about Carmen. If you want to question me properly, at least give me the chance to get dressed. My cook Jean should have arrived downstairs by now. I'll get her to rustle up breakfast for you.'

'Oh, splendid,' DC Hall beamed. 'If there's a bacon sandwich on the go, that'd be great. Now, you won't forget the brown sauce?'

'That's enough,' DS Hutchinson snapped at his colleague. He turned to Helen. 'Sorry about that, but we've not eaten in hours. It's been a long and difficult night. We'd be very grateful for a bite to eat after we've interviewed your guests.'

'Please, hang your jackets to dry in the hall. I'll go and make coffee.'

'I'm afraid we'll need to speak to your guests before you do that.'

'Now?' Helen cried. 'But they aren't due down for breakfast for an hour.'

'We'd be grateful if you could assemble them downstairs as soon as possible. We know you'll be giving them a rude awakening, but we need to be certain that none of them tries to leave, or destroy possible evidence, once they know we're here.'

'Evidence? Are you saying you think one of her castmates murdered her?'

DS Hutchinson stiffened in his chair. 'We're following all lines of enquiry,' he replied formally.

'You want me to wake them up and tell them their colleague has been murdered?' Helen said. It was too much, too difficult, too dreadful to believe.

'We'll break the news to them,' DS Hutchinson said calmly. 'All you need to do is ask them to come downstairs. Tell them it's a fire drill. I'm sure under the circumstances you won't mind telling a little white lie.'

Helen's legs wobbled as she walked away. She heard DC Hall's voice behind her.

'Salt of the earth, that woman, and this is a smashing little hotel. Did you know their breakfasts have won an award?'

Out in the hallway, Helen hesitated at the foot of the stairs for a moment, gathering her thoughts. Then slowly she began to climb, knocking on doors, apologising for waking everyone so early, asking them to come downstairs for a fire drill. She reminded herself with each door she knocked on, every cast member she came face to face with, that she was a seaside hotel landlady. She wasn't a police-woman or a detective and it wasn't her job to break news of this magnitude. She was on autopilot, stunned with the shock. Carmen had been so full of life, vibrant, the kind of woman who took life by the scruff of the neck. Granted, she wasn't to everyone's taste; even Helen knew that after spending only a few days with her. But the news that she was dead was too difficult to take in.

She returned downstairs to find DC Hall standing guard in the hallway, in case anyone tried to leave, she guessed. She felt sick to her stomach to think that the police suspected that one of Carmen's castmates might have been involved. And then she was struck by another horrible thought. Was Carmen's murder tied up somehow with the menacing phone calls she'd received and the damage to her car? It seemed too much of an eerie co-incidence that it had happened so soon after the calls had come in. She put a hand against the wall, breathing deeply, trying to calm herself down.

By now the actors were heading downstairs, milling around in their nightwear. Liza was wearing a leopard-print onesie, with ears and a tail. Audrey floated downstairs in a lemon silk gown. Chester wore a blue quilted dressing gown tied at the waist, while Paul was in flannel pyjamas. Lee strode into the dining room bare-chested, wearing only his boxer shorts and a sleepy expression, and Kate sported a matching T-shirt and shorts covered with colourful cartoon dogs.

'Please assemble in the dining room,' Helen told them all.

'Morning, Helen,' they chorused sleepily, taking their usual seats. Then their attention turned to the two strangers, who delivered the worst possible news.

Helen watched each member of the cast as the facts sank in. Chester was hit hardest, and silent tears rolled down his cheeks. Audrey's face turned deathly white; Liza fanned her mum with a napkin. Kate's mouth hung open in shock and she began to cry, her shoulders gently heaving. Lee sat in stunned silence, staring at the wall. Paul dropped his gaze, and Helen saw him close his eyes. DS Hutchinson said he'd speak to each of them privately in the lounge, to find out about their relationship to Carmen, what they knew about her, and how she'd seemed the last time they'd spoken. Through gulps of tears, Chester volunteered to go first. He wailed as he picked up one of Helen's freshly ironed linen napkins and loudly blew his nose.

Chapter 17

Helen went downstairs to make tea and coffee for the actors, and gave Jean the bad news. 'But how? When? What happened?' Jean cried.

Helen told her all she knew.

'It's too much to take in,' Jean said. 'It's tragic. Her poor family must be distraught.'

'Did she have children?' Helen asked. She couldn't recall seeing any mention of children when she'd searched online about Carmen.

Jean thought for a moment. 'No, I don't think so. She had a sister, I remember that much, and I remember reading about her getting married to her third husband, years ago.'

'I can't imagine what this will do to the rest of our guests, and what it will do to the play,' Helen sighed. 'I know I shouldn't be saying this – I mean, Carmen's body has only just been found – but Taylor Caffrey is relying on *Midnight with Maude* to save the Modernist, and if it doesn't go ahead . . .'

'How can it, after the poor woman's death?' Jean said sharply.

They sat in silence until Jean stood, straightened her skirt and pushed her shoulders back. 'Well, life must go on. Sitting here won't get the mushrooms fried, will it?' She went to the fridge and started taking out the breakfast ingredients.

'Stick some extra bacon under the grill for the detectives, would you?' Helen said. 'They've been up all night and the least we can do is offer them something to eat before they leave. Heaven only knows how Chester will take Carmen's death. The police say she was on a date with a fella last night. They were seen in the snug at the back of the North Mount Hotel.'

'Have they questioned this chap she was with?'

'I don't think so. They haven't said much, and I've told you all I know.'

Jean was about to begin slicing mushrooms when she paused with the knife in her hand. 'They mightn't be able to stomach any food after their shock.'

'Do the breakfasts as normal, Jean. They might be ravenous, who knows? Shock can affect folk in unusual ways.' Helen stood and steadied herself with a hand on the counter. 'What is it about the Seaview, Jean? What's happening here?'

'What do you mean, love?'

'Earlier this year, one of our guests, the Elvis impersonator, went missing and ended up dead in Peasholm Park. And now another guest has been found stabbed on the beach. The Seaview will be dragged through the mud in the papers again, and we'll be on the local news – they'll send television crews, and journalists will start asking questions. I can just see the headlines now; they'll call us the Hotel of Horror! The Bloody B&B! The Guest House of Gloom!'

Jean tutted loudly as Helen continued.

'It's too much, Jean, I never should have kept the place open after Tom died. I should have sold up and moved on. What was I thinking? I can't—'

Jean put her knife down, walked to Helen and threw her arms around her. Then she put her hands firmly on Helen's shoulders and gave her a hard stare.

'We'll get through this together, you, me and Sally. We got through it last time when Elvis went missing and we'll do it again. None of this is your fault and it has nothing to do with the Seaview. Nothing. Now, if Carmen had been murdered in her bed upstairs . . .'

'Oh Jean, no,' Helen cried.

'. . . that'd be a different matter, but she was killed elsewhere. We don't know what happened and I'm sure the police won't connect the hotel with the murder.'

'Won't they?'

'Now listen to me. The Seaview is your life. You and Tom spent decades building this place into a successful business. Let the police do their job and find the killer, and the news will blow over in a few days.'

'A few days? But Carmen was a big star back in the day; her death will be headline news. And you can bet the Seaview will be named. We'll lose bookings, I know it.'

'Calm down,' Jean said softly.

'Calm down? We've got the hotel inspector coming on Monday. What will she think? She'll cancel, and we'll never get our four stars. We'll probably end up being condemned, shut down. What have I done to deserve this? Nothing like this ever happened while Tom was alive. It's all my fault, Jean, there's something wrong with me . . .'

Jean manoeuvred her into a seat at the kitchen table, then pulled up a chair opposite.

'Now, breathe deeply and slowly,' she said.

Helen did as instructed.

'There's nothing wrong with you or the Seaview,' Jean said. 'Granted, it's a bad situation and one we could do without, especially after the business with Elvis. But we got through that mess unscathed and we'll get through this one too. If the newspapers get wind of what's happened, then so be it, we'll hold our heads high and deal with it. Come to think of it, aren't you friendly with Rosie Hyde, at the *Scarborough Times*? Why not have a word with her, see what she can do?'

Helen nodded. 'Well, I wouldn't say I was friendly with her, but we know each other and it might be worth speaking to her. Thanks, Jean. What you're saying makes sense, but right now it feels as if I've fallen into a pit and I can't seem to climb out.'

'Well, you can start by climbing up the stairs to give those detectives their bacon sandwiches. And if you need me for support after breakfast, let me know.'

Helen felt calmer, although her mind was still whirling and her stomach churning with anxiety.

'Do you need help serving tea and coffee?' Jean asked. 'Sally's not due in for another half an hour.'

'Thanks, Jean, but I'll be all right on my own. I don't want to subject you to what's going on upstairs, it's not nice. When Sally arrives, tell her what's happened, but break the news gently. We're going to have to get through today as best we can. Forensics are coming this morning to go through Carmen's room, so tell Sally not to go in there to clean. We'll serve breakfast once they've all been questioned and had time to dress.'

'Does Taylor Caffrey know what's happened?' Jean asked.

Helen's heart dropped. 'Crikey, no. I'll have to ring him. Although I haven't a clue how I'm going to tell him that he's lost his chance to save the Modernist. It'll break him. He's relying on *Midnight with Maude*; it's all he's talked about for months.'

Helen returned to the dining room to serve tea and coffee. She was met by the sound of crying and sniffles and saw Liza consoling Paul.

'When I saw her last, she seemed fine,' Paul said. 'You know, typical Carmen, over the top, but she was on good form.'

'I mean, she was annoying, there's no getting away from that,' Lee said. 'But who would want to kill her?'

'She was a diva all right,' Kate said. 'I bet she racked up plenty of enemies over the years.'

'Kate, how could you say such a thing?' Paul said. 'Please, have some respect for the dead.'

When Chester finally returned to the dining room after being questioned, he was shaking.

'Would you like coffee, Chester?' Helen asked.

He shook his head. 'No, I couldn't stomach anything,' he said. 'After DS Hutchinson finished with me, I called Taylor Caffrey to tell him what's happened.'

Helen felt a guilty twinge of relief that she wouldn't have to be the one to give Taylor the bad news.

'What did he say?' she asked.

'He's as devastated as we all are.'

'What about the play?' Liza asked.

Chester pulled his dressing gown belt tight. 'As we say in the business, the show must go on,' he said.

140

'But you can't possibly go on after what's happened,' Helen cried.

'Chester, dear, what exactly did Taylor say?' Audrey said calmly.

Chester looked at the expectant faces turned towards him. 'He said he understands how we must feel.'

'Bravo to that,' Kate said sarcastically.

He cleared his throat. 'But there's a catch.'

Lee banged the table with his fist. 'Damn it, what now?'

'The contract I signed – that we all signed – with the Modernist doesn't have a get-out clause. If we don't perform, not only do we not get paid, but we are legally obliged to pay the theatre for the loss of ticket sales.'

'I can't recall signing that. Can anyone else?' Liza said, looking around.

Lee and Kate shook their heads.

'We all signed it,' Paul said. 'That clause was on page three: paragraph five, subsection two. Go on, Chester.'

'It means that if the play doesn't run, we have to pay Taylor Caffrey ten thousand pounds,' Chester said.

'Dawley's Theatre Group can afford to write off that amount, I'm sure, under the circumstances,' Kate said pointedly.

Chester shook his head. 'Ten thousand pounds each.'

There was an audible gasp in the room as everyone struggled to take the news in. Audrey looked like she might faint.

'No!' Lee yelled, banging the table again.

Audrey rose to her feet, swayed from side to side, then fell back into her seat. Liza picked up a linen napkin and began fanning her face again. Paul closed his eyes and started rocking back and forward in his chair. Kate's face flushed red with rage.

'I'm afraid so,' Chester said. 'Now it occurs to me that we have two choices. The first is that we leave Scarborough today after we've all been questioned, and let the police do their job finding Carmen's killer. However, if we do that, we'll each be sued for ten thousand pounds, money I doubt any of us have. Acting is our life. We do it for the art, not the cash.'

'And what's our other choice?' Lee asked.

'We stay and put the play on; do it for Carmen and give it everything we've got. Of course we'd need a new leading lady and it won't be easy to find one at such short notice. However, if we stay in Scarborough, we're available to help the police with their enquiries if they need us. So, what's it to be, folks?'

The room was silent while looks were exchanged between Audrey and Liza. Even Kate and Lee looked at one another, the first time since they'd arrived. Paul glanced up at Helen. Then, to everyone's surprise, he pushed his chair back and stood. All eyes turned towards him. He looked around, and Helen saw his cheeks blush pink.

'I say we vote on it,' he said quietly.

Chester nodded in agreement as Paul sat back down. 'Good idea. Now, let's have a show of hands. Who wants to go home, call it a day and take their chances with being sued?'

Kate's hand shot up in an instant. 'I'm broke. I can't afford to pay Taylor. But I won't stay after such a tragic event.'

Lee's hand was next in the air. 'I'm with Kate on this.'

'Me too,' Liza said.

'And who's willing to stay, to work on the play to honour Carmen's memory and celebrate her life?' Chester asked. 'Who amongst us will vote to ensure the play's a success?'

He raised his own hand which was quickly followed by Audrey's and Paul's. Chester dropped his hand and ran a finger across his top lip.

'That's three votes to leave and three votes to stay, which puts us in something of a dilemma.' To Helen's horror, he slowly turned to her. 'We need a deciding vote, Mrs Dexter. And as you're now an honorary member of the cast, I feel it should go to you.'

'I agree, let her vote,' Paul said.

'This is absurd,' Liza said. 'She's not one of us.'

'Can you think of another way to decide?' Chester snapped.

Helen took a step back. 'No, don't make me choose,' she cried. 'I'm not an actor, I'm not part of Dawley's Theatre Group. I'm the landlady of the Seaview Hotel.'

'But you've become integral to the play, Mrs Dexter,' Chester pleaded, blowing his nose into the napkin again. 'I'm begging you, please.' He gripped the napkin to his heart. 'Think of Carmen's family, her three ex-husbands and her broken-hearted ex-lovers, like me.'

Helen took another step away. 'No . . . no, please, I couldn't possibly make the decision.'

'Please, Helen,' Paul begged.

'Helen, darling,' Audrey said at last, 'someone has to decide for us. We clearly can't do it ourselves, under the circumstances.'

Helen pushed her hands inside her tabard pockets. The Seaview was reliant on the income the group was bringing in, but that was the worst possible reason to vote for them to stay. She thought about Carmen – Janet Carstairs – about a woman's life taken too soon. She thought of her friend Taylor Caffrey; of the Modernist Theatre, which was falling apart, soon to be demolished if it wasn't saved by *Midnight with Maude*. From the corner of her eye, she saw DS Hutchinson take a step towards her. How long had he been standing there watching?

'Make the right decision for Scarborough, Mrs Dexter,' he said sagely.

That did it. She raised her hand in the air.

'I vote for the show to go on.'

Chapter 18

For the rest of the morning, Helen worked downstairs on her laptop, trying to concentrate on admin and bookings by way of distraction. She felt sick over Carmen's death, more unsettled than she'd felt in months. She was so anxious, she couldn't eat. Jean, her rock as always, kept offering tempting snacks, but Helen didn't think she could stomach anything. She stayed downstairs as long as she could to allow DS Hutchinson and DC Hall the space to question each guest. Plus, after tending to her guests' needs earlier and serving breakfast with Sally, she wanted to distance herself from the actors as the shock of the news sank in.

Once Sally had finished cleaning, she left to attend college. Helen was still working in her living room, reading the Seaview's online ratings and reviews, comparing them to the Vista del Mar's, when Jean brought her a mug of tea.

'I thought you could do with a strong brew,' she said, placing the cup on a slate coaster. 'How are you feeling now?'

Helen closed the lid of her laptop and sat back in her seat. 'Thanks, Jean. I'm still in shock; confused, upset, angry. Who would want to murder Carmen? What sort of animals are out there?'

Jean patted her shoulder. 'The police will get to the bottom of it, you'll see,' she said before walking away.

Helen's phone buzzed into life and she saw DS Hutchinson's name. She swiped it and answered his call.

'We're done up here now, Mrs Dexter.'

'I'll come right up,' she replied.

Suki made to follow her, and she had to coax the dog to stay. 'We'll go for our walk soon, I promise.'

The detectives were waiting in the hallway by the open front door. DS Hutchinson stepped forward.

'Forensics have been and gone. They've taken Miss Carstairs' belongings, which might give us some clues. The room is free now; you can go in and do whatever you need to.' He handed Helen a bunch of keys. 'These are for Chester Ford; they're the keys to the minibus. Forensics have finished with that too.'

Helen took the keys from his hand.

'We're grateful for everything you've done this morning,' DS Hutchinson said.

'And for the bacon sandwich,' DC Hall chipped in.

For the first time that morning, a smile made its way to Helen's lips. 'You're welcome,' she said. 'It was the least I could do after what you must have been through in the night.'

'But there is one more thing,' DC Hall said, casting a glance up the stairs to ensure none of the guests were on their way down. 'Keep your eyes peeled and your ears open. If you hear or see anything suspicious, anything that might help us learn more about the deceased, please let us know.'

Just then the door of the Vista del Mar next door was flung open and Miriam dashed out, stopping to do a double-take when she saw Helen with the two men.

'Oh Helen, thank heavens I've found you,' she cried. 'My

oven's on the fritz again. Could I trouble you for your friend's number? My cleaner threw the Post-it out, the one you wrote Gav's number on, and I can't find my phone. If I don't get the oven fixed, there'll be no breakfast tomorrow and my ladies on their coach holiday with the Durham gardening group will be up in arms. I can't tell you how much they like a warm curly croissant in the morning.'

DS Hutchinson smiled politely at Helen. 'We'll leave you to your business, Mrs Dexter. And remember, if you hear anything that you think might be useful in helping us find the murderer, you've got my number, right?'

'Right,' Helen said.

The two detectives passed Miriam as she walked up the path. She stared hard at Helen.

'Did he just say what I thought he said? Someone's been killed?'

Helen sighed deeply. 'Come on in. You might as well hear it from me before you read it in the *Scarborough Times*.'

Later, the remaining members of Dawley's Theatre Group were sitting in silence in the Seaview's lounge. Chester had asked Helen to join them. She took a brandy bottle from the shelf and half-filled seven glasses, one each for the actors and one for herself. She handed out the glasses, then took her place behind the bar, under the photo of Tom. In front of her was the tiny Elvis figurine. She stroked his head for luck as Chester stood and raised his glass.

'To Carmen Delray, one hell of a woman.'

'To Carmen,' the others muttered.

Another silence fell before Chester spoke again.

'It's not going to be easy. In fact, this will be one of the most difficult shows any of us will ever perform. But remember this: we're professionals, we'll get through. And most of all, we're doing it for Carmen. We need to pull together.'

Helen saw Audrey smile weakly at Paul and wondered what was going on in everyone's minds.

'Are we safe, Chester?' Kate asked.

Chester spun around. 'Safe? What do you mean?'

It was Audrey who spoke next. 'I think Kate's expressed a fear we all feel. There's a murderer on the loose and any one of us might be next.'

Paul raised his hand politely. 'After the way the police spoke to me this morning, I think they suspect one of us might have killed her.'

Chester delved into his trouser pocket, brought out a ballpoint pen and began tapping it on the table. The noise drilled into Helen's head, but it would be churlish of her to stop him today of all days.

'Nonsense!' he cried.

'It's true; the police suggested as much to me too,' Lee said. 'They asked me about every single person in this room.' He turned to Helen. 'Not you, obviously.' He looked hard at Chester. 'So you see, Chester. It seems we're all under suspicion. And some of us had more reason to kill her than others.'

Chester threw his pen on the floor, leapt to his feet and darted towards Lee. Helen reached them in the nick of time and stood between the two men, one hand on Chester's arm to keep him away from Lee.

'Sit down,' she ordered.

148

Chester snarled at Lee before taking his seat. 'I loved that woman with every ounce of my being,' he wailed.

'I think we all need to calm down,' Helen said.

'I agree,' Audrey chipped in. 'And for what it's worth, I don't think for one moment the murderer is one of us. We're professionals, we care too much about the play. What nonsense the police are putting in our heads. I can't help but feel that Dawley's Theatre Group is being targeted by an outsider. We need to look after each other, not fight within the ranks.'

Liza took her mum's hand and smiled. Paul nodded eagerly.

'I'm with Audrey on this,' he said. 'Chester, as our director, you need to lead us, and as Kate says, keep us safe.'

Chester picked his pen up off the carpet and rolled it between his fingers. 'Yes, of course.' He paced from the window to the bar and back again, with his hands behind his back. 'I'm in charge. You're my group. We'll stick together,' he muttered to the carpet as he walked. Suddenly he stopped dead and raised his gaze, and Helen saw his mouth twist in a wicked grin. He pointed at Audrey with his pen. 'You can be our new leading lady, our Maude.'

Audrey gasped, then shook her head. 'Oh no. Not me,' she said vehemently. 'No, Chester. I will not step into a dead woman's shoes.'

'But it's the lead role, darling,' Chester said.

'No. Choose someone else,' Audrey said firmly, shaking her head.

Chester looked around. 'Then who will step up to the mark and play Maude?' He pointed at Kate. 'Will it be you?'

'I'm not doing it,' Kate huffed. 'If I had my way, I'd be on the train home. This is horrible.'

He pointed at Liza. 'You?'

'I'm a bit-part actor, Chester. I don't have leading lady experience. I couldn't possibly do it. This play needs someone with gravitas. Besides, I'm nowhere near old enough.'

Chester took a step towards Audrey. 'She's right. This play needs you, Audrey. You're the only one of the right vintage, the only one who can carry this part.'

Audrey put her brandy down, closed her eyes and clasped her hands under her chin. It looked to Helen as if she was praying, and for a moment she wondered if faith was the secret to her calm manner. Finally she opened her eyes, dropped her hands and looked at Chester.

'And what if I take Carmen's role? What happens to my own?'

Chester began pacing the floor again, running his finger across his top lip. 'It's too late for a rewrite,' he muttered as he walked from window to bar. 'I could ring Taylor Caffrey, ask him if he knows another actor who needs the work. She'll need to learn the script quickly; we've done a few read-throughs already. Yes, I'll ring Taylor. He must know someone who can join at short notice.'

He stopped pacing and got down on one knee in front of Audrey. It looked to Helen as if he was proposing, which in a way he was.

'Darling, please take the role of Maude. Would you?'

Audrey picked up her glass and threw the brandy down her throat.

'Mum?' Liza said. 'If you do this, you know the press will have a field day once it gets out.'

'It's all right, darling. I know what I'm doing.'

Chester gave a little cough. 'Audrey, don't keep me waiting. My bad knee can only take so much pain.'

'Oh, all right, but only because it means so much to all of us. I'll do it.'

A respectful round of applause rippled round the room in grateful thanks. Audrey laid her hand against her cheek.

'Oh, I think the brandy's gone straight to my head,' she said with a tipsy smile.

Helen watched from her spot behind the bar as the group became animated for the first time that day. But now there was a subtle tension she hadn't noticed before. Lee was coolly eyeing up Chester, who was tapping his pen against his knee. Kate was congratulating a stunned Audrey, while Liza and Paul were running through technical details. Through the window, Helen saw a red van with *Gav's Garage* on the side. It was followed by her own car, and she breathed a sigh of relief. That is, until she saw two women in red coats walking past the Seaview. Her heart dropped at the sight of them. Carmen's fans couldn't possibly know about her death yet, could they? Had news already spread in the fan forum online? 'Excuse me a moment,' she said to Chester, and went out into the hallway.

By the time she got outside, the two women were walking off into the distance. Helen snapped her attention back to Gav, aware he was waiting to speak to her. She admired the paintwork along the side of her car – there was no trace of the scratch – and the broken window was as good as new.

'I've also given it a good clean, missus, inside and out. Changed the oil, topped up the petrol, blown your tyres up and generally given it a mini MOT. Oh, and I've put an apple-scented air freshener inside.'

He handed the keys over. 'It's all sorted with the insurance, too, I've got Sandra DeVine in the office dealing with the paperwork.'

'I thought Sandra was working in the chippy on the seafront?' Helen said.

Gav shrugged. 'She's been working for me for a month now. She's very efficient.' And with that, he leapt into the passenger seat of the red van, which was being driven by one of his mechanics.

As Helen watched the van roar off down Windsor Terrace out of sight, her phone buzzed in her back pocket, but when she saw it was Rosie Hyde, journalist at the *Scarborough Times*, she didn't answer. News of Carmen's death must have been released, but Helen hadn't prepared what to say and needed more time to think. The thought of a woman's life, Carmen's life, making headline news and being reduced to lurid clickbait on websites was sickening.

She walked across the road and sat on the bench that looked out over the bay. The storm of the previous night had blown itself out, and the day was now mild, with a gentle breeze. She breathed in the sea air, trying to clear her mind after the chaos and shock of the day. She hadn't had time to shower that morning, or even brush her hair. Her face was blotchy and pale, her normally shiny bobbed hair lank and stuck to her head. After everything that had happened, she hadn't given a thought to how she must look. She'd only just managed to get through the morning, struggling to concentrate on emails and bookings. How was she going to cope with the next few days? She had to prepare for the hotel inspector's visit – that was, if the woman didn't cancel after reading the news about Carmen. And it *would* make the news, Helen was sure of that; the missed call from Rosie Hyde at the *Scarborough Times* was proof that the papers were already sniffing after a story. She still hadn't taken Suki for a walk; the poor dog had only been out to the patio, and would be desperate to stretch her legs. Added to all of that were the worrying phone calls she'd received, her damaged car, and Carmen's obsessive fans stalking her hotel. She closed her eyes to push it all away, letting the breeze ruffle her hair and softly blow on her face.

'Is this seat taken?' a man's voice said behind her.

She opened her eyes, and when she saw who it was, her heart almost jumped from her chest.

'Jimmy?'

Chapter 19

Helen touched Jimmy's arm. After the day she'd had so far, she didn't know if she was coming or going and needed to make sure he was real.

'Jimmy?' she said again, taking in the whole of him.

'It's me all right,' he said as he sat down.

Jimmy was good-looking, rugged in a past-his-best sort of a way. When he smiled, lines creased around his mouth and his brown eyes twinkled. Helen laid a hand on her stomach, trying to calm the butterflies there and failing. She breathed in the familiar scent of his lemon spice aftershave.

'You're looking well,' she said. And it was true, he was. She thought he looked slimmer, too. 'You're very tanned.'

'Well, that's what living on a cruise ship floating around the Med for a few months does.' He ran a hand through his dark hair flecked with grey. 'It's good to see you.'

Helen winced. 'It's been one hell of a morning and you've not caught me at my best. Why didn't you text me to tell me you were coming?'

'Because I didn't know when I would arrive. I had some . . .' he faltered before carrying on, 'some stuff to sort out at home when I got back. But once that was done, I drove straight here to see you. I arrived last night in the middle of the storm. This morning, I knew you'd be busy with breakfast after I saw the No Vacancies sign in the window, so I went to see Jodie.'

An image of Jimmy's daughter flashed through Helen's mind. Jodie had been struggling, living rough in Scarborough, when Helen first met her.

'Of course. How is she?' she asked.

'She's good, thanks. She was asking after you.'

'I thought I might have seen her while you were away,' Helen said. 'I offered her food and shelter at the Seaview whenever she needed it. I couldn't bear to think about her sleeping rough. But she never got in touch.'

'She's got too much pride to accept anyone's help. She's doing OK now, even got herself a flat. She's working too, helping to get youngsters off the streets and into supported accommodation.'

'Good on her,' Helen said, impressed.

Jimmy turned to her. 'But I'm not here to talk about Jodie. I want to talk about you, about us. You were always on my mind when I was working on the cruise.'

Helen's heart pounded. 'Always?'

'Always,' he replied. 'It's been a long summer without you; it's given me plenty of time to think and to work out what I want. Did you . . . I mean, did you ever think about me that way too?'

'Every day,' she replied. It was the first time she'd admitted that to anyone. It felt as if she was taking a leap of faith, diving off a high board into a deep Jimmy-shaped pool.

He took her hand. 'We need to talk. Can I take you out to dinner tonight? We'll go somewhere nice, quiet. You choose.'

Helen looked out at the sea, where waves were crashing at the base of the cliff, the water foamy and churning. 'We don't need a posh restaurant, we just need to talk,' she said. 'Let's go for fish and chips. There's a place in town close to the railway station, Old Mother Hubbard's, they do wonderful food but they close at six.'

'Then I'll call at the Seaview for you about . . . four o'clock? We'll walk there, share a bottle of wine, and you can tell me what's upset you today.'

Helen rolled her eyes. 'Believe me, you don't want to know.'

Jimmy looked deep into her eyes. 'No, Helen. I'd like to know everything about you from now on.'

Helen felt her breathing quicken. She glanced down, and noticed Jimmy had no luggage. 'Are your bags in your car?' she said.

'No, they're in my room at the Grand Hotel,' he said. He turned and looked at the Seaview behind them. 'I booked in there for a few nights. I didn't want to presume . . .'

'Oh,' Helen said, secretly relieved. 'That's probably for the best, because I'm . . .' *Terrified*, she thought. 'I need to take things slowly,' she said, twisting her wedding ring. She did it automatically, unconsciously, but as soon as she realised what she was doing, she stopped. 'I mean, you already know that Tom was the only man I . . . Well, you know, I don't have to say it again. After he died, I thought I was destined for a life on my own, a middle-aged widow running the Seaview with my staff. I was prepared for all of that, see? And then you and your Elvis troupe turned up and somehow we fell for each other, and I soon realised I don't know how to handle a new relationship.'

'I understand,' Jimmy said. He smiled, and the little lines around his face creased and made him look even more handsome.

The butterflies in Helen's stomach returned, and this time they brought friends. 'I'm sorry, Jimmy. I know I must look a mess. It's hardly the reunion I'd planned in my head. I was woken early this morning with bad news, and I've stumbled my way through the day. I haven't even had time to walk Suki.' She covered her mouth with her hand and stifled a yawn.

'How is she?' Jimmy asked.

'Oh, same as ever. Still loves chewing things she shouldn't. She's good company, though, stops me getting lonely and keeps me fit with lots of walks.'

He brought her hand to his lips and gently kissed her fingertips. Helen felt herself blush. She yawned again, couldn't help it.

'I could really do with a nap,' she said.

'Then I'll let you go, for now.'

'But we haven't seen each other in months. Are you sure you can wait till tonight to catch up?'

'I can tell that whatever's happened is lying heavy on your mind,' he said gently. 'I should have called, or texted at least. I shouldn't have just landed on you without warning.'

Helen squeezed his hand. 'Thank you. I really do need some rest, and I appreciate your patience.'

'We've got all the time in the world,' Jimmy said. 'What's a few more hours? And I hope it's not ungallant of me to say, but you do look rather done in. I'll call for you later, and we'll have a proper catch-up over fish and chips. And maybe afterwards, if it's not too chilly, we could walk on the beach and call for a drink at Farrer's.'

I'd like nothing more, thought Helen. I've been waiting for this moment for months.

'That'd be lovely,' she replied.

Still holding hands, they stood from the bench, facing each other while the waves crashed below. A seagull screeched overhead, then the sound of the whistle from the North Bay miniature railway reached them on the breeze. Helen stepped forward awkwardly just as Jimmy stood to one side.

'If we carry on like this, we'll be dancing around each other all day,' he smiled, his eyes twinkling. 'Or we could both stand still and . . .'

Helen felt his arms wrap around her waist and gently pull her close. Slowly she put her arms around his neck. As she breathed in the subtle scent of his aftershave, she felt his lips brush hers, softly and tenderly. Their kiss was over too soon, before she was ready, leaving her wanting more. The butterflies in her stomach were fluttering their wings in time to her beating heart.

'I'll see you later,' she said.

'You will,' he replied. 'Have a good rest this afternoon. I'm looking forward to tonight very much.'

'Me too, and I promise we'll talk,' she said.

And then she turned, crossed the road and walked back into the Seaview.

Chapter 20

Helen wanted nothing more than to head to her apartment and sleep. But when she walked past the lounge and spotted Chester there, she felt duty-bound to check in on him. He was alone, sitting on the window seat with the bottle of brandy and an empty glass. He looked lost, a shadow of himself, which was no surprise after the shock of Carmen's death.

'I'm so sorry, Chester,' she said. 'Is there anything I can do?'

'Thanks, Helen, but no. I . . . We all need to process Carmen's death in our own way. None of us can face working today,' he added. 'We'll restart tomorrow. Might you still be willing to continue as our prompt? We'd understand if you'd rather not, after what's happened.'

'Yes, I'd still like to help.' She could hardly let the actors down when they were at their lowest ebb. In fact, she admired them for bravely carrying on. Chester raised the bottle.

'I need to drown my sorrows. Mind if I have another?'

'Go ahead,' she said.

He nodded at the window. 'Nice-looking man you've got there. Can he act? I've always got plenty of roles for tall, dark, handsome men.'

She realised that Chester must have seen her kissing Jimmy.

'Is he your husband?'

She was taken aback by the direct question. 'No . . . no, he's a friend. A good friend.' She walked to the bar and ran her hand along the framed picture of Tom. 'This is . . . was my husband. He died after a long illness.'

'I'm sorry to hear it,' Chester said.

'And I'm very sorry for your loss too.'

Chester poured himself a glug of brandy as Helen sat down.

'Were you and Carmen together a long time?' she asked.

He took a drink from his glass, then held it with both hands as he gave his reply. 'More than two years, which was something of a relationship record for Carmen. Two of her three marriages didn't even last that long. I thought she and I were soulmates for life, but she wanted someone younger in the end.' A faraway look came into his eyes. 'We had fun, though, oh my word, we did. She was one of a kind, that woman. I'll never find anyone like her again.'

Helen glanced at Tom's photo again. She knew exactly what Chester meant.

'She was feisty, though, sometimes too hot to handle,' he continued.

'In what way?'

'Oh, we argued like cat and dog, yelled and screamed at each other sometimes. But we always enjoyed making up.' Chester struggled to keep his voice from breaking as he carried on. 'Do you know, I was only just starting to get used to the fact that she'd dumped me, and now . . . she's dead. None of it seems real.'

Helen remembered how angry Chester had been when she'd seen him through the lounge window, arguing with Carmen – angry enough to snap his cigarette holder. And the argument she'd heard through the closed door when Carmen had thrown something at him. She still didn't know what that was, hadn't found any smashed glass or pottery. Whatever it had been, Chester must have cleared it away. She wondered how much of the truth he was prepared to reveal. She dared herself to push and ask another question, hoping the brandy might have loosened his tongue.

'I notice you don't carry your cigarette holder any more,' she said, dropping the words casually.

'Oh, that thing? Yes, I . . . er . . . It broke,' he said quickly.

'Really?' Helen replied, eyeing him coolly. 'And you don't have another?'

'I could never replace it. Carmen bought it for me on a passionate weekend in Madrid. It was unique, an antique.'

She was going to press on with her questions, but when she glanced at him again, she saw him on the brink of tears. She knew she couldn't ask any more.

He raised his glass and drained it. 'Now, if you'll excuse me, I've got calls to make, to relay the sad news to Carmen's friends,' he said, pulling his phone towards him.

Helen stood and walked down to her apartment, stifling another yawn as Suki padded towards her. She caught her reflection in the living room mirror. Being woken early by the police to be given such shocking, tragic news, and then struggling with a torrent of emotions after seeing Jimmy was taking its toll. Her eyes hung heavy, her face doughy and pale.

'Oh crikey, I look even worse than I feel. I can't believe Jimmy saw me like this. I need to sleep now, Suki. Can you wait for your walk?'

Suki padded away and lay down by the patio doors. Helen pulled her phone from her pocket and dialled Marie's number.

'What's up, love?' Marie said. 'I can't talk for long, I'm busy at work. Tom's Teas is doing a roaring trade.'

'Why aren't you working at your nail bar today?'

'I've left the place in Sharelle's capable hands. She's a dynamo.'

Helen came straight out with it. 'Look, one of my guests was found dead on the beach last night.'

'Dead?'

'She was murdered. Stabbed.'

'Oh my word, no!'

'I've had a bit of a day of it. The police came this morning to break the news. They've talked to the other guests, and forensics have been. It's horrendous, Marie. I don't think I can cope.'

'Course you can cope. You're Helen Dexter of the Seaview Hotel. You've won awards for the best breakfast on the Yorkshire coast.'

Not for the first time, Helen wished she had as much confidence in herself as Marie had.

'It's not as if the body was found inside the Seaview, is it? That'd be different, much worse,' Marie said.

'That's exactly what Jean said.'

'And Jean's always right; you should listen to her more often.'

'Anyway, I've got other news too. He's back.'

'Who?'

'Who do you think? Jimmy!'

'Oh.'

'Yeah. Today of all days. As if I didn't have enough on my plate.'

'Have you seen him?'

'We talked briefly. I'm meeting him after I've had a nap. I feel done in, Marie. I need to sleep before I can face him. I need to try to make sense of what's happened.'

There was a silence at the other end of the phone.

'Marie?' Helen said.

'I'm still here. Just wondering . . . What are you planning to wear for your date tonight?'

'It's not a date. We're just having fish and chips.'

'Then start thinking of it as a date,' Marie said firmly. 'Make an effort, tart yourself up. Don't wear that blue forget-me-not top, it does you no favours. Puts pounds on your hips and makes you look old.'

'But it's my favourite top,' Helen huffed.

'What time are you meeting him?'

'About four.' She glanced at her watch, working out that she should have enough time for a nap, then a walk with Suki and a shower before Jimmy arrived.

'Sorry, love. I'll have to go,' Marie said. 'There's a customer waiting. Have a great time with Jimmy. And if you need me for anything, I'm here.'

Later that afternoon, Helen woke refreshed after two hours' sleep. In the split second before Carmen's death intruded on her mind, the first thing she thought of was Jimmy. How gentle he'd been with her when they'd met earlier, how patient. She was grateful for those qualities. He never pushed her for more than she was willing to give. He had an old-fashioned, polite charm she admired. She clambered out of bed in her pyjamas, then quickly changed into jeans, jumper and boots.

163

In the living room, Suki was pacing the floor. 'Come on, girl, let's go.' Helen clipped the dog's lead to her collar and left the Seaview by the back door.

When she rounded the corner to Windsor Terrace, she was pleased to see the tide out and the sea calm. Once on the damp sand, she let Suki roam free, although the dog never ventured far. They walked happily along the shore and Helen breathed in the salty air. As she closed her eyes to the sun and felt the warmth on her face, she thought about her guests at the Seaview. Was it really possible that one of them was Carmen's killer, as DS Hutchinson had implied? A shiver ran down her spine at the thought she might be harbouring a murderer under her roof, serving their breakfast, cleaning their room. Surely it couldn't be one of the cast? If one of them had wanted Carmen out of the way, they wouldn't have done it so publicly in Scarborough, would they? Especially when Carmen was about to make her much-vaunted comeback in the media spotlight. Anyway, she reasoned, if DS Hutchinson really believed one of them had killed her, why was there no police presence at the Seaview? The cast could leave any time they wanted to. Helen shook her head. DS Hutchinson must be wrong.

Her thoughts turned to bright and breezy Kate with her colourful clothes. What secret was she hiding, carrying nude photos of Carmen? Or was it just a crush, as Helen suspected? She thought about shy, awkward Paul. His clothes didn't fit properly and he lost himself in technical details at any opportunity, but did that make him a killer? Helen hoped not. And then there was Lee, and the giggling women he'd taken up to his room – two women in two days, one straight after the other, and he had the gall to be giving them scores out of ten.

Helen sighed. She was being paid extremely well by Dawley's Theatre Group for their two-week stay, but after what had happened to Carmen, she had to admit she'd be relieved once they packed up and left. Chester was a mystery too. He'd been Carmen's lover and confidante and the pair had shared a tempestuous relationship. But was he capable of murder? And then there was Audrey and Liza, mother and daughter, as close as could be, separate to the rest of them, lost in their own world. It was true that Audrey and Carmen had history between them, but if Audrey had wanted to do Carmen in, she would have had plenty of opportunity over the years; no need to wait for a visit to Scarborough.

But then something occurred to her, something so obvious that it took her breath away. She stood still, the breeze ruffling her hair, the sea churning behind her. Audrey was the one with the most to gain from Carmen's death. Despite her protestations when Chester had offered her the lead role of Maude, she had taken it nonetheless. And while she didn't appear the type of woman to get her hands dirty with something as distasteful as murder, what if she'd arranged for Carmen to be bumped off? Helen shook her head to dismiss her foolish thoughts. Carmen's death was taking its toll on her state of mind and she needed to stop over-thinking. There was no reason on earth why any of her guests would have killed the woman. Perhaps Audrey was right when she said the murderer might be an outsider with their sights on the cast. Well, if that was true, Helen needed to have her wits about her too and keep an eye on anyone hanging around. Like those two ladies in the red coats.

She sighed heavily as she walked on. Having the Seaview's

reputation tainted by another connection to murder, just months after the case of the missing Elvis impersonator, was going to do her business no good. She looked up to the blue sky and exhaled as her thoughts turned to Jimmy again. And now her heart lifted and she found herself smiling. Calling Suki, she turned around to retrace her steps to get ready for . . . She didn't dare call it a date. She was just having fish and chips with a friend . . . wasn't she? Oh crumbs. It would be the first date she'd gone on since she and Tom got together. No, she wouldn't think of it as a date; she couldn't, it was too nerve-racking. She would take Jimmy's company on her own terms, not Marie's. He was a friend, a handsome, talented friend. A friend she'd kissed once or twice. A friend she'd missed – a lot – while he was working away. A friend who was now back in her life.

She picked up her pace when the Seaview came into view. She was looking forward to jumping in the shower, washing the sadness of the day off and getting ready to see Jimmy again. Her stomach rumbled when she thought of crispy fish and golden chips slathered with salt and vinegar. As she walked up King's Parade, she felt more upbeat. But when she reached the Seaview, something stopped her dead. The two women in red coats were standing outside the hotel. Both of them were on their phones, texting furiously. She suspected they were updating the fan forum with news of where Carmen had stayed. That was all she needed, a whole load of grieving fans arriving on her doorstep.

She headed to the back of the Seaview. Once inside, she showered quickly and dried her hair. She pulled the wardrobe open and her hand went automatically to her favourite forget-me-not blouse. Then she hesitated, remembering Marie's words, and chose a white linen blouse instead, along with her smartest black jeans and new pair of high heels. She'd never worn such heels when Tom was alive; it didn't feel right towering over her husband. But Jimmy was taller, and so she picked out the shoes and wiggled her feet in. Remembering Jimmy's idea of a walk on the beach, she wondered how wise it was to be going out in heels that would sink into sand, but she decided to throw caution to the wind.

Make-up done, hair shining and bobbed, she shrugged on a black jacket, wrapped a pale blue scarf around her neck to keep off the evening chill, and stowed her purse and phone in her bag.

At four o'clock exactly, the doorbell rang. Typical Jimmy, Helen thought. When he said he'd do something, he did it. She took a last look in the mirror before heading upstairs, and greeted him with a huge smile.

'Wow! Now you look more like the Helen Dexter I remember,' he said. 'You look gorgeous, well rested. Is that a new blouse?'

She pulled her jacket closed, self-conscious. She wasn't used to receiving compliments. She tried to think about what Marie would advise her to say and what Jean would tell her to do. She pulled the Seaview's door closed, and Jimmy offered his arm. How lovely, she thought. She threaded her arm through his and they walked close together. She was relieved that Carmen's fans were nowhere to be seen. There was something creepy about them being in Scarborough, especially now that Carmen was dead.

They chatted amiably as they walked towards Queen Street. From there they turned right on Newborough, up Westborough, walking through the centre of town. Scarborough was busy with afternoon shoppers, tourists and locals. Mobile carts selling leather belts and handbags were parked in the pedestrianised main street, vendors calling out to those strolling by. Helen and Jimmy talked non-stop, catching up on each other's news, lost in each other's lives. She asked him about his work on the ship, and was intrigued to hear all about it. However, the way he told it, cruising sounded nowhere near as glamorous as it looked on TV. It felt comforting to walk with him like this; she felt secure and happy in a way she hadn't done in some time.

They soon reached the restaurant, where they were shown to a window table. Both of them ordered haddock and chips. A pot of tea was brought to their table with two cups, and milk in a small silver jug. Helen took her jacket off and hung it on the back of her seat. Jimmy did the same, and she saw for the first time the cherry-coloured shirt he was wearing.

'That colour suits you,' she said.

'I bought it on the ship,' he said, looking a little embarrassed. 'It was a bit pricey, but I thought I'd treat myself. You really like it?'

'It looks nice. *You* look nice.'

He reached across the table to take her hands in his. 'I can't tell you how often I dreamed of this moment, of being with you again.'

Helen's gaze dropped to the table, and he let go of her hands.

'I'm sorry. I'm going too fast, aren't I? Trust me to get it all wrong.'

'No, you're not going too fast. It's me, I'm . . . Well, I've had one hell of a shock today.'

'I'm a good listener and I promise I won't tell a soul,' Jimmy said. He picked up the teapot and poured two cups of tea.

Helen looked at his strong hands holding the teapot, then she gazed deep into his brown eyes. All the worries she'd had, her concerns and anxiety about seeing him again, began to melt away. Of all the places it could have happened, it was in a fish and chip café that she let her defences down and realised something important. Her breath caught in her throat when the truth of it hit her. She didn't need Marie's advice, or Jean's. All she needed, all she'd ever needed, was to listen to her own heart.

Chapter 21

A huge weight lifted from her shoulders as she told Jimmy about Carmen's murder. She also told him about the mysterious phone calls and her damaged car. He listened patiently, asking questions at the right times, chipping in with advice when he could and knowing when to stay quiet. But then Helen shifted awkwardly. If she didn't tell him everything, she wouldn't be able to rest. She fiddled with her napkin, unfolding it and laying it on her lap, trying to form the questions she needed to ask.

'You know, it had crossed my mind that the woman who rang . . .'

Jimmy sat up straight in his seat.

'She was warning me away from someone, saying "he's mine" and "leave him alone", and I know it's daft, but something Marie said just won't leave me alone.'

He picked up his tea and took a long drink before placing the cup back in the saucer. 'Why? What did she say?'

'She said . . . well, she said that the woman could have been warning me away from you.'

'Me?' Jimmy said, shocked. 'But no one knows we're seeing each other, do they?'

'That's exactly what I told Marie. I think she's got it wrong.'

'I'm certain she has,' he said quickly. 'It sounds to me like you're being targeted by mistake. Someone's going after the wrong person.'

'That's what the police think too.'

'You've reported it to them?'

'Of course I have. My car window was smashed after a menacing phone call; who knows what might happen next? I had to tell the police and the insurance company.'

'Let's hope it all blows over,' Jimmy said, holding up crossed fingers.

'I hope so too. I don't know how much more my shredded nerves can take.'

The waitress appeared carrying two plates of steaming fish and chips. The delicious smell made Helen's stomach rumble; she'd hardly eaten all day. She was so wrapped up in the food that she didn't notice Jimmy's hand tremble when he picked up his knife and fork.

After they'd eaten, they walked through town to the narrow streets that led to the South Bay beach. Helen slipped off her heels, Jimmy took off his loafers and socks, and they strolled barefoot on the sand. The night air was mild, and they sat at a table outside Farrer's at the Spa, enjoying spectacular views, holding hands as the moonlight sparkled on the sea. When last orders were called, Jimmy insisted on walking her back to the Seaview, even though it meant putting him well out of his way. As they walked, they laughed and talked, neither of them wanting the evening to end. And so, when they reached the Seaview, Helen invited him in.

'Are you sure?' Jimmy asked, hesitating on the threshold.

'I think so,' she replied.

She led the way into her apartment, making a fuss of Suki, but was surprised when the dog backed away from Jimmy. She saw Suki's ears go up, a sure sign the dog felt unnerved.

'She's normally great with people,' she said. 'I don't understand what's got her so spooked. She's even met you before, although it *was* months ago and you were upstairs. It looks like she doesn't remember you now. I wonder if she's having problems with you being here in my apartment; she thinks it's her domain.'

Jimmy playfully called for Suki, but she slunk away to her spot by the patio doors. He even got down on all fours, trying to coax the dog, but Suki ignored him.

'I'm sure she'll be fine once she gets used to you being here,' Helen said, trying to convince herself. She poured two glasses of red wine and sat next to Jimmy on the sofa. They shared a long, lingering kiss before Jimmy gently pulled away.

'I want to stay, Helen, but if you're not ready for this, just tell me and I'll head to the Grand.'

'I'm . . . I think I . . .' Helen stuttered.

He stroked her cheek with his finger. 'I want to be with you, but I want you to be comfortable.'

'And I don't want the night to end,' she breathed.

'There's no need for us to rush.' He patted the sofa seat. 'I'd be happy to sleep here.'

'You would?' Helen felt more relieved than she'd expected.

Jimmy smiled. 'Very happy, especially as it means seeing you in the morning and sharing breakfast. Maybe we could go for a walk, have some lunch tomorrow? I've got nothing else to do other than visit Jodie.'

'That sounds great, Jimmy.' But then the reality of life at the

Seaview came crashing down. 'Damn, I can't. I promised to work with the theatre group.'

'You're an actor now?' he laughed.

'I'm their prompt, and I need to be here to serve refreshments and lunch.'

'Couldn't Jean do that?'

'It's too short notice to spring it on her for tomorrow; she visits her mum in the care home after work. Besides, I don't want to leave the actors with only each other for company after what's happened to Carmen. They're all in a right state, crying and grieving. I think I can be a steady hand on the tiller if I spend time with them now.'

She stood and walked to a cupboard under the stairs. She took out a duvet and pillow, sheet and blanket and left them at the end of the sofa. 'Are you sure you'll be all right?'

'I'm certain,' he said. 'Anyway, I've got Suki to look after me.'

Helen looked at the dog, who was snoring gently. Then she wrapped her arms around Jimmy, gently pulled him close and kissed him.

'Night, Jimmy,' she said, before walking to her bedroom and closing the door.

Helen woke early the next day, feeling happier, more relaxed. She was lying in bed, wondering if Jimmy was awake, when she heard a voice she recognised as Jean's. She got out of bed, threw her dressing gown on and peered around the door. What she saw made her smile. Jimmy was up and dressed, the bedding neatly folded, and was sitting with a mug in his hands, being quizzed by Jean.

173

'So, tell me about working on a cruise ship,' Jean said. 'And as soon as the bacon's ready, I'll make you a sandwich. Could you manage a couple of sausages too?'

Helen noticed Suki watching Jimmy but not venturing anywhere near him. She closed the door and headed to the shower, and within minutes she'd dressed and joined him in the living room.

'I heard Jean offer you breakfast,' she said.

Jimmy beamed. 'Five-star service. You've got great staff here, Helen.'

'Jean's more like family than staff; Sally too. The three of us are close. I couldn't run this place without them.' She nodded at the pile of bedding. 'Did you sleep well?'

'Very well, and you?'

Helen took a step towards him, reaching for him, ready to hug him. Jimmy stepped forward too. Their arms were about to slide around each other, their lips about to touch, when Suki forced her way between them.

'Suki!' Helen cried. 'What is it, girl?'

'Maybe she needs her walk,' Jimmy suggested.

'She's acting very strangely,' Helen replied. 'I think she might be jealous.'

'Of me?' Jimmy said, affecting shock.

'Well, I've never had a man stay overnight before. The only man Suki's ever known in this apartment was Tom.'

'Oh, I get it,' Jimmy said, trying to make light of the situation, but Helen picked up a note of sadness in his voice.

She kept her eyes firmly on him. 'She'll get used to you in time. That is, of course, if you'd like to come back?'

174

'I'd love to,' he said.

He reached for Helen again, and this time Suki grudgingly moved out of their way.

'Want to come for a walk with me and Suki?' Helen asked. 'I normally take her out first thing each morning.'

'Sure. What are your plans for the rest of the day?'

'Well, Jean likes to be left alone to do breakfast, then Sally arrives and between the two of us we serve it. After that, we clean the rooms, then take a breather and have coffee with Jean. And as I mentioned, I've promised to help the actors with the play. It's going to be harder than ever after Carmen's death.'

'You really are a busy lady. You make running this place look so easy, and yet there's hard work going on behind the scenes. Is there anything I can do to help?'

'Oh, I appreciate the offer, but we're like a well-oiled machine. We've got our routine, and we all know our roles to keep the place ticking over.'

'Isn't there anything I can do?' Jimmy pleaded.

Helen thought he sounded petulant, but on the other hand, there was one pressing chore she needed help with. 'Well, there is something. It's not glamorous, but it needs doing.'

His eyes lit up. 'You name it, I'll do it.'

She laughed, thinking of the bags of rubbish in the yard that needed lifting into bins for refuse collection that day. They were heavy, and she always struggled with them, but if Jimmy was volunteering, she wasn't daft enough to turn him down.

Later, Helen, Jimmy and Suki ventured out for their walk on the sandy North Bay beach. Jimmy took Helen's hand as they walked, chatting amiably, words coming easy to both of them. It felt good to Helen; it felt right to be at his side. It felt nice. Suki walked ahead, sniffing stones and trotting to the water's edge. Helen began to tell Jimmy about Carmen's fans who'd taken to stalking the Seaview Hotel, and expressed her concern that more fans might arrive once news of Carmen's death spread.

'You can handle it, Helen,' Jimmy said encouragingly. 'It strikes me you're the sort of woman who can cope with anything life throws at you.'

Helen's phone buzzed into life and she pulled it from her pocket. It was a number she didn't recognise.

'Sorry, Jimmy, I've got to answer this, it might be a booking,' she said, swiping the phone to life. 'Good morning, Seaview Hotel, how can I help?'

All she could hear was the sound of the sea as the waves frilled to the shore.

'Sorry, could you speak up a little? I can't hear you,' she said.

Still there was nothing from the caller.

'Is anyone there?' Helen asked politely. 'Seaview Hotel here, how can I help?'

And then the woman's voice again. She recognised it instantly.

'I'll get him back, he's mine.'

Then the line went dead.

'Hello? Hello?' Helen called.

'What is it?' Jimmy said, concerned.

Helen glared at her phone. This time the woman hadn't withheld her number. It was a mobile number, not a landline. Her heart began to beat wildly and her mouth went dry.

'It was her, Jimmy,' she said. 'It was her.'

Jimmy put his hands in his pockets. 'The woman who smashed your car window?'

'I think so. It must be her. I recognised her voice straight away.'

'What did she say?'

'She said, "I'll get him back, he's mine", and then she hung up.' She turned the phone towards Jimmy. 'And look, this time she forgot to withhold her number. I've got it now. I've got something to give the police.'

Suki padded towards her and stood by her side. Jimmy peered at the number on the screen.

'Could you send that to me?' he said. 'I'll take care of it, Helen. I'll pass it on to the police. Is it DS Hutchinson you're dealing with at the station?'

'No, it's a PC. I've got her email address and phone number. But I'm more than capable of handling it myself.'

Jimmy gently laid his hands on her shoulders. 'You've got a hotel full of grieving, shocked guests to deal with. The Seaview's in the middle of a murder investigation. Let me help you, Helen, please. I can do this much for you at least.'

Helen mulled his offer over. It was true she already had a lot on her plate after Carmen's death, and there was the hotel inspector's visit to think about too. The last thing she needed was more involvement with the police.

'All right, you're on. I'll send the number to you now, with the PC's details.' She swiped and tapped at her phone and sent it all across. 'Thanks, Jimmy. I appreciate your help.'

When they returned to the Seaview, Helen was surprised to see two beautiful baskets of colourful pansies. One was hanging each side of the door. And on each step that led to the door was a big navy pot planted with the same blowsy flowers. How pretty it looked. Gav must have been and hung the baskets for her. She sent a silent thank you to wherever he was; he certainly worked in mysterious ways.

Inside, Jean served Jimmy breakfast while Helen and Sally headed for the dining room. As Helen worked, it felt comforting to know Jimmy was in the building. She chided herself for the wasted months she'd spent doubting her ability to start a new relationship. All she had to do was take things one day at a time. That was all she'd ever had to do, she just hadn't been able to see it. She found herself looking forward to spending more time with him, getting to know him better, and yes, to spending the night with him too. It would all come in time. Jimmy had already told her there was no need to rush. Knowing that, hearing those words from his lips as he'd gazed into her eyes, helped calm her anxiety about moving their relationship on.

At breakfast, Helen thought the actors looked tired and distant. They were clearly still coming to terms with their shock. Chester looked like he'd been crying; his face was puffy and red. Lee was scrolling through his phone, barely acknowledging the others. The table where Carmen used to sit alone, with her back turned, was empty. There was a strained atmosphere in the room; the guests spoke in whispers, as if raising their voices would be disrespectful. Helen and Sally worked quickly, taking plates of hot food from the dumbwaiter. They served vegan sausages with beans on toast to Kate, while the rest of the actors enjoyed Jean's award-winning full English. Helen assured Chester, when he asked again, that yes, she was certain she still wanted to act as prompt. But first

178

there were rooms to clean, followed by her daily catch-up over coffee with Sally and Jean, where she guessed Jean would have questions about Jimmy.

When breakfast was over and the dining room cleared, she headed downstairs to collect her mop and bucket. A delicious smell greeted her in the kitchen, and she saw Jean, with her sleeves rolled up, standing at the counter in front of a floured board. A pan was bubbling on the stovetop.

'Thought I'd stew apples and bake one of my pies for the guests' lunch today,' she explained. 'I thought they might appreciate something to cheer them up.'

Suki was lying in her usual spot, watching Jean.

'Jimmy?' Helen called.

'Oh, he's gone, love,' Jean said, rolling out pastry.

'Gone? Where?'

She shrugged. 'Don't know, he didn't say. His phone rang and I heard him talking to someone, then he rushed off without a word of goodbye.'

'You don't know who he was talking to, do you? Was it Jodie, his daughter? She might be in trouble.'

Jean paused for a moment to think. 'No, he didn't mention the name Jodie. But I heard him telling someone to stop crying, and he kept saying . . . Well, I shouldn't be telling you this really. You should speak to him yourself and find out.'

'For heaven's sake, Jean, what did he say?'

'Whoever he was talking to, he seemed to be pacifying them. He said . . . and these were his exact words, because I heard every one . . .'

Helen wished she would get to the point.

'. . . he said, "Calm down, love" a few times, and then he said, "I promise you we'll work something out. I'll see you at home when I get back to London and I promise there's no one else for me but you."'

Helen felt her cheeks burn. 'And then what?' she asked.

'And then he ran out of here as fast as he could.'

Chapter 22

Helen had no reason to doubt Jean; she trusted her implicitly. If Jean said she'd heard Jimmy saying what he'd said, then that was what had happened. It was as simple as that. So who had he been talking to? There was only one way to find out. She decided to confront him head on. She dialled his number, but his phone went to voicemail. 'You owe me an explanation,' she said flatly before she hung up.

'You all right, love?' Jean called.

Helen stared at her phone, all kinds of thoughts going through her mind, jealous, angry thoughts. She wondered if she'd misjudged Jimmy. How could she have been so stupid as to fall for him when she didn't really know him? His home was in London, he had his own life there; who was to say he didn't have a woman there too?

'Helen?' Jean called again.

'Yeah, I'm all right, Jean, thanks,' Helen replied. She walked into the kitchen and found Jean trimming pastry around a plate.

'I'm sure there's a simple explanation,' Jean said, without pausing.

'I wish I felt as certain,' Helen muttered under her breath.

She missed the look Jean gave her as she gathered her mop and bucket. She took her phone too, in case Jimmy called back.

However, when her phone rang that day, the calls were from guests booking in, or from the linen company who laundered the hotel's bedding and towels, or from the local butcher confirming her order for sausages and bacon, or . . . well, they were from anyone other than Jimmy. Helen carried her anger inside her all day. At one point, she was so furious that she tapped out a sarcastic text and was just about to hit send when she thought better and deleted it. She was damned if she would get in touch with him. He was the one who'd run out on her, and she wasn't going to chase him. She had too much pride for that.

Later, she managed to distract herself from thinking about Jimmy while she was working with the actors in the lounge. Suki lay at her feet, her skinny body in the hallway and her head under Helen's chair. When rehearsals began, the actors were subdued at first. Smiles were forced rather than spontaneous, and conversation was hushed. Helen watched them one by one, wondering if behind their professional smiles, they still remained suspicious of each other. Chester seemed distant, not the forceful leader he'd been. Kate barely looked up from her script, and Audrey seemed embarrassed to be stepping into Carmen's role. She faltered over her lines and spoke with a catch in her voice. Liza hovered by her side, holding her hand, encouraging her to carry on. It was touching to witness. With Audrey now taking on the role of Maude, Paul was reading the role she had originally played. However, he struggled trying to read the script as well as use his laptop to type up technical notes. He got flustered easily and Helen's heart went out to him.

'It's just until Taylor Caffrey sends us a new actor,' Chester assured him. He looked at Helen. 'And I've asked Taylor again when our professional prompter is coming, I promise.'

Kate leapt to her feet and pointed out of the window. 'What on earth's going on out there?'

Helen's heart sank. What now? She rushed to the window and saw two men in dark coats sitting on the bench opposite. Normally there wouldn't be anything out of the ordinary about two men sitting on that particular bench. But these men weren't there to enjoy the view. Each of them held a long-lens camera, focused directly on the Seaview's lounge.

'Close the curtains in here and in your rooms upstairs!' she ordered. 'I'm going to sort this out.'

Kate and Chester began to pull the curtains closed as Helen stormed from the Seaview with Suki at her heels. As she neared the men, they turned their cameras on her. She waved her arms furiously, as if batting away annoying wasps. The men stared at her as if she was mad. She guessed they were both in their forties. They looked scruffy, wearing identical black hooded jackets, black scarves, worn jeans and scuffed trainers. One of them had short brown hair and a dark messy beard, while the other had blond hair swept back from his face. The blond one kept winking and squinting with his left eye. Between them on the bench was a tartan flask, two plastic cups and a large plastic box with a transparent lid. She saw white-bread sandwiches inside.

'You two! What do you think you're playing at?' she yelled.

'We're just doing our job,' the one with the beard replied.

'Has Rosie Hyde sent you from the *Scarborough Times*?' Helen demanded.

'Who? Never heard of her.' The blond man winked.

Suki began to take an interest in their trainers, and the blond man leapt up on the bench.

'Get the dog away!' he squealed.

'Calm down, Bob,' the other man said patiently. 'You know what the doctor said, you can't let this fear of dogs rule your life.'

'Will it bite?' Bob asked. He was still standing on the bench, gripping his camera with both hands.

Suki had never bitten anything in her life, apart from shoes, boots, slippers and wellingtons. She'd also chewed a pair of flip-flops that a guest once left.

'Yes, she bites,' Helen said. 'She'll bite anything I ask her to.'

Right on cue, Suki growled.

'Get down, Bob,' the bearded man said.

Bob came down gingerly off the bench but remained behind it, keeping his eye on Suki.

'If he's Bob, who are you?' Helen demanded.

'Stuart,' the bearded man replied. 'And I'll bet you're Mrs Dexter, landlady of the Seaview Hotel, where Carmen Miranda was staying.'

'Delray, mate,' Bob said. 'She was called Carmen Delray. Carmen Miranda's the woman with the fruit on her head.'

Stuart shrugged and looked back at Helen. 'All we want is to do our work. A few pictures of Carmen's grieving castmates, that's all the papers need, and we're going to stay here until we get them.'

'You're parasites, that's what you are,' Helen said. 'You won't get any pictures, I can tell you that now. We're keeping the curtains shut, so you won't be able to see inside. And I've got contacts at the police. I'll get you moved on.'

184

Her words made no difference to Stuart, who opened the plastic box and took out a flaccid ham sandwich.

'Now then, Mrs Dexter. Was there anything else you wanted?'

Helen glared at them both. 'You're disgusting.'

He popped the sandwich in his mouth and shrugged again. 'We've been called worse.'

Helen grabbed Suki's collar and started to walk towards Bob. He squealed with fear and ran around the bench.

'Calm down, Bob, for heaven's sake!' Stuart cried.

Helen left them and walked back to the Seaview. Once inside, she told the actors what had happened.

'The media vultures are gathering already,' Chester said, closing his eyes. 'That's the last thing we need.'

'Could be good publicity for the show, though,' Lee said.

Everyone turned sharply to look at him. Audrey opened her mouth in shock. Lee raised his hands in mock surrender.

'I'm sorry, but someone had to say it.'

'I'll call the police,' Helen said. 'Although I'm not sure there's much they can do. It's not as if they're causing a nuisance; they're not even littering. As long as we keep the curtains closed in here, they won't be able to get their pictures.'

'What about when we go in and out?' Audrey asked, worried. 'I won't be photographed, Helen. The last thing I want is negative publicity for taking over Carmen's role, and there'll be plenty of people who'll say I should never have done it. I feel that way myself sometimes.'

'You can all leave the hotel by the back door, through my apartment, if you need to.'

'What if the paparazzi take up position at the back?' Liza asked.

'Then we'll hunker down in here until they go away,' Chester said. 'And Audrey, dear, you're going to have to face the media spotlight at some point, whether you like it or not. We're all going to be of public interest after what happened to Carmen. We'll have to get used to it.' He walked to the window and peeked through a gap in the curtains. 'But I'll be damned if the paparazzi will get pictures of us before we're ready to face the world.'

He turned to Helen. 'I don't suppose you know any local journalists, friendly ones, who might be on our side?'

Helen thought of Rosie Hyde of the *Scarborough Times*. 'Actually, yes, I do.'

'Then maybe we should announce Audrey as our new lead sooner rather than later. If we do it through the local press, with a story for Rosie, those animals across the road with their cameras might disappear once they realise they're getting nothing from us. I'll speak to Taylor Caffrey about issuing a press release.'

Audrey sidled up to Chester, put her arm around his waist and kissed him on the cheek. 'Thank you, darling,' she said.

Liza walked to Audrey and took her hand. Kate followed and laid her arm across Liza's shoulders. Then Paul and Lee joined them and the six of them formed a circle, lowering their heads and listening as Chester spoke. Helen could hear little of it, just the odd whispered word about friendship and loyalty, about performance and art. And in that moment of togetherness, as she watched the actors, she hoped with all her heart that DS Hutchinson was wrong about his suspicions that one of them had murdered Carmen.

* * *

At lunchtime, Jean's apple pie went down a treat, and Helen warmed custard to pour over the top. It was comfort food of the best kind. The afternoon session was more focused, the actors slowly getting back into their stride. Helen was impressed with their resilience. As they read through their scripts, this time they were on their feet, reacting to each other, moving around the lounge, following Chester's direction. When they felt confident with their lines, they laid their scripts down and fully acted. It thrilled Helen to see the transformation, to watch magic happen. The people in the lounge weren't her guests any more; they were actors, professionals, different characters wearing different clothes, doing things their real-life personas never would. Audrey, normally so calm and serene, was coquettish and saucy as Maude and had a real knack for comedy. However, Paul preferred to read his temporary role from his seat, uncomfortable having to perform. His acting role continued to interrupt his technical note-taking and often threw him completely, leaving him fumbling with his script and on the wrong spreadsheet on his laptop.

When rehearsals paused for afternoon break, Helen peeked around the side of the curtains. The two men were still there, in the same position, cameras held at shoulder level, waiting. She checked her phone. There was a missed call and her heart leapt, hoping it was Jimmy, only to be disappointed when she saw DS Hutchinson's name. She went down to her apartment with Suki to call him back.

'Ah, Mrs Dexter, how are you?'

'Never mind me. I hope you're calling to say you've found the murderer,' Helen said. She just wanted the nightmare to end.

There was a beat of silence before he answered. 'Not yet. But we will. I've got my best man on the case.'

An image of DC Hall eating his bacon sandwich at the Seaview, brown sauce dripping on his trousers, flashed through Helen's mind.

'I'm afraid we've come up against a brick wall. We seem to have exhausted all avenues of enquiry, and that's where I was hoping you might be able to help.'

'Me?'

'Yes, you. Are there any more details that have come to mind since the night of Miss Carstairs' death?'

Helen sat on the sofa and told DS Hutchinson once more about the arguments she'd overheard between Carmen and Chester.

'Anything else happened you think might be useful for us to know?' he said.

Helen pressed her fingertips to her temples. She'd been struggling with the information about Kate and the nude photos of Carmen since the moment Sally had told her.

'Well, there is something, yes,' she said cagily. She hadn't wanted to tell the police as she felt it was Kate's personal business. But under the circumstances, she realised it might be details like this that might help them bring this dreadful business to a close. It was all too much; she was exhausted, done in, with Carmen constantly on her mind. Plus she now had the paparazzi outside to deal with as well as the hotel inspector's visit to prepare for. She closed her eyes, wishing her worries would disappear.

'Mrs Dexter?' DS Hutchinson prompted.

She told him about the photos. The detective remained silent as she spoke. 'And there's more,' she added, before filling him in about the list of women's names that she'd found under Lee's bed, a list that included Carmen. What a relief it was to offload this at last. She'd already told Jimmy, of course, but it was the first time she'd revealed everything to the police.

'Why didn't you give us these details before?' DS Hutchinson barked.

Helen sat bolt upright in her seat; she didn't much like his tone. 'Because I didn't think any of it was important. And because I don't like snooping on people. You're the detective, that's your job,' she said firmly. 'Plus, do you know how stressful it is running a seaside hotel, especially after the murder of one of my guests?'

'Listen, Mrs Dexter—'

'No, you listen to me. I work my socks off to keep the Seaview running. Do you think my hotel, my business, my home . . .' She was aware she was raising her voice, and she took a breath to calm herself down. 'Is any of that safe after what happened to Carmen Delray? I could lose everything once the Seaview is mentioned in the press in connection with the murder. Bookings will stop coming in! And now there are two photographers who've set up camp across the road. Isn't there anything you can do to move them on?'

'An officer has already had a word with them, Mrs Dexter, after we received a complaint from the landlady at the Vista del Mar. They've been warned and that's all we can do unless they cause a breach of the peace.'

Helen sighed. 'I'm doing all I can to protect my guests and it's very hard work. Now, excuse me if I haven't had the time to do your job for you, but I've been a little distracted.'

There was silence for a few moments before DS Hutchinson spoke again. 'I understand,' he said.

'No, you don't know the half of it,' Helen carried on, furious. 'I've also received anonymous phone calls and had my car damaged, and as if that wasn't enough to worry about, I've got those two women to deal with.'

'Which women?'

'Two fans of Carmen's; they hang around outside the Seaview.'

'This could be important. Please don't withhold any more information.'

'I wasn't withholding anything. I've told you, I've got a lot on my plate.'

'Tell me about the women, everything you know.'

'There's not much to tell, except that Carmen got upset when she saw them,' Helen said, remembering how vulnerable Carmen had looked that day. 'She said they follow her around the country, waiting for autographs, hoping for a selfie. You don't think they're involved in her murder, do you?'

'At the moment, we're keeping an open mind,' DS Hutchinson said. 'If you see them again, call me immediately. I'll send someone round.'

'Carmen said something about an online forum for fans. You might find something there.'

'I'll get our digital team on it.'

'Will you follow up on what I've told you about Kate and Lee?'

'As soon as it's possible.'

'What does that mean?'

DS Hutchinson sighed. 'Cutbacks at the station mean we're not fully staffed. You're an intelligent woman, Mrs Dexter, you must read the news and know how bad the situation is. That's why I need you to be the eyes and ears of the force.'

'Don't you have sniffer dogs for that?'

'Don't be cute,' he said. 'I'm asking you nicely, begging you. Watch your guests like a hawk, and if anything happens, if you hear or see anything you think we should know, give me a call.'

And with that, he hung up. Helen stayed in her seat for a few moments, letting his words sink in. She wasn't about to start sticking her nose into her guests' business, but despite their moment of togetherness earlier in the lounge, she had to admit there'd been some strange behaviour between certain members of the cast that she'd mostly turned a blind eye to so far. She stood, put her phone away and headed back upstairs.

During afternoon rehearsals, Helen tried hard to catch the small personal exchanges between the actors. Did the way Chester winked at Audrey each time he gave her a direction mean anything? What was the significance of the furious looks that passed between Lee and Kate? Was there more to it than a couple whose romance was on the rocks? Or was she seeing things that weren't there? Oh, it was all too confusing. She kept one eye on her script and one eye on the actors whenever there was a break in the play, or when Chester was giving direction, or when Paul was asking a question about lighting or props, or Liza discussing costumes and hats. But nothing she saw leapt out as suspicious. They all seemed . . . Well, after Carmen's death, their behaviour was anything but ordinary, of course. But they were getting on with the job in hand. The play was everything to them, and they were hard-working, dedicated, determined to get through it as best they could.

She had no clue what she should be looking for. That is, until she saw Kate reach to the floor and noticed for the first time her large canvas bag. Was it the same bag Sally had seen when the photographs of Carmen had fallen out? She watched, intrigued, as Kate took her phone from the bag, glanced at it quickly, then put it straight back, her eyes flicking guiltily to Chester to see if he'd noticed. Helen remembered that he didn't allow phones in the rehearsal room. Kate looked across the room and caught her watching; she smiled, and Helen smiled back.

For the rest of the afternoon, Helen's gaze kept falling on Kate's bag. Were the photos of Carmen inside? And then she remembered Kate arguing with Liza over which one of them would retrieve items from the room used to store costumes and props. Was Kate hiding something in there? She knew there was only one way to find out. And if she didn't speak to Kate, she knew the police would, even if they took their time about it.

When rehearsals ended, Kate slung her bag over her shoulder. 'Any chance of a quick word?' Helen said.

Chapter 23

Helen waited until the rest of the cast had left the lounge. As they filed out, they muttered darkly about the men with the cameras outside. Once the group headed to their rooms, she closed the dining room door and gave Kate what she hoped was an encouraging smile.

'Sorry for keeping you back,' she said. Her eyes automatically went to the bag hanging from Kate's shoulder, and Kate pulled it towards her defensively.

'Please, have a seat,' Helen said, as kindly as she could. Her mind was racing; she had no clue how to approach the subject of the nude photographs. Nothing in her experience of running the Seaview could equip her for what to say next. She sat opposite Kate and looked at her. The younger woman wore no make-up, and her hair was scraped back from her face with a wide scarlet headband. She wore her rehearsal clothes of black T-shirt and leggings, and her small, pale feet were bare.

'I really need to take a shower,' Kate said.

'I won't keep you long. All I want is to ask a few questions.'

'It's about my credit card, isn't it?' Kate said nervously.

The question threw Helen completely. 'Your . . . what?'

'My credit card. Chester said we had to leave our credit card numbers with you for any expenses that Dawley's Theatre Group wouldn't cover. I knew there'd be a problem with my card. I've not had work for such a long time, and you know how bills mount up. I know I'm over the limit on my card. But I don't understand what you've tried to charge to it.'

'Oh!' Helen said. 'No, it's not your card.'

Relief flooded Kate's face. 'Then what is it?'

Slowly, carefully, Helen reminded her of the morning Sally had entered her room. As she spoke, she saw Kate's face drop, saw her bite her lip, saw her left knee jig up and down. Kate sat in silence, her body language doing the talking. And when Helen reached the part about the photos of Carmen spilling from her bag, Kate was breathing fast, staring at her wide-eyed. When she'd finished, she let a silence hang between them, waiting for Kate to explain.

'You think the photos connect me to Carmen's murder?' Kate said at last. Her tone was flat, her breathing returning to normal.

'I think . . .' Helen stopped herself from saying more. In truth, she hoped with all her heart that Kate wasn't the killer, but who was she to judge who was capable of evil and who wasn't? The only thing she knew for sure was that she was out of her depth. She normally asked guests what kind of day they'd had, whether they'd been on the beach, played crazy golf or won anything in the amusement arcades. She offered advice on what to do in Scarborough when it rained, where to find the indoor market, or gave directions to Oliver's Mount for one of the best views in Yorkshire. She had no clue what to say now.

'I think . . . there's something you're hiding,' she said carefully. 'Why else would you have treated Sally the way you did when she was trying to help you pick up the photos?'

Kate buried her face in her hands and her bag slid down her

arm. Helen tried to peer inside, but all she could see was Kate's script. Then, as Kate dropped her hands, she snapped her gaze to the young woman's face, where she saw tears brimming. She hated that she'd upset her so much. She crossed her fingers and prayed again that Kate wasn't involved in Carmen's death. She seemed too innocent for that.

Kate gazed out of the window, where soft clouds scudded over the sea.

'Were you in love with Carmen?' Helen asked.

Kate snapped her gaze back. 'What?' she cried.

Helen felt herself blushing. 'I'm sorry, I had to ask . . .'

Kate shook her head. 'No, of course I wasn't in love with her. I did it because I needed the money.'

'Did what?' Helen asked.

Kate looked out of the window again as she began to reveal what had happened. 'There's an actor I know, one of Carmen's ex-lovers. When he learned I was going to be working with her, he gave me the photos. He wanted revenge after she dumped him for a younger man with a bigger moustache. Oh, I shouldn't be telling you this. I promised I wouldn't breathe a word. But I never expected her to end up dead.'

Helen searched Kate's face, reminding herself that the woman was a trained actor and good at pretending. Was she telling the truth? Helen had to know for sure; she might not get another chance to ask such personal questions. She stood and walked to the bar, where she splashed whisky into two glasses. She brought them to the table, placed one in front of Kate and took a sip from her own.

'Take it easy, in your own time,' she said.

'He wanted Carmen to suffer – financially, I mean. It was the only way he could hurt her. She's got a heart like a rock, that woman. I mean, she did have, when she was alive.' Kate picked her glass up and threw the whisky down her throat in one gulp. 'The pictures . . .'

She paused, and her lip quivered, her resolve about to give way. Helen decided that if she was faking it, she was doing one heck of a job.

'. . . the pictures were taken a long time ago, and Carmen did her best to stop them getting into the public domain. But this guy, he knew I needed money. An actor's life isn't easy. We're always broke, and I have commitments at home to take care of. I needed the cash. I wouldn't have done it otherwise.' Tears began to stream down Kate's cheeks, and she rummaged in her bag until she found a pack of paper tissues, then wiped her eyes and blew her nose.

'So you were blackmailing Carmen over those photos?'

Kate nodded between gulps of tears. 'I tried to, yes. I'm so ashamed, Helen, but I was desperate. The plan was for Carmen's ex-lover to get half of the money and I'd get the rest.'

'To pay off your credit card?' Helen said.

Kate wiped her eyes again. 'Yes, but it's not what you're thinking. I don't fritter away cash on holidays and clothes. Those jumpsuits I wear, and my boots, I buy everything from charity shops. I spend my money on something else. It's . . .' She faltered.

'Go on, you can tell me,' Helen said.

'It's to pay off a different kind of debt. My little brother Ben is . . . he's in a wheelchair, and Mum can't afford to buy what he needs. There's where my money goes, all of it; every penny I get my hands on goes to Mum for Ben.'

In that instant, Helen knew Kate was telling the truth.

'But blackmail's a crime, Kate. It's extortion. You could be sent to jail.'

'Oh, I never took Carmen's money. Things never got that far. I was too scared of her, if I'm honest.'

'But she knew you had the photos?'

'Yes, and she knew I wanted cash. She also knew who was behind it, pulling my strings, because she'd posed for those photos for him.'

'Could this man, her ex-lover, be the one who killed her?' Helen asked.

'No,' Kate replied without hesitation.

'You sound very sure.'

'I am. He's working in Florida for a year. I've been looking at his pictures online; he's posting stuff each day for all the world to see. I'm not proud of myself for what I've done, Helen, but Ben's not well and Mum needs money more than ever.'

She took out her phone and swiped it into life, bringing up a photograph of herself with a young boy in a wheelchair. In it, she was all smiles, her arm around her brother, who was grinning lopsidedly, holding an ice cream.

'I thought I could get money from Carmen in exchange for the photos and send it to Mum this week. But now Carmen's dead, I don't know what to do,' she said, tears running down her face.

'You could start by getting rid of the photos,' Helen said.

Kate's hand went straight to her bag. 'You think so?'

'I think you should let Carmen rest in peace. I appreciate you telling me all this, but while we're being honest with each other, is there anything else you're hiding? You were pretty defensive the other day when Liza wanted to go upstairs to fetch props from the storeroom.'

Kate hung her head. 'I was hiding the photos up there in a box when I first arrived. I was worried you or your cleaner might find them in my room if I left them in there.'

'I never pry into my guests' belongings,' Helen said. Well, not usually, she thought, remembering Lee's list of women.

Kate opened her bag, delved to the bottom and pulled out a handful of glossy black-and-white pictures. Helen's eyes opened wide as she began to rip them to shreds.

'Farewell, Miss Delray, sleep in peace,' she said, as her tears continued to fall.

'What about the negatives?' Helen asked. 'How can you be sure the photos won't surface in the future from someone hoping to make money from her death?'

'As far as I know, there are no negatives, no more photos. But if there are, it won't be me who exposes Carmen's past. I should never have got involved. Those photos cost me my relationship; they're the reason Lee and I split up.'

Helen was stunned to hear this. 'How?' she asked.

'Because I was being so secretive. I couldn't admit to him that I was trying to blackmail Carmen, so I backed away and told him I didn't want to see him any more. I let him go when he was the best thing that's ever happened to me.'

'Can't you confide in him now and tell him the truth?' Helen asked.

Kate shook her head. 'It's too late. I hate to think what he must think of me. What a mess it all is. Oh Helen, what will I do? Ben needs add-ons to his wheelchair and a pulley system for his room so Mum doesn't have to lift him in and out of bed.'

'Your mum needs to get social services involved; surely they pay for such things?'

Kate continued sobbing and Helen waited patiently until she was able to speak.

'Since Dad walked out, it's just been the three of us. Mum's not good at reaching out for help.'

'Then tell her she must, for Ben's sake and yours. There are people out there who can help, organisations, charities.'

Kate nodded, then gathered her bag to her side. 'Is it all right if I go now?'

'Yes, of course it's all right. Just promise me you'll speak to your mum,' Helen replied.

Once Kate had gone, leaving the torn pictures behind, Helen picked up the shreds of Carmen's past, took them down to her apartment and threw them in the bin. Then she flipped her laptop open and went through bookings, spreadsheets and emails. Feeling more relaxed after speaking to Kate, she scrolled through her emails to find the one from the PC she'd spoken to about the phone calls and her damaged car. She decided to ring to ask if there was an update on the phone number that Jimmy said he'd pass on to the police.

'I'm sorry, Mrs Dexter, no number has been reported,' the PC said. Helen could hear clicking and tapping over the phone as a computer system was searched.

'But Jimmy . . . er . . . a friend of mine, Jimmy Brown, he gave you the phone number of the most recent call I'd received.'

More clicking, more tapping. 'No, I can't find anything here, Mrs Dexter. There's nothing here about a Mr Brown, or anything since we last emailed. But if you still have the number, I'll take it from you and we'll do what we can.'

Stunned, Helen pulled her phone towards her and reeled off the number before hanging up. Then she leaned back in her seat and tried to make sense of what was going on. Jimmy had kindly offered to pass the number on to the police – in fact, he'd insisted. Had he been too busy to call the station with it? Had he forgotten? Or – and here Helen's stomach twisted when she thought of Jean's report about Jimmy running out after speaking on his phone – was there something else going on?

Chapter 24

Helen didn't sleep well that night. Had she been wrong to trust Jimmy after all? Despite leaving another message for him, he hadn't called back. On Saturday morning, she was rudely awoken by the sound of bells, lots of bells, high and low, buzzing and ringing. It took her a while to work out was happening. The doorbell at the Seaview was being pressed non-stop by an insistent finger. The landline was ringing and her phone was furiously buzzing by the side of her bed. She got out of bed to find Suki walking in circles, looking as confused as Helen felt.

'It's all right, love, I'll sort it, whatever it is,' she told the dog.

She glanced at the screen on the kitchen wall, which showed an image from the security camera by the front door. And when she saw who was pressing the bell, her knot of anxiety tightened. It was the paparazzi, with cameras, but it was even worse than she'd feared. There were more people behind; she could see a TV crew, journalists talking to cameras, taking pictures of the Seaview on their phones.

'They can ring that doorbell until they wear the battery out. I'm not answering,' she said out loud. But she knew she had to do something so that the noise didn't bother her guests. She knocked the landline off the hook to stop it ringing, then glanced at her mobile. There were fourteen missed calls, and several texts,

201

from numbers she didn't recognise. She pulled her dressing gown on, tying it tight around her waist, stuck her phone in her dressing gown pocket and stormed upstairs.

She was met by a sight that stopped her dead in her tracks. One of the men she'd had a run-in with the day before – Stuart, the one with dark hair and a beard – had his face pressed up against the glass of the front door and his finger on the doorbell.

'Mrs Dexter? Just a word from you, or anyone who knew Carmen Delray. That's all we need.'

On the steps behind him were more paparazzi, more cameras, another TV crew, all of them shouting her name, wanting a comment. Nothing like this had ever happened before, and she didn't know what to do. But one thing she was certain of – none of them were getting inside. There was a heavy green velvet curtain to one side of the door used only on the darkest, coldest days. She pulled it across.

'Mrs Dexter! Helen! We just need a quote.' The calls continued.

Helen leaned with her back against the door, thinking fast, her heart beating wildly. She reached up and yanked the doorbell off the wall. The Seaview was plunged into silence, though the clamour continued outside. Then the phone in her dressing gown pocket started to ring. She lifted it out, intent on turning it off until she saw Rosie Hyde's name. She walked into the lounge, gloomy and dark with the curtains closed, and let Rosie's call go to voicemail.

Suddenly Liza appeared at the lounge door. She was wearing her leopard-print onesie.

'Are you all right?' she asked. 'The doorbell woke me, and when I peered out of my window, I saw the media scrum outside.'

'I'm sorry it woke you,' Helen said. 'I'm not sure what to do. I'll report them for breach of the peace if they don't go away. It looks like news of Carmen's death has spread.'

'I'll call Taylor Caffrey, he'll know what to do,' Liza said matter-of-factly. 'He's a master at handling the press. Chester meant to get in touch with him to send out a press release about Mum taking over Carmen's role, but I don't think he's done it yet. I guess he's got too much on his mind, poor man.'

'Thank you,' Helen said. 'I know none of this can be easy for any of you.'

Liza sat down and folded her leopard-print legs under her.

'It's worse than you can imagine. None of us are sleeping properly; we're barely keeping it together. What you see on the surface when you're working as our prompt is a carefully controlled act. Underneath it all, we're terrified that one of us might be next on the killer's list.'

Outside, the journalists were banging on the front door. Helen ran her hand through her hair, then gave a wry smile.

'Let them knock. The paint will last longer than their knuckles. I can't apologise enough about the noise. I didn't expect any of this.'

'None of us did,' Liza said. 'But I can't help feeling that wherever she is, Carmen is enjoying it. You know, being the centre of attention, back in the public eye.' She stood, her leopard tail trailing behind her. 'I'll get showered and dressed, then I'll ring Taylor.'

Once Liza had disappeared, Helen returned to her apartment, leaving the braying crowd at the door. As she walked into the kitchen, she saw Jean coming in through the back.

'There's trouble at the front of the hotel. Lock the door after you,' she said.

'Right you are,' Jean called, but as she turned back to the door, it burst open and Rosie Hyde pushed her way in.

'What the . . . ?' Jean gasped.

Rosie slammed the door and put her back against it. 'Quick, lock it. Stop them getting in! They followed me round to the back.'

Jean locked the door, and just to be on the safe side, bolted it too.

'What the hell do you think you're doing?' Helen demanded, glaring at Rosie.

The journalist stepped forward confidently, an attractive young woman with long brown hair and an eager expression. She was wearing jeans, trainers, a beige raincoat and a blue scarf, and carried a large black satchel over her shoulder. Rosie Hyde of the *Scarborough Times* was as tenacious as the best of them. She whipped her phone from her coat pocket.

'Helen Dexter, I was hoping for a few words about the tragic murder of TV star Carmen Delray, who I understand was staying here when she died.'

She held the phone close to Helen's mouth, ready to record, but Helen was furious at the way Rosie had barged in, and she batted it away. The phone clattered to the floor and Suki raced to reach it.

'This is trespassing. You can't come in here!' Helen hissed.

'You should have more manners, young lady,' Jean said.

Rosie reached her phone just seconds before Suki.

'Put that away, you're getting nothing from me,' Helen said. 'I should ring the police, have you thrown out and report the rest of them for causing a disturbance.'

'Do you want me to ring them?' Jean asked, walking to the phone on the kitchen wall. The receiver was still dangling off the hook, and she picked it up, keeping her eye on Rosie. 'All I have to do is dial nine . . .' she pressed the keypad, 'nine . . .'

'All right, I'm sorry!' Rosie cried, looking desperately from Jean to Helen. 'All I need is a quote, just a couple of sentences. And a picture. Or two.'

Jean replaced the receiver in the cradle, but the minute she did so, the phone began to ring.

'Take it off the hook, Jean, it's unbearable. I daren't think how many bookings I'll lose if I can't even answer the phone,' Helen said. She turned to Rosie. 'You're as bad as them at the front door, picking over the bones of a dead woman. It's not right.'

'Helen, let me help you,' Rosie said.

Helen noticed a mischievous gleam in the journalist's eye and wondered what she was up to. 'You want to help me? How?'

'I can get rid of most of them out there. And they're not just at the front; there are some at your back door too.'

Jean moved to stand beside Helen and crossed her arms under her stout bosom. 'Go on, we're listening.'

'Well, if you give me a quote, a story we can use in the *Scarborough Times*, I'll announce it an exclusive. The others will have no reason to stay if they know they're not getting anything from you.'

Helen thought about this for a moment. 'You can really get rid of them?'

Rosie stood firm. 'I know most of the journalists out there and I've worked with some of the snappers. They'll listen to me.'

Helen turned to Jean. 'What do you reckon? Think we can trust her?'

Jean eyed Rosie all the way up from her trainers. 'Your surname, Hyde . . .' she began.

'What about it?'

'Are you any relation to Alfie Hyde, who worked in parks and gardens at the council?'

Rosie's eyes lit up. 'He's my grandad, lives up by Falsgrave Park.'

Jean turned to Helen. 'We can trust her.'

Helen's eyes opened wide. 'As easy as that?'

Jean nodded. 'Alfie's a gent. We grew up together. And if his granddaughter goes back on her word . . .'

'I won't, I promise,' Rosie said.

Helen ushered Rosie and Jean to the sofa. Rosie switched her phone on to begin the interview.

'I'm doing this on one condition,' Helen said firmly.

Rosie tilted her chin. 'What?'

'If I do this for you, you need to promise me something.'

'Go on.'

'I need an assurance that you'll help protect the Seaview's reputation in the article you write.'

Rosie was silent for a moment, and Helen knew she was thinking this through.

'OK. But if I agree to that, I'm going to need something more than an exclusive.'

'What more can I give?' Helen asked, puzzled.

'Well, what about a competition to put on the paper's website?

It's all about online hits and stats these days to sell ads; without those, we can't survive. What I need is a prize to offer readers – say two nights' accommodation, with Jean's award-winning breakfast thrown in.'

'You drive a hard bargain, Rosie Hyde,' Helen said, but she offered the journalist her hand. 'Now if you'll excuse me, I'm going to get dressed. We'll do the interview when I'm ready.'

Jean stood to head to the kitchen. 'Cup of tea and a bacon roll, Rosie?' she asked.

'Thank you, yes,' Rosie replied with a smile.

As Helen left·the room, Suki moved to stand to attention in front of the journalist, not letting her out of her sight.

While Helen was being interviewed, there was a loud banging at the back door.

'You're not coming in!' Jean yelled.

'It's me, Sally,' a voice shouted.

Jean unlocked the door and peered out, relieved to see Sally on her own. She quickly ushered her in and locked the door again, then told her that Helen was talking to a journalist from the *Scarborough Times*.

'Is that wise?' Sally asked.

'She'll not give anything away that she shouldn't. Helen knows what she's doing,' Jean said.

Once Rosie had what she needed and had left, Jean poured Helen a mug of coffee and slid it across the kitchen counter towards her.

'Those flaming journalists. Can't they let a dead woman rest in peace? You should have sent her away with a flea in her ear,' Sally said.

'Now don't be like that,' Helen said. 'I didn't say anything about Carmen that's not already public knowledge. The information I gave Rosie was bland, though I pepped it up with a couple of details about my opinion of Carmen. That way, it sounded like I was delivering news she wouldn't get anywhere else. It seemed to work a treat, and she's now going to that pack at the front to tell them she's got an exclusive.'

'I hope she doesn't come back,' Sally said.

'She won't,' Helen assured her. 'And what's even better is that after Jean plied her with tea and a bacon roll, and I gave her permission to run a competition to win two nights' accommodation here, she agreed that she'll protect the Seaview when she writes her article. I don't think I could cope if our reputation got dragged through the mud.'

'Whatever happens, the hotel's bound to be named in the press, love,' Jean warned. 'You need to prepare yourself for it.'

Helen took a sip from her mug. 'It's not going to be easy, is it? Oh, I saw Liza earlier. She's going to ring Taylor Caffrey to ask for his help managing the press. I expect Dawley's Theatre Group will put out a statement, something to appease those evil creatures outside.'

'Speaking of the actors, breakfast is almost ready,' Jean said.

With a heavy heart, Helen put her tabard on and headed upstairs with Sally. Before she went into the dining room, she peeked out of the front door from behind the velvet curtain in the hall. The crowd of journalists and TV crews had moved away from the steps and were now gathered in a group on the other side of the road. Some of them still had their cameras trained on the Seaview. She saw Rosie Hyde speaking to them and was impressed by the forceful way she handled them. She dropped the curtain and was about to turn away when there was a sharp knock at the door. Not another journalist, surely? She peered out again, and this time saw Miriam from next door. She quickly opened the door and pulled her inside, locking the door behind her.

Miriam stood with her arms folded and her face like thunder. 'Care to tell me what's going on?' she asked, tapping her foot angrily. 'My guests were woken by a rabble at your door. This isn't the sort of thing four-star guests like, dear. It might be all right for you and your three-star lot, but not for mine.'

'I'm sorry, Miriam. I can't apologise enough.' Helen felt close to tears. What a horrible way to start her day, as if things weren't bad enough. She gulped back a lump in her throat. 'I'll make it up to you, Miriam, I promise.'

Miriam uncrossed her arms and glared at her. 'Just make sure it doesn't happen again.'

Helen peeked around the side of the curtain again. 'They're still there, across the street. Rosie Hyde from the *Scarborough Times* is trying to get them to leave. And they will, I'm certain, although the most persistent might take more persuasion. You're safe to go out now, Miriam.'

'Safe? You make it sound like the Seaview is under siege!'

'That's exactly how it feels,' Helen sighed.

Chapter 25

Helen opened the door to let Miriam out. She was about to close it when she saw Taylor Caffrey approach the pack of journalists and photographers. She watched, intrigued, through the crack in the door. Behind her, Sally called out, 'Helen? They're coming down for breakfast.'

'I'll be there in a minute,' she replied.

Taylor strode purposefully towards the journalists. He was dressed in a grey pinstripe suit with black-and-white brogues, and wore a black fedora at a jaunty angle. Helen was too far away to hear what was said, but she watched in awe as he commanded everyone's attention. Cameras that had been trained on the Seaview now pointed at Taylor. TV and radio crews gathered around him, with Rosie Hyde leading the pack, first with her questions.

'Helen, please, I need you,' Sally called.

'I'm coming,' Helen replied.

She closed the door and locked it, then went to work, but her heart wasn't in it and her mind was far away. Instead of Carmen's murder and the heartache it had caused, why couldn't the Seaview be full of happy families with smiling children, the kind of guests Helen adored, the kind of guests the hotel was meant to take in?

As they waited by the dumbwaiter, Sally was bubbling with

news that she couldn't wait to share. 'Gav's asked me and Gracie to his mum and dad's house for dinner tonight.'

'What's that, love?' Helen replied. She wasn't concentrating, too distracted.

'I said that Gav's invited me and Gracie to his mum and dad's.'

'Sounds like he's getting serious,' Helen said.

'His mum sounds nice. She's called Ann and runs an amusement arcade on the seafront. And his dad, Ted, owns a fish and chip shop. I just hope Gracie behaves herself. She's at that age where she's asking awkward questions. You'll never guess what she said the other night. She wants Gav to be her new dad, said it right in front of him. I went beetroot and wanted the floor to open up and swallow me.'

'What did Gav say?'

'Oh, he just laughed it off. You know Gav. By the way, he asked if you were happy with the hanging baskets. They'll give a great first impression when the inspector arrives on Monday,' Sally said cheerfully.

With everything else going on that morning, the inspector's visit was the last thing Helen wanted to think about.

'Has Gav fixed Miriam's oven yet, do you know?' she asked, changing the subject.

'Think so,' Sally replied.

'You've got a good one in Gav. You should hang on to him tight.'

'What about you and Jimmy? Jean told me he was back. When are you seeing him again?'

Helen was saved from answering by the rumble of the dumbwaiter bringing up plates of sausages and beans, bacon and hash browns, fried and poached eggs, brown and white toast, grilled kippers and bowls of porridge.

The actors were quiet today, tired, she thought. And when they did speak they were unusually snappy with each other. The media attention had clearly rattled them as much as it had upset Helen. Audrey, usually so well put together, looked a little ragged around the edges. Her short grey hair, normally sleek and shiny, looked like it hadn't been brushed.

'Morning, everyone. How are we today?' Helen said cheerfully, professionally, as she laid the plates down.

'We're coping as best we can,' Liza replied, glancing at Audrey. 'Although Mum's having sleepless nights after what happened.'

Audrey lifted a linen napkin, shook it open and laid it on her knee, taking her time to smooth it out. 'It's stepping into the new role, darling. I told you, it's hard for me to deal with. The part of Maude was written for Carmen, and I don't feel I can do it justice. And think of her fans, who were expecting to see her on stage. I can't fill her shoes, I'll be a disappointment to everyone – well, to those who haven't already asked for a refund on their tickets.'

Chester leaned across the table and gently laid his hand on her arm. 'You're doing just fine, darling. Don't ever doubt yourself.'

Later, once breakfast was over and Helen and Sally had cleaned the guests' rooms, Helen prepared to take Suki on the sands. She needed some sea air to help clear her head. She felt anxious in case she met Carmen's fans, the women in red coats; she didn't want the Seaview turning into a shrine for a dead actress. Fortunately, the pair were nowhere to be seen. However, she did have to walk past the two photographers, Bob and Stuart, who were still sitting on the bench opposite. The rest of the media pack had thinned out, thanks to Rosie Hyde announcing her exclusive and Taylor Caffrey giving a statement to the press. There was still a TV crew doing a piece to camera, and three young eager journalists standing next to Bob and Stuart. As Helen walked up to the pack with Suki by her side, the TV presenter swung around to her.

'Are you ready to talk, Mrs Dexter?'

Helen put her hand up to the camera. 'No comment.'

She walked towards the photographers, and Bob leapt up and scuttled behind the bench. 'Keep your dog away from me,' he squealed.

'You two still hanging around like a bad smell, then?' Helen said.

'We're not leaving until we get a picture of Audrey Hepburn,' Stuart said.

'Monroe, mate. It's Audrey Monroe. Audrey Hepburn was the one in *Breakfast at Tiffany's*,' Bob said.

'You're wasting your time if you think you'll get photographs of my guests,' Helen said.

Stuart looked at the sea and shrugged.

She left them to it and walked down to the North Bay beach, thinking about what had happened that morning. The media frenzy had scared her half to death. And then she thought about Carmen. It seemed as if she was always thinking of Carmen, wondering who could have killed her, and why. She thought of the actors again, and then of course about Jimmy, who was constantly on her mind. She pulled her phone from her pocket and saw a list of missed calls from numbers she didn't recognise. More journalists, she reckoned. But how many of those calls were potential bookings? And that was when she saw it, a text message from Jimmy.

Meet me at Bay View café, 1pm x

She stared at the screen. There was no explanation, nothing. Not even a please or thank you. Just an abrupt request to meet. Her first instinct, after wanting to chuck the phone at the wall and smash it to bits, was to ignore him. And she managed to, for most of the rest of the morning. But the message niggled at her and refused to let go. She needed to know what was going on. Her life was in enough turmoil after the death of her guest. And while Rosie Hyde had promised to do all she could to keep the Seaview's reputation from being tarnished too much, Helen knew it would inevitably be mentioned in the news. There'd be pictures too, and they'd be on national TV.

She groaned out loud. The last thing she needed was more trouble in her life. And that was why, she told herself, she had to know the truth about Jimmy. Only then could she decide what to do. It wasn't that he'd lied to her, not exactly, but he was certainly keeping something from her. Jean had heard him speaking to someone on the phone before he ran out of the Seaview, and he hadn't passed on the threatening caller's number to the police as he'd promised. Helen felt certain he was hiding something, or someone. She texted back to say she'd be there, but she didn't return his kiss.

She set off from the Seaview wearing her old fleece jacket, with Suki on her lead. She was prepared to handle Jimmy on her own terms. She'd give him time to talk, let him explain, and then decide if she could trust him again. Outside, the late-summer sunshine had disappeared. In its place was a fine mist, and she regretted not bringing a brolly. When she rounded the corner of King's Parade, the mist turned to rain, and she retraced her steps towards the Seaview. It was quicker to run to the front door rather than go to the back, and she kept an umbrella stand in the hallway for her guests. She and Tom had bought a set of three golf umbrellas, unable to resist a promotional offer. They'd learned the hard way that when they bought telescopic ones, guests forgot they had them in their handbags or luggage and ended up taking them home.

As she picked up an umbrella, Suki began sniffing around the stand. 'Come away, girl, leave it!' Helen ordered.

Outside, she struggled against the wind, one hand holding the large turquoise umbrella with the Seaview's name and logo in white, the other on Suki's lead. She walked along Windsor Terrace, then on to the picturesque old town on the South Bay with its jumble of narrow streets. The rain began to ease off and she shook the umbrella dry. Suki's coat was soaked and the dog shook herself, spraying water up Helen's jeans. The sky began to clear, and the sun spread a gentle warmth in the air. Helen breathed in the sweet, woody aroma of rain on the grass, a scent she adored.

When she reached the seafront, she stepped on to Foreshore Road. The Bay View was a small café facing the sea, with plenty of seating outside. As she approached, she saw two staff dressed in black aprons wiping rainwater from tables and chairs. She hoped the chairs would be dry enough to sit on, as Suki wouldn't be allowed inside. She found a table, tied Suki's lead to her chair and waited. She glanced at her watch; it was five past one and there was no sign of Jimmy. She ordered a cappuccino. At quarter past, there was still no sign of him. She paid for her coffee and checked her watch. It was now twenty-five past. She texted him.

Where are you?

There was no reply. It was quarter to two when she walked off with Suki. At ten to two, she swore she'd have nothing to do with Jimmy Brown again. No one took Helen Dexter for a fool.

Chapter 26

Helen stormed back to the Seaview, furious with the world, with Jimmy, with whoever had killed Carmen, with the police for not solving the murder and arresting the culprit. She walked quickly, and poor Suki had to trot to keep up. She railed against the person, whoever she was, who had damaged her car. She fumed against the media frenzy outside her beloved Seaview and the two men with their cameras who looked set for the long haul. She was angry with them all. But most of all, she was angry with herself for falling for Jimmy, a man she barely knew. She'd been ready to commit to him; she'd confided in him, for heaven's sake! He knew all about Carmen and her guests. She bit her lip. She shouldn't have told him any of it. How foolish and stupid she'd been. What if . . . No, it couldn't be, could it? But what if Jimmy was embroiled in Carmen's murder? She shook her head to dismiss the crazy thought. How could he be tied up with that? He was a man with secrets, yes, but was he really a killer?

'I don't think so,' she said out loud.

Suki looked up and whined.

'But I'll tell you this, and I'll say it only once, Suki,' Helen continued as she neared the Seaview, 'I'm done with him. I don't care what he does, or what he says, I'm finished with him now.'

Right on cue, her phone buzzed in her pocket, and when she pulled it out, Jimmy's name was on the screen. She waited a moment, then another, hesitating, battling against answering it. She looked from the phone to Suki. 'What do you reckon?' she asked the dog, and Suki whined in reply.

'I agree,' Helen said. And with that, she sent Jimmy's call to voicemail. He'd had his chance and he'd blown it. Just for good measure, so she wouldn't be tempted to call him back after a night out with Marie when she'd had a few glasses of wine and was feeling melancholy, she deleted his number.

'There, that'll teach him,' she said.

She thought she'd feel triumphant, in command. But a sense of loss had already begun to gnaw away inside her.

The following morning, she woke feeling down in the dumps. The first thing she did was check her phone to see if there were any missed calls from a number she might recognise as Jimmy's. But there were none. At least the journalists seemed to have given up pestering her, and for that she was grateful. She played Jimmy's voicemail again. He said he was sorry for not turning up, and begged her to meet him later in the week. He said things were difficult and he'd explain when he could. Well, the last thing Helen needed was more difficult in her life. She was done with difficult and she was done with Jimmy Brown. Done and dusted, never wanted to see him again in her life. Ever. Not on your nelly. If she saw him again tomorrow, it'd be a day too soon. But she checked her phone throughout the day, just in case.

Outside the Seaview, the usual suspects sat on the bench across the road. Bob and Stuart with their cameras, flasks of tea and sandwich box, along with the TV crew and one journalist. Helen kept all the curtains closed. She was no longer afraid of the media pack outside. She was angry. Angry with them for making it feel as if the hotel was under fire. Her guests were too scared to leave in the evening for dinner in town. Instead, they ordered in take-aways and ate in silence in the dining room. She saw them reading the news about Carmen's death on their phones. She kept the copy of the *Scarborough Times*, with its lurid headlines about Carmen's past, out of sight. She didn't want to upset the actors any more than they already were.

She had her own problems with the news stories too, because not only was the Seaview mentioned, there were pictures too, as Jean had warned. How this would affect bookings coming in, she didn't yet know, and she could only fear the worst. When she'd mentioned this to Jean, though, her friend had waved away her concerns.

'It's September now, love,' she said. 'By the time spring comes around next year and the holiday season kicks in again, this will be old news, forgotten.'

'I hope you're right.'

She winked at Helen. 'Aren't I always?'

With Jimmy now positively, absolutely out of her life, she decided to do all she could to help the police find the murderer and bring this horrendous episode to an end. If it was really possible that the killer was one of her guests, as landlady of the Seaview she was determined to find out what she could, as DS Hutchinson had asked.

Later, after breakfast, when she entered her guests' rooms to clean, she paused for a moment at each threshold with her mop in one hand, bucket in the other. Was it possible the actors were hiding something, a clue to who had killed Carmen? She would not – absolutely would not – rifle through her guests' belongings; it was something she'd never do. The only thing she *was* prepared to do, even though the thought of it made her queasy, was to look around thoroughly as she cleaned.

In Paul's room, the tidiest of all, the surfaces were clear. The only signs that anyone was staying there were a phone charger on his bedside unit, a toothbrush and tube of peppermint toothpaste in the bathroom, and his beige anorak hanging over a chair. Liza's room was chaotic, with scarves and hats strewn about. Make-up spilled messily on the dressing table; Helen cleaned around it, trying not to disturb things too much. Audrey's room was tidy and calm, much like the woman herself. There was a pleasant scent in the air, and Helen saw a bottle of perfume, expensive, the same kind Marie used. In Kate's room, a line of colourful ankle boots stood to attention along a wall. Two red boots, two yellow, two black, two blue. Hair bobbles of pink and green lay on the duvet, and when Helen made the bed, she carefully placed them back where she'd found them. In Chester's room, papers and scripts were scattered on the dressing table, books of techniques for acting and directing were piled up on the bedside unit.

So far, Helen had found nothing she would describe as suspicious. Finally she unlocked the door to Lee's room. When she pushed the vacuum cleaner under the bed, no papers were sucked up this time. However, the red notepad was lying open on his bedside unit, with his list of women indecently exposed. Helen felt a growing anger looking at it; the nerve of the man! She noticed that Carmen's name had been scratched from the list in red pen. Plus there was a line of writing next to it that she was certain hadn't been there before. She leaned closer and read: *Death to the diva*. A shiver went down her spine at the chilling words. Surely Lee couldn't be the murderer? She'd seen him lose his temper when he forgot his lines during rehearsals, and he banged his fist a lot against the furniture. But a bad temper didn't make someone a killer . . . did it?

She walked down to the kitchen, alarmed by her discovery. Unsettled, she immediately called DS Hutchinson to tell him about it and to ask for an update on the investigation. She received his voicemail and left an urgent message asking him to call back.

As she sat at the kitchen table with Sally and Jean, she checked her phone constantly, waiting for the detective to ring. However, she decided to keep what she'd found to herself. If she told the two of them about it, she was afraid it might frighten them off. Admittedly, it would take a lot for Jean to up and leave and find work elsewhere – the Seaview was her life – but she couldn't take a chance on losing Sally.

Jean poured coffee into mugs and Helen took hers gratefully. She was exhausted, as she hadn't slept well again, feeling angry with Jimmy. 'Penny for your thoughts,' Jean said, breaking into her reverie.

'Sorry, I was miles away.'

She didn't want to talk about Jimmy. The situation was still too awkward and raw to discuss.

She tapped her hands on the tabletop. 'Is everything ready for the hotel inspector tomorrow?'

'Don't tell me she's still coming after what happened to Carmen?' Jean cried.

'She hasn't cancelled, so we've got to assume she'll arrive. Although what she'll make of the media scrum hanging around outside is anyone's guess. It'll go against us. It could ruin us, Jean, after all our hard work. We'll never get our fourth star.'

Jean leaned forward, eyes sparkling with mischief. 'I think I know how to get rid of them,' she said.

Helen's mouth opened in shock. 'What? How?'

Jean tapped the side of her nose. 'I met Alfie Hyde for lunch yesterday.'

'Alfie Hyde? Rosie's grandad?' Helen said.

Jean nodded. 'I took the old rogue to Bonnet's coffee shop for lunch after I'd visited Mum in the care home.'

'How are your mum's legs, Jean?' Sally asked.

'Oh, not so bad, thanks. Anyway, Alfie and I had a right good catch-up. He told me there's a singer in town, a pop star that all the kids like. She's performing at the Open Air Theatre.'

'Tilly Shilling,' Sally said.

'Pardon?' Helen said.

'That's her name. She's huge, Helen. I mean, a proper megastar. Scarborough's going to be buzzing when she plays here. The gig sold out in an hour when tickets went on sale.'

Helen turned to Jean, her patience wearing thin. 'What's this Tilly wotsit girl got to do with our problem?'

'I know where she's staying,' Jean said smugly. 'The press have been trying to find out for ages, but nobody knows where she is. Except me. And my friend Gloria, who works at the Royal Hotel. See, Alfie knows Gloria too, and he mentioned her when we were chatting yesterday. I rang her for a chat when I got home and she told me Tilly Shilling is staying in the penthouse suite at the Royal. Apparently the staff have been sworn to secrecy. But as I'm one of her oldest friends, she told me, and now I know.'

Helen could almost hear the light bulb ping above her head. 'And you think we could get the media outside to move on if we tell them where she is?' She thought about this for a moment. 'Poor Tilly, though. She'll have the press camping outside her hotel.'

'Rather her and her team of bodyguards in their luxurious suite in a prestigious landmark hotel than you and the actors under siege here,' Jean advised.

'Do you really think it'll work?' Helen said.

Jean shrugged. 'There's only one way to find out.'

'OK, leave it to me,' Helen said, thinking quickly. 'I don't want the reporters there when the inspector arrives. She's probably already seen that we're in the news. All this negative publicity can't be doing us any good.'

'We've done everything that's required of us for our four stars, Helen, that's all the inspector needs to know. Although it's probably best if she doesn't know we're using Tilly Shilling as bait to move the media pack away.'

'Her room is ready,' Sally said. 'I've put one of the new duvet covers on the bed, and the fluffiest towels I could find in the bathroom. I think we're all set.'

Helen looked at Jean. 'Think you can manage to rustle up pancakes for the inspector, Jean? I'd really love to add them to the menu if I can.'

Jean cleared her throat and sat up straight in her seat. 'You might notice I haven't baked any biscuits or cakes this morning while you two were cleaning the rooms.'

Not only had Helen noticed, she'd been disappointed that there'd been no cake to go with their coffee.

'That's because I wanted to wait until you were both here before I tried making pancakes,' Jean explained. 'I've made the batter already. I want to see if I can cook them without burning them this time.'

Helen was so happy to hear this that she clapped her hands with glee. Jean stood up, picked an apron up from the worktop and tied it around her stout waist.

Helen turned to Sally. 'How's Gav doing?'

Sally's face broke into a wide smile. 'He brought me a huge bouquet of red roses last night, and a little bunch of freesias for Gracie. She loves him to bits.'

'Sounds like you've fallen for his many charms,' Helen said.

Sally's face clouded a little. 'But what if Gracie starts to think of him as a permanent fixture, then he does a runner with someone else? Should I let him into our lives, or do I keep him separate and stop her from even calling him Uncle Gav?'

Helen patted Sally's hand. 'Only you can make that decision. But if you want my advice, I'd give him the benefit of the doubt. He's one of the good ones.'

'I could say the same about Jimmy,' Sally replied.

Helen bit her tongue. Their conversation ended when the smoke alarm began to beep and an acrid smell filled the air. Jean flapped at the alarm with a tea towel to move the smoke away.

'Think I'm going to need more practice,' she said.

Chapter 27

Later that morning, Helen was frustrated to see that DS Hutchinson still hadn't returned her call. Neither were there any missed calls or texts from a number she recalled belonging to Jimmy. Not that she wanted him to get in touch, or so she kept telling herself. Trying her best to distract herself from thinking about him, the inspector, Carmen or the press, she concentrated hard on her work with the actors, following the script with her finger.

She kept looking at Lee, wondering if she'd overreacted to finding the list in his room. The words *Death to the diva* were certainly shocking, but did they connect him to Carmen's murder? He seemed focused on the play, intense, concentrating hard, even if he still couldn't remember his lines as well as the others. He was the one she had to prompt most. When he stumbled, or forgot his cue, he shot her an imploring look. All she had to do was give him a couple of words and he was up and running, but it wouldn't be long before he needed help again. She was trying hard to give him the benefit of the doubt as troubled thoughts about what she'd found in his room hurtled around her mind. She kept glancing at her phone, hoping for DS Hutchinson's call, but it never came.

She glanced around the room and noticed Kate seemed brighter after their conversation, as if a load had dropped from her mind.

Audrey was growing in confidence in the lead role, her timing perfect and her movements graceful, and Liza seemed more relaxed too. She was no longer fussing around her mum, making sure she was all right, stroking her arm, offering words of advice. Audrey was getting into her stride and seemed to be a natural in the part – even better than Carmen, although Helen kept that thought to herself.

Since Taylor Caffrey had spoken to the press about Carmen's death and sent out an official Dawley's Theatre Group press release, news reports on the murder had begun to mention Audrey as well as Carmen. As the play's new lead, her public profile was soaring. Helen even overheard Kate and Paul discussing offers of interviews she'd received from women's magazines.

Paul sat at Helen's side, continuing to read from the script in the role that had been Audrey's. Helen could tell he was out of his comfort zone trying to act. He was embarrassed when Chester asked him to stand, and moved awkwardly when interacting with the others. He was much more at ease discussing technical details about lighting, props and sound. It was at those moments that he came to life, as if a light had been switched on inside him. Taylor Caffrey hadn't yet sent a replacement actor to rehearse with the group. And to Helen's dismay there was still no news on when a professional prompter would replace her. Each time she asked Chester, he said Taylor was sorting it out.

As for Chester, he looked done in, suffering the loss of Carmen more than anyone. Helen noticed he'd started fiddling with his ballpoint pen more, using it to point at the cast in the same way he'd used his cigarette holder. She wondered why he'd told her it had broken, when she'd seen him snap it in half. However, she felt his pain and knew that maybe he wasn't thinking straight. She understood what it was like to lose someone she loved. Her eyes went to the framed photo of Tom behind the bar and she wondered what he would have made of these guests. And then, slowly, she wondered what he would have made of Jimmy, and what advice he would give her now.

When morning break arrived, Helen served coffee with shop-bought chocolate biscuits and apologised that Jean hadn't had time to bake. Then she rang Marie and told her what had happened with Jimmy.

There was silence for a few moments.

'I'm sorry, love,' Marie said. 'He seemed like one of the good ones.'

'Yeah, he seemed it, but in the end, he was too full of secrets and I can't be doing with that. He's unreliable too, asking me to meet him and then not turning up. You know . . . Tom and I never had secrets. We were honest and open with each other all of our married lives. Will I ever find a man I can trust?'

'You're asking the wrong woman,' Marie laughed. 'Just look how me and Daran turned out. But don't you think you're being a bit harsh on Jimmy? I mean, he might have had a perfectly good reason to disappear.'

'And break a promise about reporting the threatening phone number to the police? Oh, and take a phone call from someone saying he'd see them in London and say there was no one else in his life?' Helen added.

'Sure, OK, there's a lot to unpick. But if he explains, maybe it'll all make sense.'

'I'm done, Marie. I can't give him another chance.'

'Well, just think about it, that's all.'

Helen had done nothing but think about it. 'How's business at the nail salon?' she asked.

'Bad news, I'm afraid. You know I mentioned Sharelle, my new manager? She's been offered another job and it looks like I'm going to lose her. It means I'll have to go back to working in the nail bar, and do you know what? I don't want to. I've been enjoying myself running Tom's Teas so much, it's made me realise the nail bar isn't where I want to be. I'm going to put it on the market and see what offers come in.'

'What? I can't believe it, Marie. That'd be a huge change for you. You've run that nail bar ever since we left school. Are you sure it's what you want?'

'I'm certain. I'm looking to the future, Helen; got to take care of myself, because no one else will. Listen, I've got to go, it's busy here, but promise me you'll think about what I've said about Jimmy?'

'We'll see,' Helen said, and hung up.

Chapter 28

When Jean arrived for work the next day, all she could talk about was the inspector's visit.

'Is there anything you need help with before she arrives?' she asked Helen.

Helen shook her head. 'It's all done, we're as ready as we'll ever be.'

'Did she mention what time she'll arrive?'

'She can't check in till twelve, she knows that. It says so on the website and in her booking confirmation. But apart from that, I have no clue what time she'll get here. She didn't make any arrangements for an early or late check-in, so I'm assuming she'll be here sometime this afternoon. I'll have to stay here and wait.'

Helen bit her lip and glanced at Jean.

'How do you feel about me adding pancakes to the menu for tomorrow's breakfast? Think you can manage to cook them OK?'

Jean put her hands on the countertop and glared at her. 'Flaming pancakes! Is that all you can think about?'

Helen was taken aback by the outburst. Jean's glasses began to slip down her nose and she pushed them back.

'Sorry, Helen. Mum's not well, and I've got a lot on my mind.'

'I'm sorry to hear that, Jean.'

'It's all right, love,' Jean said, squaring her shoulders. 'I'll soon have pancakes under control. If I can manage not to burn them when I try them again this morning, you can put them on tomorrow's menu.'

Jean spoke with less enthusiasm than Helen would have liked, but she knew better than to chivvy her along. The woman worked at her own pace and always had.

'Were the photographers still out there?' she asked. She crossed her fingers, hoping Jean would tell her the coast was already clear, then she wouldn't have to go out and bait them with news of Tilly Shilling. She'd never heard of the singer, but now that she thought about it, she remembered seeing posters and flyers around town showcasing the gig.

'Oh, they're still there. I think they're even sleeping out there. One of them was folding a pop-up tent away when I walked past them just now.'

Helen braced herself. 'Wish me luck then. I'm going outside.'

Jean leapt forward. 'No! Don't go yet,' she cried. 'Even if the inspector comes early – which she might do, to catch you on the hop and see how you cope – she won't come *this* early. Leave it until after breakfast. There's no point trying to get rid of them yet. Once they find out where Tilly Shilling is staying, they'll be off like a shot. You don't want to fire your cannon too early. Keep your powder dry and wait.'

'But how will I know when the time's right?' Helen asked.

Jean paused with a knife in mid-air. 'We'll know. Don't worry . . . I've got a plan.'

Breakfast was a somewhat rushed affair; Helen wanted her guests up and out of the dining room so that she and Sally could clean and get everything shipshape before the inspector arrived. She had so much on her mind that she didn't pick up on the slump in the air between the actors. She didn't spot Chester's sad face or hear his constant sighs. She didn't notice Audrey's concerned looks towards him or overhear Kate and Liza's hushed conversation. She didn't see how tired Paul was. However, she couldn't fail to notice that Lee was missing. When she asked Paul where he was, he shrugged and said no one had seen him since the previous afternoon.

She gave it little thought, as her head was fully tuned to the inspector and getting rid of the photographers and journalists before she arrived. Jean said the timing had to be right, but how on earth was she to know when that was? She was so wrapped up in this that when Chester stopped her in the hallway after leaving the dining room, she got rather a shock.

'Will you be working with us today?' he asked. 'We really could do with your help. There's less than a week before the show opens. Taylor Caffrey called last night; he said ticket sales remain strong.'

'Really? In spite of what happened to Carmen?' Helen asked.

Chester shrugged. 'Maybe it's *because* of what happened, who knows? Anyway, there's a lot of press interest in *Midnight with Maude*, although the big London agents who were coming to see Carmen have cancelled. It's understandable, of course. So, will you help us today?'

Helen glanced at her watch. 'I can give you a few hours, but that's all,' she said. 'I've got another guest arriving.'

Chester's face clouded over. 'Another guest? But Taylor assured me he'd booked the Seaview exclusively for Dawley's Theatre Group!'

231

Helen stood her ground; the hotel inspector's visit was too important to her. 'I'll square things with Taylor, don't worry. This is a special guest, someone I couldn't refuse. She won't get in your way and I'll explain to her the moment she arrives what's going on in the lounge with rehearsals.'

Chester waved his hand dismissively. 'I guess a few hours of your time is better than nothing,' he said.

Helen bit her tongue to stop herself from saying something she might regret. Something about not being paid, about feeling taken advantage of, about doing the work of a professional prompter – and where *was* the prompter Taylor had promised, anyway? The play was beginning to grind her down. Lines of dialogue from it spun around her head at night and were sometimes the first thing on her mind each morning. The dark shadow of Carmen's death was unsettling her like nothing else had done before.

'I'll be with you as soon as I've cleaned the rooms and had my morning . . . er . . . meeting with my staff,' she said. There was no way she was going to miss out on the daily ritual of coffee, cake and gossip with Sally and Jean.

Later, when Helen began to clean, she started with Lee's room this time. She wondered if he was still asleep inside or whether he'd hooked up with a woman and was lying in bed somewhere else in Scarborough. She knocked. There was no response. She took the master key from her pocket and lifted it to the lock. She was about to turn the key when she thought better of it and pressed her ear to the door, just in case. What she heard shocked her. It was a woman's voice, giggling.

'Oh, you are a naughty man.'

Those words again! The invigorating sea air really was working on Lee.

'Harder!' she heard him command, then the woman's voice repeated the words.

'Oh, you are a naughty man.'

'Give it to me faster!' Lee urged.

Another high-pitched giggle from the woman.

'You're a wicked boy. Oh, you are a—'

'Don't look at me like that when you speak. Give it to me faster! Harder!' Lee demanded. 'I want it harder!'

There was a crashing noise, a loud smash that could only be glass. Helen was stunned. It was much louder than the smash she'd heard during Chester and Carmen's fight. She hadn't wanted to get involved then, but this sounded more serious, and she had to know what was going on.

She rapped at the door, but when it opened, the sober scene that greeted her was in stark contrast to the debauchery she'd expected to find. Sitting on a chair by the dressing table was a well-dressed, attractive dark-haired young woman. She wore a fetching blue retro 1950s skirt suit, and her hair was styled with large curls pinned back from her pretty face. She smiled brightly at Helen, while Lee hovered by the door. Helen looked past him into the room, relieved but confused to see that nothing looked broken – the dressing table mirror and all the windows were intact.

'Everything all right?' Lee asked cagily.

'I heard something break, glass . . .' she began.

The woman in the blue suit was standing now and smoothing her skirt.

Helen opened her mouth to ask what on earth was going on, but stopped when a voice behind her made her spin around. It was Sally, red in the face, whispering frantically.

'Helen, a guest's just arrived. It's Jane Jones. The hotel inspector, she's here!'

Chapter 29

Helen thrust her mop and bucket at Sally and they ran down the stairs. Her heart was going nineteen to the dozen; she felt nervous, sick to her stomach. The inspector was here. The inspector! This was it, her one and only chance to impress.

'I've got to get rid of the media outside, the photographers, the journalists!' she cried.

Sally paused, panting for breath. 'It's all right, they've gone. Jean sorted them out.'

Helen's heart lurched. 'When?'

'You know Jean, she won't be rushed. She cooked breakfast, tidied up, put her hat and scarf on and left. Then she went straight over the road to give the journalist the news about Tilly Shilling and they were off like a shot. Oh, you should have seen them, Helen. I was watching through the curtains while I was cleaning upstairs. Just as they were running away with their cameras and jumping into their vans, the inspector walked around the corner. By the time she reached the Seaview, they'd all gone.'

'They've really gone?' Helen couldn't believe her luck. 'How on earth did Jean manage to time it so perfectly?'

'She had a tip-off from a friend of hers who works in Espresso Yourself on Falconers Road. Jane Jones called there this morning for a coffee and cheese scone. Jean's friend recognised her – well, you know what gossip's like here – and called Jean to say she was in town. Then it was action stations here and all hell broke loose. You missed it all while you were upstairs. Jean thought it best to leave you out of it and deal with it in her own way.'

'She's a marvel, that woman. She deserves a pay rise after this. Never mind a pay rise, she deserves a flaming medal.' Helen turned to Sally. 'How do I look?'

'Smashing. Now go and get the inspector checked in. And good luck.'

Helen continued down the stairs, slower and calmer, ready to greet Jane Jones. How long she'd waited for this, after all the work she'd put into upgrading the Seaview. The extra star glittered in her mind. Nothing could go wrong now; she wouldn't let it. She paused and straightened her tabard, and put a welcoming smile on her face.

When she reached the ground floor, she saw a woman waiting in the hallway. She had her back to Helen and was picking tourism leaflets from the display. A small pink pull-along suitcase stood by her feet, which were clad in sensible black shoes.

'I'm Helen Dexter, the landlady. Nice to meet you.' Helen's voice came out in a squeak; she barely recognised it. The woman turned. Helen extended her hand and the inspector took it with a hearty shake.

Jane Jones was short, with bobbed blonde hair that curled under her chin. When she smiled, Helen saw a gap in the middle of her front teeth. It gave her a childish look, made her look younger than the forty-something Helen guessed she was.

'I'm Mrs Jones, booked in for one night. I'm sorry I'm so early. I know your website said check-in wasn't until midday, but I found myself in Scarborough a lot earlier than planned. I'm happy to leave my case and come back later when my room's ready.'

'Actually, your room is ready for you now, and I could check you in straight away, if you wish?' Helen kept her tone friendly and light, trying to treat her new guest as she would any other, trying not to let on that her heart was racing, her palms sweating.

She busied herself with the routine of checking in her guest, making the same small talk as always.

'Have you travelled far?' she asked, and then could have kicked herself. What if Jane Jones thought she was prying? Would that go against her in the report?

'Not too far, and the traffic was light, hence my early arrival,' Jane replied.

Helen's antennae picked up on the generic reply. The woman clearly wasn't giving anything away about where she'd come from or what her business in Scarborough was.

She moved to the dining room door. 'Before I take you up to your room, let me quickly show you the dining room, where breakfast is served from seven thirty until nine thirty a.m. We offer an extensive menu.' She beamed at the inspector, waiting for a reaction, but the woman's face remained impassive. 'Our cook's been with us for many years. We've even won an award for our breakfast.' She waited for at least a smile of acknowledgement, but Jane Jones gave nothing away. 'And we have linen napkins!' Helen cried, with another squeak. She covered her embarrassment with a slight cough.

'Is this the lounge?' Jane asked, pointing at the door across the hallway.

Helen dreaded her seeing the room with the curtains closed. But to her relief, the lounge was flooded with light. Either Jean or Sally must have opened the curtains. What fantastic staff she had; what would she do without them?

'Yes, it is, would you like to see it?' she said. Without waiting for a reply, she walked into the lounge, where she hoped the view might impress Jane enough to get a reaction. But she was to be disappointed.

'A bar,' the woman noted without emotion. Usually, Helen's guests were delighted to find the bar; they normally oohed and aahed about it when they saw it for the first time.

Jane's eye was caught by the jukebox on the wall. 'Someone's an Elvis fan, I see,' she said, scanning the list of songs.

'My husband was a huge fan,' Helen replied. 'I've been meaning to change the songs, put some new tunes in there.'

Jane nodded, taking in her surroundings but saying nothing. She didn't even pass comment on the stunning view of the North Bay, which looked particularly pretty with the morning sun shining on the crescent of blue sea.

'Oh, one thing I should mention about the lounge is that I've got a troupe of actors staying with me until the weekend. They're using the lounge each day, rehearsing a play that's starting on Saturday night at the Modernist Theatre.'

'*Midnight with Maude*? Yes, I read about the tragic death of Carmen Delray.'

Helen looked at her, surprised. 'You know about that yet you still want to stay here? I was worried that the news would put visitors off.'

Jane shook her head. 'It's not as if she was murdered in here, right?'

'Heavens, no!' Helen cried. 'But still, her passing hangs heavily over my guests; they've lost a valued colleague and friend. I've been helping them rehearse. The least I could do was offer them a hand after such a tragic event.'

'Really? I'm impressed,' Jane said.

Helen snapped back into professional landlady mode, worried she'd given too much away.

'The lounge is free by four p.m., when the actors finish work.'

'I'll be out all day; I don't think I'll need to use it,' Jane said.

Helen walked from the lounge to the hallway and towards Jane's pink suitcase. 'Let me take your case and I'll show you to your room.' She lifted it easily; there wasn't a lot inside. 'This way, follow me,' she said as she headed upstairs.

Once in the room, she handed two keys to Jane on a white plastic fob etched with the Seaview's logo in blue. She explained that one was for the bedroom and the other for the front door. She showed her where the hairdryer was, then pointed out the tea tray, mentioning tea bags, milk, biscuits, coffee and hot chocolate. She told her that if she needed anything, all she had to do was call.

'I hope you enjoy your time in Scarborough,' she said before she closed the door and left.

Once outside, she took a moment to calm herself down. She'd been running on adrenaline ever since Jane arrived. It felt as if she'd been hyper-aware of every word she'd said, every move she'd made, every gesture. She'd tried her absolute best not to let on that she knew who Jane was. But the pressure of having the woman arrive so early and catch her on the hop meant that she'd acted anything but normal.

As she headed downstairs, she heard footsteps behind her and saw Lee with the woman in the fetching blue suit. When she reached the hallway, she stood to one side, watching Lee open the front door to let the woman out.

'Will I see you again?' the woman asked.

'I'll call you,' Lee replied, and with that the woman left. Helen heard him mutter something under his breath.

'A definite seven out of ten.' Then he turned to face her.

She cocked her head at the lounge door. 'I want a word with you.' She knew she had to be quick, aware that the rest of the cast would be coming down to rehearse at any moment.

Lee sat on the window seat and Helen stood in front of him with her arms crossed.

'You already know my rules about having overnight guests in your room, and yet you went ahead and brought in another young lady last night.'

'I didn't,' he said.

Helen was nonplussed. 'What?'

'I didn't have anyone in my room overnight,' he said calmly.

'But I've just seen her with my own eyes.'

'No. What you saw was an actor who turned up this morning for a seven a.m. audition.'

Helen's head swam. An actor? Was she the one Taylor Caffrey had sent to replace Audrey in the play?

'But I heard something smash in your room. What on earth were you up to? You know all breakages must be paid for.'

Lee pulled his phone from his jeans pocket. He swiped it, pressed it, then held the screen towards Helen. There it was again, the same noise of breaking glass that she'd heard from his room, coming out of his phone.

'Please sit down,' he said. 'There's something I should explain.'

Helen remained standing. 'Whatever it is, be quick, before your colleagues arrive.'

Lee put his phone on the table. 'I've been auditioning actors for the supporting female role in a play that I've written.'

'You've been doing what?' Helen said, shocked. She sat down on a stool.

'I've been doing it in my room. I had nowhere else to take them and we needed privacy. I met one of them in a pub the other night, the Angel Inn, but it didn't work out, there were too many people around. Some of the actors could only meet me in the evening, others first thing in the morning; all of them had to fit auditions around their day jobs. The noise you heard was part of the sound effects. Helen, look, I haven't told any of the others I'm writing a play, so please don't say anything, especially to Chester; he'll be furious if he finds out. He sees himself as the group's writer.' He raised his eyes to her. 'See, I've written the lead role for Kate. I hoped it might be a way for us to get back together.'

'So those women I saw you taking up to your room, they weren't overnight guests?' Helen said, the pieces falling into place, the same line of dialogue repeated over again. *Oh, you are a naughty man.* 'Why didn't you tell me when I gave you the spiel about overnight guests not being allowed?'

'I was afraid if you knew the truth, you'd tell Chester. I was hoping to audition Carmen; she was on my list of actors I thought would be perfect for the supporting role. Once Carmen and Chester split up, I felt I could approach her and confide in her about my play. But then she died. And now I've decided to name it in her honour.' Lee looked a little flustered. 'It's silly really, it's just a working title; it's a murder mystery called *Death to the Diva.*'

Helen felt the weight of the world drop from her shoulders. The title of a play, that was all. It was just as well DS Hutchinson hadn't called her back; she'd be far too embarrassed to explain this.

'Were there . . . er . . . many women on this list?' She felt uncomfortable asking this, knowing she'd seen the list in his room. She wouldn't normally be so brazen, but a guest had been murdered, and these were exceptional times.

'Just a handful, but none of them came up to the mark.'

'What mark?'

'I score their acting ability out of ten. The best I've seen so far was an eight.'

Relief flooded through Helen's body, making her feel light-headed. 'Have you told Kate you've written a lead role for her?'

Lee dropped his gaze to his lap. 'She won't even look at me now. You've seen how she is with me; she ignores me at breakfast, shuns me in rehearsals. And she sits at the other end of the table when we all go for dinner in town. I don't know how to put things right.'

Helen leaned towards him. It was on the tip of her tongue to tell him she could help. She was ready to spill the beans about what Kate had said about Ben, but stopped herself in time. She'd never interfered in her guests' lives before, and she wasn't about to start now.

Once Lee had left, she stayed in the lounge for a while, with a lump in her throat and a heaviness in her heart. She remembered Kate's tear-stained face when she'd spoken about her brother and her mum. Maybe, she thought, just maybe, it was time to break her golden rule about not getting involved.

* * *

Later that day, Helen had shopping to do in town. She left Suki at the Seaview and walked up Eastborough. As she was about to step inside the newsagent's, she saw a familiar figure. A young woman was walking towards her, slim, with long dark hair, talking animatedly into her phone. Helen couldn't believe her eyes.

'Jodie?' she called.

The last time she'd seen Jimmy's daughter, the girl had been gaunt, with a dark, haunted look. Back then, she'd been battling her drug addiction and living rough on the streets. Now she looked healthy and had put on weight. She was more like Jimmy than ever.

'Jodie?' she called again.

Jodie looked up. It took her a few moments to recognise Helen. When she did, she took her phone from her ear.

'Helen! Hey, it's good to see you. Dad's been telling me all about you since he came back from the cruise. You're all he talks about.'

Helen was stunned to hear this. 'He has? I am?'

Jodie pointed to her phone. 'Sorry, I can't stop, there's an emergency at the hostel. I've got to get there as soon as I can.'

'Your dad, Jodie . . .' Helen said. 'Where is he? What's going on?'

Jodie opened her mouth to reply, then shook her head. 'He's in London. I'm sorry, Helen. I can't say, I shouldn't . . . He asked me not to. You need to speak to him, let him tell you himself.'

'But—'

'Sorry, Helen, I've got to dash.' And just like her dad had done, Jodie disappeared.

Chapter 30

The following morning, Helen's phone rang at exactly five minutes past seven. This was unusual, as nobody called her that early. The caller's number was withheld, and a flash of anxiety stabbed her. She hesitated a moment as a chilling thought went through her. Since the last time she'd seen Jimmy, she'd received no more of those threatening calls. He must've been connected to them; it seemed too much of a coincidence otherwise. Was this him on the phone now, withholding his own number? If it was, she decided, she'd give him a minute to explain himself. Sixty seconds, no more. Or was it the woman again, with another menacing message? There was only one way to find out. She wasn't going to let anyone scare her from answering her phone. Her livelihood depended on it. She swiped it into life.

'Good morning, Seaview Hotel.'

'Good morning, it's Mrs Jones here, I'm staying in Room 9.'

Helen stiffened. Mrs Jones. The hotel inspector. 'How can I help?'

'Could I possibly have a bottle of water in my room, please?'

'Water?' Helen said. 'Of course, I'll bring one up to you now.'

She rang off, puzzled by the request. She couldn't remember any of her guests asking for water before. If they wanted a drink, they ran the tap in their en suite and used one of the glasses provided.

'Who was the early caller, someone trying to book in?' Jean called from the kitchen, where she was taking plates from a cupboard.

Helen explained the inspector's request and Jean glanced at her watch.

'She knows our reception opening hours, doesn't she?'

'What do you mean?'

'Well, the Seaview is officially open from seven a.m., so she rings you at five minutes after, to check that you're there. She puts in an easy request, say for tea bags, biscuits or a bottle of water. It's what they do, Sally mentioned this to you before about her friend at the North Mount; you should've been prepared.'

'I've had a lot going on,' Helen snapped. She bit her lip. 'Sorry.'

'Water off a duck's back, love. She'll be timing you, recording how long it takes for you to arrive. You'd better get your skates on.'

'Oh crikey!' Helen cried.

She grabbed a bottle of chilled water from the fridge and ran up the stairs to Room 9. She was panting by the time she reached the door and stood a moment getting her breath back. Then she knocked, smiled and handed the bottle over.

'Is everything else all right?' she asked. 'You've got plenty of hot water? Enough biscuits? The TV works fine? Hairdryer powerful enough for you?'

'Everything's fine,' Jane replied politely before closing the door.

Helen went back downstairs and opened up her laptop to prepare and print out the breakfast menu. She hesitated a second, unsure whether to add pancakes. Was Jean up to the challenge? The last thing she wanted was to cause her any stress.

'Well, shall we add pancakes to the menu?' she asked. 'Because if you've got any doubts about making them this morning, I won't put them on. Speak now or forever hold your peace.'

Jean havered for the briefest of moments. 'Put them on,' she said decisively. 'Nothing's beaten me yet, and I'll be damned if milk, eggs and flour will get the better of me at my age.'

Helen smiled warmly. 'You're a star.' With a final flourish of the keys on her laptop, she added pancakes to the menu for the first time in the Seaview's history.

Suki walked up to her and nudged her leg.

'Sorry, Suki, we can't go on our walk yet. I've got to stay here in case our special guest needs me.'

Suki whined at the tone of Helen's voice and slunk away outside to the patio, where two sparrows were splashing in the birdbath. Helen watched as Jean busied herself in the kitchen, pulling metal trays from cupboards and eggs from the fridge.

'What's happening with you and Jimmy?' Jean asked. 'I haven't heard you mention him for a while.'

Helen glanced out of the patio doors at the cloudy September day. 'Oh, I don't know. I think maybe he and I are done.'

Jean paused in what she was doing. 'Oh, now that's a shame,' she said. 'I thought you were well suited.'

'Well, turns out we're not. I rushed into things. And every man I meet, I realise now I'm going to compare him to Tom. That's a lot to live up to. Anyway, I don't think Jimmy was the right man for me, and I'd rather not talk about him, if you don't mind.'

'Have you heard anything more from the police?' Jean asked, changing the subject.

Helen glanced at her phone. 'Not a sausage,' she replied.

Jean slapped a hand against her forehead. 'Oh, that reminds me . . .' She walked to the fridge and pulled out the vegan sausages to go under the grill for Kate.

Half an hour later, Helen and Sally were waiting outside the dining room for their guests to come down. Chester was first as usual. Helen thought he looked like he hadn't slept well, which was no surprise. She noticed he was carrying his ballpoint pen again, twiddling it in his fingers, passing it from one hand to the other. He stopped when he reached the bottom of the stairs and smiled brightly.

'I've got good news to share,' he beamed. 'Taylor Caffrey has secured an actor to take over Audrey's role. She's arriving today, Anabel Craven. She's a Scarborian, lives locally and won't need a room.'

Small mercies, Helen thought. She could do without another thespian under her roof while she was trying to cope with the tragedy of Carmen's death.

Sally's face lit up. 'Anabel Craven? Really? Oh, I love her! She's famous. I've seen her on the telly. She plays Suzette in *The Archer's Wife*.'

'I don't think I know her,' Helen said.

'I couldn't . . . I mean . . . would it be all right if I stayed behind today to say hello? Mum would love her autograph, if that would be all right.'

Helen looked at Chester's tired face. 'Now then, Sally, I'm sure Chester doesn't want his actors bothered in that way.'

Chester prodded his chest with his pen. 'Nonsense. We thespians are used to such things. I'm sure Anabel would be honoured to sign.'

Sally beamed from ear to ear. 'Oh, thank you. She's one of Mum's favourite actresses.'

Chester shot her a look. 'Please don't call her an actress. We're all actors now; there's no gender difference in the term these days, in professional circles at least.'

Paul was the next one down, looking happy and relaxed.

'Anabel Craven's arrival can't come quickly enough,' he whispered to Helen. 'I don't know if you've noticed, but I haven't taken well to the acting side of things. It's really not my cup of tea.'

Audrey and Liza drifted downstairs arm in arm. Liza wore a turquoise beret cocked at a jaunty angle over her cropped hair, while Audrey was dressed in shades of lilac. Helen admired the effect and wished she could put together an outfit like that, something to highlight her assets, if only she knew what they were.

Kate came down next in her rehearsal outfit of black leggings and T-shirt, hair scraped back with an orange headband. Helen recalled the conversation she'd had with Lee the previous day. He was hopelessly in love with Kate and desperate to win her back. Lee was last down and nodded shyly at Helen as he took his seat in the dining room. Helen saw him cast a glance at Kate as he wished his colleagues good morning, but she didn't reply.

The actors didn't need to pick up the breakfast menu; they knew it off by heart. Had they done so, they would have seen pancakes on offer. Helen didn't get a chance to tell them about the new addition, however, as they all ordered their favourite items so quickly.

As she worked, a noise upstairs startled her. A door opening, closing, footsteps on the stairs. It could only be Jane, heading down for breakfast. She hadn't expected this; she'd hoped the inspector would take her breakfast after the actors. She wanted to lavish her attention on her to ensure everything went as smoothly as it could. But she also knew she didn't have a choice. If the inspector wanted breakfast right then, she would have to oblige.

'Come on, Helen, pull yourself together,' she said out loud. Then she raised her eyes to the stairs, where Jane was coming down. 'Morning!' she said brightly. 'Did you sleep well?'

'Like a log, thank you. The room is lovely.'

Helen's heart lifted to hear this. 'Please, take a seat. I've put you on a table by the window.'

She and Sally watched as Jane settled herself and picked up the breakfast menu.

'Do you want to serve her, or shall I?' Sally whispered.

'Let me, then if anything goes wrong, it's my fault,' Helen whispered back.

'Good luck,' Sally said. 'Here's to getting our extra star.'

Helen crossed her fingers on both hands as she walked into the dining room. She smiled warmly at Jane.

'Help yourself to fruit, juice and cereal from the buffet,' she said, indicating with a sweep of her arm the range on offer. 'Now, would you like tea or coffee this morning?'

'Tea, please,' Jane replied, scanning Helen's printed menu.

Helen took her notepad and pencil from her tabard pocket, ready to write down the next request. 'And for your cooked breakfast, what would you like from the menu?'

'Your sausages, are they local?' Jane asked.

'They're so local, you can hear the pigs snuffling in the woods when the wind's in the right direction.' Helen wanted to take the words back the minute they left her lips. She was feeling nervous, too anxious to please, and was getting it all wrong. 'Sorry, what I mean is—'

'And the black pudding, where does that come from?'

'From the same farm on the Wolds,' Helen said, more confidently now. 'All of our meat is local; we support Yorkshire farmers as much as we can.'

'And your eggs?'

'From a dairy farmer in the East Riding.'

Jane ran a short, stubby finger down the page, and in that moment, Helen chided herself for putting pancakes on the menu when Jean wasn't fully prepared. She hadn't given her cook the attention she deserved. She should have worked with her closely to ensure the pancakes were turning out well before even thinking of adding them as a house special. She'd been selfish. What on earth had she done? Although Jean was confident she could make a success of them, everyone had their Achilles heel, and Helen was worried that she might have found Jean's. Jane continued to peruse the menu.

Please don't choose the pancakes, Helen thought. *I'm sorry, Jean, forgive me.*

'I think I'd like to try your house special,' Jane announced at last, and Helen's heart dropped to the floor. 'The pancakes, please. Two, if I may. With lemon and sugar on both.'

Helen swallowed hard. 'Of course, that's fine. Two pancakes coming right up.'

She walked from the dining room making two mental notes. The first was to send a get-well bouquet to Jean's mum in the care home. And the second was never to take Jean for granted again.

Just as she was about to break the news about the pancakes to Jean, the doorbell rang. She straightened her tabard, walked along the hallway and opened the door. It was Miriam from the Vista del Mar. Her next-door neighbour, usually so calm and unflappable, immaculately made up and well groomed, looked completely undone.

'Miriam? Are you all right?' Helen said.

Miriam pushed past her and leaned against the wall. Her long grey hair fell about her shoulders; her face was red and puffy.

'Miriam? What's happened?'

'I'm ruined,' she cried. 'Ruined!'

Helen quickly ushered her neighbour into the lounge and closed the door. She forced Miriam into a seat and sat opposite. 'What is it?'

'My oven, it's broken again. I've called Gav and he's on his way now.'

Helen looked aghast at her. 'Your oven? Is that all? Look, I'm in the middle of breakfast service. I've got . . . a special guest in, I can't handle this right now.'

Miriam buried her face in her hands. Helen quickly glanced at the door, aware the inspector was waiting. She wondered briefly if she should explain the urgency of the situation. As a fellow hotelier, surely Miriam would understand. But she quickly dismissed the thought, because she wouldn't be able to bear her neighbour's gloating if she knew the inspector had been and the Seaview wasn't upgraded.

Miriam's shoulders shuddered, then she pulled a handkerchief from her pocket and loudly blew her nose. 'It's Taylor's Bar and Kitchen,' she cried.

'Taylor's? What do they have to do with your oven?' Helen said, growing impatient. 'Look, Miriam, I don't mean to be rude, but I really need to get back to work. Sally's on her own out there.'

'I've had to send all my guests there for breakfast. I can't serve them myself. I can't cook a thing. I can't even boil the kettle – the whole kitchen's kaput. Heaven only knows what this'll do to my online reviews.' Miriam started sobbing.

Helen put her arm around her and waited a few moments for her tears to subside. 'Have you eaten this morning?' she asked.

'How could I stomach anything with the stress of what's happened?'

'Then stay here, I'll bring something for you with a mug of strong tea.'

Miriam looked at her with tears in her eyes. 'You'd do that for me?'

'Of course I would. How long have we known each other?'

Helen was about to leave the lounge when she felt Miriam's hand on her arm.

'It's not that I'm not grateful, dear, but this breakfast you're going to bring . . . I don't want any of those cheap three-star sausages you serve.'

Helen was stung by her words. 'Just because you've already got four stars doesn't mean you're any better than me. You know fine well that we both buy our sausages from the same farm.'

She hurried from the lounge, closed the door behind her and headed downstairs to see Jean.

'What's got into you? You look frazzled,' Jean said when she clapped eyes on her.

Helen's heart was beating too fast. She laid a hand on the worktop to steady herself. 'Miriam's kitchen's not working; she's upstairs in a state. I've promised her a mug of tea and something to eat – a sausage sandwich ought to do it, if you're not too busy. And there's something else I need to tell you.'

Jean paused with a wooden spoon in her hand. 'What?'

'The inspector's put her breakfast order in.'

'And?'

'And . . . she's asked for the pancakes.'

'Pancakes?' Jean gasped.

'Pancakes,' Helen confirmed.

There was a beat of silence before Jean leapt into action, rolling up her sleeves and straightening her back. She turned to the fridge, took out two eggs and cracked them into a bowl.

'Right. If it'll help us get our extra star, then I'm going to stand here and keep cooking them until I get the blasted things right.'

Chapter 31

Helen returned upstairs, but when she popped her head around the lounge door, she was shocked to find the room empty.

'Where's Miriam gone?' she whispered to Sally in the hall.

Sally pointed at the dining room, and Helen's heart dropped to the floor. There, sitting at a table near the hotel inspector, was Miriam. The nerve of the woman! The inspector was reading a romance novel while eating a bowl of cereal. Sally busied herself at the dumbwaiter. 'Who's the mug of tea for?' she asked.

Helen took it from her hands. 'Allow me,' she said.

She took the mug across to Miriam's table.

'Your tea,' she said.

'Thank you, dear,' Miriam said. 'I trust my food will arrive very soon?'

Helen bit her tongue. If the hotel inspector hadn't been within earshot, she'd have given Miriam short shrift. As it was, all she could do was smile through gritted teeth and be polite.

'It's on its way,' she said.

'Be sure it's cooked all the way through,' Miriam replied. Helen turned away and busied herself serving the actors, removing plates, bringing toast and pats of butter, tiny jars of honey and jam, and fresh pots of tea. The group seemed animated that morning, she noticed. News of the arrival of Anabel Craven, the new addition to the cast, seemed to have reinvigorated their collective energy, and she was glad to see them so happy. Well, not all of them were happy, of course. Lee and Kate were still studiously avoiding each other.

She brought more tea for Jane Jones and a promise that her pancakes were being freshly cooked. She crossed her fingers for luck. As she turned away, she overheard Miriam speaking to the inspector and her heart dropped again. The last thing she needed was for her neighbour to say the wrong thing.

'Of course, next door at the Vista del Mar,' Miriam brushed a hand across the linen tablecloth, 'I use a superior cotton blend for my cloths and napkins. None of this cheap rubbish.'

Helen saw Jane peek over the top of her novel at Miriam, and was relieved that she didn't encourage more conversation. However, this didn't stop Miriam, who continued to waffle on about the shortcomings, as she saw them, of the Seaview.

'The guests who stay with me next door are of a better sort, shall we say. I have my Durham gardening group in at the moment; they're very particular. I offer them a quality service the likes of which they'd never receive somewhere like this.' As she looked around the dining room, appraising every corner, from the high painted ceilings to the window blinds and buffet table, her face curdled with distaste.

Jane lowered her novel and nodded politely at Miriam to acknowledge she'd heard her before raising the book even higher. Miriam, however, didn't get the message.

'And she keeps that dreadful dog in here too,' she said, almost in a whisper.

At this, Jane laid her novel down. 'The Seaview allows pets? I didn't know that.'

Miriam shook her head. 'Oh no, pets aren't allowed. But there's a dog downstairs. I see her walking it on the beach. It's a vicious creature, if you ask me.'

Jane's eyes widened. 'You've seen it attack other dogs?'

'Well, no . . . but . . .'

'Does it bark a lot? Does the noise disturb you next door?'

'No, I don't think I've ever heard . . .' Miriam stumbled.

Helen felt her neck and shoulders tense. She had a good mind to grab Miriam and yank her out of the dining room. How dare she say such things about Suki and the Seaview? She pushed her feet into the carpet to steady herself against the anger she felt building inside.

Just then, the dumbwaiter rumbled into action and two plates arrived. One small plate had Miriam's sausage sandwich on it, while a larger one held two perfectly round golden pancakes and two lemon wedges.

'Oh Jean, you've done it!' Helen cried out loud. 'I always knew you could!'

She took the pancakes into the dining room and set them down in front of Jane with a flourish. Then she brought the sausage sandwich in and held it tantalisingly close to Miriam without handing it over. She knew how delicious Jean's sandwiches were.

'I heard you mention my dog Suki earlier,' she said, just loudly enough for Jane to hear. 'You and I have known each other many years, and in all that time, have you ever known Suki to be vicious?'

'No,' Miriam said, shaking her head.

'Have you ever known her to bark loudly?'

'No.'

'Does she upset your guests, or mine?'

'No.'

Helen made to place the sandwich on the table, and Miriam's nose followed the plate before Helen whipped it away again. 'Just one more thing . . .'

Miriam looked at her, annoyed. 'What now, dear?'

'I'd like to thank you for recommending the linen company. It's where I bought these tablecloths and napkins. The lady in the shop said they were the exact same ones that you buy for the Vista del Mar.'

She finally put the sandwich in front of Miriam, then walked from the room, leaving Miriam speechless. She turned at the door to see a smile make its way to the inspector's lips as she tucked into her pancakes.

After breakfast, Gav and his team arrived in a convoy of vans to fix the kitchen at the Vista del Mar, and Miriam returned home. The actors had gone to their rooms, and Sally was downstairs with Jean. Helen was straightening dining room chairs when she heard a cough behind her. She turned, surprised to see Jane wearing her coat, ready to leave, her pink pull-along suitcase on the floor beside her sensible shoes.

'Oh, sorry, Mrs Jones, I didn't see you there,' she said. 'Would you like to check out now?'

'Yes, please,' Jane replied.

'Has, erm, everything been all right for you? Was your room warm enough?'

'Everything was fine,' Jane said, giving nothing away.

'And how was breakfast?'

A huge smile appeared on her face, and Helen's heart lifted.

'Please give my compliments to your chef; the pancakes were delicious. It's easy to see why the Seaview won its award for best breakfast.'

'Thank you, I'll pass on your comments to Jean – she's my cook,' Helen said proudly.

She processed Jane's card payment and handed her a receipt. 'I hope we'll see you again,' she said, still pretending she didn't know who the woman was.

'Thank you for a most pleasant stay. It's been very nice,' Jane replied, picking up her suitcase. 'And I have to say, I particularly admired the way you handled such a difficult guest this morning at breakfast.' She gave Helen a subtle wink before turning and walking along the hallway.

Helen followed and opened the door.

'Such a beautiful view,' Jane said, nodding at the bench opposite, facing the sea. 'It must be wonderful for your guests to sit there and enjoy the scenery.'

'Oh it is, yes, they love it,' Helen replied. She looked at the bench where just moments before Jane had arrived, the media had had their cameras trained on the Seaview. She'd heard on the hoteliers' grapevine that they were now camped outside the Royal Hotel, hoping for a glimpse of Tilly Shilling. But although the bench was clear of photographers and journalists, two women sat there now, both of them wearing red coats.

Chapter 32

When the door closed behind Jane, Helen fell into the nearest seat in the lounge, relieved and exhausted. The adrenaline that had kept her going since the inspector had arrived now left her in an almighty rush. She put her head in her hands and sat quietly, breathing deeply as she ran through the last twenty-four hours. Had she done enough to earn the extra star that she craved and the Seaview deserved? She looked across the room at the picture of Tom on the wall behind the bar.

'What do you think, Tom?' she said out loud. 'I mean, she seemed nice enough, polite, professional. She liked Jean's pancakes, so that was a good sign. I bet you never thought we'd see the day when Jean would cook pancakes. She even cooks porridge now, although that took a bit of persuading – you know what she's like. And she's cooking kippers too, the one thing she swore she'd never do.'

She looked at Tom for a very long time, remembering his voice, the way he moved, his mannerisms. Meanwhile, the clock ticked on the wall. The postman walked up the path, then mail rained on to the mat. The noise broke into Helen's thoughts, and she was heading to the hall intent on collecting the post when she saw Audrey drifting downstairs.

'The lounge is ready for you,' she said.

'I'm going outside for a breath of fresh air before we start rehearsing,' Audrey replied. 'Care to join me?'

Helen considered the offer as she picked up the post. Of all of the actors, Audrey and Liza were the ones she had spoken to least. Mother and daughter had always been together, happy as a twosome, and Helen hadn't wanted to intrude. But this was a chance to speak to Audrey alone, and the opportunity might not come again. She placed the mail on the hall table.

'I'd love to,' she said.

As they stepped outside, Helen shivered. The day wasn't as warm as it looked. The warmth of summer was disappearing now, a nip in the air ushering in autumn. She noticed the two women in red coats had gone from the bench. Audrey was wrapped in the pale blue pashmina she'd been wearing when the actors had first arrived. The material fell in graceful folds around her shoulders and the colour complemented her beautifully. Helen felt a pang of envy as she looked down at her tabard and the old jeans she wore for work.

They sat down on the bench, and she breathed in the scent of Audrey's expensive perfume.

'It's so beautiful here,' Audrey said, looking out over the bay.

'It is, I'm lucky to live in such a wonderful place,' Helen said. She decided to plunge straight in, and tried her best to sound casual, not wanting to appear nosy. 'Liza not with you this morning?'

'No, she's taking a phone call and could be some time. She's been offered some freelance costume work in London once we finish in Scarborough.'

'Freelance? So she's not a regular member of Dawley's Theatre Group?'

'Heavens, no, none of us are, apart from Lee and Paul. And Chester, of course, who does his best to keep it together,' Audrey said. 'The rest of us are jobbing actors. We go wherever the work is, and simply sign up to join whatever theatre group will have us. Liza works abroad quite a lot, and she loves big city life. She'd be no good staying too long in somewhere like Scarborough or anywhere on the coast. She's a city girl through and through.'

'You seem very close. You must miss her when she's working away,' Helen said.

Audrey kept staring out over the sea and didn't reply at first. When she did, her tone was neutral, her face stern.

'I don't see her very often, and when I do, we stick close together and make the most of the time we have.' She turned to Helen. 'Do you have children?'

Helen bit her lip. She'd been asked the same question hundreds of times, and each time she felt its pain. 'No, it wasn't to be for me and my husband. We tried, but . . .' She shook her head.

'I'm deeply sorry to hear that,' Audrey said.

'Thank you,' Helen replied. She was silent a moment before she pressed on. 'Do you have other children, or is Liza your only child?'

'She's my one and only. Her father brought her up after we split. As soon as Liza was old enough to decide which one of us she wanted to live with, she chose him. Oh, I understood her reasons. I was away a lot of the time when she was growing up, on tour with one play or another, and I couldn't take her on the road with me. Things were different back then, much harder for women and impossible for a mother with a small child. Her father offered a more stable home life, as well as a swimming pool and a pony.' Audrey smiled wryly. 'I couldn't compete with that. So whenever we do spend time together, we make the most of it, become inseparable; there's so much to catch up on.'

'I see,' Helen said, and she did. Audrey and Liza's closeness made sense now.

A few moments of silence passed. Helen rubbed her arms as a cold breeze made her shiver.

'I must say, I admire the way you've handled things since Carmen died,' she said.

'It's not been easy, dear,' Audrey replied.

'I know, but you have a special way about you; there's something still and tranquil that you bring to the group. As an outsider, I've been able to watch you all together. You're the calming influence.'

Audrey gave a beatific smile. 'Well, it's taken me a lifetime of acceptance and contemplation to reach this Zen-like state. Carmen's death has hit us all hard. I just hide my feelings better than the others. I retreat into myself; go to a place I keep just for me where I handle my emotions. It's a technique I learned early in my acting career, one that's stood me in good stead for all kinds of situations.'

'Has it helped you cope with taking on Carmen's role under such tragic circumstances?' Helen asked.

Audrey pursed her lips. 'Taking the lead is something I never expected or wanted. I'm struggling with the fact that I've stepped into Carmen's shoes – they're an extremely uncomfortable fit – and I haven't made my peace with it yet. There's something indecent about taking the role just days after she died.'

Helen let a silence fall between them, and it was Audrey who broke it.

'As a woman, I feel I'm taking something from Carmen that was hers and hers alone,' Audrey continued. 'But as an actor, it was too good a role to turn down. However, that doesn't mean it's easy for me; in fact, it's one of the most difficult things I've done in my life. I'll have to draw on every ounce of my acting ability to get me through the first night.'

'Is it true about the interview offers from the women's magazines?' Helen dared herself to ask. 'I overheard some of the others talking about it.'

'It's true,' Audrey replied gently. 'And I've turned every single one of them down. I have no wish to talk to the press. I'm not a celebrity and nor do I want to be. Besides, they'd only ask me questions about the past, about Carmen. I'm sure you must have heard by now what happened between us.'

Helen kept quiet, not wanting to admit that she'd Googled Carmen to find out.

'Oh, how good it is to sit here with you, Helen. I feel we've been cooped up indoors far too long. I'm pleased the photographers have gone and we can open our curtains again.'

'Mum!'

Both of them looked round at the sound of the voice behind them. Liza was walking across the road. She was still wearing the turquoise beret, this time with a gold sheriff's badge pinned to one side.

'Mum, are you coming in? Chester wants to start warming up.'

Audrey stood, and she and Liza made their way back to the

Seaview. Helen was about to follow when a police car pulled on to Windsor Terrace. She recognised the driver and its passenger immediately. DS Hutchinson climbed out of the driver's seat, DC Hall from the other side.

'Morning, Mrs Dexter,' DS Hutchinson greeted her.

'Morning,' she replied. 'Any news?'

DS Hutchinson nodded towards the hotel. 'You called me, Mrs Dexter, and I'm sorry I haven't had time to return your call. I'd like to speak to you in private, not here on the street, and I'm afraid I need to ask you more questions.'

'But you've questioned me already,' Helen protested. 'Do I really have to go through it again?'

'You were in a state of shock last time we spoke. We'd like to go through things again, and we'll be speaking to your guests as well.'

'Sounds as if I have little choice. You'd better follow me,' Helen said.

She led the way inside, where DS Hutchinson headed towards the lounge. Helen stopped him.

'Sorry, we can't use this room. My guests are working in here and I won't have them upset. We'll talk downstairs instead.'

When Helen walked into her apartment with the detectives, Jean and Sally stood and stared.

'I'll take DS Hutchinson and DC Hall into the living room,' she told them, 'and I'll need to close the door.'

'Would you like coffee bringing in, with some of my double chocolate cake? It's fresh out of the oven this morning,' Jean said.

'That sounds perfect,' DC Hall said, licking his lips.

Once seated, DS Hutchinson took a beige folder from a large black leather wallet. He laid it on his knee, then looked at Suki lying by the patio doors.

'Is that a greyhound?'

Helen nodded. 'I've had her for years, she's a good companion.'

'Do you race her?'

'No, she retired a long time ago.'

DS Hutchinson cleared his throat. 'Anyway, we've had more news from the North Mount Hotel, where Miss Carstairs was last seen. We've had a good look through the pub's CCTV from the night she was murdered. We've also interviewed the couple who run the place.'

'They do a smashing pint in there; they've even got their own brewery,' DC Hall chipped in.

Before DS Hutchinson continued, there was a knock at the door.

'It's all right, Jean, come in,' Helen called.

A tray appeared with three mugs of coffee, three plates and three slices of cake. Jean handed mugs and plates to the detectives. Helen took her mug but left the cake where it was. She needed to concentrate. Once Jean left the room, DS Hutchinson picked up again.

'The CCTV clearly shows Miss Carstairs drinking with a younger man—'

'A much younger man,' DC Hall interrupted.

'She appears to be enjoying herself, laughing and joking, stroking his leg, kissing his neck, running her fingers along his moustache. According to the landlord, she knocked back quite a lot of vodka that night. And then things turned sour; they argued,

265

she stormed out and he followed. The couple who run the North Mount have now accounted for their customers that night, all of whom were captured on CCTV. They were either regulars or locals they knew.'

'Apart from one person,' DC Hall chipped in between mouthfuls of cake.

'Yes, I was just coming to that,' DS Hutchinson said, a touch peeved. 'There was a man sitting alone. Now, he could have been a tourist; it's a popular little pub, there's no crime in going out for a pint. But this chap nursed half a pint of shandy for over an hour while doing a crossword.'

Helen was somewhat confused. 'What did he look like, this man?'

'Fair-haired, short, wiry,' DC Hall said. 'Someone who likes drinking shandy, and that's all we know.'

DC Hutchinson pulled out a large grainy black-and-white picture of a man in a flat cap. The image wasn't clear. The man's hair was hidden under the cap, and he had his collar up, shielding much of his face.

'This is a still from the CCTV. Recognise him?' he asked Helen.

Helen took the photograph and stared hard at it, then shook her head. 'I'm sorry, I don't. I've never seen him before.' She handed it back to DS Hutchinson, who replaced it among his papers.

'Miss Carstairs and her gentleman friend left the pub at nine fifteen p.m. As you know, Mrs Dexter, the North Mount Hotel is located on Scarborough's North Bay. What we don't understand is how the victim ended up, stabbed to death, on the other side of Scarborough, on the South Bay beach. You see, there's no CCTV to show us her movements once she left the pub.'

Helen shifted in her seat. 'I appreciate you telling me all of this, but I don't understand . . . Is there something more you need my help with?'

'I'm afraid so, Mrs Dexter. You told us that on the night of the murder, the dead woman went into town for dinner with her colleagues and the manager of the Modernist Theatre.'

'That's right. And I've already told you she left the dinner early to go on her date. I remember Chester was particularly upset by that.'

'And you said they all came back here to the Seaview except for Miss Carstairs.' DS Hutchinson flipped open the beige folder and lifted out a notepad of lined paper, then took a ballpoint pen from his jacket pocket. 'I need to go over the events of that night once again. This time, I want you to remember every single detail, leave no stone unturned.'

'I'll try my best,' Helen said.

DC Hall rattled his fork against his empty plate. 'Before you start, Mrs Dexter, any chance of more cake?'

Chapter 33

Once again Helen ran through what had happened the night Carmen died. DC Hall asked who had returned first, and Helen cast her mind back.

'Lee arrived first on his own, drenched through, about nine thirty. He'd walked back from town; said he couldn't afford a cab. Then Kate and Paul arrived together – Paul had paid for them to travel in one of Gav's Cabs. I served drinks at the bar to the three of them. I remember that, because Paul asked for a cocktail that needed blue curaçao, but I never buy blue curaçao, I mean, who does? So he had a glass of Rioja instead. Then Audrey and Liza came into the lounge together. They'd had the sense to take one of the Seaview's umbrellas from the stand in the hall. Chester, the director, was last in, about ten thirty, by which time the rain had eased.'

'And did Chester Ford give any indication of why he'd returned so late?'

'No, I've told you all of this. And if you don't mind me saying so, I think you should cut Chester some slack. He's grieving over the death of his lover.'

DS Hutchinson eyed Helen coolly. 'Did any of them seem out of sorts? Was their behaviour at odds with what you'd learned about them so far?'

'They seemed fine, in good spirits. They'd clearly had a drink or two with dinner in town. In fact, we put the jukebox on and had a singalong to Elvis. That reminds me, I really should get around to changing those records.'

'Well, we appreciate your time, Mrs Dexter, and we don't want to hold you up any further from your work at the Seaview.'

'Thank you,' Helen said as the men stood to leave. 'Let me show you out.'

Once the detectives had left, Helen's phone buzzed into life with a text message. She was stunned when she read it.

Please let me explain, Jimmy x

She couldn't handle this right now. Her head was spinning after talking to the police. She sat at the kitchen table, where Jean and Sally were waiting to hear what had gone on, and put her phone out of sight as she revealed some of what the detectives had said – though not everything, as she didn't want to unsettle them. When she had finished, Jean tapped her watch.

'Shouldn't you be upstairs working with the actors by now?'

'I should, but I haven't taken Suki out for her walk yet.'

'I don't mind taking her out,' Sally offered.

'I couldn't ask you to do that, love.'

'You're not asking, I'm offering, because you've got another visitor upstairs to deal with.'

Helen shot her a look. 'Oh no, who now?'

'The new actor, Anabel Craven. She signed her autograph for my mum.'

Helen's shoulders slumped. 'I suppose I should go up and introduce myself.'

'You might want to make yourself presentable first,' Jean advised, nodding at Helen's tabard.

'I cleaned all the rooms while you were with the police,' Sally said. 'So there's nothing left for you to do.'

Helen looked at them both and a lump welled up in her throat. 'I don't know where I'd be without you two.'

She removed her tabard, brushed crumbs from her jumper, ran a comb through her hair and slicked her favourite lipstick across her lips while puckering up in the mirror.

'You'll do,' she told her reflection.

Walking upstairs to the lounge, she found the actors in full flow. Audrey was centre stage, her arm linking Chester's, reciting dialogue that Helen knew word for word. Before she knew it, she was mouthing along with the words. And then a voice she hadn't heard before filled the room, and a woman strode across the lounge, in character, arguing with Audrey, pulling her away from Chester.

Anabel was tall and thin – a little too thin for Helen's liking; she looked like she could do with one of Jean's breakfasts inside her. As Helen watched her perform, she realised that she was exceptionally good. In fact, she'd go so far as to say she was the best in the room. She'd learned her lines, too. While Lee was still occasionally reading from his script, Anabel needed no support. She was mesmerising to watch, commanding, filling the room with her energy, long limbs and auburn hair. Helen tried to guess how old she was and settled on late thirties.

When the scene they were rehearsing ended, Chester waved a ballpoint pen in Helen's direction. 'Ah, here she is, our wonderful landlady.'

Helen stepped into the room, and Anabel walked towards her with her hand outstretched.

'Anabel Craven, pleased to meet you. I understand you're working as our prompt?'

Helen shook the woman's thin, bony hand. 'Only until Taylor Caffrey sends a professional,' she said quickly. Before she could say more, Chester clapped his hands to bring the room to order.

'Next scene, please. Kate, you start. Lee, darling, give it a bit more oomph if you could. Paul? The spotlight will be on Kate in this scene.'

'Right you are, Chester,' Paul replied, making a note on his laptop. 'I just hope there's a chance to do a couple of technical run-throughs at the Modernist before the play starts on Saturday. Otherwise, I'll be spotlighting the wrong parts of the stage.'

'Helen, are you ready?' Chester asked.

Helen pulled a chair to the doorway and took her script from the bar. 'I'm ready.'

'Then . . . action!' Chester called dramatically.

Helen saw Liza roll her eyes at Audrey, who tried to stifle a smile.

And so the day went on, with newcomer Anabel bringing a fresh energy to the group. It cheered Helen to see the actors working better together, trying harder. Their dialogue sounded fresher, more nuanced, and they appeared to have stepped up a notch – all except for Lee, who seemed downcast. When lunchtime came, Helen brought sandwiches from the kitchen, along with a cherry and almond cake Jean had baked that morning. She was cutting the cake into slices when Chester appeared.

271

'Well now, doesn't that look delicious?' he said approvingly. 'Might be just the thing to cheer me up a little.'

'You're still in shock. It'll take a while,' Helen said gently.

Chester smiled weakly and laid both hands on his heart. 'I'm broken, truth be told. But as the old saying goes, the show must go on. And that's exactly what Carmen would want. I'm throwing myself into *Midnight with Maude*; it's devouring every spare moment and it stops me from thinking too much.'

'Do you think the play will be ready for Saturday night?'

'It has to be. There can be no ifs or buts,' he said firmly.

'Well, I'd like to wish you all the luck in the world.'

Chester recoiled in horror. 'No! No, you must never say that. Never! It's bad luck to say good luck to an actor. If you want to wish us well, say "break a leg".'

Helen realised her faux pas. They really were superstitious. 'Sorry, Chester. I should have known better. Where does it come from, that phrase?'

'It's an old saying from variety. Performers only got paid if they made it on stage. To get there, they had to break the line of the theatre legs which marked the edge of the stage.'

'Interesting,' she mused as Chester walked away.

As she was serving cake on to plates, Kate walked into the room. She was followed by Lee, and Helen found herself caught between the troubled twosome. She decided to strike while the iron was hot. She turned to Kate on her left.

'How's your brother doing? Did your mum manage to get in touch with social services?'

To her right, she felt Lee stiffen. His hand reached for a plate, but stopped in mid-air.

'Your brother?' he said. 'Kate? Is Ben all right?'

'Helen? Tell Lee it's none of his business,' Kate said.

'Helen, tell Kate I'm asking because I care,' Lee said.

Helen looked from one to the other. 'I think it's about time you two talked, and I mean to each other, not through me.'

'No,' Kate said, shaking her head.

'Please, Kate,' Lee cried.

'Kate, don't you think Lee deserves an explanation?' Helen said.

But Kate was already walking away.

Helen sighed. 'I'm sorry, Lee, I tried.'

'What's wrong with her brother?' There was concern in Lee's eyes.

'I think you need to ask Kate. I don't want to upset her more than she already is. I've spoken out of turn. You should talk to her, Lee.'

'She won't speak to me, you know that.'

'Then . . . oh, I don't know . . . write her a letter, slide it under her door. Tell her how you feel. Tell her you've written her a starring role, and if your play's a success, the world could be your oyster. No more working for Chester, or Dawley's. Just think of it, your name and Kate's up in lights. It could be the Lee Cooper Theatrical Group, with Kate Barnes as your star.'

'I haven't dared think about that,' Lee said softly. 'Kate's passion is to work in children's TV; she dreams of being a presenter. I don't have contacts in that world, I don't know anyone I can introduce her to. I'm not sure I can be any use.'

'Well, you could do a lot worse than let her know you've written a lead role for her. It might be a stepping stone to her dream. Confide in her about the play, flatter her, give her no reason to refuse, then take things from there. Begin again with her, gentle and slow. If Carmen's death has taught us anything, it's that life's short and we should grab happiness where we can. Talk to her, Lee. What's the worst that can happen?'

Chapter 34

As Helen walked Suki on the beach the next day, the strong wind whipped her hair into her eyes. There was a sharp coldness to the air, autumn making itself felt. The waves out at sea were dark grey, and a shudder went through her as she watched them roll in. It brought to mind Carmen's body being found on the beach by the surfer. What a dreadful way to die.

She remembered DS Hutchinson telling her that Carmen had been found with her handbag still on her shoulder and the murder weapon close by. Something about this puzzled her, although she couldn't put her finger on exactly what it was. She called Suki to her side and headed back to the Seaview.

Once home, she had admin to deal with, so she fired up her laptop. The first thing she did was scan news reports about Carmen's death. There seemed to be fewer of them now that Tilly Shilling was headline news. Mentions of the Seaview were sporadic, and Helen hoped with all her heart that Jean was right about bookings not being affected long-term. However, when she checked the booking app and her emails, she was saddened to see that bookings had dropped off. The Seaview had weathered many storms, but she felt this one might be her trickiest yet.

She scanned her emails, replying where needed, filing others away. It was while she was trying to pacify a guest cancelling a mid-winter break because of news about Carmen that another email popped into her inbox. It took her a moment to process what she was seeing when she spotted the sender's name. She finished writing her email, crossed her fingers that she could convince the guest not to cancel, then tentatively opened the new email.

Darling Helen, forgive me for contacting you this way, but it's the only thing I can think of as you won't answer my calls or texts. Please give me a chance to explain. Love, Jimmy x

She stared at it for a few moments. He was there, out in the ether, at the other end of whatever tin-and-string-can arrangement the internet was. But *where* was he? What was it he had to explain that he couldn't write in an email? Couldn't he at least give her a clue? Her fingers twitched over the laptop keys. How easy it would be to reply. But she'd made a deal with herself not to invite trouble into her life. And she'd already decided that she was done with Jimmy Brown . . . hadn't she? On the other hand, Marie had warned her not to rush to conclusions. Her fingers twitched again, with her friend's words buzzing in her head. She didn't know what to do. She reached for the keyboard. And then she deleted his email.

Later, Helen was upstairs with Sally cleaning the rooms while the actors gathered in the lounge for rehearsal.

She picked up her mop and bucket and knocked on the door of Liza's room. There was no answer, so she unlocked it. The room was its usual mess, with scarves and hats strewn about. Shoes and boots covered the floor and make-up spilled from a neon-pink bag. Papers and books were piled messily on the bedside unit. Helen didn't like to interfere with her guests' belongings, but in order to clean, she needed to tidy up first. She decided to begin by putting the books into a neat pile.

A startling black-and-red cover caught her eye. It was a book of set pieces to read at auditions, placed face down with the pages spread wide. Helen picked up the book carefully; she didn't want to lose Liza's page and would replace it the same way she'd found it. She was curious to see what was inside. With the book in her hand, she scanned the lines on the page. It was an interesting scene, a monologue, it seemed. An idea struck her. She felt silly at first, but throwing caution to the wind, she decided to give it a go and read the passage out loud. She'd worked with the actors for over a week now and knew she should project her voice. She was curious to see if she had it in her to perform. How hard could it be? It was only pretending, after all. She stood straight, with the book in one hand, cleared her throat, lifted her chin and read.

'It was a Thursday afternoon when I left Roger at the church. I walked out; it was as simple as that, nothing complicated about it. I was in my wedding dress, my bouquet in my hands, roses and freesias. Roger cried, "Stop!" I could hear him behind me. Blood was rushing in my ears; I saw the organist gasp in horror. He was halfway through the bridal march. His hands left the keyboard as I pushed the door open and escaped. I ran down the path, I had to get away from the storm in my mind and I . . .'

She shook her head, tutted loudly and laid the book back down. She didn't reckon much to Roger, whoever he was, and wished the runaway bride all the luck in the world. A flicker of guilt went through her for peeking at her guest's book, and she shook her head.

'Don't do that again,' she said.

She carried on cleaning, singing along to the radio, trying to push all thoughts of Jimmy away. But every song she listened to brought him right back to mind. Songs of happiness and love, of wanting, longing, romance.

When the rooms were done, her phone rang. She slid it from her tabard pocket.

'Seaview Hotel, good morning.'

'Helen, darling, it's Taylor. How are you?'

'Taylor! It's good to hear your voice. How's it going at the Modernist?'

'Well, we've got the damned media camped outside the stage door; they're determined to get shots of the cast when they arrive on Saturday night. But it's nothing I can't handle.'

'How are the roof repairs coming on? Will it be ready for the play's opening night?'

Taylor gave a huge sigh.

'What's wrong?' Helen asked.

'Don't mention that wretched play! *Midnight with Maude* will be the death of me. Oh, I shouldn't have said that. Poor Carmen Delray. I didn't mean it to come out the way it did.'

'It's all right, Taylor, calm down. Has something happened?'

'No, and that's the problem. Something *was* happening, but now it's not, and I rather think it's your fault.'

'*My* fault? What are you talking about?'

'Your pal Gav and his gang of merry men finished the roof

repairs, but I need a health and safety certificate. I'm desperate for it, Helen. Gav promised to bring it to me, but he was called away to fix a kitchen at the Vista del Mar and I haven't seen hide nor hair of him since. When I called to ask where he was, he said the landlady at the Vista del Mar told him you'd recommended him to her. This means that he's working for her now when he should be here with me.'

'It's not my fault Gav can't be in two places at once,' Helen said.

'But he should be *here*, Helen. You know we can't open without building control signing off the works on the roof.'

'Have you tried ringing him this morning?' Helen asked.

'Yes, but my calls go to voicemail. I know how busy he is with all his different businesses, but I really need to speak to him,' Taylor moaned. 'Can you help at all?'

As Helen was listening to Taylor, Sally walked towards her carrying her mop and bucket.

'I'll be down in a few moments for coffee,' Helen told her.

'What's that, Helen?' Taylor said.

'Nothing, Taylor. Please, go on.'

'I said is there anything you can do to help?' he continued, exasperated. 'This is serious. If the roof repairs aren't signed off, the theatre can't open and the play won't go on! Gav's a friend of yours; he'll answer your call. I'm frantic here. The stress has brought out my rash, and poor Mr Phipps has picked up on my unease and lost his appetite. He's very sensitive, you know. I can't even tempt him to eat his luxury tuna chunks, and he normally devours those.'

Helen was surprised to hear Taylor speak like this; she'd never heard him so upset. She watched as Sally walked away, and an idea came to her.

'Leave it with me, Taylor. I might not have any influence over Gav, but I know someone who does.'

Chapter 35

'Gav's on his way to the theatre now,' Sally said once Helen was settled at the kitchen table with coffee and a slice of Jean's apple cake. The cake was warm from the oven, moist and tangy with fruit.

'Beautiful cake, Jean,' Helen said appreciatively.

Jean nodded in response.

'It really is gorgeous, you've excelled yourself today,' Sally agreed, before turning back to Helen. 'Once Gav knew how important it was to hand the certificate to Taylor, he didn't need to be asked twice.'

'I dare say there's not a lot Gav wouldn't do for you and little Gracie if you asked him,' Jean said, lifting her coffee mug. 'He's clearly smitten.'

'How are you feeling about him now, Sally? Are you still having doubts?' Helen asked.

Sally shrugged. 'Well, he's good to me, I'll give him that, and Gracie thinks the world of him. But there's a part of me that's scared of letting myself trust him too much in case I get hurt. Because it's not just me I have to protect, it's my daughter; we come as a package. Anyway, he's asked me out on Saturday night for dinner and has bought tickets for *Midnight with Maude* at the Modernist afterwards.'

'I'm sure I could have got you free tickets from Chester,' Helen said. 'Gav could have saved himself some money.'

'Oh, he won't take anything for free. He insists on paying for things himself, doing everything by the book. He's straight down the line is Gav.'

Helen noticed Sally's eyes light up when she spoke about her boyfriend.

'Have you got a babysitter for Gracie on Saturday night?' she asked. It had been a long time since she'd spent time with Gracie, whom she adored.

'Yeah, Mum's offered to look after her.'

'Well, you know if you ever need me for babysitting, I'm here for you too.'

'Thanks, Helen. But what about you and Jimmy? We bumped into him last night, by the way.'

Helen was about to take a bite of cake, and stopped with the slice in mid-air. 'What? You've seen him? Where?' Hadn't Jodie said he was in London?

'Me and Gav took Gracie to feed the ducks in Peasholm Park. He was sitting on a bench and we stopped to chat with him. He's such a lovely bloke. He was asking after you, of course.'

Helen put her cake down on her plate. 'What did he say?'

Sally shrugged. 'Just that he hadn't heard from you for a few days and was hoping you were all right. I said you were really busy and that was probably the reason you hadn't been in touch.'

'Right,' Helen said, taking it all in. She could feel Jean's eyes on her.

'Are you all right, love?' Jean asked.

'In all honesty, Jean, I don't know.'

Jean put her mug on the table and pushed her empty plate away. She looked from Helen to Sally.

'You two are lucky, you know that? Both of you with fellas who want you.' She turned to Sally. 'Has Gav got a grandad, with his own hair and teeth? You could fix me up on a date. Actually, I'm not too fussed about hair. I like bald men, and even dentures I can cope with. It's about time I got myself back in the dating game. I'm sure there are plenty of men out there who'd like a cuddly little woman like me. Having you two mooning about men while we have our morning coffee is making me feel romantic.'

'Is it giving you all the feels, Jean?' Sally laughed.

Jean looked shocked. 'All the feels? Don't be so dirty. I was just hoping for a night at the bingo with a bit of male company, that's all.'

'What about Alfie Hyde?' Helen asked, grateful that the spotlight had been taken off her and Jimmy. 'You seemed to enjoy having lunch with him the other day.'

A twinkle came into Jean's eye. 'He's a nice man, Alfie. A very nice man indeed.'

Helen and Sally shared a smile as Jean gathered plates and mugs from the table and tidied them away, then bustled away to get her coat, calling over her shoulder as she went.

'I've made pea and ham soup for lunch, and mushroom soup for the . . . veganarian, or whatever she calls herself. I thought the actors might appreciate a change from sandwiches. There's home-made bread under the tea towel.'

'Jean, you're fantastic,' Helen replied, trying to suppress a chuckle.

* * *

Once Jean and Sally had left, Helen called Marie. She needed to talk to her friend. She could feel her resolve about Jimmy threatening to give way, and she needed some advice. It didn't feel right to land all her problems on Jean; the woman had already done enough to help her with the press and the inspector.

'Fancy playing truant?' she asked. 'I need your wise womanly words more than I've ever needed them before.'

Marie laughed out loud. 'What did you have in mind?'

'How about a ride on the North Bay railway around the park?' Helen said, dangling the bait she knew her friend would never refuse. Marie adored Scarborough's miniature railway.

'It's a date,' Marie replied.

The colourful carriages of the little train were waiting at the station in Northstead Manor Gardens. A small, perfectly restored engine named Georgina was steaming at the front. The two women had to walk through the gift shop to buy tickets before they could board. Once they were seated, Marie linked her arm through Helen's while they waited for the train to move. It ran to a strict timetable, and there were still ten minutes to go before the train was allowed to leave.

'Come on then, what can I help you with?' Marie said. 'Is it Jimmy?'

Helen poured everything out. She told Marie about Jimmy's email, bumping into Jodie in town, what Sally had said when she'd met Jimmy in the park. And then she told her about the stress she was under looking after her guests, the hotel inspector's visit, DS Hutchinson asking her to keep an eye on the actors, and the Seaview being in the news. It was a relief to get it all off her chest.

'Blimey, you're really going through it, Helen,' Marie said.

'I don't know how much more I can take,' Helen said. 'If it wasn't for Jean and Sally's help at the hotel, I think I might be considering a change of career, just like you.'

'Now don't talk like that. You can't sell up and move on; you *are* the Seaview Hotel. You love that place.'

'I know . . . and I want to keep it, of course. But my word, it's tough. I've never gone through anything like this in my life.'

'You know, if you're starting to think about giving Jimmy a chance to explain, letting him back into your life, remember that a problem shared is a problem halved. Speaking to him might ease some of the worries about everything else you've got going on,' Marie said.

Helen looked at her. 'Or it might just make them worse.'

Just then the train began to chuff its slow way from the station and brought their conversation to a close. Passers-by waved as it made its way around the park, and Marie waved back enthusiastically.

'I've been riding on this little train since before I can remember. I love it,' she beamed.

'I know you do,' Helen replied, waving too, caught up in Marie's infectious enthusiasm.

The train followed a narrow-gauge track along the beach to Scalby Mills, a journey of less than a mile but packed with beautiful scenery. At first it ran along the edge of a lake before heading under the historic water chute that dunked thrill-seekers into a lake, soaking those brave or daft enough to sit at the front. And then came the tunnel, plunging the train into darkness. Whoops and screams went up from the passengers, the loudest scream coming from Marie. Helen couldn't stop herself from laughing. She hadn't felt so happy and carefree in days. No sooner had the train entered the tunnel than it emerged into daylight at the other end, Helen's heart beating in time to the clattering wheels on the tracks. On it went past the Open Air Theatre, through more gardens and a crazy golf course until it reached its destination.

'Should we call at the Old Scalby Mills pub for a drink and a chat?' she said.

'Sounds wonderful,' Marie replied.

They walked from the train station to the prom, past the Sea Life Centre with its penguins and sea lions, past another crazy golf course, this one with a pirate theme. There were wooden benches and tables outside the pub. Helen secured a seat while Marie went inside for the drinks. As she sat and gazed at the sea, feeling more relaxed than she had for some time, a flash of red caught her eye: two women in red coats sitting at a table in front of her. They had their backs to her, but from their body shape, their hair, she had no doubt they were the women who'd hung around the Seaview. Carmen's obsessive fans. Then she noticed who they were talking to, a man Helen could see clearly. A man wearing a beige anorak.

She caught Paul's eye and waved, trying her best to hide her confusion. What was he doing with Carmen's fans? A shiver went through her. Surely he wasn't caught up in anything to do with the murder? He'd seemed so friendly and nice, had even joined her on a walk with Suki after confiding he was homesick. He waved back, then said something to the ladies in red, and both of them turned to look at her. They nodded and smiled before turning back and carrying on their conversation.

Marie returned with two pints of North Bay Ale from the local Wold Top brewery. Helen took her glass and raised it.

'Cheers,' she said. She took a long drink to quench her thirst, then set her glass on the table. 'See that guy over there, the one in the beige anorak?'

Marie subtly turned her head.

'He's one of my guests, Paul, one of the actors – well, he's not an actor really; he's the stage manager, who looks after lighting and props. But see those women he's with? They've been hanging around the Seaview since before Carmen Delray died. It was Carmen who pointed them out to me, she was anxious about them. She said they were obsessive fans who followed her when she was on tour.'

'Have you seen them at the Seaview since she died?'

'A couple of times,' Helen replied. 'And now I'm wondering why Paul is talking to them.' Then she stiffened, her body alert. 'Don't look now, they're coming over.'

It was the first time she had seen the women close up, and she realised how much younger they were than she'd first thought.

'Hello, Helen,' said Paul. 'I'd like you to meet my mum.'

Helen rocked back in her seat. His mum? What the . . .

The woman with the brown shoulder-length hair and glasses offered her hand. 'Pat McNally, nice to meet you. Paul's been telling me all about the Seaview. Thank you for looking after him, Mrs Dexter. He says your breakfasts are amazing. What a relief it is to know he's being well fed. I always worry about him while he's away.'

Paul rolled his eyes and Helen saw him blush. 'Mum, please,' he said through gritted teeth.

The woman with the short grey hair held out her hand. 'I'm Paul's aunt Margaret. Pat's sister.'

Helen looked from Pat to Margaret. Of course. She could see the resemblance now, and saw Paul's soft features mirrored in his mum's face. Her mind scrabbled to make sense of their connection to Carmen, and Carmen's connection to Paul, but none of the pieces of the puzzle would fit.

'I'm Marie Davenport, I run Tom's Teas tearoom. You should come in some time and bring your mum and auntie.' Marie shook hands with Paul.

'Sorry, I forgot to introduce my friend Marie,' Helen said, still struggling to understand what was going on.

'Well, we won't stop, Mrs Dexter, but I had to come and thank you for looking after my boy,' Pat said. 'I can't tell you how glad I am to know he's staying somewhere decent. You should see the state of some places these touring groups stick him in. Some of them aren't fit for a dog, never mind my favourite son.'

'She always says that, and I'm her only son.' Paul laughed awkwardly.

'He's a good boy, our Paul,' Margaret said, patting his arm. Pat beamed with pride. Paul looked mortified and shuffled his feet awkwardly.

'Aren't you eating out in town with your castmates today?' Helen asked quickly, desperate to know what was going on.

'Oh, after we finished rehearsals, Chester was struggling – you know how he's been after what happened with Carmen. Lee was talking about her and Chester got upset and started crying. Anyway, Kate and Audrey are supporting him; they took him for a stroll on the beach. And I spotted Mum and Auntie Margaret waiting for me outside the Seaview, so I took them up on their offer of a drink.'

Helen looked from Pat to Margaret. 'You were waiting outside the Seaview . . . for Paul?'

'Oh yes,' Pat said proudly. 'We follow him everywhere when he's on tour, don't we, Margaret?'

'We do, Pat.'

'I like to keep my eye on him and make sure the hotels he stays in are nice and clean,' she continued. 'If they're not, I put a complaint in.'

'Mum, please. Helen doesn't need to know this,' Paul said.

Yes I do, Helen thought. She cleared her throat and decided to dive straight in.

'It was tragic news about Carmen Delray, wasn't it?'

She searched Pat's face, then Margaret's, but saw no reaction.

'Sad news indeed. I can't imagine what her family are going through,' Pat said.

'Were you fans of hers?' Helen asked.

There, she'd said it. She could feel Marie's eyes on her.

'Not especially,' Pat said, wrinkling her nose and looking at her sister.

Margaret shrugged. 'Well, I've been watching reruns of *The Singing Nurse* on classic TV, but I can't say I was ever a fan. I much prefer Audrey Monroe. Now that woman's got class.'

Helen's head spun. If the two women weren't fans of Carmen's, as Carmen had thought, then what was going on?

'Did you ever meet Carmen when Paul was working with her on productions in the past?' she pushed.

'Oh yes, we met her a few times, twice in York, once in London, and two, no, three times in Torquay,' Pat said. 'She kept insisting on giving us her autograph or a signed picture. It seemed rude not to take them. But it always felt like she was forcing them on us. I felt a bit sorry for her, didn't you, Margaret?'

'I did, Pat.'

'I reckon she thought we were waiting to see her, you know,' Pat carried on. 'She must've thought we were clamouring for her attention when in fact we were waiting for Paul.'

Now it all made sense. Helen and Marie exchanged a smile. Paul shuffled awkwardly again.

'I wish you wouldn't interfere, Mum,' he said, before turning to Helen. 'I'm sorry to have interrupted you and your friend. We'll leave you in peace to enjoy your drink, and I'll see you tomorrow.'

Pat and Margaret said goodbye, and the three of them turned to leave. As they did so, Paul's mum linked arms with him on his right-hand side. On his left-hand side, his aunt Margaret did the same. Paul was stuck in the middle, a tall pole in a beige anorak between two short ones in red.

Once they were out of earshot, Marie raised her glass. 'Bravo. I take my hat off to you. I think you can cross those two ladies off your list of suspects, and Paul too. It must be a bit creepy for the boy, though, having his mum and aunt following him whenever he works away.'

'No, it makes sense. Paul's more sensitive than the others, and now that I've met his mum, I understand why he's the way he is.'

'So you don't think he's got anything to do with Carmen's murder?' Marie asked.

Helen sighed, then took another long drink.

'I hope not. He seems like such a nice guy. To be honest, I don't know what to think any more.'

'Well, just remember, you're not being paid to solve a murder. Let the police do their work while you concentrate on being landlady of the best hotel in Scarborough.'

'Amen to that,' Helen said, raising her glass.

Chapter 36

Helen would have loved to be certain that such a gentle soul as Paul wasn't involved in Carmen's death. After she'd spoken to Kate and learned the truth about her failed blackmail plan, she felt sure that Kate at least was no murderer. She was a carer, not a killer; all her energies and money went into looking after her family. If only she could be sure about Paul. Plus, there was costume designer Liza and her mum, calm, serene Audrey, to think about. Those two seemed a separate unit to the others somehow, a partnership of two, sticking together and looking after each other.

Helen shook her head and reminded herself she was taking a rare few hours off work. But something niggled away at her each time she thought about Carmen's body lying on the damp sand.

Later, back at the Seaview, Helen was surprised to find the cast still rehearsing in the lounge. They'd normally finished by this time. However, as opening night was just days away, she supposed they needed all the rehearsal time they could get. Paul wasn't there, and she wondered if he was eating out with his mum and aunt.

She pulled up a chair and sat quietly in the doorway, watching.

Oh, how wonderful they all looked now they were fully dressed in character. She marvelled at the outfits, colours and designs. They were wearing jackets, hats and scarves, some that she recognised from being strewn on the floor in Liza's room. They carried umbrellas and briefcases. She caught Liza's eye and smiled; the young woman had done a wonderful job.

She soon noticed that Anabel was not only acting, she was also giving the cast directions, and Chester didn't look too pleased. In fact, he seemed rather peeved. As the newcomer dished out words of wisdom, he stood motionless, then he dipped his hand into his trouser pocket and pulled out his pen, which he began tapping against a tabletop. No one apart from Helen seemed to notice; they were too much in awe of Anabel, concentrating on her advice. Even seasoned actor Audrey was taking her words on board, nodding and agreeing. Still Chester didn't speak, just kept tapping the pen on the table, then against his leg. Helen watched, intrigued, as Anabel walked towards him. No, she thought, surely she wasn't going to give Chester notes on his performance? That was definitely overstepping the mark. She leaned forward in an effort to hear whatever was said between them at the other end of the lounge. Anabel was taller than Chester, and she bent down to whisper in his ear. Chester gripped the pen with both hands, then raised it and jabbed it at her. Helen could see he was rattled.

Anabel drifted back to the centre of the room and acknowledged Helen with a generous smile. Then she clapped her long, thin, bony hands.

'Right, cast, let's get back to it. Kate, let's start with you, from the scene where you've just come out of hospital. And . . . action!'

But it wasn't Anabel or Kate that Helen was interested in, it was Chester. His face reddened, then he turned away from the others and, quick as a flash, snapped the pen in half. It was the same angry gesture she'd seen him make before, when he and Carmen had argued and he'd broken his cigarette holder. She glanced away when she met his eye, embarrassed to be caught watching, and looked down at the script in her lap, stabbing her finger at the page and trying to focus.

When it was time for Chester to join in, she could tell he wasn't on good form. His voice sounded too high, and he kept shooting daggers at Anabel. A chill went through her. What if . . . ? No, she thought, surely not. But it was a thought that refused to go away. What if Chester was the one who'd murdered Carmen? And if he'd been furious enough to kill Carmen, after being jilted for a younger man with a bigger moustache, then who was to say he wouldn't go after Anabel next? Helen's stomach turned over, and she felt sick. She had to get out of the room; it suddenly felt too stuffy, too warm. Her head swam when she stood from her chair. She put her hand to the door frame to steady herself.

'Going somewhere, Helen?'

It was Anabel. Helen didn't turn around.

'I need some fresh air,' she muttered.

She stumbled along the hall to the front door and out into the cold day. There was a spit of rain in the air, but she didn't care. She had to get away from Chester, from Anabel and Kate and Lee; she'd had it up to here with the whole flaming lot of them. She walked across the road and sat on the bench overlooking the beach. But this time she didn't notice the view. She closed her eyes and took great gulps of air, one after the other, trying to calm her racing heart, trying to make sense of what she knew about Chester. Was he really a killer? Or had Carmen been murdered by someone else – perhaps her date, the mystery moustachioed man?

Helen wished, oh how she wished with all her heart, that she'd never clapped eyes on Dawley's Theatre Group. Yes, they were good for business, on paper at least. Her bank manager would be overjoyed with the income going into the Seaview's account. But how she longed for normal guests again: families with children, couples enjoying a cheeky weekend, friends meeting up and spending time together. She'd even welcome back the coachload of ladies from Nottingham obsessed with playing bingo each night in the lounge; they'd be a welcome relief after what'd happened to Carmen. She wanted normal guests, regular guests, guests who didn't use her lounge as a rehearsal space, guests who didn't need pampering with sandwiches at lunchtime, who didn't have sensitive egos or mothers in red coats hanging around outside her hotel. She wanted guests who didn't go around being murdered.

She buried her head in her hands, trying not to cry, the stress of the week working its way through her, and that was when her phone buzzed. She let it ring, too upset to answer, and not until she'd pulled herself together did she take it from her pocket. The call had been from DS Hutchinson, and he'd left a message asking her to ring back.

Within a minute, she was speaking to him.

'Ah, Mrs Dexter, it's good of you to return my call,' he said. 'How are you?'

'Believe me, you don't want to know,' Helen replied.

There was a beat of silence before he spoke again. 'We've, er, had some news from the autopsy carried out on Miss Carstairs' body and have received confirmation of how she was killed.'

'Confirmation? But you've already told me she was killed by a knife found next to her body,' Helen said.

'No, Mrs Dexter. I never said it was a knife. I told you she'd been stabbed. The autopsy confirmed our suspicions that the item left beside her body on the beach was indeed the murder weapon. It was a long, sharp weapon that made very deep wounds. It was exactly a foot long, unusually thin and round.'

Helen's mouth went dry. 'A foot long? Thin and round?'

'Yes, it's most bizarre,' DS Hutchinson said. 'In all my years on the force, it's the first time I've ever known anyone stabbed to death by a sharpened cigarette holder.'

Act III

Chapter 37

Helen's mouth fell open in shock. 'A cigarette holder?'

'Yes, an unusual weapon, Mrs Dexter, and as I say, not one I've seen before. I thought I'd ring to tell you before you read it online. We're giving a press conference this morning.'

'No! Don't!' Helen cried. She couldn't bear the thought of photographers and journalists setting up camp outside the Seaview again. She needed to protect her hotel; her livelihood was at stake.

'I'm sorry?'

She swivelled on the bench to face the Seaview. 'I said please don't say anything to the press about the weapon.'

'Is there a reason for this, Mrs Dexter?'

'There's something I haven't told you. It's about one of the actors, the man in charge, Chester Ford.'

'Miss Carstairs' ex-lover?'

Helen girded herself. 'Yes . . . He used to have a cigarette holder.'

'What do you mean, he used to?' DS Hutchinson's voice took on a more serious tone.

'I mean he had one when he first arrived, but he snapped it, I saw him do it. Before he broke it, he used to carry it around all the time.'

'He was a smoker?'

'No, he didn't smoke it, he liked to poke it.'

'He did what?' DS Hutchinson barked.

'He used it to keep his hands busy, that's all, poking people with it to get their attention. I saw him snap it in half when he argued with Carmen.'

'Where is he now, this Chester Ford?'

Helen looked at the actors moving back and forth past the window. 'He's in the Seaview, rehearsing.'

'Can you keep him there until we arrive?'

'Yes, but—'

'Mrs Dexter, you have just found our killer. He's certainly got the motive – a jealous jilted lover – and he had the weapon too. We'll be there as fast as we can. Make sure he doesn't leave, but be aware that he could be dangerous.'

Helen opened her mouth to reply, but DS Hutchinson had rung off.

When she tried to stand, her legs wobbled. The shock of it all was too much. She took a moment to pull herself together. How she would stop Chester from leaving if he chose to, she had no idea. However, she didn't get the chance to even leave the bench, because at that moment, the Seaview's door was flung open and Chester appeared. He waved at her, and her heart began to fight its way out of her chest. Using the back of the bench to steady herself, she pushed herself up to standing.

'That flamin' woman!' he growled as he walked towards her.

It was all she could do to smile weakly. Was he really the killer? He had a bad temper, yes. He'd argued with Carmen, yes, a few times that Helen was aware of. And he'd snapped his cigarette holder in half. She had seen it with her own eyes. But what if he'd lied to her about not having another, one that he'd used to kill Carmen?

With each step Chester took, Helen inched back, trying to delay the moment he'd reach her. She thought fast. All she had to do was keep him close; the police were on their way. She glanced up and down Windsor Terrace, relieved to see people about. If he pulled a weapon and she called out, people would hear her. If she screamed, they'd come running, wouldn't they? She sank back down on to the bench, slid her hand into her pocket and pulled out her phone. Tapping a couple of buttons, she placed it by her side, microphone on, red light proof of recording, and waited for him to reach her.

'That flaming Anabel Craven! Who does she think she is?' he snarled, sitting down at the other end of the bench.

Helen glanced at her phone. The red light was steady. She had to keep him talking, she had to say something, but what?

'Are you all right, Chester?' she asked at last.

'No, I'm not all right, Helen. I am definitely not all right.'

She risked a glance at him; he looked as tense as he sounded. He began drumming his fingers on the armrest.

'Care to talk about it?' she said over-loudly, for the benefit of her phone. 'You seem angry about something.' She leaned slightly to her side where the phone lay by her thigh. 'And I have just witnessed you snapping a pen in the lounge of the Seaview Hotel on Windsor Terrace, Scarborough.'

If Chester was perturbed by Helen's formal speech, he didn't show it. Instead, he buried his head in his hands and promptly burst into tears. Helen was shocked, but managed to gather her thoughts, aware she had to act quickly and take her chance to record his response. She leaned to her left and spoke loudly.

'Now, I can see that you're crying. Would you care to talk about that?'

'Talk?' he sobbed. 'Talk? I've no one to talk to, not since Carmen died. My life is over without her, Helen, over. She was everything to me.'

'Were you jealous, Chester Ford, that Carmen Delray left you for another man?'

This time he gave her a funny look. He wiped the back of his hand across his eyes, then took a cotton handkerchief from his pocket and blew his nose loudly.

'I'm grieving for the woman I love, Helen, please have some respect. I can't take any more. I don't know what to do. And on top of all of that, I've got Anabel flaming Craven to deal with. She's been desperate to join Dawley's for months. She's trying to take over in there.' He gestured towards the Seaview with his hand.

'When you say *in there*, I see you indicating the Seaview Hotel,' Helen said to her left thigh.

Chester looked at her, puzzled. 'Sorry, Helen,' he said at last. 'I shouldn't be dumping my problems on you. You've shown me and my troupe nothing but kindness under the worst possible circumstances since Carmen died.'

She kept her gaze straight ahead, focusing on the churning grey sea, hoping her phone was picking up their words against the roar of the waves below. 'Why did you snap the pen, Chester? It looked to me as if you did it in anger,' she said.

'Oh, I snapped it in anger all right,' he replied. 'You saw Anabel in there, trying to undermine me in front of my troupe. She wants

Dawley's for herself! Well, she's not getting it!' He slapped his hand on the armrest.

Helen leaned left. 'For the record, that noise was a slap of anger.'

'Yes, it was,' Chester said, oblivious. 'Oh, I wish I had my pen. I need to have something to do with my hands! My word, I miss my cigarette holder.'

'Ah, the cigarette holder,' Helen said, eyeing the phone, relieved to see the red light still on. 'What happened to your cigarette holder?' she said loudly.

Chester shot her another look. Helen waited a moment before she turned and looked him straight in the eye.

'I put it to you, Chester Ford, that you snapped your cigarette holder in half in a fit of temper after an argument with Carmen Delray.'

'You saw that?' he said.

'Yes, I saw you arguing with the deceased, Carmen Delray, otherwise known as Janet Carstairs.'

'What? Why are you talking like that, Helen? Will you stop using my surname, there's really no need. We're friends now, aren't we? Are you feeling all right? You're looking a bit peaky, if you don't mind me saying so. A bit frazzled.'

Helen had her back to her phone now and hoped it was still picking up the conversation. She'd never used it to record anything before; she'd never needed to. From the corner of her eye, she saw a red car pull up at the kerb behind them and two men get out. One was tall with silver-grey hair, the other short and round.

'Chester Ford?'

Chester swung around at the mention of his name, and Helen

saw the blood drain from his face. He looked at her, eyes wide and confused.

'What's going on?'

DS Hutchinson stepped forward. 'Mr Ford, I'd be obliged if you would accompany me to the station.'

'Me? Why?' Chester squeaked.

'I'm arresting you on suspicion of the murder of Janet Carstairs.'

As the police drove Chester away, Helen picked up her phone and sent the recording to DS Hutchinson. Then she sat in stunned silence. Above her gulls screeched, around her people walked by, but she didn't notice any of them. She could only think of Chester. If he was the murderer, her nightmare was over. She dreaded going into the Seaview to tell the rest of the troupe what had happened, but knew that she must. However, she wasn't ready to move yet. She couldn't. She felt exhausted after what had just happened.

Her phone buzzed in her pocket. She pulled it out, not too surprised to see another message from Jimmy.

I understand what you're going through, but I need to explain. Please let me. I'm at Bay View café, meet me? If you don't arrive or reply, I'll take it as my sign to return to London and never contact you again. It's now or never. Love, Jimmy x

Helen tilted her face to the sky, where grey clouds scudded over the sea. She let the breeze ruffle her hair, felt the faint warmth on her face. She stared at the sea, mesmerised, watching the waves, listening to seagulls screech above as they circled the castle walls. She was lost in her thoughts, letting the tension she felt over Carmen's death fly away. She felt her shoulders drop and closed her eyes, relaxing into the moment. Was it really over now that Chester had been taken away by the police?

With her eyes closed, her other senses were heightened. She felt the sharp tang of salt on her lips, felt the ground under her boots keep her steady and straight. She thought of Jimmy, and the subtle scent of his lemon spice aftershave. There could be no putting this off. Tomorrow would be too late. She decided to take Marie's advice and give him a chance to explain. She quickly texted him back.

See you there.

She walked back to the Seaview to see Chester's castmates huddled at the lounge window, staring out. She realised then that they'd seen him being taken away. When she entered the lounge, they all turned to face her.

'Has Chester been arrested?' Liza asked.

'Surely he isn't the murderer!' Audrey swooned before fanning herself with a beer mat.

Helen looked at the worried faces around her. All of them were waiting for her to speak, but she didn't know what to say.

'But why?' Lee asked.

'Because the murder weapon was . . .' She hesitated; this was more difficult than she'd expected. 'Because Carmen was killed by . . . She was stabbed, you know that already, and it turns out the police think that Chester was the one who killed her. With his cigarette holder.'

Audrey's hand fluttered to her heart. 'Are you all right, Mum?' Liza asked, fussing around her.

Lee put his hand on the bar to steady himself against the shock of the news. Meanwhile, Kate's mouth dropped open, and she fell into the nearest seat.

Chapter 38

Helen arrived at the Bay View café with Suki on her lead. Jimmy was waiting outside. He had his back to her, but she recognised the height of him, the way he stood, the back of his dark hair flecked with grey. She felt sick when she saw him, nervous about what he had to say and whether she could believe him. Was it over between them before it had even begun? Did he really have someone else in his life, and if so, had everything he'd said been a lie? How stupid she felt for falling so quickly, letting herself be easily charmed. She could only imagine what Tom would have thought, and felt guilty for betraying his memory.

'Helen!' Jimmy beamed. 'You came, thank you. I wasn't sure if you would. You remember my daughter, Jodie, right?'

Helen looked from Jimmy to Jodie, confused.

'Look, Helen, I'm sorry about all this,' he said. 'I should have told you earlier. I mean, I wanted to, but I couldn't find the words. We were having such a good time and I didn't want to spoil it, and—'

Helen stood firm. 'And then you ran off after taking a phone call. Jean heard every word you said.'

'Every word?' He ran his hand through his hair.

'You still haven't told her?' Jodie said, sounding appalled.

'Come on, let's sit down and get a coffee,' Jimmy said quickly.

'I don't want coffee, just an explanation,' Helen said.

'Dad, you've got to tell her,' Jodie urged.

Jimmy looked deep into Helen's eyes. 'Helen . . . I don't know how to say this . . .'

'Dad, for heaven's sake,' Jodie sighed. 'If you don't hurry up and tell her the truth, I'll do it for you. She deserves to know.'

'She does, you're right. Helen, I'm sorry. But I want you to know I'm doing something about it. I've put things in motion.'

'What the heck are you talking about?' Helen cried, exasperated.

He dropped his gaze to the pavement, then looked her straight in the eye.

'I . . . haven't been honest, about us . . .'

'Dad, will you just spit it out,' Jodie said, raising her voice now.

'Jimmy, tell me,' Helen demanded.

'This isn't easy . . . It'll hurt you, it could destroy what we've got.'

'Oh, for heaven's sake, Dad,' Jodie cried.

'Helen, I . . .'

'Jimmy!' Helen snapped.

But it wasn't Jimmy who delivered the shock news. It was Jodie.

'What Dad's trying to say, in his pathetic way, is that he's still married to Mum.'

'Married?' Helen cried.

Passers-by turned to look, but Helen didn't see them or care.

'Married?' she exclaimed again.

'Helen, listen, it's not as bad as it sounds,' Jimmy pleaded.

'Good grief, Dad, could you make things any worse?' Jodie slapped her hand against her forehead.

Helen needed to get away. She couldn't breathe. He'd lied to her all this time. All those calls from the cruise ship, the bouquets he'd sent her, the texts, funny little messages with hearts and kisses at the end telling her how much he was missing her, they'd all been a sham. He had a wife; he was married and he'd lied. What an idiot she'd been. All she wanted was to rush back to the Seaview, have a good cry and get him out of her system for good. But even in her rage, as she stormed away from the Bay View, she was fully aware she was walking in the wrong direction. However, she was damned if she'd turn around and give him the satisfaction of seeing her upset.

'Helen, come back!' Jimmy shouted.

Helen didn't hear his shoes hitting the pavement behind her; all she could hear was the blood pounding in her ears and one word: *married.*

'Helen, listen to me,' he said as he caught up with her. Still she marched on, facing forward, face stern, teeth clenched, pulling Suki behind her. Jimmy was out of breath but determined, and he managed to race ahead. He turned, running backwards now, facing her, and the absurdity of it almost made her laugh out loud. She bit the inside of her mouth to stop herself from smiling. As he ran, trying not to trip up or bump into anyone, he begged her to listen, to let him explain. She couldn't even cross the road to get away, because they were so far along Foreshore Road they'd reached the point where it narrowed and the footpath ran only on one side. There were too many other people, too much traffic; she couldn't force her way past him. People stopped to stare at them, laughing and smiling, thinking it was a joke when it was anything but.

Curtain Call at the Seaview Hotel

Suddenly Jimmy stopped running and stood completely still, and because Helen was walking so fast, she couldn't stop in time and ended up slap bang in his arms. This confused Suki, who walked around them, wrapping the lead around their legs, tying them together. Jimmy whispered in Helen's ear, 'Please, Helen, I'm begging you, let me explain.'

Helen unwound the lead and stared hard at him. 'I'll give you ten minutes. Start talking.'

He looked around, desperate. 'Let's find a seat. This deserves a proper explanation and an apology too.'

'You can say that again.' She nodded ahead. 'There are seats in the Italian gardens. It's quiet there, we can talk. But I'm warning you, Jimmy, don't tell me any more lies.'

He held his hands up in surrender. 'Lead the way,' he said.

Helen and Suki set off with Jimmy behind. They walked along the seafront, past the Spa, to a winding path that led up the cliff. Not a word was said, but Helen's mind worked overtime. She was prepared to listen to him; she'd give him one chance, as Marie had advised her to do.

'In here,' she said, leaving the path and heading into a large, secluded sunken garden surrounded by ancient trees and woodland. In the middle was a pond with a statue of Mercury with wings on his heels.

'What an incredible place. I've never been here before,' Jimmy said.

Helen ignored him and walked to a stone bench in an ornate Edwardian shelter. She sat down and Suki lay at her feet. Jimmy also sat down, a respectful distance away. Helen tapped her watch.

'You've got ten minutes, starting now.'

309

She was so angry she couldn't look at him and instead stared ahead, waiting for him to speak. She'd expected his words to come tumbling out, but he was silent for a very long time. She kept her head still, and when she could take his silence no more, she peeked from the corner of her eye, just in time to see him wipe the back of his hand across his eyes.

'Eight minutes left,' she said, trying to quell the lump in her throat that had taken her by surprise.

'I don't know where to start,' he said softly.

'At the beginning, with the truth,' Helen said, more gently now, the sting of anger leaving her slowly. 'Who were you talking to on the phone in my kitchen. Was that her? Your wife?' She turned to him as he began to speak.

'I've been separated from Jodie's mum—'

'Your wife,' Helen chipped in.

He nodded sheepishly. 'My wife, Diane, yes. We've been separated for years, but we never got around to getting divorced. I never thought it was necessary, see? I didn't think for one minute I'd meet anyone I'd want to . . . I mean, I never thought I'd meet someone like you. Being away on the cruise gave me time to think. Once I realised I wanted a future with you, I knew I had to completely sever ties with her. When I flew home, the first thing I did was call her to tell her I was going to see a solicitor to file for divorce. It's fair to say she didn't take the news well. I've had to lie to her and pretend there was no one else. I'm sorry you got hurt in the crossfire.'

'But if you've been separated so long, surely she knew things were over between you?'

'She still hoped for a reconciliation. She begged me many times to take her back and try again – she still does – but I feel nothing for her. She left us when Jodie was a kid. It was when Jodie started having problems at school, getting in with the wrong gang, taking drugs and bunking off. Diane couldn't handle it and left me to cope on my own.'

'Does Jodie ever see her?' Helen asked.

'No, their relationship was over the day Diane walked out. Jodie wants nothing to do with her. Diane, well, she battles demons every day, alcohol mainly. She's been in and out of rehab. Each time she needs help, she calls me, and fool that I am, I go. I couldn't see her suffer. Her sister helps when she can, but apart from her, I'm the only person she's got. Being away on the cruise made me realise I can't go on with that life any more. I don't want to.'

Jimmy inched his way along the bench towards Helen, but she remained unmoved. She glanced at her watch.

'Four minutes left, Jimmy. Is there anything else you want to tell me?'

'Well, there is something, yes,' he said.

Her heart dropped. What now?

'It's about your car,' he said. 'Diane was the one who damaged it.'

Helen's mouth hung open in shock. '*She* did that? Why?'

'I told her I'd started seeing someone in Scarborough and I mentioned the Seaview. She knew I was coming here and I guess she wanted to see you with her own eyes. It seems she reached Scarborough before I did and smashed up your car. When she called me, she admitted what she'd done.'

'Was she the one who made the threatening calls, warning me away from you?'

Jimmy nodded. 'I'm sorry, Helen. I knew it was her when I saw the phone number on your mobile that day on the beach. I went back to London to talk to her. I thought I could fix things before telling you the truth. I realise now I was stupid.'

'How do I know she won't come back to smash the windows at the Seaview next?'

'She won't,' Jimmy said calmly. 'Her sister called me this morning; she's arranging to get her under care at the hospital again. I've told Diane from now on, I'll refuse to go to her if she calls. Speaking of which, I'll get my number changed so she can't call me any more.' Helen detected a note of bitterness in his voice.

A silence hung over them for a few moments.

'You lied to me, Jimmy,' she said. 'You could have told me all of this at the start.'

'I know, and I'm kicking myself that I didn't. There's not a minute that goes by when I don't regret not being honest, but I didn't know how things would work out. When I saw you again after I returned from the cruise, I just knew, in that moment when I saw you sitting on the bench outside the Seaview.' He laid both hands on his chest. 'I knew then, in my heart, that it's you that I want.'

Helen felt herself softening, tears springing to her eyes.

'Diane's promised not to contest the divorce, according to her sister,' Jimmy continued. 'My solicitor reckons it'll be straightforward; he can't see any reason why it shouldn't go through quickly.'

Helen let his words sink in. 'Is that everything?'

'Believe me, if there was more, I would tell you. I know I've made a mess of this and I'd understand if you never wanted to see me again.'

She looked at his open, earnest face, tears brimming in his eyes, and sniffed back her own tears. She stood, pulled a tissue from her pocket, and dabbed her eyes. 'I need time to think, Jimmy.'

'Yeah, I understand.'

'I'll call you,' she said, and then she stood and walked away, back through the sunken gardens, past the pond with its water lilies and fountain, past the trees, a squirrel, two blackbirds on the grass. Just before she headed up the steps, she turned around. To her surprise, Jimmy was still there, sitting with his head in his hands. How easy it would be to forgive, forget and move on. But she felt betrayed. He had hidden the truth so convincingly; was there a danger he might do it again?

Chapter 39

The next morning, over a plate of expertly scrambled eggs on a slice of granary toast, Helen told Jean about the police taking Chester in for questioning.

'They've arrested Chester Ford?' Jean said, pausing as she took milk from the fridge.

'Remember, what I tell you in the basement of the Seaview . . .'

Jean waved her hand dismissively. 'Stays in the basement of the Seaview. I know, love. After all these years, you don't need to remind me.'

Jean fired up the gas hob, then looked at her. 'Do *you* think he killed her?'

Helen thought for a moment. 'In all honesty, Jean, I want this whole mess to be cleared up as quickly as possible. Yes, Chester owned a cigarette holder, but I saw him break it. Of course, it doesn't mean he didn't lie to me about not having another, which he could've sharpened into a weapon. But it seemed to me that he was really grieving for Carmen. I can tell how genuine his grief is; I've been through it myself with Tom. It's all-consuming. On the other hand, Chester is a professional actor; he knows how to present one side of himself in public, when in private he's a different man. What I do know is that he's got a fiery temper. So had Carmen. I heard them arguing a few times. But does that

314

make him a killer? I hope not, Jean. I thought he was a really nice man. A bit of a nuisance with the pen-tapping and whatnot, but he seemed like a decent sort.'

Jean raised her eyebrows and shot her a look. 'That's what they said about Crippen. Speaking of which, have you heard anything from the hotel inspector?'

'Not a thing. Every time I get an email, I think it might be her, but nothing's come through yet.'

Jean stopped what she was doing and planted her elbows on the countertop. 'If Chester didn't murder Carmen, do you think one of the others might have done it?'

'Well, that's one avenue the police are investigating, but I hope none of them are involved. Can you imagine if they are? It means we've housed a murderer since Carmen died. It means you've cooked sausages for them and I've put clean sheets on their bed.'

'My money's on Chester,' Jean said. 'A spurned lover, crime of passion. It's got all the right ingredients. Oh, speaking of which, I'd better pop vegan sausages under the grill for Kate.'

'I saw Jimmy yesterday,' Helen said.

Jean paused at the fridge door and turned. 'Oh? And?'

'And . . . it turns out he's married.'

She didn't miss a beat, carried on preparing breakfast as Helen told her everything, not holding back.

'What do you reckon, Jean? Should I trust him and give him another chance?'

'Do you want to?' Jean asked, pausing with a knife in her hand.

'I've been asking myself that question all night. And I've come to the conclusion that . . . yes, I think I do.'

Jean beamed a wide smile. Helen pulled her phone towards her and composed a text. Her finger hovered over the bottom row of characters. Then, decision made, she sent the message, sealed with a kiss.

Meet me at the castle 1 p.m. X

When breakfast was almost ready to serve, Helen and Sally walked upstairs to the dining room to wait for their guests. Helen was stunned to see Chester standing there. Why had the police let him go?

'Can we talk, Helen? In private?' he asked urgently.

Helen nodded to the lounge, then turned to Sally. 'I'll be ten minutes, tops.'

'No problem,' Sally replied.

Helen ushered Chester into the lounge and closed the door. Chester looked broken, crumpled, as if he hadn't slept. He headed straight to the window seat and sat down.

'There's something I need to tell you before you hear it from anyone else,' he said. He ran his hands through his dark hair, and looked at Helen from red-rimmed eyes.

'On the night when . . .' He faltered a moment before carrying on. 'On the night Carmen died, there was a big storm, remember?'

Helen nodded, waiting for him to carry on.

'We'd all been in town having dinner with Taylor Caffrey. You might remember I was the last to return.'

'I remember. Go on.'

He began drumming his right hand on the seat, a nervous tic that betrayed his calm tone.

'I arrived last for a reason. I'm no murderer, Helen. I don't have it in me to do anything so cruel. Yes, I was hurt beyond belief that Carmen had dumped me, but I'm not capable of killing anyone. The police know the truth about where I was that night. It's important that you do too. You've looked after my troupe well and I owe you that much.'

Helen wished he would get to the point; she had breakfast to serve. 'OK then, where were you?'

Chester tapped his hand against his knee. 'I went somewhere after dinner. The police have confirmed it. I'm not proud of this, Helen. It's something I try to battle, but it gets the better of me now and then. We'd argued so much, Carmen and I, that I needed a release.' He hung his head, unable to look Helen in the eye. 'I went to the casino.'

'The one in the old Opera House?'

He nodded. 'I spent a small fortune, wanted to lose myself, to think about anything other than being dumped by Carmen.'

Helen rocked back in her seat, taking this in. 'Does that mean the police have ruled you out of their enquiries?'

Chester nodded. 'It proves beyond a doubt that I couldn't have killed her. When my darling Carmen was murdered, instead of being close by to help her, I was throwing twenty-pound notes on to a poker table. The casino manager confirmed my identity to DS Hutchinson and the casino's got me on their security cameras. It's been a rotten night, Helen. I wasn't released until midnight and I haven't slept a wink.'

'I expect the police told you about the murder weapon?' Helen said.

Chester nodded. 'Oh, they told me all right. And they showed me the picture of a man sitting close to Carmen and her boyfriend in the back of the North Mount Hotel. I didn't recognise him, though. Couldn't see much of his face, and the photo was grainy. Thank you, Helen, for letting the police know you saw me snap the cigarette holder in half before Carmen was killed. You've saved me from being dragged further into their enquiries. DS Hutchinson said the wound on . . .' He paused, closed his eyes before starting again. 'The police said the weapon used was an unbroken cigarette holder.'

'Yes,' Helen said, rubbing her chin. 'But if you didn't kill her, who did? And why did they use a cigarette holder?'

'It can only have been to frame me, that's what the police think, although there were no fingerprints on it.'

'Chester, can you remember who else was in the lounge with you when you snapped it? Apart from Carmen, I mean?' Helen asked.

He thought for a moment, then shook his head. 'I was so furious with Carmen that the red mist descended on me. I can't remember anything about who else was around.' He dabbed at his eyes with a handkerchief. 'Look, would you mind if I went in for breakfast? I need something to eat, energy to get me through the day, with plenty of strong coffee. And please, I beg you, not a word to the others about my gambling habit.'

Once he'd gone, Helen gazed out of the window at the churning sea. Thoughts were running wild in her mind. Something didn't make sense. She tried hard, forcing herself to remember who else might have been in the lounge on the day Chester snapped his cigarette holder. She and Paul had been walking Suki when she saw it happen. But the reflection from the window had made it impossible for her to see further inside. Who had seen him do it? Who knew he had snapped it? And more importantly, who didn't? Who thought it was still in one piece, and hoping to frame him for Carmen's murder?

Chapter 40

That afternoon, Helen told Chester she had business in town and couldn't work as their prompt. Besides, the actors were more or less word-perfect by now, apart from Lee, and she didn't think they'd miss her too much. She was a little concerned that no one in the group, or Taylor Caffrey, had mentioned when the professional prompter would arrive to take over. She shrugged it off; it was up to Dawley's to sort it out, not her. She had too many other things on her mind.

It had been many years since she'd visited Scarborough Castle. She'd forgotten how exhilarating it was standing on the promontory looking out to sea, overlooking the beautiful sandy beaches of South Bay to her right and North Bay to her left. The old town, with its shops and offices, houses and narrow streets, fanned out behind her. Suki stood by her side, woman and dog looking at the sea. When Helen turned, she saw some of Scarborough's most prominent features; the market hall, the high ground of Oliver's Mount, and of course the magnificent Grand Hotel, once the biggest hotel in Europe. Ahead of her was the North Sea, glittering in the sun that bounced off the waves, making them sparkle like diamonds. She breathed in fresh, salty air as her hair blew across her face in the breeze.

She closed her eyes, listening to the roar of the sea. When she opened them again, Jimmy was standing at her side. He was so close she could smell the subtle scent of his lemon spice aftershave. She felt his arm brush hers, and then he reached for her hand. They stood for a few moments in silence before he spoke.

'I don't deserve this. Thank you.'

'Let's be clear, Jimmy. This is your one and only second chance, understand?' Helen spoke firmly.

'Perfectly,' he said.

He apologised again. He told her more about Diane and how her dependency on alcohol had soured their marriage, how he'd felt obliged to keep on looking after her even after they'd separated.

'She should receive the divorce papers next week,' he said. 'Once it's all signed and sealed, that's it. Her sister in London can look after her from now on.'

He kissed Helen on the cheek. 'How are things at the Seaview? Have the police found the murderer?'

'I'd rather not talk about it, if you don't mind,' she said. 'It feels good to take time off and get away from it all. It feels good to be here with you.'

'It does?' Jimmy said, turning towards her.

She brushed her lips against his. She breathed in the scent of him, and butterflies fluttered in her stomach again.

'What are your plans for the rest of the day?' she asked. 'I thought we could ride on the funicular and walk around South Cliff Gardens.'

He shook his head. 'Sorry, I can't, Helen. I've got a job interview in half an hour.'

'Where at?'

'The Red Lea Hotel. It's a singing gig, as Elvis.'

'You're thinking of staying in town?' she asked.

Jimmy shrugged. 'I'd be near Jodie . . .' he said, his voice trailing off. Helen didn't push him for more; it was too soon to think about him living here in Scarborough.

They walked down the hill hand in hand, and kissed goodbye when they reached the seafront.

'Good luck with your interview,' Helen said.

'When will I see you again?' Jimmy asked.

'I'll call you,' she replied, feeling certain that this time she would.

With Suki by her side, she walked along Sandside until she came to the harbour. Fishermen's boats were moored around three piers. Brightly painted signs offered fishing trips and boat rides along the Yorkshire coast. There was even a pirate ship, *The Hispaniola*, ready to take tourists on a joyride around the South Bay. Helen ignored the signs touting for business, walking past speedboat moorings, lobster creels and crab pots along the old pier. By the lighthouse, she could make out three men sitting together, heads down, fixing a lobster pot. As she walked towards them, one of them noticed Suki.

'That's a beautiful greyhound,' he called out.

'Thank you,' Helen replied.

'Is she a racer?'

'She was once. I got her from the rehoming centre when she stopped winning and her owner got rid of her.'

The man held something out to the dog. 'Here, girl,' he said.

Helen held tight to Suki's lead. 'What is it?'

322

'Just a piece of fish off the boat.'

She slackened the lead enough for Suki to walk forward and take the fish from his hand. As they turned to leave, the fisherman threw another bit of fish towards Suki, who lapped it up greedily.

Helen returned to the Seaview with much on her mind. A red car parked outside made her heart sink. She knew whose it was by now. She walked around to the back of the hotel, unleashed Suki in the yard, then immediately went upstairs to the lounge. All was quiet, no rehearsals taking place. Instead, the cast were milling around in the dining room and hall.

'What's going on?' she asked Chester.

He pointed to the lounge door. 'The police turned up; they want to speak to everyone again, and they're showing them the picture of the man from the CCTV in the North Mount Hotel. Obviously, they don't need me this time. I can't give them any more than they already know. They've got Paul in there now. Lee, Audrey and Kate have already been grilled. Liza will be next. She's waiting in the dining room with her mum.'

'I can't believe they just turned up!' Helen said, anger creeping into her voice. 'No one rang me to tell me.' She looked around. 'Where's Anabel?'

'She's gone home; we're to ring her when we start rehearsing again. She said there was no point in her hanging about.'

'And where are Kate and Lee?'

'They've gone for a walk.'

Helen was surprised but happy to hear this. 'Together?'

Chester nodded. 'I think they're starting to thaw towards each other. Carmen's death has had strange effects on us all.'

She nodded at the closed lounge door. 'When Paul comes out, let me go in before Liza. I want a word with DS Hutchinson. He can't just turn up and take over the place. I'm going to give him a piece of my mind.'

She walked into the dining room, where Audrey was reading a copy of the *Scarborough Times* in which neither Carmen nor Tilly were front-page news. Liza was sitting opposite, tapping on her phone.

'Ladies? Would you like coffee and biscuits?'

'That'd be great, thanks,' Liza replied without looking up.

Helen walked downstairs, fuming at the detectives for not having the decency to call her. When she pulled her phone out, she saw the reason why: the battery was dead after recording Chester the previous day. She quickly plugged it into the charger, where it lit up immediately with alerts, texts and missed calls, three of them from DS Hutchinson. She listened to his messages. The first asked her to ring him. The second said that he'd spoken to Jean, who'd given him permission to enter the Seaview, saying she was sure Helen wouldn't object under the circumstances. And the third said he was on his way to the hotel to question the guests. Well, there was nothing she could do about it now. She made two cafetières of coffee, laid chocolate wafers on a plate, then sent the whole lot up in the dumbwaiter.

Back upstairs, she served the coffee and sat with Audrey, Liza and Chester in the dining room. As soon as she heard the lounge door open, she leapt to her feet, marched into the lounge and closed the door. DS Hutchinson and DC Hall were sitting on the window seat behind a table, phones and paperwork spread out in front of them.

'I had no idea you were here until just a few minutes ago, and I can't say I'm too happy about—' Helen began, but DS Hutchinson disarmed her with a beaming smile.

'Mrs Dexter, you're just the woman we were hoping to see. We decided to speak to all of your guests again, in light of what Mr Ford told us about his whereabouts on the night of the murder.'

'What we're thinking,' DC Hall added, 'is that there can't be many people outside of the Seaview or Dawley's Theatre Group who knew that Chester Ford used a cigarette holder. That's why we're speaking to Carmen's colleagues again.'

Helen's heart skipped a beat. Then another. She put her hand to her chest to help absorb the shock and sat opposite the detectives. She was too stunned to speak, scared too, and her legs began shaking as DS Hutchinson continued. 'Because if Chester Ford didn't kill Miss Carstairs with the cigarette holder he was so fond of . . .'

'. . . then who did?' Helen said, getting her breath back. She leaned forward and nodded at DS Hutchinson. 'Yes, that's something I've been wondering too. Because I don't think Chester's cigarette holder *was* the murder weapon. I've already told you that I saw him snap it in half during an argument with Carmen. You said the murder weapon was a foot long. Half a cigarette holder is only six inches. Whoever wanted to frame him for Carmen's death believed that his cigarette holder was still intact. It couldn't have been anyone who saw him break it.'

'Do you have any idea who did see him snap it and who didn't?' DS Hutchinson asked.

Helen shook her head. 'All I know is that Paul was with me

when Chester and Carmen argued, and he saw Chester break the cigarette holder as clearly as I did. But the reflected light on the window didn't allow us to see further inside. The others could have been in the dining room, the hall, or in their rooms upstairs. It was break time, they could have been anywhere.'

DS Hutchinson and DC Hall shared a look. DC Hall blew air out of his cheeks.

'Well, let's crack on with these interviews, boss,' he said.

'Helen, could you do us a favour and ask Ms Carter to come in?'

'Liza? Yes, of course.'

Helen returned to the dining room. 'Liza? They're ready for you now.'

Liza looked up from her phone. Helen led her to the lounge and opened the door. This wasn't easy for any of them, she knew, and the least she could do was ask if anyone would like more coffee. DS Hutchinson replied that he would, while DC Hall patted his stomach and said that if there were any biscuits going spare, he wouldn't say no.

Helen closed the door, returned to the dining room and picked up the tray of coffee and biscuits. She was trying to balance the tray in one hand and knock at the lounge door with the other when she heard Liza's voice from inside the room. She sounded sullen, monotone, not her usual self, which Helen put down to her being nervous. Well, being quizzed by two detectives after a colleague had been murdered would set anyone's nerves on edge. Helen's nerves were shredded too. She pressed her ear to the door and listened as Liza replied to a question that DS Hutchinson had asked about the night of Carmen's murder.

'I went for dinner with the cast, then walked back here with my mother. It's as simple as that, nothing complicated about it. I'd worn my favourite hat that night, the one with roses and freesias. It was a windy night; the blood was rushing in my ears.'

As simple as that, nothing complicated about it. It took her a few seconds to recall where she'd heard those words before. Then it came to her in a flash; a horrible, terrifying flash. They were from the book in Liza's room, the monologue for an acting audition. Roger, the jilted groom at the church, the bride's bouquet with roses and freesias, the blood rushing in her ears as she ran from the church. She stood still with the tray, listening as Liza carried on.

'I ran down the path, I had to get out of the storm, and then I . . .'

There they were again, more of the same words. Helen was horrified. Slowly she turned and placed the tray down in the hall, her stomach turning in shock that Liza was lying. But why? Her heart began beating too fast. She knew she had to do something, but she couldn't storm in with all guns blazing or DS Hutchinson would think she'd gone mad. She needed proof and she knew where to find it.

She ran downstairs, taking the stairs two at a time, hanging on to the handrail for support. In her apartment, she took the master key from the box, then she ran back upstairs, out of breath already. She ignored Chester in tears in the hallway, ignored Audrey's plea for a pot of tea, and ran past Paul without a word as he made his way upstairs.

'Helen, are you all right?' he called, but she didn't stop; she had to get to Liza's room. She was in such a rush that she didn't notice Suki bound up the stairs from her apartment behind her and settle in the hallway.

327

She unlocked Liza's door and flew inside. The books were no longer by the bed. Where were they? She looked around, desperate. Where was the book she needed, the one with the red-and-black cover? She lifted scarves and hats, rainbow colours flying through the air as she searched frantically. And then she found it, she had it. She recognised the cover the minute she saw it.

She ran back downstairs just in time to see a red car pulling away from the kerb.

'Where are they going?' she cried. 'They can't leave!'

'They were called away urgently.'

It was Liza who answered. It was Liza who was standing in front of Helen now, with her hands on her hips, a scowl on her face, glaring at the book in Helen's hand.

Chapter 41

Helen's heart pounded. Her hands shook so much she thought the book would slip to the floor. She was cornered. On her right was the door to the lounge. On her left the door to the dining room, where she caught sight of the back of Chester and Audrey's heads. Suki was standing to attention ahead of her. Helen hadn't a clue what to do next, but it was Liza who broke the impasse.

'That's mine,' she said, grabbing for the book.

Helen quickly snapped it away. Suki padded along the hall and stood beside her, facing Liza. Helen saw the dog's ears go up, alert. Liza took a step forward, her face contorted with anger.

'Well? Care to tell me what you're doing with it?'

Helen held tight to the book.

'I heard you talking to the police, Liza, I know you were reading from a script.' Helen's shock gave way to fear, because if Liza was lying to the police, what did it mean about her involvement in Carmen's death?

Liza pursed her lips and clenched her hands into fists. 'Give it to me,' she hissed, swinging for the book.

Once again Helen was too quick, raising it in the air, out of Liza's reach. But this time Liza jumped at her, knocking her to the floor, and the book fell from her hand. Suki bared her teeth and gave a throaty growl.

'What on earth's going on out there?' Audrey called from the dining room.

'Nothing, Mum,' Liza replied, glaring at Helen. 'Everything's fine, isn't it, Mrs Dexter?'

Helen tried to get up, but Liza pressed her heavy Doc Marten boot on top of her hand. Helen winced with pain. 'Audrey!' she cried. 'Chester! Anyone! Help! I need help!' She batted at Liza's legs with her free hand. Liza stepped back, freeing her, but when Helen tried to stand, the younger woman lunged again. By now Suki was running up and down the hall, barking loudly.

Audrey and Chester appeared from the dining room. Chester rushed to Helen's side and pulled her to her feet.

'My word, are you all right? What happened?'

Audrey looked at her daughter, who was red in the face. 'Liza?'

Quick as a flash, Liza pulled herself together. Helen was sweating, in pain, but she recognised the way the woman composed herself so quickly. Liza had gone into acting mode; she'd seen it during rehearsals many times – the way her body straightened, the way she lifted her chin, the way her voice went high and soft.

'Oh, nothing. Helen's had a fall, but I'm sure she'll be all right.'

Helen pressed her hand against the wall. She watched Suki walk along the hallway, sniffing the umbrella stand. If she hadn't been in shock, she would have called the dog away; it was likely Suki would start chewing something. She turned her attention back to Liza.

'I did not have a fall and you know it!' she cried. 'I know you lied to the police.' She turned to Audrey. 'Your daughter read from that book when the police grilled her. She didn't answer their questions about the night Carmen died; she read lines from a script.'

Audrey's face clouded over and she turned to face Liza. 'Is this true?'

Liza laughed a little too loudly, too brightly. 'As if I'd do anything like that. It's ridiculous. I think our landlady is delusional. She must have hit her head when she fell.'

A clatter at the end of the hall caught everyone's attention, and they spun around to see that Suki had knocked the umbrella stand over. But it wasn't the stand she was interested in; it was one of the umbrellas. She pulled it out with her teeth, thrashing it on the carpet.

'Leave it, you stupid dog,' Liza snarled.

Helen straightened her shoulders, took a step towards Liza and poked her on her shoulder.

'Now listen to me, no one speaks to Suki like that.'

'Helen, please don't shout,' Audrey said, her hands fluttering to her heart.

Helen remained unmoved. 'I've just about had enough of you,' she told Liza, hackles rising now. 'I don't know what you're up to, but I'll get to the bottom of it. I'm going to ring DS Hutchinson and tell him to get himself back here as soon as he can, and—'

Helen stopped. Suki had ripped the umbrella open and was now standing with what looked like a shaggy piece of cloth in her mouth. Liza saw it too and lunged for the dog, trying to take it off her. Suki dropped it and barked, then bared her teeth, making Liza back off.

'What's going on, darling?' Audrey demanded.

'Mum, stay out of this,' Liza warned.

Helen stepped forward and picked up what Suki had found. It wasn't cloth at all. It was a wig, a short fair wig. A man's wig.

331

She held it aloft and faced Liza, who looked horrified. Slowly Helen remembered the grainy picture of the slight, short, fair-haired man who'd been in the North Mount Hotel on the night Carmen died. The man with his collar turned up, hiding much of his face.

'It was you, wasn't it?' she hissed.

Liza edged backwards to the front door.

'You wore this wig on the night Carmen died. It was you in the North Mount Hotel when Carmen and her lover were there. You nursed half a pint of shandy for over an hour. I'm right, aren't I?'

'I thought I'd lost the damn thing,' Liza growled.

Audrey looked like she was going to pass out. She put her hand on her heart. 'Darling, please, tell me what's happening!'

'It's best you don't know,' Liza hissed.

The pieces of the jigsaw from the night of Carmen's death were falling horribly into place.

'You killed Carmen,' Helen said.

'No!' Chester cried a tortured howl, before he slid down the wall to the floor, sobbing loudly.

'How dare you accuse my daughter of such a dreadful thing!' Audrey yelled. Her usual calm demeanour had been replaced by an anger so vicious it took Helen by surprise.

'Stay out of this, Mum,' Liza growled.

Liza was breathing fast, getting ready to run. Helen recognised the signs and she glanced at the door. Could she get there first and stop her from leaving? She had to try or she'd never forgive herself.

As Liza turned, Helen leapt forward, her dander well and truly up. She grabbed Liza's arm to stop her turning the handle. She had more strength in her than she knew, after years spent lugging heavy vacuum cleaners up and down stairs. Suki joined in and clamped her jaws around one of Liza's boots. Liza kicked out with her free foot, making the dog yelp, but she wouldn't let go. All the while, Chester was crying and Audrey was shouting.

Helen managed to grab Liza with both hands, and with all the strength she could muster, she frogmarched her into the lounge, forcing her on to a chair. Liza struggled at first, but Helen was firm, and when Audrey followed them, the fight immediately left her body. She slumped in the chair, sobbing like a child and calling out for her mum.

'Chester, call the police!' Helen shouted to the hallway. Chester was still lying crumpled on the floor, but she was relieved to see him pull his phone from his pocket. Audrey laid her arm around her daughter's shoulders, taking Liza under her wing. Helen sat opposite, while Suki stood in the doorway, alert, teeth bared.

'You killed her, didn't you?' Helen said again.

Liza closed her eyes and nodded.

Audrey gasped. 'No . . .' she whispered. 'This can't be true. Liza, tell me it isn't true.'

'But it is true, isn't it?' Helen said.

Audrey blanched and began to shake. 'Why, Liza? Why?'

Liza sniffed long and loud, trying to make her tears stop, then finally looked at her mum. 'Oh Mum, don't you know?' she wailed.

Audrey shook her head. 'No, darling, no.'

Liza wiped her eyes with the back of her hands. 'Mum, I killed her for you.'

Chapter 42

'Oh, darling,' Audrey said, holding Liza tight. 'But why?'

'Because it should have been yours,' Liza sobbed. 'Everything Carmen Delray had should have been yours.'

She straightened in her seat and a steely glint appeared in her eyes. Helen noticed the change. Liza had gone into performance mode again, and she watched her closely.

'The role in *The Singing Nurse* was meant for you, Mum, you always told me that. Carmen took it from you after she slept with Daddy. You were never angry, though. You never wanted revenge on her for what she did. But I did. All my life I wanted you to be Wendy "Songbird" Wren. I wanted you to have the fame and fortune Carmen stole from you.'

Helen watched in astonishment as Liza laid her head on Audrey's shoulder and Audrey stroked her hair.

'Darling, darling girl . . .' she cooed.

'I hated Carmen Delray. Each week Daddy and I would watch her on TV and he'd tell me what a great actor she was, and all the time, I knew they'd slept together. Everyone in the business knew what she'd done; she'd seduced him to get the part of Wendy Wren. She took your role. She took your husband. She took your whole career!' Liza wailed. She banged her hand against her chest. 'Well, *I'm* angry! I carried your rage all my life; it's been burning me up. All I ever wanted to do was to avenge your reputation.'

In the distance the sound of a siren could be heard. Helen quickly glanced at Audrey, who gave a subtle nod. She'd heard it too. Helen noticed her grip on Liza's shoulder tighten as she began to speak.

'When I found out about your father's affair with Carmen, I left him. I had to, for what he did would have festered inside me just as it's done to you. Yes, I lost my home when I left, and I also lost you, my darling girl. But I was not a good mother; we both know that. I was on the road all the time, on tour with theatre groups. You were better off with your father. And yes, I lost the starring role in *The Singing Nurse*, but I was damned if I would let Carmen Delray destroy me. I forged my own career in the theatre, far away from the tawdry world of TV. Many years passed and decades went by and I pushed Carmen to the back of my mind. When I found out she was joining Dawley's Theatre Group for this production of *Midnight with Maude*, of course I had doubts about whether to join up . . .'

Outside, the siren grew louder.

'. . . but I took the role for three reasons. One, because I'm a professional, darling. I need the work more than ever now I'm an age where meaty roles don't often come along. Two, because what happened between me and Carmen happened a lifetime ago. I'm a different person now. I've learned to let go and live for today. And the third reason was the most important of all . . .' She paused. 'I took the role because I haven't seen you in over three years, Liza. Once I knew you'd signed up for this tour, I didn't think twice about Carmen Delray. You were far more important than her. This was a rare chance for us to work together, and we had so much catching-up to do.

'Oh Liza, my Liza. There are more reasons than you'll ever know why I left your father. You could say that Carmen taking him from me even did me a favour in the end. You see, there was a cruel streak in him that I prayed would never manifest in you. But I know now that it has. You have his temper, his darkness. It's taken me a lifetime to put myself above what happened between him and Carmen Delray. Do you know how much time and money I've spent on yoga, health gurus, meditation, wellness retreats and . . .' Audrey gritted her teeth. '. . . awfully expensive therapy? I disappeared from public life after the news of his affair came out. I took myself to a retreat in the Pyrenees. Of course, the papers reported that I'd suffered a breakdown, and they weren't far wrong.'

The sirens grew louder, and then suddenly the lounge was flashing blue and white. Outside, a police car screeched to the kerb along with a red car with two men inside. Helen heard the front door open, Chester's voice, urgent, then the scuffling of feet in the hall. Suki barked, then backed away to lie under a table as DS Hutchinson and DC Hall strode into the lounge.

'Liza Carter?' DS Hutchinson said.

'She's here,' Audrey said, letting her arm drop from her daughter's shoulders.

'Liza Carter, I'm arresting you on suspicion of the murder of Miss Janet Carstairs.'

Helen and Audrey stood side by side at the Seaview's lounge window with Suki, watching Liza being led away.

'I love you, Mum!' Liza called as she was lowered into the back seat of the police car.

Chester came and stood next to Audrey. He laid his arm around her shoulders and gently kissed her cheek. Paul joined them.

'I was upstairs in my room when I heard sirens. Is everything all right?' He peered out of the window, curious to see what the others were looking at. 'Is that Liza in the back of the police car? What's happened? Audrey, are you all right? You look—'

Helen shook her head, a silent warning to say no more.

She went to the bar and grabbed the whisky bottle. She poured generous measures into four glasses and carried them to where Audrey had collapsed on the window seat, her face deathly white and her hands trembling. She fanned her with a beer mat, then pushed a glass into her hand. 'Drink, Audrey, it'll help with the shock.'

Audrey sat up and stared straight ahead. 'My daughter, a murderer,' she said, her words coming out in a broken whisper.

'Liza murdered Carmen?' Paul said, incredulous.

Helen nodded. Paul picked up his glass and downed the whisky in one.

'It's too tragic for words,' Chester said, taking a long swig from his own glass.

Helen looked from Audrey's ashen face to Chester. 'Look, would you like me to leave you alone for a while? I'm not sure what to do for the best.'

'Please stay,' Audrey said.

'We need you, Helen,' Chester said with a kind smile. 'Perhaps now more than ever.'

'What do you mean?' Helen asked.

He glanced at Audrey, who gave a brief nod.

'I know now's not the right time, and I hate to say this, but someone has to. Could you ring Taylor Caffrey to let him know what's happened?' Chester said.

'Of course,' Helen said quickly, her heart breaking for Taylor and the Modernist. 'He'll need to cancel the play.'

Both Audrey and Chester turned sharply towards her, and something in Audrey seemed to snap into action. The change in her astonished Helen. One minute she'd looked as if she was about to wither away and die, the next she was sitting bolt upright, staring at Helen as if she'd gone mad. She took a long drink from her glass, placed it firmly on the table, then cleared her throat.

'The play will go ahead, Helen. If ever there was a reason to stage *Midnight for Maude*, this is it.'

'You can't be serious,' Helen said, aghast.

'I'm deadly serious,' Audrey replied.

Helen winced at the choice of words, but Audrey was unfazed.

Chester nodded in agreement. 'We're professionals, we'll act our way through the pain. It's what we do best, what we train all our lives for, and we'll do it . . .' he reached across the table and squeezed Audrey's hand, 'together.'

'Thank you, darling,' Audrey replied. She raised her glass and Chester responded by lifting his own. Audrey smiled weakly, then turned to Helen.

'You see, Helen, acting is more than just a job, so much more than what we *do*; it's who we *are*. We know no other life. No matter what happens in our personal lives, quite simply, we must rise above it.'

'But your daughter's just been arrested for murder,' Helen cried. She turned to Chester. 'And you're grieving for Carmen. You can't honestly still be thinking about going on stage. Liza's confession changes everything, surely?'

Audrey and Chester shared a wry smile, then Audrey took a sip from her glass.

'Helen, darling, admittedly this is the most extreme thing that's happened in my entire life, but no matter the circumstances, it's quite simple.' She and Chester glanced at each other before turning to Helen, speaking as one. 'The show must go on!'

Chapter 43

When the actors came down for breakfast the next day, Helen hugged them one by one. She gave especially warm hugs to Audrey and Chester. She was very happy to see Kate and Lee sitting together, although no one said much, and the atmosphere was understandably subdued as they tried to process the news about Liza.

After breakfast had been served and the rooms cleaned, Helen sat at the kitchen table with Sally and Jean. Suki was lying by the patio doors. Helen picked up her blue mug and told Jean and Sally everything that had happened. An iced carrot cake sat untouched on the table; none of them could face eating. Jean closed her eyes and leaned back in her chair, while Sally rested her chin in her hands.

'How did Carmen's body end up on the South Bay beach after she'd been drinking in the North Mount Hotel?' Sally asked.

Helen remembered what DS Hutchinson had told her in his phone call the night before.

'She left the North Mount with her new fella—'

'The one with the moustache?'

'Yes. He's still not been found, but after Liza's confession, the police don't need him now.'

'He couldn't have loved Carmen if he's done a runner,' Jean sniffed.

'Anyway, they left the North Mount after arguing,' Helen carried on. 'Carmen headed in one direction and the man in another. Liza, disguised in the wig, followed Carmen, who was very drunk.'

'But you said Liza and Audrey returned to the Seaview together after the dinner in town,' Sally said.

'That's what I thought had happened,' Helen replied. 'Because I saw Liza and Audrey walking into the lounge together, both bone dry even though it was raining outside. I knew Liza had taken one of the Seaview umbrellas, and you know how much protection they give from the rain. But in fact, Audrey had returned on her own earlier and was upstairs in her room. Liza had told her she was meeting friends from a rival theatre group after dinner, then called her when she was on her way here. I was busy working in the bar and the jukebox was going, so I didn't notice her coming in. Audrey met her in the hall, where the wig fell out of Liza's pocket into the umbrella as she folded it up. She placed it in the holder and they walked into the lounge together. Audrey never breathed a word to the police about where Liza had been that night because she wanted to protect her daughter. She fully believed her lie about the rival group.'

'She never suspected that Liza was involved in Carmen's death?' Sally asked.

'No, the police are certain she's innocent,' Helen said.

'How did Liza know Carmen was in the North Mount Hotel?' Jean asked.

'Ah, well,' Helen said. 'DS Hutchinson told me that she overheard Carmen on the phone arranging her date with the man with the moustache. She slipped away after dinner with Taylor

Caffrey to follow Carmen and didn't let her out of her sight. Remember, Liza was the mistress of disguise, with hats, wigs and experience of stage costume. Also, she'd spoken privately to Carmen days earlier, offering to set up a meeting with Monty Meehan, entertainments manager at the Spa. She lied to Carmen and said Monty had arranged a meeting with a top TV producer he knew. After Carmen left the North Mount, Liza whipped off her wig, collared her and told her Monty wanted to see her right then. They took a cab to the Spa.' She looked at Sally. 'It was one of Gav's Cabs.

'Anyway, the storm was raging by the time they arrived. When they got out of the cab, they were shielded by the umbrella. Their faces weren't picked up on any of the security cameras. All that was captured was the back of our umbrella.'

'With the Seaview's logo on it?' Jean said.

'No, Jean. It was raining too hard; the logo was obscured. Well, what happens next isn't good because we know Carmen's body was found washed up on the shore. Under cover of our umbrella . . .' Helen shuddered. '. . . I'll have to buy new ones, of course . . .'

'Good idea,' Jean said.

'That's when Liza stabbed Carmen, killed her outright. While Carmen had strength of character, physically she was weak, and that night she was very drunk. It was too easy for Liza.'

Jean winced.

'Sorry, Jean. Shall I go on?'

She took a sip from her mug and nodded.

'Liza planned to push Carmen into surging waves during the storm. I remember, not long after they all arrived, she heard me talking about how dangerous the waves at the South Bay could be. She thought the body would be swept out to sea. But by the time they got to the Spa, the tide had turned and was heading out. She'd timed it wrong; she knew nothing about tide times, being a city girl. She didn't even bother to check. She assumed that because it was stormy, the tide would be in, crashing over the prom. Anyway, she panicked, as she now had a dead body on her hands and needed to get rid of it. She pushed Carmen down the steps by the Spa wall and ran. Instead of being taken by the waves, though, the body was left rolling in the shallows. The murder weapon stayed by her side, her handbag around her body.'

'Oh, what an awful way to die,' Jean said.

'Liza knew about Chester's affectation with the cigarette holder,' Helen continued. 'She hoped to frame him for the murder as a jealous jilted lover who killed Carmen in a crime of passion.' She paused for a sip of coffee. 'What she didn't know was that Chester had broken his cigarette holder. I saw it with my own eyes, but Liza was upstairs in her room when it happened.'

'Oh, poor Carmen,' Jean sighed.

Sally sat back in her chair. 'It's too awful for words.'

Helen could only agree.

'I can't believe Liza stayed in Scarborough after what she did,' Sally said. 'That's as cold-hearted as it gets.'

'Well, she did vote to leave, that day Chester gave me the deciding vote on whether the play should go on,' Helen remembered. 'It wouldn't have looked too suspicious if she'd left then. But if she'd left afterwards, it would have been obvious she had something to hide.'

Jean stood, sniffed back a tear, then picked up the plate with

343

the carrot cake on. 'I think we'll save this for another day, when we've got our appetites back. Would you mind if I took a few slices to the care home when I go to visit Mum? I need to see how her legs are doing.'

'Help yourself, Jean, take as much as you like.'

Jean walked away to find a plastic box. Sally turned to Helen. 'Are you all right?'

Helen laid her hand on Sally's arm. 'I will be in a few days, but this business has knocked me for six.'

'Are you seeing Jimmy today? That might cheer you up.'

'I don't think so, love,' Helen replied. 'I've got too much to do here. The police want to come back and ask the actors more questions to tidy up the loose ends. Both Audrey and Chester have asked if I'll stay with them for support. It's the least I can do. What about you and Gav, are you going out with him tonight?'

'He's invited me and Gracie to his mum and dad's house again, said he's got something special planned. Gracie's beyond excited.'

Later that day, when Helen stepped outside with Suki, heading for a walk on the beach to help clear her head, she bumped into Chester on King's Parade.

'No rehearsals today?' she asked.

'On the contrary, it's business as usual. We must carry on, for the sake of the play. I'm just taking a breather before we begin. I find the sea air restorative; it helps clear my mind.' He turned and looked at the stunning view. The tide was out, the sand exposed, and breaking waves frilled on the shore. He cleared his throat. 'Speaking of the play, there's something I've been meaning to ask, a favour if I may.'

'Oh?' Helen said. What now?

'Taylor Caffrey has found a replacement for Liza's role in the play. It's very last-minute, of course, but the woman is excellent, he says. She'll cram her lines before the show opens tomorrow, but we're going to need help. The new actor, I mean, she'll need help in case she . . .'

Helen could tell what was coming. 'In case she forgets her lines?'

'Would you work as our prompt, Helen? It'd just be for opening night. There's a chap coming to take over, but he's prompting in Bridlington and can't start until Sunday.'

'Oh, Chester. I'm not a professional,' she said.

'No, but you know our actors, you know our way of working. You know when Lee needs support with his lines. And heaven only knows, the new actor will need all the help you can give. Please, Helen, I'm begging you.'

She sighed. 'For one night only, you say?'

Chester nodded and laid his hand on his heart. 'One night, I promise. Please, Helen. Do it for Carmen. Do it for poor Audrey, who's suffering more than she'll ever let on. Do it for Taylor Caffrey and the Modernist Theatre. *Midnight with Maude* is its last chance.'

After everything Helen had been through with the actors, how could she refuse their final request?

Chapter 44

On Saturday morning, Helen stood on the doorstep of the Seaview Hotel with a lump in her throat. Ahead of her, Dawley's Theatre Group were packing up their minibus, ready to head off to the theatre digs next to the Modernist. The mouse infestation and other problems in the digs, Taylor had been assured, had all been taken care of. While Helen was relieved to see the actors go, she was heartbroken they were leaving under such a tragic cloud. Seven of them had arrived; now one was dead and another was in custody after being arrested for murder. Too much had happened in the last two weeks and Helen didn't want to experience anything like it again. She felt exhausted, done in, emotionally battered and bruised.

The door of the Vista del Mar opened and Miriam emerged with her arms crossed and a gloating look on her face. She nodded at the minibus. 'I see your actors are leaving.'

Helen was in no mood for Miriam after everything she'd been through. 'Very astute,' she replied.

'I see the Seaview is in the papers again today.'

'Oh no, what're they saying about us now? More murder and mayhem? More bookings cancelled? More tourists refusing to stay here because of what happened to Carmen?'

Miriam looked askance at her. 'No, dear. There's a lovely write-up from Rosie Hyde, singing your praises and offering a competition to win two nights' accommodation with Jean's award-winning breakfast thrown in. And by the way, if Jean ever wants to jump ship, there'll always be a place for her here at the Vista del Mar.'

'She's happy where she is,' Helen said curtly.

Miriam tutted loudly. 'Well, there's no need to be rude. I'd expect you to be humble after what happened with those actors. I can't say I've ever had a murderer staying at the Vista del Mar. But then I'm a cut above with four stars, you see. Speaking of which, I heard a rumour that the hotel inspector's in town.'

'She is,' Helen replied.

Miriam turned sharply. 'How do you know?'

'Because she stayed here.'

'When?'

Helen tried to stifle her smile. 'Remember Tuesday morning, when your kitchen packed up and you had to send your guests to Taylor's Bar and Kitchen for breakfast?'

'Remember it? I wish I could erase it from my memory. You should have seen the complaints left in the online reviews.'

Helen had already read the Vista del Mar's reviews and they weren't pleasant. She'd actually felt sorry for Miriam when she saw them, although Taylor's came out of it very well. She had made a note to have breakfast there one morning with Jean the next time they had no guests. She might be able to pick up some breakfast ideas.

'Well, that morning when I took you in and gave you breakfast, and in return you complained about, oh, just about everything, including my dog . . .'

347

Miriam had the decency to look embarrassed as Helen carried on.

'. . . that was the morning the inspector was here. She was sitting opposite you, the woman with blonde hair, in a bob.'

Miriam inhaled sharply. 'Why didn't you warn me who she was?'

'Ah, don't get your knickers in a twist about it, Miriam.'

'How dare you! I've got a good mind to—'

Whatever Miriam was going to say was lost when Chester bounded up the path.

'I think we're ready to go,' he said, waving his ballpoint pen at the bus. Helen saw Audrey in the passenger seat. Her face was pale, the skin under her eyes dark, but she looked as dignified as ever. Kate and Lee were sitting together in the next row back. Behind them was Paul in his beige anorak. He waved at Helen, who raised her hand and waved back.

'We'll see you tonight at the Modernist,' Chester said. 'Arrive about six, if you can. Taylor's putting on a spread and drinks for the after party.' He looked at Miriam, then back at Helen. 'Bring a friend or two, if you wish. The more the merrier.'

Miriam accepted the invitation before Helen could reply. 'How kind, thank you very much,' she said.

'I'll leave half a dozen complimentary tickets for you at the box office, under the name of the Seaview Hotel,' Chester said.

Miriam sniffed, then disappeared into her hotel.

'Thank you, Chester,' Helen said. 'I'll ask Jimmy to come, and he might bring Jodie, his daughter. I'll invite Marie and

Jean too. Sally's already got tickets; her boyfriend Gav bought them.'

'Well, thank you for everything you've done for us, Helen. I know it hasn't been easy. And you'll be great tonight, working as our prompt. We're lucky to have you.'

'Good luck for later,' Helen said, then shook her head. 'Sorry, I mean *break a leg.*'

Chester jumped into the driver's seat and started the engine. Audrey, Kate, Lee and Paul waved as the bus pulled away. Helen closed the door, went into the lounge and sat on the window seat. She sat there a while, gazing at the view of the beach. The sea was dark and grey, the clouds hanging low, a threat of rain in the air. She pulled her phone from her pocket and called Jimmy, who answered straight away.

'Helen. It's great to hear your voice. I'm at the hostel with Jodie, we're decorating. How are you?'

Helen thought for a moment. The truth was, she didn't know how she was. She felt as if she'd just limped away from a battle-field. 'How do you fancy coming to the theatre tonight? I've got free tickets. Ask Jodie if she'd like to come too. It's *Midnight with Maude* at the Modernist. I've promised to work as the prompt, just for tonight, but I'll see you afterwards. There's a bit of a do with the cast, free drinks and a spread.'

'Sounds good to me. I'll ask her. It'd be good for you to get to know her better before I—' Jimmy stopped dead.

'Before you what?' Helen said. She heard him take a breath.

'I'll speak to you tonight, Helen. I don't want to say this over the phone.'

'What's going on?' she demanded.

'I'll see you at the theatre,' Jimmy said, and hung up.

Helen stared at her phone, lost for words. Would things ever be straightforward with that man?

Helen was almost ready to head to the Modernist. She'd arranged for Marie and Jean to go with Miriam and sit next to Jimmy and Jodie. Gav and Sally would be there too, and she found herself looking forward to seeing everyone. However, a knot of anxiety in her stomach kept reminding her of Jimmy's cryptic words.

She was about to leave when she remembered something Audrey had told her when they'd first met. She'd said that for good luck, she always took Cyril, a tiny brooch in the shape of a squirrel, on stage with her, pinned to her bra strap. Helen went into the lounge and picked up the tiny Elvis figurine from behind the bar. 'You're my good-luck charm tonight. Don't let me down.' She glanced at the framed picture of Tom. 'Goodnight, love,' she said, and blew him a kiss.

She walked out of the lounge, past the jukebox with its Elvis songs, each one a favourite of Tom's that she still couldn't bring herself to change. Maybe one day she would, but not yet. Then she straightened her shoulders, pushed her feet forward in her boots and headed to the Modernist for the premiere of *Midnight with Maude*.

Chapter 45

The play's opening night was a resounding success. The audience even gave a standing ovation, and refused to sit down until each member of the cast had taken not one, but two bows. Bouquets were thrown on to the stage, along with a wreath with *RIP Carmen* spelled out in red roses. Chester gathered the cast to him; they formed a line and held hands. He looked at Audrey on his left and Kate on his right, then the whole lot of them bowed for one final time to rapturous applause. Finally Taylor Caffrey told the stage manager to bring the curtain down as the house lights went up and the audience filed out.

Helen stayed where she was at the side of the stage, where she'd sat all the way through the show. To her relief, and surprise, the cast hadn't needed any prompting at all. Even Lee had been word-perfect, and the new actor hadn't faltered. She picked up tiny Elvis and popped him in her handbag. 'Thanks, Elvis,' she whispered. Then she stood and made her way backstage, where Taylor Caffrey caught her and kissed her on both cheeks.

'Helen, darling, that was superb. We couldn't have done it without you. Anyhoo, are you coming to the after-show party?'

'I wouldn't miss it for the world,' she replied.

She followed Taylor along low, dark corridors to a room tucked away at the back. Audrey was waiting by the door, still in costume and make-up. She gathered Helen to her.

'I wanted to say thank you for all your support. And I wanted to say goodbye.'

'Goodbye? Aren't you coming to the party?'

She shook her head. 'I'm not in a party mood. And it might be some time before I ever party again.'

As she drifted away along the corridor, Taylor called out to her. 'Darling Aud! The press want a word, and there's one of the top agents from London who want to speak to you. She mentioned TV work, something that'd been lined up for Carmen.'

Audrey stopped dead in her tracks. She turned her head slightly, and Helen could see tears streaming down her face.

'I won't speak to the press. No publicity, nothing,' she said quietly, then she faced forward again and walked away. Helen stood rooted to the spot. She'd never met such a dignified woman in her life.

Jimmy and Jodie appeared, and Jodie shot her hand out to Helen.

'It's good to see you again.'

'It's great to see you too,' Helen beamed.

Jean and Marie were the next to arrive.

'Bravo!' Marie called.

'Well done, love,' Jean said.

Helen eyed Marie's tight-fitting black catsuit and high heels. Her normally sleek, shiny hair was styled in a messy updo.

'You look stunning as always, Marie,' she said, giving her friend a kiss on the cheek.

'Any chance of introducing me to Anabel Craven?' Marie said. 'I'm a huge fan of hers; she plays Suzette in *The Archer's Wife*.'

'Come on, let's go in,' Taylor said, waving his arm, gathering the group. 'All the drinks are on the house!'

They headed into a small, dark room with a low ceiling. Helen stood with Jimmy and Jodie, Marie and Jean. Across the room she could see Sally and Gav, kissing. Everyone she cared about in the world was right there, and her heart swelled with love for them all.

Taylor took her arm, gently moved her to one side and whispered in her ear. 'I've just spoken to Rosie Hyde from the *Scarborough Times*; she's going to give the play a five-star review. Ticket sales have shot up since the news about Liza was released. It's morbid, I know, but there it is. What I'm saying, Helen, is that *Midnight with Maude* has saved the Modernist; the theatre won't close and we couldn't have done it without you. I'm so happy, my rash has cleared up, and Mr Phipps has got his appetite back.'

He waved to someone across the room, excused himself and disappeared into the throng. Two women in red coats took his place next to Helen. She recognised them instantly.

'Thank you for all you did for my Paul,' Pat said.

'The new place he's staying in isn't a patch on the Seaview,' Margaret added, shaking her head. 'He says the breakfast's not up to your standard.'

As the women walked away, a glass of champagne appeared in front of Helen.

'I'm not much of a champagne man, but it's all they're serving,' Jimmy said.

'Thanks, Jimmy,' Helen said, taking the glass. 'Where's Jodie?'

'Oh, she's having a chat with Taylor Caffrey about getting young people from the hostel involved here to learn theatre skills.'

Helen was impressed. 'Good on her,' she said, raising her glass. She looked at Jimmy for a few moments. 'Earlier, you said that tonight would be a good chance for me to get to know Jodie before you did something. You didn't tell me what it was and you promised you would.'

Jimmy pulled awkwardly at his shirt collar. 'Oh yeah, that.'

Helen took a sip of champagne, the bubbles fizzing on her tongue. 'Come on, no more secrets.'

Jimmy put his champagne flute on a table, took hold of Helen's hand and looked deep into her eyes. 'You know I've been looking for work, right? Well, the guy I met at the Red Lea Hotel had already filled the singing spot, but he knew someone else who needed an Elvis impersonator. It's good money, exceptionally good, otherwise I wouldn't have considered it, not for one moment.'

'I feel like there's a *but* coming,' Helen said, trying to keep the catch from her voice.

'Well, yes, I suppose there is a slight problem.' Jimmy paused. 'This guy who wants to hire me owns a Las Vegas bar.'

Her heart plummeted. 'Las Vegas?' she cried. 'America?'

'Let me finish, Helen, please,' he said gently. 'It's a Las Vegas show bar in Spain, on the Costa del Sol.'

'Spain? You're going away again, just when we've reunited?'

'The money's too good to turn down; it's far better than anything I'd earn if I stayed in Scarborough. And it's just for three months. I'll be back after New Year. I was thinking, if you wanted, you could fly out and join me, have a holiday. Let Sally run the Seaview for a week. Fly direct from Leeds and you could be with me in a couple of hours. Will you think about it?'

'Spain?' she repeated. She felt as if she'd had the wind knocked from her sails. 'Just when we're getting to know each other, it feels like I'm losing you all over again.'

'It's three short months. And when I return, my divorce will be finalised. Diane's signed the papers already. My house in London is now up for sale and the estate agent's already had interest. So when I get back, I'll be cash rich from the sale of the house, and I'll have no ties in London. I'll be a free agent, Helen. I'll be yours . . . if you want me.'

Helen lifted her chin, moved her lips to Jimmy's, breathed in the scent of his lemon spice aftershave and kissed him for a very long time.

'There's something else, Helen. This job in Spain, it starts very soon.'

She shot him a look. 'How soon?'

'Tomorrow night. I'm flying out in a few hours; the plane leaves at four a.m.'

She let this bombshell sink in. 'Why didn't you tell me before?'

'Because you had a lot on your plate with the police and the murder, and because I only found out just before you called me today. I was still taking the news in when you rang.'

Helen couldn't reply, because Lee and Kate were walking towards her. She plastered a smile on her face. Well, she'd learned a thing or two about acting over the last couple of weeks.

'How are you both?' she asked.

'We're . . .' Kate began, then hesitated.

'Getting along,' Lee said.

'Better,' Kate added.

'Much better,' Lee said. 'And we wanted to say thank you for everything you've done.'

Helen raised her glass to them. 'I'm happy to have played my part.'

Jean bustled over, glass of champagne in one hand and a sausage roll in the other. She was followed by Sally and Gav, both of them beaming from ear to ear.

'You two look like the cats who've got the cream,' Helen said. 'What's going on?' Sally shot her left hand towards her. On the third finger was a whopper of a diamond nestled in a white-gold band. Helen's mouth opened in surprise. She stared at Sally, then at Gav.

'I only went and asked her to marry me, missus,' Gav said. 'And she only went and said yes!'

'You're engaged?' Helen cried.

Sally nodded, tears in her eyes. Helen hugged her hard.

'That's fantastic news!'

Jimmy shook Gav's hand. 'Congratulations, mate,' he said.

'Thanks, Jim,' Gav replied, then he turned to Sally. 'Go on, ask her,' he said, nodding at Helen.

'Ask me what?' Helen said, puzzled.

Sally stepped forward. 'Gracie's going to be my bridesmaid . . . and I wondered, Helen, would you be my matron of honour?'

Helen thought her heart would burst with pride. 'I'd be delighted,' she replied, choking back a tear.

'Thanks, missus,' Gav said. 'And there's something else we'd like to ask too.'

'We don't want a big wedding, see,' Sally explained. 'And there won't be many guests, so I was thinking, if it was all right with you, could we hold the party at the Seaview?'

'We were hoping for an Elvis theme, with the jukebox and all,' Gav said with a twinkle in his eye.

Marie swanned up in a cloud of expensive perfume. 'I'll do the catering, free of charge. Consider it my wedding gift, courtesy of Tom's Teas,' she said.

Jean waved her sausage roll in the air. 'And I'd be honoured to bake your wedding cake.'

Helen put one arm around Marie's slim waist and the other across Jean's shoulders. 'Then it sounds like we've got a party to arrange.'

On Sunday morning, all was quiet at the Seaview Hotel. There were no guests due in, nothing for Helen to do except catch up on admin. She'd arranged to meet Marie at the Scarborough Arms for lunch and was looking forward to catching up with her friend. She glanced at the clock on the kitchen wall. Jimmy would be in Spain by now, and she wondered when she'd see him again.

Her phone rang and she swiped it into life. 'Good morning, Seaview Hotel.'

'Good morning. My name's Alice Pickle. I'm secretary of my local crazy golf club. Our team's taking part in Scarborough's crazy golf tournament and I'd like to make a booking, please.'

Helen sat down and fired up her laptop. She'd heard about the crazy golf competition being held on the seafront. It was taking place on a brand-new themed course where the nine holes were decorated with models of Scarborough landmarks, including the castle, the Grand Hotel, a lighthouse, a windmill and even the *Hispaniola* pirate ship. She'd also heard that some of those who took part were obsessed with winning rather than playing for fun. She hoped that Alice Pickle was the latter. She could do with some lightness in her life after her draining experience with Dawley's Theatre Group.

'There's a big group of us and we'd like to book in for ten days,' Alice continued.

'But the tournament only lasts one day,' Helen said, puzzled.

'Oh, but we'll be practising day and night before the main competition,' Alice said. Helen noticed a dark note creeping into the woman's voice. 'I should warn you that we're quite a competitive bunch,' she continued. 'And we'll be doing all we can to ensure that we win . . . by any means.'

Helen took the booking and confirmed it to Alice by email.

Her phone beeped with a message, a missed call that'd arrived while she'd been talking to Alice. It was from a number she didn't recognise. She swiped the message open and listened.

'Hello? Mrs Dexter, it's Jane Jones, the hotel inspector. I'd like to thank you again for the warm welcome you gave me when I recently stayed at the Seaview Hotel. I'm calling to say that I've now written up my report, which you'll receive in due course. I'm pleased to tell you that I've recommended the Seaview be upgraded from three stars to four. My office will be in touch soon.'

Helen couldn't believe what she'd heard. She played the message again, to be sure. Then she played it a third time before the news began to feel real. She punched the air with delight. She couldn't wait to tell Sally and Jean.